THE
Stolen Child

THE
Stolen Child

———

A NOVEL

Ann Hood

W. W. NORTON & COMPANY

Independent Publishers Since 1923

Copyright © 2024 by Ann Hood

For information about permission to reproduce selections from this book, write to Permissions, W. W. Norton & Company, Inc., 500 Fifth Avenue, New York, NY 10110

For information about special discounts for bulk purchases, please contact W. W. Norton Special Sales at specialsales@wwnorton.com or 800-233-4830

Manufacturing by Lakeside Book Company
Book design by Chris Welch
Production manager: Delaney Adams

ISBN: 978-0-393-60980-6

W. W. Norton & Company, Inc.
500 Fifth Avenue, New York, N.Y. 10110
www.wwnorton.com

W. W. Norton & Company Ltd.
15 Carlisle Street, London W1D 3BS

This one is for Sam, of course

Come away, O human child!
To the waters and the wild
With a faery, hand in hand,
For the world's more full of weeping than you can
   understand.

FROM "THE STOLEN CHILD"—W. B. YEATS

THE

Stolen Child

The Museum of Tears

Enzo, 1935

Enzo Piccolo, master craftsman of *presepe*, hurried along the streets of Naples with a box of glass tubes. It was April, and in April Enzo and his brother, Massimo, were working day and night to complete the figures for the Nativities. They wrapped the wire bodies in twine. They carved arms and legs from wood. They molded heads from terra-cotta. They sewed and pressed silk from San Leucio for the clothes. And they painted the expressions on the faces, the delicate features, the glass eyes, for yes, of course, the Blessed Virgin and Joseph and the three Wise Men. But also for the pizza maker, the sausage maker, the pasta maker; the fruit and vegetable vendors; the fishmongers, butchers, carpenters, *acquafrescaio*; opera singers and politicians; even Pope Pius—God bless him—and Totò, *il principe della risata*, the prince of laughter. The *presepe* was not just Bethlehem, it was Naples.

Back at the shop on Via San Gregorio Armeno, Massimo mixed the paints. He created black, yes, but also *nerissimo*, black as night. He created every subtle shade of white: *bianco sporco*, which was off-white; and *pasta in bianco*, which was the color of pasta with cheese and olive oil and butter; and the white of someone who is sick, the white of someone who is frightened. Massimo's reds! *Rosso brillante, vermiglio, porpora*. He created the red of a blush, the red of lobsters, which was different from the red of crayfish, which was different from the red of peppers. His blues! Pale light blue, baby blue, cobalt blue, deep sea blue. Even *Madonna blu*, used only for the Blessed Virgin's cloak.

All of these colors and more Massimo was mixing as he waited for the glass tubes in which to store them. The glass tubes that rattled in the box Enzo clutched as he hurried toward Via San Gregorio Armeno. By summer, the figures would be finished and they would begin to carve the wooden stables and the other items needed to set the scenes. But for these past four months and for several more to come, all Enzo could think about were the figures. How to capture Totò's distinctive chin? The pope's holiness? How to make Santa Lucia's eyes on the platter look like eyes and not two fried eggs?

These questions so perplexed Enzo on his journey back to the shop that he almost didn't hear the woman crying. The sound was so soft that at first he thought it was a cat meowing. But as he neared the park, he realized that it wasn't a cat at all. It was a woman sitting on a bench with her face dropped into her hands and her shoulders moving up and down with sobs.

Enzo hesitated.

At eighteen years of age, he still did not know how to talk to women. *Soft*, his father used to call him. Soft, his father believed, because his mother coddled him. Enzo ran from balls thrown in the schoolyard, from stray dogs and lightning when it flashed across the sky. And from women. They frightened him. Their soft skin and tumbling hair, their tinkling voices and delicate hands, all of it so different, so foreign. And a crying woman? That was even more terrifying. Massimo, a decade older and immeasurably more handsome, with gray eyes and a booming voice and an impressive mustache, knew exactly what to do with women. What would he do now? Enzo wondered. What would Massimo do with a crying woman?

This crying woman was large, with a helmet of dark curls and bare shoulders beneath an exceedingly long feathered boa.

As if she sensed Enzo's presence, she looked up, her face a blur of makeup smeared by her tears. Black rivers moved down her cheeks, and her eyes shone from black smudged lids.

"Are you all right?" Enzo asked her, his voice small in the warm late afternoon air.

"No, you fool," the woman said harshly.

As if her words reminded her of her own heartache, she began to cry again, harder and louder than before.

Enzo carefully set the box of glass tubes on the ground beside the bench, and sat down next to her. He had the desire to pat her on the back, a gesture of comfort that his mother had used when he'd had nightmares as a child. (He had been a child who had nightmares, a bed wetter, and allergic to things no one could see: dust, pollen, changes in the weather.) But he couldn't bring himself to touch the white flesh of her back.

"What happened?" he asked.

She looked up again and Enzo realized that he was looking into a face he had painted on terra-cotta many times: Luisa Tetrazzini, the greatest opera singer who had ever lived—except, of course, Caruso.

"Oh," he said.

But the woman didn't seem to be aware that he was still sitting there. She shook her head and mumbled about a man who had said he loved her but was a liar. In fact, he loved someone else, a woman younger and more beautiful.

"Perhaps," Enzo said, "but not a woman with the voice of an angel."

Luisa Tetrazzini almost smiled. Her lips curved gently upward, and her eyes grew warm and less haunted.

"Here is my handkerchief," Enzo said, reaching into his pocket. "I would be honored if it could dry your tears."

She extended a plump hand toward him.

"Ah," Enzo said, embarrassed. "In fact, I do not have a handkerchief with me because today is laundry day and all of my handkerchiefs are being washed."

For some reason he did not understand, this made Luisa Tetrazzini cry again, harder still.

Enzo looked around for something to catch her tears. He considered the green leaves on the trees, the newspaper someone had left behind on another bench. Then his gaze landed on the box. He opened it and took out one of the small glass tubes.

"Here," he said gently.

Luisa Tetrazzini looked at him, bewildered.

He placed the tube against first one cheek, then the other, catching the tears as they fell from her dark, sad eyes.

Up close, her face had many lines, filled in with thick, flesh-colored makeup. Her skin sagged. Still, there was something in her eyes that looked young and innocent and vulnerable to him. He thought of Massimo and all of the shades of brown he had made. *Marrone chiaro. Marrone rossiccio. Marrone scuro.* Yet none of these captured the color of Luisa Tetrazzini's eyes.

She frowned at him as he held the vial to her cheeks. It was the size of an apothecary's test tube, so her tears barely filled the small rounded bottom. But Luisa Tetrazzini seemed like she did not want to give him even these.

"What are you doing?" she demanded, suddenly not angry but indignant.

"I don't have a handkerchief," he explained again, foolishly. "Laundry day," he added.

She didn't seem to know what to say to this, and just shook her head. Then, unexpectedly, she rested her head on his shoulder.

"Signore," she said softly, "will no one ever love me?"

Enzo had no idea how to answer such an enormous question. He raised the glass tube aloft, as if it held something precious, which, in fact, it did.

"Is such a simple thing impossible?" she murmured.

"I," Enzo began, but he could not finish his sentence because he honestly had nothing more to say.

Luisa Tetrazzini did not move for a very long time. So long that finally he patted her head and slipped away from her. Once on his feet, he put the cork into the glass tube and placed the tube into his pocket, into the very spot where a handkerchief should have been.

"*Buon pomeriggio,*" he said softly.

She did not answer him. Instead, she looked like he was already gone. Or, Enzo thought as he moved away from her, as if he had never existed in the first place.

Later, back at the shop, he got lost in creating the face of Benito Mussolini and almost forgot about the crying opera singer and the vial of her tears he'd placed in his pocket.

"Enzo, there's a tube missing," Massimo said. "Go and get our money back. We're not paying for something we don't have."

Enzo frowned. In his hand he held Mussolini's head, the eyes looking back at him. He placed the head on his worktable and patted his pocket.

"I broke it," he told his brother.

Massimo sighed and returned to his paints. "Of course you did," he muttered.

From a drawer in his worktable, Enzo took out a small piece of paper. On it he wrote: APRIL 18, 1935. LUISA TETRAZZINI. BROKEN HEART.

CHAPTER TWO

Somewhere on a Farm in France

Nick, 1917

Nick Burns didn't walk. He swaggered. His eyes were brown and his hair was brown, which sounded dull or ordinary. But not on Nick Burns. His hair was a rich chestnut brown that developed golden highlights from the sun, and his eyes were gold-flecked too. It was as if King Midas himself had touched Nick's head when he was born and anointed him. Six feet five, barrel-chested, broad-shouldered, he looked like someone who had played a sport in college and been very good at it. He had—rowing, at Harvard—and he was, winning the Henley two years in a row. If it weren't for this war, he would probably be training for the Olympics in Antwerp right now. Instead, he was dug into this trench, waiting for the Germans with five other soldiers on a farm near a village in France, no sunlight, no rowing, no swaggering. Just the stink of men who hadn't washed in too long and the iron smell of blood.

What Nick had with him was a small tin of paints and a brush. He spent endless hours painting on the stone wall. A mural. That's what he was painting. A mural of the Charles River on a summer day, people strolling along its banks, a band playing, a crew team rowing past. He gave all the figures the faces of his family and friends back home. The man in the Panama hat was his father. The woman beside him holding a parasol was his mother. The younger woman beside her with the adoring eyes was Lillian, the girl he might marry. The crew team was his old team, even though two of them had died in France. The band was made up of his brother and his buddies from high school. Nick Burns was painting his world, right here in a stinking trench on a farm near a village in France.

That's what he was doing when sunlight burst in and the face of an angel peered down at him.

"You," she said to Nick. "Go home. Get out of here."

Nick laughed. "Sure," he said. "I'll just walk out and escape German fire and catch a ship home."

The woman frowned, perhaps struggling with his English. Or just struggling with him, an American dug in deep on her land.

Nick reached his hand out, as if they were meeting at a dance or a party. "Nick Burns," he said.

She frowned even more deeply, this time directing her irritation at his outstretched hand.

"I don't want the war in my backyard," she said gruffly. "Nick Burns," she added, sounding as if she'd just eaten something that tasted very bad.

"Mademoiselle," Nick said, and he noticed that she flinched when he said that. His pronunciation wasn't awful; he'd gotten A's in French straight through high school and into college. "If I could be home right now in beautiful Little Compton, Rhode Island, drinking an ice-cold martini with two olives instead of eating food out of a tin in a hole in the ground, I would be. *Croyez-moi.*"

"Why would I believe you?" the woman said. "A man in a hole? On my land? Also," she added, "your French is awful."

"No it isn't," Nick said, surprised. *"J'ai d'excellentes notes—"*

"What are you doing?" she asked him, peering at his mural. Before Nick could answer, she was lowering herself into the trench.

"Ma'am?" Private Jimmy Reilly said in his big southern drawl. Jimmy, one of the other soldiers with Nick, was smoking a cigarette in the farthest corner of the trench. "You can't come down here."

"Ha! You dig a . . . a hole in my yard and you tell me I can't come down here?" She moved closer to Nick and studied his painting.

Nick studied her.

Dark hair in a messy braid. Dark eyes with impossibly long lashes. Very pale skin with very red lips. And, Nick realized, she was pregnant. Very pregnant.

"Ma'am?" Jimmy said again. "It's dangerous down here. And you're . . . well, you're having a baby."

She waved her fingers at him dismissively. "Baby," she muttered. "The last thing I want is a baby."

Surprised, Nick didn't know what to say to that. Most girls he knew wanted babies. They cooed and giggled and grew dreamy whenever they saw one.

"You're painting?" the woman said, equally surprised.

"What do you think?" Nick asked her, gesturing toward the wall. He said it with a certain amount of smugness because he knew his painting was a masterpiece.

"Amateurish," she said matter-of-factly.

Ken Bell and Marty Fusaro laughed.

"You an art critic?" Marty asked.

"You are trespassers," she said, and hoisted herself back out.

"What the hell was that?" Ken said as the hem of her blue skirt and her feet, tucked into men's work boots, disappeared.

"An angel," Nick said.

Nick wanted her to come again. But then he'd hear the distant gunfire of nearby troops and he'd wish her back inside her house, safe. He didn't have a girl waiting for him back home, like Ken and Jimmy and Marty did. He had been happily single, taking Addie out dancing and Katherine to a show, visiting Lillian at her family's cottage on Cape Cod. No one person had caught his fancy. Until that angel had dropped into hell.

Four days passed before she appeared again.

"Here," she said, passing him something wrapped in a cloth. "I baked bread."

The men pounced on it; it was still warm and yeasty. But not Nick.

"Look," he said, "you know hands are the hardest things to paint, right?"

There was that frown again.

"And see how well I've painted them here?" He pointed to the hand of the woman with the face of Lillian, reaching out to touch a flower—a peony, to be exact.

She shrugged. "You are a good amateur painter. That's all," she said.

The smell of that bread almost wiped away the smells of body odor and blood. Nick inhaled.

"What makes you such an expert?" he asked her.

"I am a painter," she said. Then she added, "A *real* painter. When this baby is born and this war is over, I am taking my paintings to Paris and showing them to the nephew of the great Monsieur Louis Leroy. He runs his uncle's gallery." She pointed to her chest, tapping lightly. "Camille Chastain. Remember that name. Someday you will be back in Little Congdon, Rhode Island—"

"Compton," Nick corrected, but she kept right on talking.

"—and you will hear the name Camille Chastain and you will think, 'Ah! The painter whose yard I dug a hole in!'"

Now Nick was the one frowning. He looked from her to his painting, which suddenly seemed all wrong. The light on the river, the perspective, the proportions, all of it wrong.

"Why is that woman with the umbrella so big?" she asked, pointing.

"It's a parasol," Nick said, cross.

"Ah," she said. "It looks like an umbrella."

"Well, it isn't. A parasol is an umbrella for the sun."

"I would wear a hat," she said. "A straw one."

She was right. His mother always wore hats in the sun. The parasol was stolen from that famous Seurat painting.

"Before you dug a hole in my yard, what did you do?" she asked.

Nick shook his head. Everything he'd ever done seemed so small suddenly. So insignificant.

"I am Camille," she said, and disappeared.

Nick decided to add a dog to his painting. A dog like Bandit, his long-dead childhood dog, a spotted mutt with long, glamorous ears. But the woman—Camille—had made him unsure of his ability to capture Bandit, or anything, just right. He needed to get the perfect shade of brown—reddish but not red. Damn her. Nick was not a man who doubted himself.

"Hey, Rembrandt," a voice from above him said.

Nick looked up and into the face of that angel.

"This is what real art looks like," she said, handing him a small square painting.

Nick took it from her. It was smaller than a book, maybe six inches by six inches, but the intensity of the colors and the vividness of the scene—a cow in a field—had the impact of a much larger painting. The cow seemed almost real, the hay and grass behind her almost alive. In the distance, a swish of blue, the vague outline of a person.

"Here," Camille said, and handed him another one, of a farmer at a plow, with the same size and intensity. The same blue swish, this time by the farmhouse.

"Why so small?" Nick asked her.

"At first it was because of this stupid war. How could I get canvas for large paintings? So I made many canvases out of what would have been just one painting. But eventually I came to prefer this size. It has more . . . " She struggled for the word in English, frowning because she couldn't find it.

"Impact," Nick said.

"Impact," Camille repeated, nodding. "I have dozens of them."

"Wow," Nick said. "They're really impressive."

"I know," she said.

Nick laughed. "Pretty sure of yourself, aren't you?"

He thought of Lillian deferring to his taste—in food and art and books. It used to make him feel puffed up to be so in charge. But this confidence, this certainty, was far more interesting.

"Why wouldn't I be?" she asked him. "I've spent my life working to become an artist. That's all I've ever wanted since my aunt took me to Paris to see Mary Cassatt's show of ten prints of women attending their toilette."

She paused, frowning again.

"You do know her work?" she asked.

"Mary Cassatt?" Nick repeated. He did not in fact know her work.

"You know Degas?" she demanded.

"Yes."

"Renoir?"

"Yes."

"Monet?"

"What's your point?" Nick said.

"No one knows the women painters. Only the men. Cassatt is as good as any of them. Better in some cases," she said. "Cassatt's *Woman Bathing* struck me dumb," she continued, her voice quiet now. "I was only six years old, but somehow I understood something important was happening to me as I looked at that painting."

He knew what she meant. He had felt that too, standing in front of Winslow Homer's painting *The Fog Warning* at the Museum of Fine Arts in Boston on a dreary March afternoon a few years ago. He'd gone there with a girl who went to Pembroke, the sister of his roommate, visiting from Providence. He was mildly bored with her and the museum until he walked into a gallery and saw that painting and something in him shifted. Should he share this with this woman? Would she believe he really did understand?

"All I want, all I ever wanted, was to go to Paris and paint. But here I am"—her hands swept across her belly—"like this, in a war."

"Surely you want this too," Nick said. "A family? A home?"

"My parents wanted this for me," she said.

"Don't women . . . " Nick began. But he couldn't finish his sentence.

He thought all women wanted children and a husband and nice things, but maybe he was wrong.

Camille reached out her hand for her paintings, which Nick was still holding.

When he gave them back to her, she said, "You are an American man who has had an easy life, no?"

"Well," Nick said, "I wouldn't call life down here easy."

"I mean before this. You never had to think hard or work hard. You never had to make a hard decision, did you?"

"I worked hard," he said, but he didn't say it with much conviction. Rowing had been hard, he supposed, but it had come naturally to him. He'd even liked getting up at dawn to practice, the sound of the oars as they hit the water, the way the boat glided across the surface.

"What would you do if you had to make a life-or-death decision? Would you make the right choice?" she asked.

"Look," Nick said, "we're in the middle of a war. Everything is life or death."

"I don't think you'd be able to do it," she said with that same confidence. "I think you are too weak."

"Hey," he said. "Where do you get off saying things like that?"

Camille narrowed her eyes at him, studying his face long enough to make him uncomfortable.

"I mean, you don't know anything about me," Nick said.

"I know you are a man," she said. "That is all I need to know. Men are all talk, but when they have to actually do something—"

"With all due respect, ma'am, men are the ones out here fighting this war."

"Men caused this war, no?"

"Well," Nick began.

"In that house," Camille said, "is my husband, waiting for his dinner. What kind of world is this where a man cannot make himself even a simple egg?"

"I can make eggs," Nick said. "Scrambled."

"In some ways, it is my misfortune that I was a born a woman," Camille said. "And it is your misfortune that you were born a man."

Nick wanted to defend himself, to prove to her that he could do whatever was asked of him, no matter how difficult. But she was hoisting herself up, her big belly pushing against the thin striped cotton of her dress.

"Don't go," he said.

She paused, half in and half out. "Why?"

Nick shrugged. "I like talking to you."

That wasn't entirely true. After all, she made him feel like an idiot. But he felt a pull toward her, embarrassingly sexual even though she was so hugely pregnant.

He stared up at her, from her feet in those ridiculous work boots, past the thick socks with ragged tops poking from the boots, to her pale calves, to the hem of the thin striped dress. Blue and white, those stripes. Then the enormous belly and heavy breasts, the slender long neck, the red lips and dark eyes.

"Do you believe in . . . in—"

"God? No," she said definitively. "God wouldn't make this horrible war."

"Not God," Nick said. "*Coup . . . coup de foudre?*"

But she was out of the trench already, her boots dangling briefly, then gone.

"Camille," he said softly, although he knew she couldn't hear him.

He didn't see her again for a week, until the night the Germans finally arrived.

All those weeks down here, waiting, waiting, for this? Nick thought. Around him, gunfire lit the sky and memories of the Fourth of July back home flooded him. The Roman candles spouting pink and blue and the bright white sparks of sparklers. Strange, he knew, to be facing death and thinking of something so beautiful, so joyful. He stood, unable to retreat or to move forward. He would add fireworks to his painting, he decided, ridiculously. Men shouted, in English and German. Guns exploded. And still Nick could not move.

Then: a woman's voice.

"Take them," she said.

Her face in the strange light of war was beautiful, round and pale. One morning, Nick had heard the screams of childbirth and then, finally, the thin wail of a baby. She hadn't come out since then. Until now.

"Camille," he managed to say.

Her eyes, darting from his face to the encroaching soldiers, were wide with terror.

"Save them," she said, and she placed two small bundles into his arms.

Nick glanced down, not knowing how he could do what she asked, how he could possibly save anything. One bundle, wrapped in coarse beige linen, had the corners of canvases jutting from it. The other, in a soft white blanket, revealed half of the sleeping face of a baby.

"He is Laurent," she said softly.

Nick couldn't take his eyes from the boy's face. The ridiculously long lashes. The impossibly tiny nose. Eyebrows so fair they looked like shadows of eyebrows. But when he finally did look back up, Camille was gone.

He squinted into the darkness, knowing that calling her name would only alert soldiers to her presence. A fresh burst of artillery fire lit the sky, and in the flash of light he saw her running. Her long dark hair spread around her, her blue dress tangled in her legs. She was barefoot. Smoke surrounded her, but she did not stop. Nick watched her until she disappeared in the distant woods.

His heart banged against his ribs. He could taste gunpowder and smoke and blood. He should go back into the trench. He should leave both bundles and pray that the Germans wouldn't go down there. But of course they would. And they would destroy the paintings and do what to the baby? Kill him? Leave him to die? *He is Laurent.*

Ahead of him, Nick saw what he thought were fallen trees. But no, they were bodies. Dozens of them. He had to do something. Anything.

If Camille had gone to the woods, perhaps she knew it was safe there.

Carefully, he lifted his gun and looped it around his shoulder. An eerie silence filled the air now, cut only by thick coughing and the hum of moans. Nick went in the direction Camille had gone, the sky dark except for a waning moon shrouded in clouds. The paintings rocked against each other in the linen; the baby remained still and warm.

Then more gunfire, this time from the woods, from the direction in which Camille had run.

Nick was shaking so hard that he could hear the canvases banging against each other. He had to think. He had to do something.

He stumbled in the smoke that was filling the air, its rotten stink gagging him.

He had to save them, these paintings, this tiny baby.

But how?

More gunfire. Closer. The sounds of German soldiers shouting.

I don't want to die. God help me, I don't want to die, Nick thought. Or maybe he said it out loud?

He should drop the paintings and run with the baby. But run where? There was, he realized, nowhere to run. Firing was all around him.

Slowly Nick began to walk in the opposite direction of the gunfire. He walked and he walked and he walked, fast, until the smoke was gone and the air was still. He was in a village, a village that seemed empty, deserted. But someone would return, surely, to his home. And that person would walk down this cobblestoned street and see this baby and rescue him. Yes. That would be the safest and smartest thing to do. Leave the baby here, safe, to be found.

Nick walked to a well in the center of the town square. It was dawn and birds were singing. He looked around again. The villagers had fled, he supposed. But they would come back. Of course they would come back.

He laid the small bundle in the grass by the well. If he'd had paper and a pen, he would have written a note explaining everything. But all he had were his paints, so he took out the reddest paint and wrote *Laurent* on the well above the baby's head. Laurent's small rosebud lips were sucking at nothing. *Please find him,* Nick thought. Or perhaps he'd said that out loud too. He tightened his grip on the other bundle, Camille's beautiful paintings. Without thinking, he pulled a few out and tucked them snug beneath the baby. A thank-you for whoever saved Laurent. *No*, Nick thought. *A bribe.*

Slowly, he walked away from the baby. Somewhere not too far away, a rooster crowed, as if this were an ordinary day.

Nick kept walking until he reached another village, this one full of triumphant soldiers. Thankfully they were Italian, on his side. He sat on a park bench, stunned, silent.

A soldier approached him, spoke in Italian. Nick shrugged, tried to indicate that he didn't understand.

The soldier was pointing. In the distance, Nick saw what he was trying to tell him. There were Americans over there.

CHAPTER THREE

Providence, Rhode Island

Jenny, September 1973

Jenny had read that in Italy there were bars that weren't bars. Instead, they sold coffee, so many kinds with such exotic names, and you stood at these bars and drank your *cappuccino*, your *macchiato*, your *caffè latte*. Standing up! The money was called *lira* and it took buckets of *lire* to equal one dollar. Italy, Jenny knew, because she had studied it in the atlas at the library, was shaped like a boot. Its capital was Rome. Mount Vesuvius had erupted in A.D. 79 and buried the city of Pompeii in ash, killing over a thousand people. One day in 1592, Pompeii was discovered, more or less intact, and even today you could go there, to Pompeii, which was only about twenty miles from Naples—she had figured that out on the map—and see a dog with bread in his mouth, a man sitting and looking thoughtful, a woman clutching her child and screaming, all of them preserved in ash.

She heard about Pompeii early one morning at the end of her all-night shift at the International House of Pancakes on Thayer Street. Drunk or high Brown University students came in early and ordered stacks of pancakes, sausages, bacon. They slathered everything with blueberry syrup and talked in languages she didn't understand. Dutch to the Dutch apple pancakes, Swedish to the lingonberry ones.

Jenny hated the students. She hated them for their indifference to her, the casual way they dropped twenty-dollar bills into her hand. She hated them for what they knew. Sometimes one of them, the cutest or most obnoxious one, read her name on her name tag and used it too often, saying *Jenny* with sarcasm and scorn. Just two years ago, Jenny had been a person going places. She was Most Likely to Succeed and class president and yearbook editor. She'd had a full scholarship to college, even though it was the state school. She was somebody, the girl everyone looked up to. Sometimes she wanted to tell all this to these buffoons, itemize all she'd accomplished, but in the end, she was here, wasn't she? The girl going nowhere.

That was how she fell in love with Italy, the country shaped like a boot where a thousand people were covered in ash. She'd known about Italy, of course, but not in the way the entitled students who came in talked about it. They did semesters abroad in Florence, where they bought leather bomber jackets cheap at flea markets and saw Michelangelo's *David* and drank red wine at lunch. They took trains to Rome and ate spaghetti made with pig jowls and heard the pope pray from his balcony on Sunday mornings. The adventurous ones went even farther south, to Naples, a crumbling, beautiful city on a glistening bay with Vesuvius looming above it. Or beyond, to Sicily, with its Greek ruins and its own volcano, Mount Etna.

Once, she'd overhead a four-top talking about Mount Etna, how one of them had bought a souvenir ashtray made from its lava.

"I read about that," Jenny said, her order pad in one hand and her pencil poised above it.

The boys all stopped talking and stared up at her.

"In 1971? The lava almost wiped out entire villages and covered five miles."

They kept staring at her.

Jenny felt her cheeks flush. She wanted to tell them why she would never forget that eruption, timed to perfectly match her own life blowing up. She wanted to tell them that she knew a lot of things, that she spent afternoons at the library reading magazines and newspapers and novels.

She'd read Gore Vidal's *Burr* and Vonnegut's *Breakfast of Champions*. She bet they hadn't. They just read whatever was on their syllabi. *Ask me anything*, she wanted to say.

"Anyhoo," one of the boys said, "I'll have a grilled ham skillet. That comes with pancakes, right?" He was looking at her now, with his bangs falling into his eyes and his Hapsburg jaw jutting.

Jenny tapped the menu, right under the category "IHOP Skillets."

" 'Served with two fluffy buttermilk pancakes,' " she recited without having to read the smaller print beneath it.

"So it says," the boy said.

Get me out of here, Jenny thought, not for the first time.

Jenny saved her tips, the quarters and dimes that jingled in her pink polyester apron pocket. If she took a plane to Iceland, she could connect to a flight to Rome, then take a train from Rome to anywhere—Florence, Naples, Milan. This, she learned from the bored travel agent at College Hill Travel on Thayer Street, was the cheapest way to get to Europe.

"Do you have a student ID?" the travel agent asked her. "Because it's even cheaper with your ID."

The woman—hair high and stiff with hair spray, coral lips, oval nails painted pink—did not look at Jenny, did not see her shake her head no. Briefly Jenny wondered if a two-year-old expired student ID might work.

"And a Eurail Pass will get you all around. Not just Italy, but all around," the travel agent added. "Kids like Austria and Switzerland. Hiking in the Alps, et cetera."

Jenny wrote the information down in the little blue pad where she took pancake orders. *Icelandair. Eurail Pass. Student ID.*

"You have a passport, right?" the woman said.

Before Jenny could shake her head no, the woman was pushing a passport application across the desk.

"Fill this out and take it to the post office. You know the main post office on Corliss Street?"

PO, Corliss Street, Jenny wrote.

"You need two pictures," the woman said. "It's all explained on the form."

"Thank you," Jenny told her.

The woman swiveled her chair around and picked up the phone. She was finished with Jenny.

How many pancakes would she have to serve before she earned enough tips to get herself there? A lot, that was how many. Stacks and stacks. She asked Fred, her manager, for extra shifts. Fred was short and sweaty and pasty-skinned, his Adam's apple big above the knot in his tie. When he was under pressure or angry, which was most of the time, that Adam's apple bobbed up and down furiously.

"Why should I give you extra shifts?" he told her. "You ain't got kids or a mortgage or even a car payment."

While he talked to her, his eyes flitted from table to table, waitress to waitress, watching for coffee mugs that needed filling and crumbs that should be wiped up, sticky syrup containers, disgruntled customers.

"Bev! Table six!" he hissed over his shoulder at Bev, slouching against the counter next to him.

"I still have to live," Jenny said softly.

Fred turned toward her. "What?" he demanded. One of his eyes had the unnerving habit of drifting off all by itself in the wrong direction.

"I still need to make money," Jenny said.

Fred frowned. His eye drifted.

"You want to switch to all midnight-to-eight shifts?" he said. "Because if you want to make money, I can give you five midnight-to-eights."

He turned away from her again.

"Diane! Do I see empty cups at that four-top?" he said, and Diane grabbed a coffeepot and hurried to the table.

"Okay," Jenny said.

"Weekends," Fred added. "Wednesday through Sunday. Midnight to eight."

Weekend nights meant students, cops, thugs, bums.

"Sunday night's slow," Jenny said. The brochure she'd gotten at the travel agency with a picture of the Colosseum on the front seemed to burn in her apron pocket.

Fred swung toward her again. "Slow, huh? You want Sunday *morning*?"

She thought of all the families that came in on Sunday mornings in their church clothes. Squirming kids and mothers in hats and proud fathers. The kids always ordered the Mickey Mouse pancakes: whipped-cream mouse ears and a chocolate grin.

"You want a double shift? Midnight to eight Saturday, eight to four Sunday?" Fred was saying, his Adam's apple bobbing and his eye floating back in focus.

Jenny thought of the picture in the brochure of the Bay of Naples glittering beneath Mount Vesuvius. "Sure," she said.

He shook his head. "You got it," he said, and walked away from her. She watched him stop at every table and ask, "Is everything okay? Is our girl taking good care of you?"

She went to the waitress station to refill the syrups: boysenberry, strawberry, fake maple. But first she took out the brochure, unfolded it, smoothed the creases. She looked at that picture on the cover, then the ones inside: the Leaning Tower of Pisa, a man in a striped shirt and straw hat rowing a gondola, a cathedral with a red tiled dome.

"We need syrup!" she heard Fred say, and she folded the brochure, put it back in her apron pocket, and picked up the sticky plastic jug of boysenberry.

"You see," the boy said softly, "I don't have any money."

Jenny frowned. He was beautiful, this boy. His hair was long and blond, just skimming his collarbone. And his eyes were a pale blue that made her think of a crayon she'd had as a child, the one that she cried over when it broke. Cornflower, that's what it was called.

She looked down at his empty plate. He'd had three buttermilk pancakes and sausages and two eggs over easy: $3.29 worth of food.

"I left my wallet in my apartment," he explained, as if that would make her forgive him.

"But you have to pay," Jenny said.

He tilted his head back and looked up at her. "Did you ever see the movie *The Graduate*?"

"Yes," she said, knowing what he was about to say.

"Anyone ever tell you that you look like that actress? The one who played Elaine?"

"Yes," she said again. People were always telling her that.

"Katharine Ross," he said.

"If you don't pay, then I have to pay," she explained. "From my tips." *And I am saving these tips to get the hell out of here*, she added to herself.

It was four o'clock on a Sunday morning and she'd been here for four long hours. A drunken boy had puked right on the table. A bum had fallen asleep and she hadn't been able to wake him and had had to call the cops to get him out. Two tables hadn't left any tips at all. And she had twelve more hours before she went home.

"I could give you something more valuable than change," the boy said. "Because you'd only make what? A thirty-cent tip on my bill?"

Sure, if he left ten percent. Some people left less.

"The point is," Jenny said, trying to keep her voice even, "I would lose three twenty-nine. Three twenty-nine of *my* money."

"But there are things more valuable, more important than money," the boy said. "That's part of why this country is going to hell. We've become a nation of consumers. I'm considering getting the hell out of here. Becoming an expat. Maybe in Mexico. Or Chile."

"Okay, well, I'm not going to do that," she said, her voice a little too loud. Luckily, the place was practically empty. Luckily, Fred didn't work on Saturday nights.

"You might," the boy said, smiling. "I might convince you to come live with me. Maybe in Italy. You ever been to Italy?"

"You can go home and get the money. I'm here all night," she said.

He had a well-thumbed paperback on the table beside his plate. *Stones of the Sky.*

"Have you read him?" he asked when he saw her notice it. "Pablo Neruda?"

"I—" Jenny began. She was always embarrassed by how little she'd read, how little she knew. One semester of college, and she'd learned nothing. She had imagined that she would get to college and spend long afternoons reading all kinds of things—British novels and philosophy books and Shakespeare's plays. But she'd mostly sat in big auditoriums with hundreds of other kids, listening to lectures in introductory psychology, sociology, and earth science. The good classes came junior year, when all of the required ones were finished. Jenny hadn't made it that far.

"He's a poet for our generation," the boy was saying. "Positive and romantic and political. My dissertation compares him to Whitman. It's called 'Joyous Impulses.' You like Whitman?"

" 'I am large,' " Jenny said. " 'I contain multitudes.' " She'd read *Leaves of Grass*, or parts of it anyway, in Honors English in high school.

"Yes! 'I celebrate myself!' Whitman wrote. And Neruda answered, 'I'm coming, I'm coming, wait up, stones'!" the boy said, poking a page in the book. "He won the Nobel Prize for Literature a couple years ago. 'For a poetry that with the action of an elemental force brings alive a continent's destiny and dreams.' "

The door opened, letting in a burst of cold air and the smell of beer, breaking the spell. Jenny turned and saw six drunken Brown students spill in, stumbling and laughing and pushing each other. One of them caught her eye and said, very seriously, "We've come here for pancakes."

That made the other five burst into laughter.

"Pancakes," another one repeated, and they all laughed again.

"Three twenty-nine," Jenny said to the boy with the book.

"Okay, okay," he said. His eyes landed on her name tag. "Jenny," he added. "I'm Daniel. Don't forget me, okay? I'm leaving in three days."

"I won't forget you because you will be back here in twenty minutes with my money."

"Research," Daniel said. "I got a grant to visit Neruda's houses in Mexico and Chile and Italy."

At the sound of the word *Italy*, Jenny straightened.

"For the Isle of Capri. You know Capri? The Blue Grotto?" he was saying. "Neruda lived there in exile in 1952."

But it was Jackie Kennedy who came to Jenny's mind at the mention of Capri. Her mother had been obsessed with the black-and-white newspaper photos of her having special sandals made there. *Fifty dollars! For sandals!*

"In the Bay of Naples," the boy—Daniel—was saying.

"I know where it is," Jenny said. Then she added, "That's where they make Canfora sandals."

He grinned. "Sure," he said. "But it's also the island of exiles. Emperor Tiberius. The historians Tacitus and Suetonius. Vladimir Lenin. And Pablo Neruda. He wrote *The Captain's Verses* there, in Via Tragara at Edwin Cerio's villa."

Jenny tried not to show him how captivated she was. The names that rolled so easily off his tongue. The things he knew.

"What did he do?" she managed to ask. "Neruda, I mean. Why was he in exile?"

"Political reasons," Daniel said. "Capri's the last place I need to visit for the dissertation. I spent last year in Argentina, so now I need to go to Mexico and, of course, Chile." He said *Meh-hi-co*. He said *Chee-lay*.

Jenny pressed her fingertips to her temples. The drunken college kids were making a lot of noise and laughing too loudly. What was this boy talking about? She just wanted her money.

Daniel stood and leaned in close to her.

"Did you know that just a few years ago they discovered statues of Neptune and Triton in the Blue Grotto dating from the first century?"

"Hey! We want some pancakes, miss!" one of the drunken boys called out.

"The water there is a brilliant azure," Daniel said. "If you put your hand in it, your hand glows blue."

He grinned again and stuck out his hand, offering her something, but she didn't take it.

"Maybe you'll meet me there, Princess Jenny of IHOP! We'll go to the Blue Grotto and Casa di Arturo, the villa where Neruda stayed."

"You're not going to pay me, are you?" she said.

Jenny turned away, already deducting that damn three dollars and twenty-nine cents, and went over to the drunken students, all crammed into a booth. She took out her order pad and waited as they discussed what they should get, reading aloud the descriptions of the pancakes in fake accents. Swedish. French.

Out of the corner of her eye, she saw Daniel walk out. Even though he'd stiffed her, Jenny knew that he was exactly the kind of boy she wanted to go out with. Someone who knew poetry, who traveled the world, who was smart and romantic. She thought of that line from the Simon and Garfunkel song "The Dangling Conversation": "And you read your Emily Dickinson, and I my Robert Frost . . ." That sounded like the perfect couple to her, one of them reading Dickinson and the other one Frost, pausing to say lines out loud to each other.

Despite the chilly early autumn night, Jenny saw that Daniel didn't have on a coat, just an army-green pocket T-shirt and faded jeans and sneakers. She found herself wishing he'd come back tomorrow, that he'd want to keep talking to her. *Stop*, she told herself. The last thing she needed was a boyfriend, especially one who was about to move out of the country. What she needed was to earn enough money to leave here and start a new life. A real life.

When she cleared his table, she found the napkin he'd tried to give her tucked into the book of poems. On it he'd written: *we shall be stone, borderless night, unbending love, unending brilliance . . . the only star that is ours.*

She stuck the napkin into her pocket. Just as she'd figured, he didn't come back with her money.

At home, the television blared some movie, a western. Her mother always watched *Sunday Afternoon at the Movies*, no matter what was playing. The smells of fried hamburgers and cigarette smoke filled the air. Jenny sighed. She'd read in a magazine that people should eat more salads and fresh vegetables. In the library, she'd torn a recipe out of an issue of *Good Housekeeping*; it was for a Cobb salad, which had been invented in Hollywood at the Brown Derby restaurant, where Clark Gable proposed to Carole Lombard. It had chicken, lettuce, avocado, bacon, hard-boiled eggs, and cheese. "A traditional Cobb salad," the recipe read, "has blue cheese, but most people prefer a milder cheddar." The salad was served with Russian dressing.

"Mom," Jenny said, entering the living room. She turned on the light that sat on the end table and dropped onto the couch, kicking her shoes off as she did. Her mother didn't answer, just kept her eyes on the television screen.

"Mom!" Jenny said again.

"Shhh. This is the best part," her mother said. "The climax."

Jenny rubbed one foot, feeling the bump of a corn on her little toe, the hard calluses on her sole.

"You've seen this a million times," she muttered.

"Go get some dinner. It's in the oven."

"Tomorrow night I'm going to make dinner," Jenny said. She imagined the beautiful Cobb salad in her mother's good china bowl, the one she never used, a wedding gift. And candles. And wine in the crystal wineglasses her mother also never used, also wedding gifts. The way dinners looked in glossy magazines. The way dinners looked inside houses on Love Lane.

Now her mother sighed. "You're not going to let me watch the end of this, are you?"

"I am," Jenny said, getting to her feet. "Watch away."

She went into the kitchen and took one of the hamburger patties and a scoop of buttery canned corn out of the oven, then sat at the table, with its cheerful yellow-and-white checked tablecloth topped with plastic and the bowl of plastic fruit in the center—pears and apples and purple grapes and one banana—and emptied her apron pocket. All the change and one-dollar bills spread out before her like a promise.

"Russ called!" her mother shouted over the sound of gunshots. "He'll be here in time for *60 Minutes*!"

Jenny rolled her eyes. *Russ. Russell.* Why didn't he just go away? Leave her alone already. She suspected he kept coming over out of guilt, some misplaced sense of responsibility. Or maybe he too was simply bored.

"I told you I don't love Russ," Jenny yelled back. "I don't even like him much," she added to herself.

When her mother didn't answer, Jenny called, "I told you I'm saving up to go away."

She began to stack the coins, all the quarters and dimes and nickels in their own neat columns. The pennies—*Really? Pennies?*—and the one half-dollar. Next she sorted the bills, facing them in the same direction. Mostly ones and a few fives and . . . Jenny frowned. And a paper napkin? She unfolded it. Right. The boy who left his wallet at his apartment.

we shall be stone, borderless night, unbending love, unending bril-liance . . . the only star that is ours.

What was she supposed to make of that?

CHAPTER FOUR

The Museum of Tears

Enzo, 1942

E nzo stared down at all of the vials of tears he had accumulated. Luisa Tetrazzini's, of course. But also his own mother's: Rosa Piccolo. SAD-NESS OVER ALL THE THINGS SHE REGRETS. A man he heard crying by the bay one night: Benito Piazza. LOST EVERYTHING GAMBLING. There were tears from a lost child, from a woman in the neighborhood who had a still-born baby, from a young woman whose husband died in the war. So many tears that Enzo had to figure out what to do with them, how to honor them.

His own tears could find a place here too, he thought.

This was the truth about Enzo: although he was considered by some to be quite handsome, and known around town for being kind and thought-ful, a good son, a good uncle, a devoted worker, he had never been in love. Had never, actually, even had a girlfriend, unless he counted Lucia, his childhood friend, whom he adored. They had been inseparable from the time they'd started school until Lucia grew breasts and other boys took her attention. That long-ago autumn when they were twelve and Lucia arrived back in school taller, more long-legged, and with the breasts of a woman, Enzo was tortured watching other boys, older boys, even his own brother, flirt with her. Boys flocked around Lucia the way the seagulls flocked around the bay when there was an especially tasty treat there.

Instead of meandering home together after school, wandering the alleys and hills of Naples, Lucia would look at him and without regret say, "Not today, Enzo." And Enzo would watch her go off with whichever boy, his heart ripping more each day. He knew that she had never gazed at him the way she gazed up at those boys, her eyes soft and sparkling. She took her lunches with boys who were not him, and when he went to her apartment building and called up to her, it was her mother who flung open the window, stuck her head out, and told him Lucia wasn't home.

One night, after months of this torture, Enzo walked the streets alone, determined to come up with a plan to win her back. He realized, however, that she had never really been his. It was dark, and the streets away from the piazzas were empty except for the occasional prostitute leaning against a wall beneath a Mussolini poster or a drunk zigzagging his way home. Enzo turned this way and that, dreaming up plans and then discarding them. But then he realized how simple this was. All he had to do was tell Lucia that he loved her! In all of their years of friendship, he had never actually said this to her. Perhaps she didn't think he loved her. Perhaps she was feeling rejected too.

Ecstatic with this realization, he decided to cut through an alley, practically humming out loud. And there, right in front of him, pressed against a building, stood a boy with Lucia draped around him, her thin arms clutching his waist, her beautiful face softly lit by an apartment window's light from above. Although Enzo did not yet know the mechanics of how these things actually worked, he understood what he was seeing, and he understood too that Lucia would never be his. Afraid that she would open her eyes and see him, Enzo slowly backed out of the alley, careful not to make any sounds. Once he turned the corner, he ran the rest of the way home. Had there been a Museum of Tears then, Enzo sometimes thought when the memory resurfaced, he would have collected his own and placed the vial there: BROKEN HEART OF A TWELVE-YEAR-OLD BOY.

Enzo sighed at the memory. He took a cracked piece of terra-cotta and carefully carved into it: MUSEUM OF TEARS. Then he hung it on the door of the workshop, beneath his and his brother's names. Enzo fussed with it, making sure it was straight, before he went back inside and arranged the tubes on a shelf in the alcove in the back. He told his brother not to move them.

"This is a museum," he said.

His brother just shook his head.

"The Museum of Tears," Enzo said.

"You will need lots more room then. In a war, many tears are shed."

"In a lifetime," Enzo said, wanting to explain all the ways hearts break but not finding enough words.

Yesterday his brother had said, "Under Mussolini, we were hungry for a day. Under the Americans, we are hungry for a week."

Enzo thought he saw a tear glisten on his brother's cheek. He knew better than to try to collect it. That was just the sort of thing about him that irritated Massimo.

"People cry because they're hungry," Enzo said now. "And sad. And mourning. And—"

"I know why people cry," his brother said, but he said it gently.

CHAPTER FIVE

Jenny, 1973

S ometimes at night, alone in her childhood bed (white furniture, trimmed in gold; sheets covered with lilacs; feather pillows), Jenny let herself think of that one semester at college. She closed her eyes and re-created the dorm room—Barlow 401—with its cinder-block walls, which she and her roommate painted a yellow that reminded Jenny of pineapples, and the Marimekko sheets they'd bought for too much money, leaving Jenny short of cash for textbooks. But how could she say no to the exotic girl who had burst into that small room wielding two pails of that paint (not plain yellow, as Jenny thought of it, but *sundance*) and rollers and brushes and said, "Okay, doll face, let's get to work."

Doll face. Also: sweetie pie and cutes.

As in "Sweetie pie, Vera thinks we should go to the Glass Mall and get matching Marimekko sheets and duvets, n'est-ce pas? Unikko."

She was Vera. And she always referred to herself in the third person like that.

Vera stood back and studied the one wall they'd painted, nodding, satisfied. "Yes," she said. "Unikko."

Jenny felt dizzy, like she'd just stepped off a boat and into a foreign country. Glass Mall. Marimekko. Unikko. She had no idea what any of it meant.

"Or Vera could just pick them up when she's home this weekend?" Vera said.

"Where's home?" Jenny managed to ask.

"Boston," Vera said with a sigh. "Somehow BC, BU, and Emerson did not accept me. A clerical error, surely. But alas, here I am."

Vera was a theater major. She took Mime, Introduction to Theater, The Alexander Technique, Voice, Introduction to British Literature, and Beginners Stage Combat. She always wore a black leotard and black tights with a jersey wrap skirt in magenta or chartreuse or metal gray, her dark hair either pulled into a ponytail or wound into a tight bun. Her shoes—flat, soft, black—came from Chinatown in Boston. To Jenny, Boston seemed as distant as Rangoon or Zanzibar, even though it was only a ninety-minute drive from Barlow 401.

Jenny's family did not go to Boston. They did not go anywhere. In July, when Jenny had asked for permission to see John Sebastian perform in Providence, her mother had told her absolutely not.

"You want to go to Providence alone? To a hippie concert?" her mother said. "Absolutely not."

She went anyway, telling her mother that she and Russ were going to see the movie *Joe* at the Midland Mall and then to Chelo's for strawberry pie.

"You better be home by midnight. Not a minute later," her mother said as Jenny and Russ were leaving. She didn't even bother to look at them, just kept working the jigsaw puzzle of kittens she'd been doing all summer.

In Russ's white VW Bug, Jenny pulled off her chamois shirt and then wiggled out of her bra without removing her skinny tie-dyed T-shirt, a trick that always pleased him. He reached over and pinched her left nipple with one hand as he shifted into drive with the other.

"You're hot, college girl," he said, pinching again.

"Hey. That's attached," Jenny said, swatting his hand away.

Russ was boorish, not very smart, and beautiful. When he'd asked her

out in tenth grade, she thought she was the luckiest girl in the entire sophomore class—a gorgeous senior had wanted to go out with her. On that
very first date to see *Bullitt*, she was so dazzled by the way his dark hair
curled around the collar of his suede jacket. The bluish shadow on his high
cheeks. The one dimple in his left cheek. The smell of him: suede, soap,
and something deep and mysterious. By Halloween, she was his girlfriend.

After he graduated in June, he went to work for his uncle at their family's golf course. He mowed the grass and caddied and sold golf balls and
shirts with the golf course logo on them at the shop. "Don't you think you
should go to college?" she asked him. "What for?" he said. "One brain
in the family is plenty," he added, nudging her in the ribs with his elbow.
Family? The thought made her queasy. They weren't a family. She didn't
want them to be a family.

By the time she was back in school that fall, she knew that Russ was
the wrong person for her. She wanted to go to college, travel the world, *be*
something. He was content riding around in a golf cart or drinking beer
with his friends. She avoided Russ as much as she could. There were yearbook meetings and school newspaper deadlines and student council votes
and SAT prep classes and homework and the fundraiser she ran to break
the Guinness World Record for hot dog eating. There was chorus practice
and making sets for the school play and studying and anything, anything,
she could think of to avoid meeting Russ at the golf course.

By the summer of 1973, she was counting the days until she gave Russ
the breakup speech she'd been practicing since graduation. They'd been
together for three years. She would tell Russ it wasn't fair to either of them
to stay together when she was leaving for college in just four days. She
would say that it was hurting her more than it hurt him to break up, but she
had to do the right thing. She would cry, but just a little, and she would let
him make love to her one last time. Then she would take the bus the thirty
miles to the University of Rhode Island and she would start her real life,
the one she'd imagined for practically ever. In this life, people read books
and discussed poetry and art. They ate fresh fruit and vegetables, went to
the ballet and maybe even the opera. In this life, people were happy.

On the way to the concert in Providence, Russ pulled over and lit a joint. Jenny had been smoking way too much pot and drinking way too much beer that summer, mostly to dull her hours with Russ, who bored her more with each passing day.

"Come here, Professor," he said when she was good and stoned, pulling her onto his lap.

Lately, having sex with Russ was fun only if Jenny was this stoned—sloppy, goofy, dumb stoned. She closed her eyes, almost enjoying it, him thrusting into her and her knee banging into the stick shift and the hot summer night air filling the car.

It wasn't until after that she thought, *Shit*, because he hadn't put on a condom. At college there was an infirmary where they gave out birth control pills like candy. That's what her friend Wendy, a year older and already about to be a sophomore there, had told her. Day one she would get a prescription, Jenny decided as she dropped back onto her seat. She tugged her T-shirt back down and leaned her head against the headrest, letting the whoosh of the breeze wash over her as they continued driving to Providence.

"You are wasted," Russ said happily.

"Mm-hmm," Jenny said, smiling to herself.

Jenny left out most of these details when she mentioned to Vera that she'd seen John Sebastian in concert that summer. Vera was playing his solo album and singing along to "Darling Be Home Soon" in their sundance-painted room with the Unikko sheets, which Jenny now knew were just sheets with big blue flowers on them designed by a woman in Finland, of all places, and sold at a store in Cambridge.

"But wait," Vera said. "Vera was at that concert too!"

They both squealed with delight at the kismet of it, both of them at the same concert. Surely they were meant to be roommates and best friends.

"Destiny," Vera said, taking Jenny's hand in hers and squeezing it. "We'll live together all four years, but we'll leave the dorms and move down the line, maybe to Bonnet?"

Bonnet Shores was a small beach community where students rented summer houses during the school year.

"Bonnet," Jenny repeated, imagining one of the small houses where she'd gone to a party one weekend; it had had nautical-themed furniture and decorations. Vera had held up a needlepointed blue pillow with white stitching and read, "Life's a Beach" off it.

"And then we'll get apartments together after college, in San Francisco or New York or somewhere," Vera continued, "and I'll be in plays at La MaMa and you'll work for *Vogue* or something and then we'll be each other's maids of honor and I'll name my first daughter Jenny and you'll name yours Vera and eventually our husbands will die because the husbands always die first and we'll live together again!"

Jenny grinned and nodded, seeing it, all of it. Seeing her life unfold. Her real life.

CHAPTER SIX

Rhode Island

Nick, 1974

S omeone was knocking on the door, relentlessly.

 Goddamnit, it took Nick forever just to get up from his recliner and walk across the kitchen to answer the door.

His knees ached. His hips ached. His mouth was dry, his eyes blurry. *Goddamnit.*

And at the door? Two men in military uniforms.

Nick blinked, trying to clear up the blurriness.

"Sir," one of the men said. "It's an honor to meet you."

One eye's vision came suddenly into sharp focus, sending Nick backward a few steps.

"What?" he said, his lips smacking together loudly.

The other guy had his hand out. Nick didn't shake it.

"May we come in?" the first one asked.

"Why?" Nick said as his other eye slowly focused.

The men glanced at each other.

"To talk?" the one with his hand out said, dropping his hand.

"About?" Nick said. *Smack smack.* He licked his dry lips with his parched tongue. Then he turned from the men and went back inside, achingly, slowly, to get a beer.

The men followed him in.

Nick was acutely aware of the house, tired and dusty since Lillian had died. Which wasn't yesterday, or last month, or last year, but almost ten years ago, right here in the kitchen. A stroke. Just like that. She was putting the coffee on and he was opening the newspaper and she dropped to the floor, her eyes frightened and one side of her mouth drooping and by night she was gone. Now the ruffled curtains with the pattern of ripe, red, almost cartoonish cherries were dulled with time and bleached from sunlight. There were ashtrays with old cigarette butts everywhere, more than one square of the harvest-gold linoleum had a scorch mark from a dropped cigarette, and—Nick realized as he looked around, almost for the first time in years—everything made him seem like a pathetic old man.

Nick puffed his chest out and straightened his shoulders, sending a sharp pain down his spine.

"I guess you can sit down," he said, pointing to the kitchen table and chairs.

They did. So did Nick.

"You went to school with my grandmother," one of the men said. "Julia Mareaux?"

The name didn't ring a bell, but Nick grunted something that sounded like an affirmative.

"She remembers you too! Said you were a big athlete?"

"Did you come here to go over my high school yearbook? Or you got some other business?" Nick said.

The guy blushed. He was the younger of the two, pink-cheeked and shaggy-haired.

"I . . . we—"

The other guy interrupted: "We're here about the veterans' parade." Older. They could almost be father and son.

"Sir," the younger one said, "we at the American Legion would be honored if you would march with us in the Veterans Day Parade. We can provide a car for you to ride in, if that would be easier—"

"A Caddy," the older one said, nudging Nick with his elbow like they were in on a secret together. "Nice one too. We put the top down and you can sit up on the back seat or all comfy up front."

"I hate parades," Nick said, fumbling a cigarette from a pack and lighting it. He always had. Lillian had loved them though, the marching bands and heavily decorated floats. She never missed the Macy's Thanksgiving Day Parade on TV, or the Tournament of Roses Parade on New Year's Day. *Eighteen million flowers on these floats! Can you believe it, Nick?* He used to indulge her, feigning enthusiasm. *Eighteen million? Will you look at that!* Who would have thought that he'd even miss watching those darn parades with her?

The men were staring at him.

Nick cleared his throat.

The warm feelings that had washed over Nick as he'd thought of Lillian happily watching that parade faded. That's how it was these days—the good part of him, the happy parts, showed themselves less often.

"I can't," Nick said, hearing the harshness in his voice and wishing he could explain how fleeting kindness had become for him. "I've got things to do."

"I served," the older guy said. "In the Pacific. Nothing compared to what you guys went through—"

Nick coughed one of his deep, phlegmy coughs. The men looked at their laps until he caught his breath.

"Matthew here was in Nam. Lost his leg."

Nick glanced at the kid. Prosthetics had come a long way. He would have never guessed.

The guy leaned closer to Nick. "Did you know you're the last World War I vet in the county?"

They all listened as the clock noisily clicked into the silence.

Nick's ears started to ring. Around him, things began to fade—the pink-cheeked guy and the ticking clock and the stale smell of cigarettes. In their place: a farm in France, a pregnant woman, a poorly painted mural. He did not want to go back there. He did not want to see the woman, wild eyed, frightened, struggling to speak English. The Germans nearing. Artillery. *Save them.*

Slowly, things came back into focus.

But Nick was no longer at the kitchen table. He was flat on his back on the linoleum, just like Lillian, one of those god-ugly afghans Lillian used to crochet draped over him.

"Stay put," the young guy was saying.

In the distance: the sound of a siren, getting closer.

For a moment, Nick thought it was the Germans, nearing. He was clutching those two blankets, one soft and warm, the other sharp and bulky.

"Don't make me save them," he mumbled.

Outside, doors slammed and footsteps pounded.

He heard the older guy say, "He's right here."

Then he was lifted and rolled onto a stretcher, his arms reaching, grasping, for what he left behind.

___

CHAPTER SEVEN

Jenny, 1973

The day Jenny's passport arrived in the mail, after she flipped its empty pages, imagining all the stamps that would fill it someday, and studied her little square picture on the front page and repeated her passport number to herself as if it were a magical incantation, she got in her Bug and headed south. It was maybe the craziest idea she had ever come up with, but what did she have to lose? Nothing, that's what. She would find Vera and ask her to go to Italy with her this summer. She would present it as a brilliant adventure, something they were meant to do together.

Jenny tried not to focus on the fact that she hadn't really spoken to Vera since that afternoon almost two years ago when she left for winter break and never came back. There had been a few awkward phone calls, some brief letters exchanged, a postcard from New York City of the bright lights of Broadway that said, *Hey Doll Face, Remember how we were going to move here together??? Saw COMPANY. Stephen Sondheim is a genius and someday I'm going to star in one of his plays. Hope you're having fun, Babycakes! Vera*

Jenny had looked up Stephen Sondheim at the library, and even listened to the album of *Company* there. Was he a genius? Was this what people like

Vera believed? Jenny didn't think the play had any plot, but maybe that was the point.

One of the consequences of getting pregnant—that one night in Russ's car without a condom—and dropping out of college after only one semester was an immediate and seemingly permanent shortage of friends. Her high school friends—Colleen, Linda, and Karen—were all at Rhode Island College, studying to be a teacher, a nurse, and an accountant. When they came home for spring break, Jenny was too pregnant to go out with them. What pregnant nineteen-year-old went to bars anyway? No one. Linda visited her, but every time she glanced at Jenny's big round belly she blushed and stammered. For most of the visit, Linda kept her gaze focused somewhere vaguely above Jenny's head.

"Good luck," she said as she slipped into her pink ski jacket at the front door.

Ski passes dangled from the zipper, and when she saw Jenny notice them, she blushed again.

"I guess you weren't able to ski this winter," she said.

Jenny glanced down at her belly pressing against one of Russ's old sweaters. "Not this winter," she said, trying to sound breezy.

"Well then, next year maybe," Linda said, and then shook Jenny's hand, surprising both of them, and walked out into the cold January night.

Jenny's neighborhood friend Annette still lived up the street. Annette was a year older and worked as a hairdresser at Julius Scissor at the mall. Jenny's pregnancy had left her unfazed. "It happens," she'd said, shrugging and puffing on one of her Virginia Slims. Annette did Jenny's hair for free, and sometimes the two of them sat in her basement rec room and drank screwdrivers or smoked pot. They had absolutely nothing in common, which Jenny found oddly comforting.

When Jenny told Annette about her dream to go to Italy, Annette said, "Some people like doing things like that." Annette was apparently not one of those people.

She did, however, get very excited about Daniel and meeting him in

Capri. "So romantic!" she said, and they spent a pleasant night stoned and trying to find him in the White Pages and through the operator. Even though it seemed he didn't exist, or at least didn't have a phone number, Annette latched onto the possibility of Jenny finding him and falling in love.

"I don't want to fall in love," Jenny insisted.

"Of course you do," Annette said. "Everyone does."

Jenny didn't even try to explain how she wanted to be back in that dorm room with Vera, listening to her run lines for a play. Or sitting on the quad watching other students walk by carrying heavy textbooks and wearing blue jeans with butterflies or hearts embroidered on the pockets. Or going to the Ram's Den for coffee with the other girls on her floor and eating Hostess cupcakes for lunch. Or drinking beer on Friday afternoons at happy hour at the Pub, flirting with the mustached bouncers and the frat boys and Andy, the boy from her Intro to American Lit class she had a crush on.

"Don't worry," Annette said dreamily, perhaps from being stoned or perhaps from her romantic notions, "you'll fall in love. Just wait."

Jenny didn't protest this time. She just let Annette pat her arm.

How could she explain to Annette, or to anyone, how much she'd loved these simple things? How she'd felt like a different person there? How she had lost something more than time and schooling and her reputation? She had lost herself, or the self she was trying to become. She had lost her future.

The house where Vera lived in Bonnet Shores was a Cape with weathered shingles and periwinkle-blue shutters on the windows. The lawn was overgrown, spotted with dandelions. Jenny knew it was ridiculous, but she wanted to prove to Vera that she was the person Vera had thought her to be. Sometimes she even dropped Vera a postcard with the picture of a writer on the front and a few lines written on the back about a book she had read or a movie she'd seen. Of course, Jenny didn't mention IHOP or anything else about her life. Just the things that might impress Vera, who had taken on ridiculous proportions in her mind as some kind of arbiter of what was cool and important. If Vera thought Jenny was cool, then maybe Jenny would actually live up to it. Jenny shook her head. It was ridiculous. She knew that. But of everybody she'd met in her brief time at college, Vera was the one she wanted to impress.

Jenny sat in her car and looked at the house long enough that a face appeared at one of the downstairs windows and stared out at her. Then the front door opened and Vera stood on the top step and put one hand above her eyes like a salute, except that Jenny realized she was just blocking the glare.

"Jenny?" Vera said, walking down the next two steps. She was barefoot and she had on those black tights she always wore and an oversized white button-down shirt. Her feet were dirty.

Jenny rolled down the window. She knew she should get out of the car and hug Vera or at the very least say something. But she was glued to her seat, unable to move. She tried to smile, but it felt wrong on her face.

"Hey," Vera said.

"Hey!"

"I got that card you sent. With Flannery O'Connor and all those peacocks?"

"College Hill Bookstore has all these really cool author cards," Jenny said. College Hill Bookstore on Thayer Street was really cool, but she didn't know if Vera knew that.

"You said you read, um, *The Painted Bird*?"

"Yes! You've read it already, I bet."

Vera shrugged. She looked back at her house as if she was considering going back inside. As if she was getting bored.

"I listened to *Company*," Jenny said. "The soundtrack."

"Yeah? Did you like it?"

Jenny didn't answer. She hadn't liked it, but if she said so Vera would think she was unsophisticated or something.

"I could be April," Vera said. "Don't you think I could be April?"

"Sure," Jenny said.

"*Barcelona*," Vera sang, and Jenny remembered what a beautiful voice Vera had. "*Flight Eighteen.*"

"You sound just like the girl on the soundtrack," Jenny said.

"Are you back?" Vera asked. "In school?"

Jenny almost lied and said yes. But then Vera would ask where she was living and what classes she was taking, so she shook her head. "I lost the scholarship and my mother won't pay."

"That sucks," Vera said.

"I was saving up to come back, but I'm going to go to Italy instead."

Vera looked at her, surprised. "Wow. That's really cool."

"I got my passport and everything," Jenny said, reaching into her hobo bag.

"You going alone?" Vera asked her.

Jenny hesitated, her hand wrapped around the stiff passport. "I was thinking," she began, but then the front door opened again and out came a curly-haired girl in overalls with a skinny T-shirt underneath and no bra.

"What's going on?" the curly-haired girl said.

"Jenny was my roommate," Vera explained. "First semester freshman year."

The girl squinted at Jenny, sizing her up. "The one who dropped out," she said.

"She was just," Vera said, and laughed. "I was going to say she was just in the neighborhood, but maybe you were actually coming here? To visit?"

"Oh, no," Jenny said. "I'm visiting some friends nearby and I was like, isn't this close to where Vera's living?"

"We have to run lines," the curly-haired girl said to Vera. She looked at Jenny. "Pirandello," she said.

"Right," Jenny said, and she thought, *Pirandello Pirandello Pirandello* so she could remember to look it up at the library. If she were still in college she would already know.

"Jenny's moving to Italy," Vera said.

"That's wild!" the girl said, impressed.

"I'm not actually moving there," Jenny said, but Vera and her room-mate had stopped listening.

"This was great," Vera said. "Seeing you again. Who did you say you were visiting?"

"My friends," Jenny said. She pointed vaguely down the street.

"Not Jessica and that crew?" Vera said.

"No, not them," Jenny said dismissively.

"That's good. I mean, really. Jessica."

"Right." Jenny rolled her eyes. "Jessica."

"Send me a postcard," Vera said, wiggling her fingers in good-bye.

"Sure. I will," Jenny said.

"Send me a million!"

"Okay!" Jenny said.

Vera and the curly-haired girl were already walking back to the house, both of them barefoot and slender and carefree.

"I named my baby after you, like we promised," Jenny said softly after the door closed. "I named her Vera."

But Vera didn't even know there had been a baby. Jenny just went home for Christmas break and never came back.

"Why are you such a sourpuss?" her mother asked her later at dinner.

They were sitting at the table for a change, instead of eating off TV trays and watching whatever program her mother couldn't miss. Jenny stared down at the Shake'n Bake pork chops and Rice-A-Roni and canned string beans. Somewhere in Italy, people were eating delicate hand-shaped tortellini, vegetables like ramps and fiddlehead ferns, things Jenny read about in *Gourmet* at the library.

"Some boy called for you," her mother said.

Jenny looked up, surprised. "Really?"

"That got your attention, didn't it? My boy-crazy daughter," her mother said, shaking her head. She took some rice onto her fork, then pierced a green bean and a piece of pork chop and put it all in her mouth.

"I'm just surprised someone called at all, since all I do is work and sit in Annette's basement or watch television with you," Jenny said.

"So you don't know any boys? You've given all that up?"

"Forget it," Jenny said, getting up and taking her plate of barely touched food into the kitchen.

"Said his name was Daniel," her mother called after her. "Said he'd call back."

Jenny stood in the doorway between the kitchen and the dining room. "Daniel?"

"Ah! Suddenly you do know a boy!"

"Did he leave a number?" Jenny asked.

"Nope. Just said he'd call back. So who is this Daniel?"

"He owes me money," Jenny said, and went back into the kitchen.

"You be careful," her mother said. "You don't need to get in any more trouble."

Despite her mother's words, Jenny smiled. He'd called her, and just a few days later, which meant he went back to the restaurant and got her number from somebody there. Which meant he was thinking about her too.

Sometimes, when Jenny's feet in the ugly white nurse shoes she wore for work really ached, she imagined running on the beach. How the sand felt beneath her bare feet. The sound of the waves. The salty air in her nose and mouth. Once, during her brief semester at college, she and three other girls from her dorm had flown kites on Narragansett Beach. It was a breezy afternoon, midweek, and they'd gone right after their two o'clock classes ended. Barefoot, they had run along the sand, the kites lifting higher and higher, whipping in the wind.

Standing at this table at IHOP, squeezing her sore toes inside her shoes as she took down the order, she thought about flying that kite, running along the shore as the kite lifted. She'd watched it flutter up there, bright red against the pale blue sky.

"Did you get that?" the girl at the table said. "Sausage instead of bacon."

"Yes, I got it," Jenny said.

She hadn't. She wasn't even listening. Instead, she was back on that beach on a perfect autumn afternoon.

It might have been exactly two years ago, she realized as she called out the order to the kitchen and put up the slip. Today was September 24, and two years ago on September 24 she'd most definitely been in college, maybe even jumping into the VW of that girl from her floor whose name she no longer remembered, clutching a red kite.

Finally, Jenny cleared her last table, wiped it down, and refilled the salt and pepper shakers, the syrup containers, the napkin holders. Then she limped to the time clock and punched out. Her shift had started at eight and it was after eleven. She stuck her hand in her apron pocket and pulled out her tips. Not even twenty bucks. It was going to take her forever to save up enough for a plane ticket and a Eurail Pass, she thought as she hurried out the door, afraid that Fred would think of something else for her to do if he saw her leaving.

Outside and safely away from the restaurant, Jenny paused. Thayer Street was empty, the only light from the streetlights and the marquee at the run-down Avon Cinema, across the street. *La Nuit Américaine*, it said. Jenny took off her shoes and walked across the street, the asphalt sharp beneath her bare feet. Directed by François Truffaut, she read on the poster at the entrance. Starring Jacqueline Bisset and Jean-Pierre Léaud. Had the theater been open, she would have bought a ticket and gone inside. There would be subtitles, of course, but she would try to not read them and listen to the French instead. Jenny had always gotten an A in French, though she hadn't spoken it since high school. One of her plans had been to study it in college. She'd signed up for French III for the spring semester and had even taken the test to determine which class she qualified for. But by spring she was back at home, waiting to have her baby.

Roger Ebert gave the film four stars and Vincent Canby from the *New York Times* called it "hilarious, wise and moving." She would go to see this film the very next day, she decided. There was a nine o'clock show, and she had picked up hours and was working until seven. Which meant she would be lucky if she was out by eight. Then she'd cross the street and buy a ticket and watch *La Nuit Américaine*. She'd get a buttered popcorn too, and she would sit in the dark and be the kind of person who went to foreign films alone.

"Jenny?" said a voice from behind her, startling her.

She turned, and there stood the boy writing his dissertation on Pablo Neruda. The boy who owed her three dollars. Daniel.

"I went in there looking for you," he said, motioning across the street at the restaurant. "They said you'd left."

"You brought my money?" she asked. He had a nice face, she thought.

"He died," Daniel said. "Neruda. He died last night."

"Oh! I'm so sorry. You must feel upset," she said.

"I wanted to talk to someone about it." He shrugged. "To you."

Surely he had dozens of brainy friends, all writing their dissertations on obscure things. People who would love to talk about the importance of a Chilean poet no one had heard of.

"Me?"

"You just seemed to get it," he said. "The way you quoted Whitman was . . . marvelous."

Jenny didn't know how to respond, but thankfully he pointed to her shoes and said, "I was going to ask you if you wanted to take a walk, but you seem to have no shoes on."

"I like being barefoot," she said.

He nodded. "Okay. Then let's find you some grass to walk on."

They walked in silence down Thayer Street to George Street, then through the iron gates onto the Brown University green. Even though it was mostly dark, two students were playing Frisbee in the light from the streetlamps. Music drifted through the air, unfamiliar.

"Blue Öyster Cult," Daniel said, maybe seeing her trying to identify it.

"Ah," Jenny said, pretending to know of the band. When she'd been at Annette's a few nights ago, they'd played Jim Croce's new album, *Life and Times*, over and over again. Jim Croce was probably not who students here listened to.

"With a little Lou Reed thrown in," he said, taking her hand.

"Are you still going on your trip?" she asked him. "Even though he died?"

The grass felt soft and cool under her feet, a sensation so pleasant she kept bending her toes into it to better feel it.

"It's even more urgent now that I go. Neruda is the most important thing to me. I just had this fantasy that I'd meet him when I was in Chile, you know? That I'd get to ask him all these questions I have about his poetry."

You read your Emily Dickinson, Jenny thought, shivering slightly, *and I my Robert Frost* . . . How foolish it was to think that she'd actually met the person she used to conjure in her mind, that he'd walked into a crappy IHOP on Thayer Street, that she was holding his hand right now.

"I feel like it's my purpose. What I'm meant to do, you know?" Daniel said.

She nodded.

"What's yours?" he asked her.

"My purpose?"

She almost said *To get out of here. To not work at IHOP. To find a real life somewhere.*

But instead she said, "I don't know yet. I'm still looking for it."

This time he nodded. "You're a seeker," he said.

"I know that whatever my purpose is, it doesn't involve pancakes," Jenny said.

"Don't."

"Don't what?"

"Make jokes," he said.

They walked across the green, passing the stately brick buildings that lined it.

"How did he die?" Jenny asked. "Was he very old?"

"Not very old. Sixty-nine. They're saying it was cancer, but I bet it was that bastard Pinochet. Neruda dies twelve days after a military coup by Pinochet? Really?"

Jenny tried to remember all of these details so she could look them up in the library and have something to say about them the next time she saw Daniel. *Pinochet*, she repeated to herself.

"I've been thinking about you a lot since that night at the IHOP," Daniel said, pausing.

The air smelled slightly floral, like something beautiful and fragrant was blooming. Jenny breathed it in.

"Confession?" Daniel said. He was standing in front of her now, both his hands on her arms. "I've been in to see you."

"Into IHOP?" Jenny said, surprised. "When?"

He laughed. "Maybe twice. Or three times."

"Impossible. I work all the time. I live at that place."

"No, you don't. Or I would have found you."

He was coming closer, leaning toward her as if he planned on kissing her.

"Do you have my money? Is that why you were looking for me?" Jenny said, maybe to sound sassy, maybe to delay what was about to happen.

"I do not have your money," he said.

Then he kissed her.

"You called me at home," she said.

"Twice."

"I only got one message."

"I didn't leave one the second time," he said. "Also, the other five times the phone was busy."

"You called me seven times?"

He shook his head. "More like a dozen," he said. "There were also all the times no one answered."

"You know that's kind of creepy, right?" she said, thinking that it wasn't at all creepy. It was, in fact, wonderful.

They were silent for a few minutes; then he said, "I like you. I kind of can't stop thinking about you, which I know sounds potentially scary, since I don't even know you really, but it's true."

"I've thought about you too," Jenny said.

"Not just about getting that money? Like other ways too?"

"Maybe," she said.

He squeezed her hand. "Good."

It was almost light when they arrived back at her car, sitting alone on Thayer Street. The sky was streaked violet, and they paused to stare up at it before he kissed her good-bye. They had walked for hours, through neighborhoods with run-down houses built in the late 1700s, past stately Victorians and contemporary square houses with sharp angles, and down a boulevard with a tree-lined promenade in the center, where they stopped to kiss some more. He tasted of a spice she didn't recognize.

"Your feet," he whispered.

She looked down. They were so dirty and grass-stained from walking that she felt embarrassed. At some point, she'd lost her shoes.

"I love your feet," he said. "Neruda wrote a poem about loving someone's feet."

"What's it called?"

" 'Your Feet.' "

"It's not."

"It is!"

Somewhere between there and here, Daniel had told her that he was leaving on his trip the very next day. Mexico and Chile and then Capri, in Italy. The disappointment that flooded her when he told her this made her lose her breath. But now he said, "Meet me there."

"Where?"

"Italy. Capri. I'll have a pair of those sandals made for you if you come."

She was shaking her head, but he said, "Why not?"

"You won't even remember me by then," she said.

"I will so. You will always be the girl I spent the night walking with on the night after Neruda died. I'll never forget you."

She just shook her head again.

"Do you have any paper?" he asked her. Before she could answer, he reached into her ridiculous apron pocket and pulled out her order pad and the little pencil she used.

"There's an information kiosk when you get off the boat," he said, drawing a map of water and a boat and a dock and a rectangle, which he wrote the word KIOSK inside. He drew hills behind it, and a smiling stick-figure boy running toward the kiosk.

"I'll be there in July, but what if I'm delayed? Let's say August?" he said.

"You're crazy! That's a year away."

"Eleven months, actually," he said. He wrote *August 24* on top of the paper. *Noon.*

"It's the twenty-fifth," Jenny said, and she crossed out the *4* and wrote a *5* beside it.

"We've walked all night," he said. "There's a poem, 'The Infinite One,' that describes walking so beautifully. I'll memorize it and recite it to you someday."

She understood that it was a Neruda poem too. "You don't even know me," she said.

He tipped her chin up and bent to kiss her again. "I do know you, Princess Jenny of IHOP."

Her lips tingled from so much kissing. "If I come, will you give me the money you owe me?"

"Yes! But in lire," he said, grinning.

One more kiss, the paper folded and put back into her pocket, and then he had to go; he hadn't even packed yet and his flight was at noon out of Logan.

"August twenty-fifth at the information kiosk at noon," he said, walking backward down the sidewalk, away from her. "Like *An Affair to Remember.*"

Jenny smiled. He even knew romantic movies, this boy. "August twenty-fifth," she said.

She got into her car quickly, not wanting him to see her cry. It was too ridiculous, she thought as she started the car and pulled away. Hope was a thing with feathers. Wasn't that what Emily Dickinson wrote? And hadn't Jenny's hopes flown away? But still, something deep inside her fluttered.

CHAPTER EIGHT

Nick, March 1974

"Jeez, Uncle Nick," the doctor said, "when was your last physical?"

The doctor was married to Lillian's brother's youngest daughter, Eileen. That's why he'd come to the hospital, because they were sort of family. Nick had never liked the kid. He was too impressed with himself. Once, at Easter breakfast, he'd proudly told Nick he was a double-dipper: Harvard undergrad and medical school. Big fucking deal, Nick had said, because he was known to be a miserable bastard. Also, he'd gone to Harvard himself, and it hadn't really mattered at all.

"I don't like doctors," Nick said. The hospital bed was narrow, and the tray of food in front of him smelled like his elementary school cafeteria.

"But if you'd been getting your yearly physicals . . ." the kid said, looking embarrassed. "You wouldn't be in this . . . uh . . . predicament."

"Which is?" Nick said. He couldn't for the life of him remember the kid's name. His name tag said Dr. Casey, which was funny because what if the kid's name was actually Ben?

Dr. Casey let out a low whistle. "Which is very, very bad," he said.

Nick stared right into Dr. Casey's brown eyes, as if he was expecting to find something there. But all he saw was awkwardness and embarrassment.

"Surely you had some pain? Some discomfort?" the kid was asking.

"I'm seventy-six years old," Nick said. "Of course I have pain."

Dr. Casey ran his fingers through his wispy straw-colored hair. He looked like he'd rather be anywhere else than here.

"What are you doing such a bad job trying to tell me, kid? That what? I'm dying?" Nick said.

Relief washed over the doctor's face. "Yes. Yes. That's what I'm trying to say."

Nick laughed. "That's impossible," he said.

Dr. Casey shook his head. "The blood work and X-rays show metastasis. At this point, it's probably not worth trying to figure out where it started . . . I'm so sorry. Susan and I will do anything we can to help."

Susan? Nick thought. He was trying to hold on to something, anything, solid. Surely the kid was wrong. He'd get a real doctor, Nick decided. A grown-up one.

"We know you're alone," the kid said.

He was. All alone. And now maybe dying. The realization hit him like a kick to the gut. He'd watched Lillian die right in front of his own eyes on the gold linoleum floor, and his own mother, and so many young boys in France so horribly. Like Jimmy Reilly, killed less than a foot away from him. But they hadn't been alone. People had held them. He'd done it himself, cradled Jimmy Reilly's head in his arms. He was going to go home and die alone in his bed. The kid was talking about medicine to ease the pain and visiting nurses, but all Nick could think about were angels. Would angels come to usher him into death? Of course not. Angels meant you were going to heaven, and Nick knew he was not going to heaven. Not after what he'd done. He tried to catch his breath, but he couldn't.

"Anything at all," the kid said. "Susan can maybe put some meals in the freezer, and all you'll have to do is heat them up."

Nick gasped for air, finally got some. Susan was of course this kid's wife, the daughter of Lillian's sister Eileen. A round-faced girl who taught first grade. Susan.

"How long?" Nick asked.

That embarrassed look came over the doctor again. "Only God can say that—"

"Take a wild guess," Nick said.

"Six months?"

Six months. Not even a year. He'd already had his last miserable Christmas, seen his last first snowfall of the winter, watched the last crocuses he'd ever see pop their heads up. Those things were already gone.

"Or less," Dr. Casey said softly.

"Bill," Nick said. "Your name is Bill."

The kid looked surprised. "Well," he said, "yes."

"We went to your wedding," Nick said. "It was at night."

"A candlelight ceremony," Bill said.

Nick started to get out of the bed. "I've got to go home," he said, reaching for his shirt, which was neatly folded, along with his pants, on a mustard-yellow vinyl chair.

"You're not discharged yet. We're still waiting for some tests."

"Kid," Nick said as he buttoned his shirt, "I've got six months. And I've got to find something before I die. Can't waste time in here."

"Is it something I can help you find? Or maybe Susan can stop by the house on her way from school and help you look for it?"

Nick pulled on his pants, tucked in his shirt, buckled his belt.

"Kid," he said. "Bill. I wish Susan could find it. But this one, I've got to do myself."

Trembling and weak, he sat down on the bed. He thought of those bundles. He thought of that woman, Camille. He could smell dirt and bread and metal, and the smells made him dizzy, so dizzy that he had to lie down. Someone was asking him something, but he couldn't make out the words.

He wanted angels to come for him. But was it too late for that?

"He's talking about angels," someone said. "Poor guy."

No! Nick said. No! Or he thought he said it. He needed to make a plan. Where to start? He squeezed his eyes shut, tried to think. Around him people scurried, whispered. An intercom screeched.

Nick opened his eyes. The doctor was still here, and beside him a nurse with a perky starched cap atop shiny brown hair.

"France," Nick said.

The nurse looked down at him sympathetically.

"That's where to start," he said.

WANTED:

Girl/Assistant. Must not talk much. Must stay out of the way. Must be organized. Must get things done. Must be free to travel. Must have passport.

Nick hesitated. He still had three words. The ad was thirty words for three dollars for one week. *No strings attached?* He shook his head. What did that even mean? Who had no strings attached? *Must be unencumbered?* No. No one was unencumbered, not really. He reached for a Lucky Strike, lit it with his Zippo, and took a drag. Then he wrote: *Smoking preferred.* But what if the perfect girl, quiet and efficient and ready to go to France, didn't smoke. Then she wouldn't even answer the ad. He crossed out *Smoking preferred* and wrote, *Smoking okay.*

Nick read the ad out loud.

WANTED:

Girl/Assistant. Must not talk much. Must stay out of the way. Must be organized. Must get things done. Must be free to travel. Must have passport. Smoking okay.

It was still one word short. And the newspaper probably wouldn't give him his dime back; he'd have to pay the whole three bucks. Nick took another drag of his Lucky Strike, read the ad silently, then wrote: *Hurry.*

WANTED:
Girl/Assistant. Must not talk much.
Must stay out of the way. Must be organized.
Must get things done. Must be free to travel.
Must have passport. Smoking okay. Hurry.

CHAPTER NINE

Jenny, 1974

There were two girls around Jenny's own age in a booth. They were dressed in jewel-toned silk evening dresses, even though it was almost noon. They both smoked Virginia Slims, like Annette, cigarettes made just for women. *You've come a long way, baby,* the ads said.

"Do you think he's a pervert?" the one in the emerald-green dress asked.

"Maybe," the one in sapphire blue said, nodding and blowing a puff of smoke from her mouth, which was tinted with the remains of pink lipstick.

Jenny thought she could stand there by the coffeepots and listen to them forever. She imagined herself in that emerald-green dress, sitting in a booth at IHOP at noon after dancing until morning.

"You on vacation?" Fred said, appearing out of nowhere with a tray of sticky syrup pitchers. "If you are, what the hell are you doing here?"

"I was just getting fresh coffee," she said. She whisked a pot off the burner and walked to the booth with the girls.

"Finally," emerald green said without looking up. With the red pen in her hand, she circled an ad in the Help Wanted section.

"Job hunting?" Jenny said.

Both girls looked up, startled.

Jenny filled their cups with hot coffee and smiled at them.

"For the summer?" she asked.

Emerald green shook her head, not as a response but in disbelief. But sapphire blue pushed the newspaper toward Jenny and tapped the circled ad with a fingernail painted ballet pink.

WANTED:

Girl/Assistant. Must not talk much.

Must stay out of the way. Must be organized.

Must get things done. Must be free to travel.

Must have passport. Smoking okay. Hurry.

"What do you think, Jenny?" the girl said, reading Jenny's name from her name tag. "Is this guy for real?"

"It's kind of weird," Jenny agreed. " 'Smoking okay'?"

"Do you think he's looking for a sex slave?" the other girl asked, smirking.

Jenny was sure the girls went to Brown. They'd probably been at a formal dance with boys from there. She tried to picture that life but came up blank. That was her problem: she couldn't picture a life for herself. She'd tried to imagine being a single mother in a tiny apartment with lemon-yellow walls and a Gerber baby on her lap. She'd tried to imagine working in an office, taking night classes, being the person who could actually save up enough money and buy a Eurail Pass and fly to Italy. But all she got when she tried was a one-dimensional image, like a picture in a magazine, not anything real.

"I don't know," Jenny said, sliding the paper back toward them, her eyes lingering on "Must have passport."

She took out her little order pad and pencil. "Ready?"

They shared one order of pancakes and left two untouched. Probably on a diet so that they could fit into those shimmering dresses. Jenny still hadn't been able to lose all the weight she'd gained with the baby. Her hips, once slim and straight, were round, and her stomach had a little puff to it.

They also left the newspaper, still folded into thirds with the Help Wanted ad on top.

WANTED:

Girl/Assistant. Must not talk much.

Must stay out of the way. Must be organized.

Must get things done. Must be free to travel.

Must have passport. Smoking okay. Hurry.

She did not smoke, but otherwise she had the qualifications. Jenny folded the newspaper again, so that it would fit in her apron pocket. Maybe she'd call. Maybe the person who'd posted the ad was a tragic young man who smoked too much and needed someone to be his companion—his *boon* companion, as Vera used to say—to listen to his sad story without judgment or comment, to maybe travel somewhere exotic, somewhere faraway from this IHOP. Maybe Jenny was just what he was looking for.

She remembered a picture of F. Scott Fitzgerald and his wife, Zelda, she'd seen in a book at the library. They were sitting in a convertible, with Scott smiling from the driver's seat, looking handsome and young, and Zelda behind him in her flapper hat, with bobbed hair. This man who'd placed the ad was probably like that, romantic and tragic. Jenny would ride around Paris with him, and they'd have a mad affair. By the time her shift ended, she was certain she would get the job.

Her mother liked to talk about Barbra Streisand. "A girl who's not so pretty, but look at her!" The implication, Jenny assumed, was that Jenny— who was considered pretty and therefore had advantages others did not— had messed up her life. Her mother also liked to talk about Julia Child, who had a TV show on Channel 2 called *The French Chef*, where she made strawberry soufflés and beef bourguignon and French bread. "Look at her! So tall! And not very attractive. But she's really made a life for herself." What her mother never talked about was Jenny's baby.

Jenny had come home from college for winter break, her jeans unbuttoned and only half-zipped to accommodate the bulge of her not-so-long-ago flat belly. She had hoped her mother wouldn't notice that small bulge, hidden beneath an oversized URI sweatshirt. But Jenny's first night home, as she'd undressed for bed, her mother had burst into her room, wild-eyed and pointing.

"Are you kidding me? Pregnant?" her mother shouted at her. She picked up a notebook from the bed and swatted it at Jenny, hitting her arm and her shoulder and her back as Jenny turned away, embarrassed in just her little white cotton underpants and suddenly too small bra, that bump seeming larger in her nakedness, swelling over the waistband of her panties.

"What? You went to college and slept around with boys?"

"No!" Jenny said, reaching for the sweatshirt, which her mother swatted out of her hands.

"Turn around," her mother ordered.

Jenny did, trying to suck in her stomach the way she used to when she and her friends went to Scarborough Beach in the summer, making it almost concave between her sharp hip bones. Except nothing would make this bump go away. Jenny sucked in her breath, trying, but there it was for her mother to see.

"Oh, Jenny," her mother said sadly. "You have ruined your life."

Her mother sat heavily on the bed, staring at her stomach.

"Ma," Jenny said, "its Russell's. I didn't go with any strange boys in college."

"Okay," her mother said, considering. "Okay. So you'll get married then."

"Russ and I broke up, remember? We broke up because I don't love him."

"It's not the worst thing to get married at your age," her mother continued. "I was only twenty when I got married—"

"Yeah, but look at how that turned out," Jenny reminded her. Jenny's father had left when Jenny was three, appearing infrequently with oversized stuffed animals and things that sparkled—hula hoops and fake tiaras and sequined music boxes. And then he'd died when she was ten and even the erratic child support had stopped.

"But Russ is a good kid. Not like your father, the bastard."

When Jenny was little she'd actually thought her father was Your Father the Bastard, like Richard the Lionhearted or Alexander the Great. Her mothers and aunts still laughed about that.

"And he's already supporting himself. He's got a good job at the golf course. Assistant manager," her mother was saying, calmer now. "You'll get married. That's the solution."

Her mother stood, smoothing her dress and hair as if she were going to an appointment.

"Let's call him now. Have him come over."

"Ma," Jenny said. "I don't love Russ. I'm not going to marry him."

"You should have thought about that before you did this. Never mind having relations with someone you don't even love."

"I could go to New York," Jenny said softly.

"What's in New York?"

"An abortion. It's legal there."

"What kind of person have you become?" her mother said, eyes wild again. "Having relations with a boy you don't love, getting knocked up, and now this. Killing your baby."

"It doesn't feel like a baby," Jenny said. "It feels like the end of my life."

CHAPTER TEN

Nick, 1974

The girl was all wrong. Nick knew that immediately. For one thing, she was too pretty. Pretty could be distracting. Not to him, not anymore. But others might find her a distraction. He thought about the ad and those extra words he'd added. He should have said something like *Ordinary looks* or maybe *Bookish*. But he hadn't, and now there was this girl on his doorstep with long auburn hair blowing in the breeze and bewitching green eyes and a big smile. She was holding the ad in one gloved hand.

"Sorry," he said. "You're all wrong for this position."

That smile—dazzling, lots of big white teeth—disappeared and confusion replaced her optimistic look.

Nick closed the door.

Also, she was too fresh-faced. The kind of girl people didn't take seriously. The kind of girl who wouldn't be able to navigate airports and maps and the myriad other things he needed her to do.

She knocked. Repeatedly.

"Hello?" she called to him. "Can you at least interview me?"

For another thing, she was too young. He should have asked for someone middle-aged or at least over thirty. He should have been more specific.

What if he got sick on the trip? This girl couldn't handle that. She'd be too scared. Too inept. Too, well, young.

"Sir?" she was saying. "My name is Jenny and I am perfect for this job because I have no responsibilities tying me down and I am free to travel as early as next week."

Her words came out in a rush, making Nick think of waterfalls. See? he told himself. Distraction.

"Which isn't to say I'm irresponsible, because I'm not," she continued. "I work double shifts at the International House of Pancakes on Thayer Street in Providence and I studied liberal arts at the University of Rhode Island for one semester."

A waitress. A college dropout.

Nick opened the door.

Her smile returned, just as big and optimistic. "I was forced to leave college for a health concern that has been resolved," she said, and he could tell she'd practiced that line a lot.

"You're too young," he said.

"I may be young, but I have had lots of life experiences."

"Have you ever been out of the country?" Before she could answer he added, "Canada doesn't count."

"My dream is to go to Italy and visit Pompeii. That's why I work double shifts, to save up enough to go there."

"Pompeii," he repeated.

"Near Naples," she said. "It was destroyed in 79 A.D. after a catastrophic eruption of Mount Vesuvius."

"I know what it is," he said. "I'm just wondering why a fresh-faced girl wants to go to a place of such destruction?"

She nodded thoughtfully. "I guess I'm interested in the secrets of history," she said. "Actually, I'd like excavating that city. Maybe I'll study archaeology when I return to college."

"But it's sad," Nick said. "All those people died there. Burned to death."

"Actually," she said, "they were buried in ash and suffocated."

Nick peered at her more closely. See? She'd shown up for a job interview and somehow they'd ended up talking about Pompeii. He needed someone who could stay on task. She was smart, he had to admit that.

"Suffocated," he muttered to himself.

"Imagine walking down the street with your baby in your arms on a hot August afternoon and suddenly the sun is blocked by ash. It turns as dark as night and—"

"Volcanoes erupt lava," Nick said.

"Not all of them," Jenny said.

"Hmmm."

"Am I hired?" she asked.

She looked him right in the eyes, which was unsettling.

"You're all wrong for the position," he said again. With less conviction.

"What exactly is the position?"

One thing he liked about her was that she hadn't shown up in blue jeans. Everybody these days wore blue jeans all the time. But she had on a simple black skirt and a wool car coat and fuzzy green gloves.

"Sir?" she said. "The position I'm so wrong for? What is it?"

"I need to find a baby," Nick said.

For an instant she looked startled. She even took a step backward, as if he'd thrown something at her.

"In France," Nick added.

The girl took two deep breaths.

"Sir," she said, "I am perfect for this job. I took three years of French and got an A each year."

"I don't think—" he began.

"I promise you"—and she even held up the gloved hand clutching the ad, as if she were taking an oath—"we will find that baby."

For reasons Nick could not understand, he found himself opening the door wider and shaking her hand.

"We leave a week from tomorrow," he heard himself say.

From the bag slung around her shoulder she produced a résumé of sorts: a single piece of paper with her name and address and telephone number typed in the upper left corner and her experience, such as it was, the one semester at college and the waitressing job at the International House of Pancakes, outlined below.

That smile was back, maybe even bigger than before.

"Thank you, Mr. . . . "

"Burns," Nick said.

"I await further instructions," she said. She shook his hand, with a firm, hard handshake not at all like a girl's, and walked away, down his front steps and into one of those tin-can VW Bugs. He had to admit she walked purposefully. He liked a person who walked like that. Showed confidence.

Nick closed the door and went into the TV room. He sat at the telephone table and pulled out the Yellow Pages, flipping to "Airlines." His finger slid down the listings until it landed on "Trans World Airlines." Surely they flew to Paris. He lifted the heavy receiver and slowly, carefully began to dial. As he listened to the phone ring on the other end, he remembered the feeling of that baby boy, wrapped in cloth, so light in his arms. *He is Laurent.*

When the woman answered, professional and efficient, he was momentarily confused. But he recovered enough to tell her he wanted to buy two tickets to Paris, France. He could hear his voice crack as he spoke, feel tears running down his cheeks. How would he ever find that baby, fifty-seven years after he'd left him in that village? It was ridiculous. Foolish. Bound to be disappointing. What were the chances of success? Slim, Nick thought. None. Possibly heartbreaking. He had little information to go on. And the world had changed so much in a half century—another war, urbanization, fires, natural disasters. He thought of the girl on his doorstep. *Imagine walking down the street with your baby in your arms on a hot August afternoon and suddenly the sun is blocked by ash. It turns as dark as night . . .* What if no one had found the baby? What if he'd left him there to die?

Still, despite everything, Nick found himself thinking—foolishly, desperately: *I'm coming, Laurent. I'm coming.*

CHAPTER ELEVEN

Jenny, 1974

J enny, still in her good skirt and car coat—kept on to hide the holes at the elbow of her sweater—hovered beside her mother at the stove, trying to work up the courage to ask her. She watched as her mother stirred applesauce in a small pot on the stove. It was made with just apples and sugar and cinnamon, the only really homemade thing her mother liked to cook. The green beans came from a can, the rice from a box (always *Rice-A-Roni, the San Francisco treat!*), and the chicken breasts required nothing more than some salt and pepper and a preheated oven. But that applesauce, with its carefully peeled and pared Granny Smiths and all that stirring and tending, would be the centerpiece of an otherwise bland meal.

"You have to watch it," her mother was saying. "The apples release their water and then thicken, and if you're not careful, you can burn it. Someday you'll be making this for your own family."

Beneath her frilly yellow-and-white apron, her mother wore a lavender skirt with a matching sweater, a pin of a cat with green rhinestone eyes at the collar.

"And why are you standing there with your coat on?" her mother said, shaking her head.

Instead of explaining about the holes, Jenny slipped off the coat and draped it over her arm.

Even though it seemed her mother's gaze stayed on that applesauce, she said, "Are those holes in your good cashmere sweater?"

Jenny sighed. "Yes."

Her mother shook her head again.

"Mom," Jenny said. She took a deep breath, going over again in her mind what she'd practiced saying in the car. "Where is it?" She grimaced at the word *it*.

"Where is what?"

"No. I mean she. Where is she?"

Her mother turned off the burner and slid the pot off the stove. She reached into the cupboard, took down a blue-and-white bowl, and began to scoop the applesauce into it.

Jenny placed her hand on her mother's arm, to stop her.

"I think you know where she is," she said softly, her prepared speech gone, replaced by desperation. "Please."

Although her mother stopped filling the bowl, she didn't turn to look at Jenny.

"It's done," she said. "You've got to stop thinking about it. You will have more babies, and I promise this will fade away, like a bad dream."

"Does Dr. Wells know where she is?" Jenny asked.

Her body felt heavy, like it did that last month, her belly and breasts and legs swollen and big. But this heaviness was different. It came from somewhere deep inside her, made her wrap her arms around herself, as if she could carry it. She remembered the feeling of her daughter's foot or elbow lodged against her ribs, the slow tumble of her rearranging herself.

"Jenny," her mother said. "He did us a favor. He knew a lawyer who knew a family—"

"So she's here somewhere? Nearby?" Jenny's heartbeat quickened. Maybe her daughter lived on Love Lane. Maybe she had a house surrounded by hydrangeas and a father who mowed the lawn on Sundays.

Finally her mother turned and looked at her, still holding the wooden spoon, glistening with sugar.

"I believe the family was from Florida. But the lawyer never told Doc their name. It's better that way," she said again. "For you and for them and, well, for that baby."

Jenny nodded. She licked her lips and nodded again. She thought of oranges, and palm trees, and white sand beaches.

"I got a job," she said.

Her mother looked confused. "You have a job."

"A new one."

"Okay?"

The timer on the oven dinged, but her mother didn't turn it off. The pork chops would be dry.

"I'm going to accompany a man to France on business," Jenny said.

"A man?" Her mother's eyes grew cloudy. "What man?"

The timer dinged again, and this time Jenny turned the oven off.

"His name is Nick Burns." That heaviness was lifting, slowly, slowly, ever so slowly. "I leave in a week."

The cloudiness in her mother's eyes was replaced with panic. "What's gotten into you? You can't go off with another man and leave just like that."

"That's why I've taken this job. To get away from all this." She swept her arms around, as if to indicate everything from the applesauce cooling in the blue-and-white bowl to the small kitchen and beyond.

Now it looked like her mother was about to cry. But Jenny didn't even care. In her prepared speech, she'd ended with *I hope you can be happy for me.* But Jenny realized she didn't care if her mother was happy for her.

"I'm sorry if this disappoints you," she said instead.

Her mother sighed. "Oh, Jenny, all you've done is disappoint me," she said. She bent to open the oven and pull out the pan of pork chops, all six of them dried out.

Jenny let her mother's words settle on her. They should wound her, those words. *Oh, Jenny, all you've done is disappoint me.* But they didn't. Standing there in that warm kitchen in her sweater with the holes in the elbow and watching her mother carefully place the overcooked pork chops on a platter, Jenny felt even lighter still, like that kite lifting higher and higher in the air. Free.

CHAPTER TWELVE

The Museum of Tears

Enzo, 1950

The first time Enzo met Sofia Lazzaro was right after the war. Naples was bombed more than one hundred times during the war, and his beautiful city was in ruins. The Nazis even destroyed the port, and Neapolitans were without water or gas or electricity. Starving on the one hundred calories a day the Allies gave them. Not many people were buying Nativities. How could they, when even the most basic elements of survival were beyond their reach? His brother knew people, rich people, who left the city for Sorrento or one of the islands in the bay, and sometimes Massimo managed to get an invitation to a dinner or a party. That was where he heard about the bar in Pozzuoli run by four beautiful women.

The bar, Massimo explained as they drove along the bay and past the Phlegraean Fields, was famous for the homemade cherry liqueur that the owner, Luisa, made.

"But it's the granddaughters that really brings in the customers," Massimo said.

Enzo looked out the window, hoping to glimpse one of the fumaroles that sent steam into the air here. But it was already too dark, and all he saw were the lights of Naples fading.

"The one who waits tables is called Sofia Lazzaro, because her beauty is so great it can wake Lazarus from the dead," Massimo said. "The men who told me to go there claim this is true," he added.

"Interesting," Enzo said, even though he didn't find it interesting. It was difficult to think of pretty girls and cherry liquor when all around him people were hungry and barefoot. Their own mother had made a soup last night with just bones and a few carrots.

"Maybe those men in Sorrento——" Enzo began.

"Capri," Massimo corrected. "I was in Capri with a family who has a villa there. The lemons are as big as your head, Enzo. And they had veal for dinner. Can you believe it? Veal!"

"Maybe those men on Capri will buy a Nativity," Enzo said, looking out the window again, into the darkness. Somewhere out there was an ancient amphitheater, from Roman times. "I can make lemon trees for it. Lemon trees with giant lemons."

Massimo sighed. "No one is thinking of Nativities these days."

"I think we should make one with Allied soldiers."

"Ah," Massimo said with a laugh, "my baby brother is getting political."

The bar was not a bar. It was just a house, and everyone was crowded into the living room, where a beautiful woman played the piano and a girl sang along. She sang "Faniculì, Funiculà" and "Tammurriata Nera," but her version had verses Enzo didn't know, in English, about putting down your guns.

"Imported from the American soldiers," Massimo told him. "Some American song."

Enzo spotted the beautiful girl right away, the one who could wake Lazarus from the dead. The men from Capri were right: her beauty was that magnificent. Even dressed in a worn cotton polka-dot dress, she looked elegant. Even in this crowded, smoky bar that wasn't really a bar, she looked like royalty.

When she brought them glasses of the cherry liquor, Enzo saw a dark red scar on her beautiful chin. Without thinking, he reached up and touched it.

"Enzo!" Massimo said.

But the girl didn't even recoil. She turned her gaze on Enzo, and he understood that those eyes had seen terrible things during the war.

"Shrapnel," she said simply. "From an air raid."

The woman at the piano was singing that American song, "I'm Looking Over a Four Leaf Clover," so optimistic and exuberant. The crowd joined her, and the small room shook as they belted, "*One leaf is sunshine, the second is rain!*"

These people, who had just months ago begged for a crust of bread, seen neighbors shot dead in the street, fought the Nazis during the four days of Naples, were here singing this ridiculous happy song.

Enzo opened his mouth and sang along too: "*I'm looking over a four-leaf clover that I overlooked before.*"

The second time Enzo saw the girl known as Sofia Lazzaro was a few years later, in 1950 in Naples. By then, people had started to buy Nativities again. They zipped around the city in little Fiats and women wore red lipstick—though not in church. In other words, Enzo believed that the optimism he'd witnessed in that bar in Pozzuoli had been contagious and Naples had grabbed on to it. Even though there were still bombed-out buildings everywhere he looked, and barefoot children begging for bread, and women who turned to prostitution to survive, and American soldiers, Naples was starting to smile again.

Many mornings Enzo went to sit in Piazza Trieste e Trento, near the fountain of the artichoke, to sip a coffee and draw, or in Piazza Bellini to watch the students and artists. But it was in Piazza Gesù Nuovo, the small piazza that lacked the grandeur of Piazza Dante or Piazza del Plebiscito, that he saw Sofia Lazzaro. He recognized her immediately by the scar on her chin.

He was sitting at a table near the giant white obelisk, sipping his coffee, his sketch pad in his lap and his pencil waiting on the table for him to get inspiration and pick it up to draw. But this morning Enzo was not feeling inspired. His gaze settled on the front of the church, with its three portals and diamond-shaped ashlars. There, leaning against the stone church, stood a girl with her head thrown back, gazing skyward. Something about her was immediately familiar, and Enzo stood and squinted to get a better look. What he saw was a scar on her beautiful chin. A scar from shrapnel.

Slowly he walked toward her. The girl's eyes were closed, and to his surprise and dismay, Enzo saw that she was both laughing and crying at the same time.

As if she felt him nearing, her head shot down and her eyes opened and she glared at him.

"Can't you see I am having a private moment?' she said.

Enzo didn't state the obvious: that it was impossible to truly have a private moment in a busy piazza.

Instead he said, "Why are you laughing and crying at the same time?"

The girl tilted her head at him, as if he were an exotic bird that had just landed in front of her.

"Because," she said simply, "I am about to be famous."

This didn't surprise him.

"Bravo," he said.

"I was about to go into the church and light a candle of thanks when all of a sudden I was overwhelmed with tears. And then I said to myself, 'Why are you crying? This is the happiest time of your life.' And then I thought about how when I was a girl, people used to tease me. Do you know what they called me?" she asked him.

Enzo shook his head.

"The Toothpick," she said. "And remembering that made me start to laugh. And this is the condition you have found me in here."

Enzo looked at the beautiful woman in front of him. "Why the Toothpick?" he asked.

"Because I was so skinny. From hunger."

Enzo nodded to let her know he understood.

"Do you see these eyes?" she said, but she didn't wait for him to answer. "I stood on our little balcony with my mother and my sister and watched the Germans round up Jews and drive them away. These eyes saw people shot in the street."

Enzo wanted to reply, but he didn't know what to say.

"Do you know the most delicious thing I've ever eaten? The rations some GIs and Scottish soldiers shared with me when they arrived in Naples. I was a little starving street urchin," she said, and her eyes brimmed with tears. "But now I am Miss Elegance."

"Miss Elegance?" Enzo repeated.

"Last night in the Miss Italia contest I was named Miss Elegance, and a film producer approached me and said he was going to make me famous."

"I believe it," Enzo said.

"I came here to thank God for this," she explained.

When he asked her for her tears, Sofia did not even seem startled. She just agreed, saying, "Why not?" Later, back in the shop, he labeled the vial SOFIA LAZZARO, even though she hadn't told him her name. She didn't have to; he knew her by her scar. Beneath her name he wrote: MISS ELEGANCE 1950. TEARS OF HAPPINESS.

——

CHAPTER THIRTEEN

Jenny, 1974

To her surprise, Jenny's mother went shopping with her to buy an outfit to wear on the flight to Paris. Jenny had quickly let go of the idea of her and this man as the Fitzgeralds. For one thing, he was old. For another, he was very possibly sick, what with his yellow-tinged skin and skinny body. The outfit had to be sophisticated but comfortable (the flight was more than eight hours, overnight, which both excited and terrified her), wrinkle-free, pretty without being sexy or flashy, stylish, and able to double for dinners in Parisian restaurants. Though Mr. Burns had not mentioned any such dinners—or, really, anything at all—Jenny couldn't help but imagine herself eating fancy French food and window-shopping in Montmartre and dancing in the Eiffel Tower like Audrey Hepburn in *Funny Face*.

Her mother thought a skirt with a matching blazer was the perfect thing. "You can bring different blouses and a few scarves to make all kinds of different looks," she said, holding up a mustard-colored suit.

Audrey Hepburn would never wear something like that, Jenny thought. Especially with the moss-green flowered blouse her mother was thrusting at her.

"No, that's all wrong," Jenny said. Although as she flipped through the racks of clothes, nothing seemed right.

"You look good in these colors," her mother said, adding a mustard-and-cream striped blouse to the clothes draped across her arm.

In the movie, Audrey Hepburn wore a lot of black—those skinny ankle-length pants with a turtleneck, and the strange boxy tunic over that.

"I was thinking something black," Jenny said.

"Black?" her mother said, incredulous. "You're not going to a funeral. You're going to start a new life!"

In the end, Jenny did get black pants and a black turtleneck and a black-and-white striped top. She bought black flats too. But her mother won about the skirt and blazer. "It works for day and night," she told Jenny. "It's versatile." It wasn't quite so bad in navy blue, Jenny decided, even though her mother sighed and shook her head and muttered, "Why all the dark colors?"

Now she was wearing that navy blue suit with a cream-colored blouse and a scarf tied jauntily around her neck, waiting for Mr. Burns at the TWA ticket counter at Logan Airport. She wished she had splurged on a new suitcase, like the poppy-colored three-piece set she'd seen at Jordan Marsh. But her mother had convinced her that she should save her money for souvenirs or, God forbid, a ticket home should this Mr. Burns make trouble. Her mother's scuffed beige suitcase from her honeymoon trip to Florida would have to do.

Jenny watched as a woman not much older than herself checked in for a flight. She wore a long Indian-print skirt, a skinny ribbed T-shirt, and had one long braid down her back. Her suitcase, Jenny noticed, had a sun-and-moon decal on it. Suddenly, Jenny felt old or just so behind the times that she would never catch up. She was dressed like a secretary or a high school teacher, not someone on an adventure. That woman, with her batik and the bracelets that lined her arm, she looked interesting. Somehow, in the two years since Jenny had left college, everything had changed. The world looked completely new, and she was still in the old one.

She turned to watch the people entering the terminal. A feeling of dread coursed through her. What if Nick Burns didn't show up? What if he had decided she was all wrong for the job? She couldn't go back home, not now, not after telling Russ and Annette and everyone at work that she was leaving for a new life in Europe. Already she'd had to deal with every-one's smug looks and whispers when she'd dropped out of college. Most Likely to Succeed—ha! Somehow, her mother had changed her mind and decided that going away was the best thing Jenny could do. Forget Russ, forget this town, and go have adventures. If she showed up back home, once again she would disappoint her mother.

The woman in the batik skirt was all checked in, and she pulled a cig-arette from her macramé handbag and lit it. As she took a long drag on it, her eyes met Jenny's, making Jenny quickly look away. But it was too late. The girl was walking straight over to her.

"Jenny?" she said, surprising Jenny. "It's Kim Mayo. From school?"

"From URI?" Jenny said.

"From high school! You probably don't remember me, because you were in the smart crowd. I was the one hiding in the back of the classroom."

Jenny shrugged. "I'm sorry—"

"That's okay. No one remembers me, which is fine. You're at URI, right?"

Jenny hesitated. "Well, I was. I left."

Kim looked surprised. "Like, transferred?"

"I'm moving to France, so—"

"France! Wow! With Russ? Didn't you go out with Russ . . . I can't remember his last name. He was so dreamy."

"No, actually I'm—"

Nick Burns's raspy voice interrupted her. "Goddamn traffic," he said. "Come on, let's get in line."

"We've got to check in," Jenny said, embarrassed.

"Right," Kim said, narrowing her eyes at the sight of Nick Burns. "I'll see you on the plane, I guess. I'm going to Paris too. I have a Eurail Pass."

Jenny did not want to see Kim Mayo on the flight. She wanted that

Eurail Pass. She wanted to be wearing a batik skirt and have her hair in a braid down her back.

"Then I was thinking Switzerland and Italy and Greece," Kim was saying.

"I've got to go," Jenny said, hurrying after Nick Burns.

"I hope you're not going to make friends everywhere we go," Nick said when she came to a stop beside him in line.

"I'm not," Jenny said.

"In case you haven't noticed, I pretty much hate just about everyone."

"Great," Jenny said.

Nick folded his arms and stared straight ahead. Jenny, defeated, confused, already homesick, did the same.

CHAPTER FOURTEEN

———

Nick, 1944

I f someone had asked Nick how he managed to live with himself after
what he'd done, he would have said he didn't think about it. When
images of that day threatened to intrude—the woman thrusting those
bundles into his arms, the baby staring up at him, the smell of battle—he
pushed them away. Except at night. At night they came to him as he
slept. *He is Laurent.* Nick would wake up, thrashing, fighting, pushing
Camille away. At first, Lillian would sit with him or bring him a cup of
tea with milk and honey. "Tell me," she'd say. But Nick couldn't bring
himself to tell her. Eventually, Lillian either lay beside him, awake but
unmoving, or the liquor ensured that she didn't wake at all when the
nightmares came.

She used to treat him extra kindly in the morning after a night like that.
She would keep the shades drawn, give him toast with the beach plum
jam he liked so much, climb back into bed with him and make love, which
calmed him. But then the hangovers started and she couldn't rouse early.
Instead, he was the one bringing her aspirin and coffee and toast. She'd
stopped putting up the beach plum jam by then.

Nick used to love watching her make it in the warm kitchen on the Cape
on a late August afternoon. Lillian picked rose hips and blackberries too,

and turned them magically into jam. But it was the beach plums he liked best, showing up just when it seemed summer was over. Lillian, still slim, her long blond hair in two braids like a schoolgirl's, with a faded pink apron tied over her summer dress, would wash, de-stem, and pit pounds of beach plums, sitting at the kitchen table, humming along with the radio. Then she'd cook them in sugar and wine, her face glistening with sweat, which somehow made her look younger and even prettier.

"What are you looking at?" she'd tease him.

"You," he'd say, which always made her blush. After she'd worked the plums through the old silver food mill and simmered them some more, she'd take a small dish from the cupboard and spoon some jam onto it.

"Is it ready?" she'd ask him, lifting the spoon to his lips.

Once, when the rest of the family was away, clamming at a nearby beach, he'd lifted her onto the kitchen table and made love to her right there, before she'd even put the jams in jars. After that, it had become their secret code. "I wish we had some beach plum jam," he'd whisper to her, and then that beautiful blush would make her cheeks pink.

Oh, Lillian, he would think as he held her head to help her swallow the aspirins he'd brought her. Some mornings, he ached for her, even when she was right there beside him.

It was the war, what FDR called the Second World War, that made it impossible for Nick to push away the memories of those days in France. After the Great War, he had been certain men would never do this to each other again. When he'd gotten home, he'd joined in with everyone else having fun—reckless, continuous fun. He and his buddies drank too much and danced too much and went skinny-dipping under the full moon. There were always women and always someone willing to drive fast to Manhattan or to a house up in Maine or the Adirondacks. Eventually he'd settled on marrying Lillian, and despite everything that had happened, despite what he had done, he'd believed in their future.

But then there was the problem of him working with other people, of taking orders, of being nice. There was Lillian's problem, what they'd started referring to as Lillian feeling *peaky*. There was their empty, quiet house. When the United States invaded France in '44, Nick couldn't hold it back any longer. The nightmares, which used to strike at night, stayed with him all day. He broke things—dishes, glasses, a stupid china cat that Lillian loved. He paced, trying to figure out how to find the woman, the baby, both of them. How to fix it.

"Do you ever wish you could do it all over?" he asked Lillian one night.

They sat across from each other at the red-and-white enamel kitchen table, cold chicken and potato salad on their plates, a fan whirring noisily, blowing the hot air around.

"No," Lillian said. "You don't get that in life."

"But do you ever wish you could?" he asked. Sometimes, like now, he could feel the weight of that baby in his arms. He shook them, as if that could make it go away.

"No," Lillian said.

They had been married twenty years that February. It was hard for him to picture her at twenty-five, in her satin gown, surrounded by brides-maids wearing dark red velvet.

She refilled her glass from the straw-covered bottle of Chianti. When had she let go of the pretense of seeming to drink just a little and started to use a tumbler, one of the everyday ones with the red and blue rings around it?

"I guess I'm too pragmatic," she said. "I don't think like that."

"If I could do things over again, one thing I would—"

"But you can't," she said. "It's a waste of time to think like that."

He wanted to tell her, but after she said *that*, he couldn't manage it.

He went to a doctor, the same old doctor he'd been seeing for years.

"I have all these thoughts," Nick told him. "From the war. And they won't go away."

The doctor prescribed sleeping pills, but they made him feel like he'd been hit with a hammer, all woozy and thickheaded.

Autumn arrived in the East Bay, with its usual Technicolor splendor. Nick sat on the porch, looking out at the bright orange and yellow and red leaves, trying not to scream. From inside the house came the sound of Lillian humming along with the radio while she made supper. It used to be nice to sit out here together on an evening like this one, wrapped in sweaters, having a martini and some salted nuts before dinner. They would talk about the news, about the small things of their days. Lillian would divulge neighborhood gossip; she could perfectly mimic the voices of their neighbors, sending Nick into a fit of laughter and hushing her. "She's going to hear you," he'd sputter as she imitated the beleaguered Celeste Martin next door.

Nick stood and went to the screen door.

"Lillian!" he called. "Come sit with me, darling. It's such a lovely fall evening."

The humming stopped.

"Bring your cocktail," he added, more softly.

She didn't answer. Nick sat back down heavily. From somewhere down the street came laughter, and Nick leaned toward it, as if he could catch some of it. The door opened and there stood Lillian, holding a tray with a pitcher and two glasses on it, a small bowl of olives, and another of nuts.

"Lillian," Nick said. He felt he might burst with happiness at the sight of her. "Here, let me take that," he said, opening the door and taking the tray from her.

"It is a lovely evening," Lillian said in the overenunciated way she had after a drink or two too many. "Glorious," she said.

Nick set the tray down and poured the drinks, being sure hers was a short pour.

"Isn't this nice," Lillian said, smiling up at him.

He touched her cheek. "It is."

Once he'd sat again, he said, "Now tell me about your day."

"Hmmm," she said. "Let me think." She chewed on the olive from her drink. She shook her head. "There was a thing," she said.

Nothing more.

Nick looked out at the trees again. "So pretty, aren't they?" he said.

"Oh, I know, darling," Lillian said. "Celeste dropped by. Her daughter is selling something, I can't remember what, for the *war effort*. That's how she said it. The *war effort*. I told her I was feeling a little peaky and she'd have to come back."

He touched her cheek again. "Have you been peaky today?"

"Not now. Now I feel grand." She refilled her glass, sloshing some on the tray. "Grand." She clinked her glass with his, too roughly, sloshing more.

There was no supper that night. Nick cleaned up the mess in the kitchen, the meat sitting in the sink and the half-peeled potatoes and the bowl of flour and who knew what else. Maybe the makings for biscuits?

Alone with a sandwich, Nick sat at the red-and-white enamel kitchen table and wrote on a legal pad.

> *Dear Camille,*
> *I am the soldier from your farm whom you entrusted with the safety of*
> *Laurent. Please write to me at this address. I would very much like to*
> *discuss with you the events of that night. It is urgent.*

He signed it and put it in an envelope, on which he wrote the exact location of the farm. He didn't have an address, but by God he knew where it was, and anyone in that town who saw this description would immediately know too.

The next day he went to the post office to send it.

"It'll be slow," the clerk told him. "What with the trouble over there."

"That's fine," Nick told him.

After six months with no reply, Nick decided that even with the *trouble over there*, Camille had not received his letter. Because surely if she had, she would have answered him. Surely she was, just like him, tortured by what had happened, by what had become of her Laurent.

——

CHAPTER FIFTEEN

Paris

Jenny, 1974

"You have to stay awake," Nick told her in the taxi from the airport to their hotel. "Otherwise you'll be asleep all day and awake all night. Got it?"

Jenny's head was pressed against the window, her eyes shut. Even though her head was bouncing around with the taxi's stop-and-go driving, she couldn't stay awake. It might be early morning in Paris, but to Jenny it was the middle of the night. Nick's voice felt like sandpaper scraping her brain.

"Got it?" he repeated.

She thought of Kim Mayo, in her batik skirt, moving into the city on her own. She could sleep if she wanted to, or stay up all night, without this crabby old man bossing her around. *Maybe I could find her,* Jenny thought. *I could find her and escape Nick Burns.*

"You're no good to me if you're asleep all day," he said.

Jenny forced her eyes open. "It's three in the morning," she said.

"No, it's nine in the morning. We'll get some breakfast and I'll give you all the information I have, and tell you the plan. You can nap for a couple hours after that."

Miserable, Jenny looked out the window. She never would have imagined that Paris was so ugly: concrete buildings, traffic, noise.

"I thought it would be prettier," Jenny said.

"Well, nothing is ever what you hoped," Nick said.

Off in the distance, Jenny glimpsed a flash of silver in the early morning sunlight. She narrowed her eyes to see if it was what she thought it might be. The taxi turned and suddenly, just like that, the Eiffel Tower was in full view.

"Oh!" Jenny said, and without thinking about it she grabbed Nick's hand and squeezed. Just as quickly, she dropped it.

"It is something, isn't it?" Nick said softly.

Even though her brain was cottony and her head ached, a surge of energy shot through her. She was in Paris, looking at the Eiffel Tower. Tears sprang to her eyes as she felt the last two years start to fade.

Ever since the day at the college infirmary when a stern-faced nurse had given her the news that she was about fourteen weeks pregnant, Jenny had come to a halt. She'd stopped feeling and thinking and caring about anything, like she was a robot just moving through her life. The nurse had handed her a bunch of brochures about what foods to eat (iron-rich vegetables and lean meats) and things not to do (clean cat litter boxes, eat soft cheese, take drugs), a giant bottle of prenatal vitamins, and an appointment with the doctor in two weeks. Jenny went back to her dorm room with the happy yellow walls and bright flowered sheets, Vera's clothes tossed everywhere and Jenny's final paper for her Intro to American Literature class still in the typewriter. She already knew she no longer belonged here. She was not the girl who would move down the line to Bonnet Shores with Vera and date shaggy-haired philosophy majors or make the dean's list.

But now, as the Eiffel Tower grew closer and larger, Jenny glimpsed that lost part of herself for the first time in two years.

"We are going to find that baby, Mr. Burns," she said.

The outskirts of Paris may have been ugly, but now that they were actually in the city, it was everything Jenny had imagined. Before she left, she'd gone to the library and studied the pictures in *Fodor's France* and taken notes from *Let's Go: France*. All the Brown students used the *Let's*

Go books when they traveled, and even jotting down tips from it had made Jenny feel like she was a part of something. Now, just like in *Fodor's France*, there was a boulangerie bursting with baguettes and croissants, people rushing about with brightly colored market bags with newspapers and bread and flowers sticking out from the tops, and outdoor cafés where customers sat drinking coffee and eating omelets. The exhaustion that had overtaken her in the taxi disappeared as she and Nick walked from their hotel to the bistro the hotel clerk had recommended. The hotel was small, its lobby filled with overstuffed sofas and chairs in rich silks and a faded Oriental rug.

"It looks just like Paris," Jenny said.

Mr. Burns shook his head. It was very possible that this girl would drive him mad.

Her room had an iron bed and blue shutters that opened onto a small balcony, which overlooked rooftops. "I'm in Paris," she'd said as she stood staring out.

To her surprise, when they entered the café, Nick spoke to the maître d' in French, and he did so again when the waiter approached their table.

"You speak French?" Jenny said.

"I studied it all the way through college," he said. He opened the menu. "And of course I was here during the war."

"I took French in high school," Jenny said, "but I haven't ever actually spoken it. Lose it or use it, Madame Tillis used to say." She looked at the menu. "Oh, eggs and ham and—"

"It comes back to you," Nick said.

"It does, doesn't it?" she said, recognizing *champignon*. "I'll have an *omelette aux champignons et jambon*." She grinned at him.

"Are you always so cheerful?" he said.

"Not for a very long time," she said.

"Same," Nick said.

"You said you studied French in college? Where was that?"

"Harvard."

"You went to Harvard?" Jenny blurted.

"Yup."

Jenny waited for him to say more, but he didn't. He didn't talk again until after they'd eaten and their plates were cleared away. To Jenny, Nick Burns was as mysterious as this mission they were on. When she thought of someone who went to Harvard, she imagined someone more elegant, more successful than him.

After the waiter brushed the crumbs off the table and Nick took out a notebook and a pen and laid a small picture down between them.

"We're trying to find the woman who painted this picture—"

Jenny frowned. "I thought we were trying to find a baby."

"It's complicated," Nick said.

In the silence that followed, Jenny studied the small painting. The colors were so vibrant that it almost looked like a photograph, except that the brushstrokes reminded you that this was a painting. She noticed the small figure dressed in blue in the background. It looked like a woman fleeing, Jenny thought. Fleeing what?

"Interesting," she said.

"The artist is Camille Chastain. The baby we're looking for is hers."

Jenny couldn't tell if he was getting upset or if something was wrong with him. He had grown suddenly very pale, and he was sweating.

"Mr. Burns?" Jenny said. "We can talk about this after we rest. Let's go back—"

"This gallery might know something about her," he said, his voice weak. He was pointing to a page in the notebook. "I looked for her years ago, and the dealer I spoke to mentioned this gallery." His voice had grown even weaker, and his eyelids were fluttering, as if he couldn't keep them open.

"Okay, we'll go there this afternoon."

She tried to get the waiter's attention, but he ignored her. At IHOP, she slapped the check down right after she served the food. She refilled the coffee too, a lot.

"*Garçon!*" Jenny said, the word returning to her.

The waiter looked up, then took his time coming over to the table.

Nick had started to shake, as if he'd gotten suddenly very cold.

"Check, *s'il vous plaît*," Jenny said, motioning with her hands as if she were writing.

As the waiter tallied their bill, Nick pulled some francs from his pocket. "Got to go now," he sputtered.

"Yes, yes," Jenny said, sliding the coins into her hand and offering them to the waiter, who shook his head and muttered as he plucked three from her.

Jenny stood, ready to help Nick get up. But he just looked up at her, his usually hard-set face softening.

"Mr. Burns?" she said.

Oddly, he smiled. Then his eyes rolled back and he slid off the chair, landing with a soft thud on the black-and-white tiled floor.

CHAPTER SIXTEEN

Nick, 1952

Of course, Nick had looked for her before. But one spring day—
beautiful with pink dogwood blossoms and daffodils—Lillian had
given him an ultimatum: *Fix whatever it is that is torturing you or I am leaving*. She was done with it, she said, and he knew that by *it*, she meant *him*.
He shouldn't have married her. He shouldn't have married anyone. When
you've done something like that, left a tiny baby and walked away from it,
all you have left is darkness. But he'd come home from the war and Lillian
had been pretty and kind, a benign presence in his darkness. And the darkness and guilt and regret that grew over time was small in the beginning.
Small and private. Lillian stroked his hair and held his hand so tenderly.
They spent weekends at her family's house in Truro, where they walked
along the beach, took sunset sails, and ate salty clams, which she brought
to him in silver buckets.

At first, he was forgiven for his moods because of the war. Later, Lillian was less tolerant, especially after he lost his third job. He just couldn't
get along with people, couldn't hold his temper, couldn't satisfy the clients.
"Nick," Lillian said, "you went to Harvard. Act like it." Which he understood to mean that men who went to Harvard stayed on the straight path it
allowed them to walk on: get a good job—his field was advertising—and

move up the ranks until you become a partner, or, if you're entrepreneurial, start your own company. Get married to the right kind of woman, like Lillian, who was from a good family in Westchester County, with a summer house on the Cape and a Vassar education. Buy a house. Buy a Cadillac. Join a country club. Have children, two or three or four. But Nick Burns could not even hold on to a job for more than a year. The thought of having a child terrified him; he didn't deserve that, would surely be punished for having a child of his own after what he'd done back in France. No job, no child. The more things he achieved, the more that dark thing in him grew. Lillian crying in the bathroom more and more often, drinking gimlets with lunch, gin on the rocks before dinner, wine with dinner, and brandy for dessert. Nick would look at her, his once-pretty wife, and see how her mouth stretched into a tight line, see the sloppy face and thick waist that came with too much drinking. He'd had to ruin her too, he supposed. Her and their love. He could not remember the last time he had kissed her.

One Monday morning that spring, the threat of Lillian's ultimatum hanging between them, Nick woke up and decided he had to tell her. She was prepared to leave him anyway, wasn't she? This thing that he had been too ashamed to say out loud would either drive her away or help her understand him.

"Lillian," he whispered, touching his hand to her cheek. His heart beat hard from the shame and fear he'd built up inside him all these years, ready now to tumble out.

Her eyes fluttered open, but as soon as she saw him she frowned.

"It was in the war," he began.

By the time he'd told her everything, she was frowning even more, her hand held to her mouth.

"So go find her," she said when he finished.

"How?"

"I don't know, Nick. Just do it."

Instead of going to his dead-end job, where he was the guy who'd been there too long and was never getting a promotion, he drove straight to New York City and the gallery on Madison Avenue that his old buddy Walt Moss from college had told him about when Nick asked where he might sell a piece of art. Walt had followed all the rules. He was a partner in a fancy law firm in Manhattan, he lived in a sprawling house in Katonah, and he had four kids who all excelled at sports and academics and life in general. Nick hated the bastard.

Once, when they were all young and not even married ten years, he and Lillian had gone on a skiing weekend with Walt and Peggy. Walt had spent money so easily, ordering steak dinners and expensive wine, overtipping and splurging on things they didn't need—the hotel's s'mores party and room service breakfasts and a goddamn sleigh ride through the snowy fields. Every time Nick had to put in another twenty, his stomach clenched. Then, on their thankfully final night, Lillian, who he'd watched quietly refill her wineglass and say yes to an after-dinner Drambuie or three, got so drunk that her words slurred and her eyes drooped and she sloshed her Drambuie onto the front of her white cashmere sweater. He watched Walt and Peggy exchange a glance.

"Time to turn in," Nick said, trying unsuccessfully to keep his voice neutral.

"Yes," Peggy said. "We need to call my mother and check in on the kids."

"Aww," Lillian said, "the kids. That must be nice. Isn't that nice, Nick?"

Another glance shot between Walt and Peggy.

Nick stood, grabbing Lillian's arm maybe a bit too roughly. "Okay, let's go."

"I want a nightcap," she said, shaking free of him. "You'll join me, won't you, Walt? These two can go and check on the kids." She smiled: a drunken lopsided grin, brown splotches on that white sweater.

"Well, if you want, Peggy and I can have another—" Walt began.

"Nope," Nick said. "She's done."

This time when he took her arm, he managed to lift her off her chair, and he held on tight as she tripped her way out of the chalet bar.

Walt hadn't invited them away on any more weekends after that. They kept getting those Christmas letters, though, all the smiling kids in color-coordinated outfits. "Don't they look nice?" Lillian always said, her voice so wistful it broke Nick's heart. "We should invite them for a weekend. Remember that time we went to Vermont? The sleigh ride?"

Now Nick was at the gallery where Walt bought art. It was the kind of place where a man in a suit opened the door for you and brought you coffee or whiskey, and spoke in a hushed, almost reverential tone.

"I have this painting," Nick said, after the ceremony of pouring a god-damn cup of coffee was over.

From his briefcase he produced the small canvas and carefully unwrapped it. He had not looked at it in almost thirty-five years, since the day he'd pulled it from the bundle of paintings and shoved it in his jacket pocket.

The art dealer took in a breath.

"It's magnificent," he said.

With white-gloved hands he picked it up and studied it, the colors still as vivid as Nick remembered: the dirt and haystack and speckled chickens. In the distance, a bent figure in blue.

"Who is the artist?" the dealer asked.

"That's what I'm hoping you can help me with. She's French—"

"A woman," the dealer said, letting a low whistle out from between his teeth.

"This was painted in 1917 or '18, and I think . . ." Nick swallowed hard. "I hope she continued to paint, to get some recognition."

"A talent like this surely had some success." He held the canvas at arm's length, still studying it. "Though that would have been difficult then for a woman."

"If she survived," Nick added.

The dealer looked at him sharply.

"It was France. The First War," Nick said.

"And you don't know her name."

"Camille," Nick said, the name almost too painful to say out loud. "Camille Chastain."

"Camille Chastain," the dealer repeated.

Nick waited for almost a week before the dealer called him at the Hotel Taft, where he was staying. He'd tried to distract himself from the possibility that Camille couldn't be found as much as from the possibility that she could. In the first case, he would have to return home to Lillian and tell her that he could not fix what was wrong with him. In the other, he would have to go to France and find her and tell her what he had done with her baby. *He is Laurent.* Nick had eaten at the Taft Grill, allowing himself one martini and a small club steak for dinner. He'd gone to hear Artie Shaw play and had taken in a matinee of *The King and I.* He'd even eaten dinner at Lüchow's, on Irving Place, Lillian's favorite restaurant whenever they came into Manhattan. She always ordered the sauerbraten with red cabbage, but Nick just had a wurst platter with mashed potatoes and sauerkraut, two German beers, and a piece of apple strudel. Full, with memories of past dinners there with Lillian pinching his heart, on a whim he bought a copy of the Lüchow's cookbook as a gift for her. "Any messages?" he asked at the hotel desk again when he returned. Day after day it was "Nothing, Mr. Burns."

The next morning the art dealer called.

"I'm afraid I have very little information on your Camille," he said. "I located another painting of hers, in Paris. Also very small. Same vivid colors, same farm, I believe. It's of a cow, and there is also a figure in blue in the background. I'm afraid it's slightly damaged, as if it was in a fire."

"And Camille?" Nick asked.

"She is Camille Chastain," the dealer said. "She was scheduled to have a show in Paris back in the early twenties, twenty-one or twenty-two. But it never happened, and the trail ends there."

"Camille Chastain," Nick repeated. Vanished.

———

"Then put it behind you," Lillian said when he got home. "Behind us."

"But the baby," Nick said.

Lillian shook her head. "Leave it alone, Nick. It was all long ago. It was the war. People did inexplicable things. They were extraordinary times."

Nick couldn't quite believe that this was what Lillian thought. But she was practical, his wife. How often had he heard her say it was no use crying over spilt milk? How often had he seen her forgive what others judged—adultery and harshness and all manners of ill behavior. People do what they do, she'd say.

Lillian was busily seasoning veal cutlets with salt and pepper, heating margarine in a skillet. She was already thinking about dinner.

But Nick could not leave this alone. He knew it right then as they stood in the kitchen with the hiss of the meat dipped in flour and dropped into the frying pan. She was already making the Wiener schnitzel from the *Lüchow's German Cookbook* he'd brought her from New York. A peace offering.

"The sauerbraten takes five days," Lillian was saying. "Five!"

No, he could not put it behind him or write off his poor judgment as the fault of extraordinary times. He thought of the weight of that baby in his arms, a weight he still felt almost every day. A weight, he realized, he could not lighten.

CHAPTER SEVENTEEN

Paris

Jenny, 1974

Jenny woke from the deepest sleep she could ever remember having. Yet she still felt sluggish. The clock radio on the bedside table read 2210, and it took her a moment to subtract twelve from that and realize that it was after ten p.m. She'd slept almost twelve hours. Her stomach growled, reminding her how long ago she'd eaten that ham-and-cheese omelet.

She needed food. And she needed to find out how Mr. Burns was. Remembering the long ambulance ride to the hospital with him, she shuddered. The emergency workers paid no attention to her as they administered oxygen, took his blood pressure, and shouted in rapid-fire French to one other.

"Is he going to be all right?" Jenny asked them from her place in the far corner of the ambulance.

"*Il est dans un état grave,*" one of them said, making brief eye contact with her before returning to Nick.

She didn't understand what he said, except that *grave* meant *serious*. At the American Hospital, she kept asking the same question to any nurse or doctor she saw. The reply was always the same: *grave*. Finally, a nurse who spoke English came to the little room where they'd told her to stay, and confirmed that he was in serious condition. They were running tests, she said. "You should go home and we will call you when we know something."

The nurse called a taxi for Jenny, and when she got to the hotel she fell immediately into bed. Now she tried not to panic about what she would do if they had to return home or, worse, if Nick died. He was old and frail. Anything was possible. She thought about how he'd smiled just before he lost consciousness. The strange sound of the siren—so different from the ones back home—as it wove through the Paris streets toward them still echoed in her mind. Food, she thought again. Food would help.

There were no messages from the hospital for her at the front desk, so she went back to the place where she and Nick had breakfast and ate a *croque monsieur* and *pommes frites* and a salad. Everyone around her seemed to be drinking carafes of wine, so Jenny ordered one too. Despite the dread she felt, sitting in this bistro sipping wine alone in Paris soothed her. She made up stories about the people around her: the detached couple over there were bored with each other and they were both thinking of their lovers. The old man with the beret eating mussels was a painter. The young couple laughing and sharing *steak frites* were on a first date.

What would they guess about her? she wondered. How did she look to others as she sat alone sipping wine? She was glad she'd worn the black cigarette pants and white shirt. It was already obvious that the suit her mother had urged her to buy was all wrong. Once Nick got out of the hospital—he would get out, she decided; he must—she would buy new clothes. She'd buy a dress like the one the happy girl feeding her lover French fries had on. It was mustard-yellow linen—hadn't her mother said that color looked good on her?—with short sleeves and a little collar and buttons to the waist. The hem fell below her knees, revealing bare legs and brown Mary Janes. Yes, Jenny could see herself walking down the streets of Paris in a dress like that. And the outfit the bored woman wore too, with its white peasant shirt top and red knee-length skirt and white espadrilles. For a while, daydreaming about becoming a Parisian woman, she almost forgot about her predicament.

But when there was still no message from the hospital the following morning, her dread returned. Of course she hadn't slept much at all, because she'd slept most of the day before. Hadn't Mr. Burns warned her not to do that? Now she was turned upside down, tired when the rest of Paris was awake.

She would call the hospital herself, she decided, and got her purse to find the card the nurse had handed her. There it was. And there was the notebook with the name of the gallery and its address written in it and the small painting they'd been looking at when Nick got sick. Jenny opened the notebook. Camille Chastain. Nick wanted to find Camille Chastain. She took a deep breath. That was why he had brought her here, to help him. So that was what she would do. She put on the black cigarette pants and white shirt again, pulled a comb through her tangled hair, and even brushed pale pink lip gloss across her lips. Then she made a list: *Call the hospital. Have breakfast. Go to the gallery.* The pencil hovered above the page as she hesitated. *Buy a dress*, she wrote. Feeling lighter now that she had a plan, Jenny closed the notebook and headed downstairs.

Armed with a map that the hotel concierge had carefully marked—fat blue circles around the American Hospital, the gallery, the hotel, and two dress shops—Jenny made her way to the gallery. She kept getting lost, but she didn't mind. Each street held new treasures. One was lined with kitchen supply stores, enormous copper pots and knives in all sizes gleaming from the windows. Another had a cheese shop that sent its stink into the street. A *boucherie* displayed chickens still with their feathers and rabbits with their fur, and a *poissonnerie* had shrimp and mussels and whole fish on a long table out front. Jenny thought she could wander these streets forever and never see the same thing twice. Thayer Street, with its store that sold clothes from India and another that stocked Levi's and all the record stores—Tom's Tracks and In Your Ear and Mother's—and, of course, the IHOP where she'd spent more hours than she cared to remember: all of it already seemed quaint and provincial.

Jenny paused in front of a flower shop with silver buckets of hot-pink hydrangeas and apricot roses and enormous sunflowers.

On a whim, she bought three sunflowers. The clerk tied raffia around them. "*Prendre plaisir*," she said as she handed the flowers to Jenny. *Enjoy.*

Jenny felt foolish standing in the gallery holding three enormous sunflowers, but no one seemed to notice her anyway. As she stood awkwardly studying the abstract paintings on the wall, she tried to figure out how to say "I am looking for an artist named Camille Chastain" in French. Her high school French vocabulary was limited to food, body parts, and simple verbs, so even "I am looking for an artist" proved impossible. *Regarder? Vouloir? Chercher?*

By the time a stick-thin woman wearing green-framed cat-eye glasses with a smattering of rhinestones on them approached her, Jenny had given up. She knew *Parlez-vous anglais?* and had decided to go with that.

To her surprise, the woman immediately spoke to her in lightly accented English.

"Interesting work, isn't it?" she said, motioning with her chin toward the black, gray, and white painting in front of them.

Even though it looked like someone had thrown big globs of paint on a canvas, Jenny said, "Yes, interesting."

"The painter is Louise Dubois. She's quite young, only twenty-six. She works exclusively in black, gray, and white."

The woman had very short blond hair and a dress similar to the mustard-yellow linen one Jenny had admired at the café yesterday.

"I am Chloe Marchand," the woman said, extending her long, bony arm.

Jenny shook hands with her and introduced herself.

"Miss . . . Mademoiselle . . ." she stammered.

"Chloe. Please."

"I'm actually here looking for an artist," Jenny said.

"I see. You know that we specialize in twentieth-century female artists only, yes?"

"I have a painting to show you," Jenny said.

Chloe raised her thin eyebrows. "You have a painting? Where?"

"It's really small," Jenny said, holding up her purse.

"I'm intrigued. Let's sit in my office so we can talk privately."

Jenny followed her into a small room off to one side, with a perfect view of the entire gallery.

"Would you like a coffee?" Chloe asked as soon as they sat down in matching modern lime-green chairs.

"I would love some coffee," Jenny said. "I just arrived yesterday and I was up all night."

"Ah. The jet lag." Chloe pressed a button on the glass-topped desk and asked for two coffees.

While they waited for them, she asked Jenny where she was from and what had brought her to Paris, and Jenny heard herself telling Chloe the strange circumstances of this job she'd taken with a cantankerous old man who had ended up in the hospital almost as soon as they'd arrived.

"*Mon Dieu!*" Chloe said, her eyes sparkling. "You are the most interesting person to walk into my gallery in a very long time."

I am? Jenny thought, feeling a blush rise on her cheeks.

The coffee was delivered by a young man as thin as Chloe, dressed all in black.

When he left, Chloe said, "He is my assistant, Gabriel. Very sullen."

Jenny pinched her thigh very lightly. A reality check that she was actually sitting in an art gallery in Paris with a woman who had a male assistant and thought that she was interesting.

"So. This painting?" Chloe said.

Jenny took the painting from her purse and handed it to Chloe, who studied it very carefully. First, she held it at arm's length, then she held it close to her eyes, then away from her again.

"This figure in blue," she said softly. "It is running away? Very evocative."

Again she brought the painting close.

"I seem to remember something from a few years ago," she said finally. "Another gallery owner came to me with a similar painting to see if I recognized the artist. That one was two cows. The same size. The same vivid colors. And off in the distance, a small bit of blue. I thought it was a flower, but now I wonder if it was this figure, just farther away."

"Was the artist Camille Chastain?" Jenny asked.

"That was the thing. They didn't know who the artist was. And neither did I."

Chloe moved her chair closer to the desk and flipped through the Rolodex, almost impatiently, until finally she said, "Yes. Here." She picked up the receiver of the telephone and dialed. When the person on the other end answered, Chloe spoke fast, in French that Jenny was unable to follow.

"Are you available this evening at six?" she said when she hung up. "We can go to discuss with Jules Aveline, the one who has the other painting. You can bring this one with you."

"Okay, sure," Jenny said.

Chloe smiled. "Good. Maybe we will find your Camille Chastain, yes?"

She wrote down an address and handed it to Jenny. "This is a little wine bar in Montmartre where we will meet Jules, yes?"

"Yes," Jenny said, her head spinning. How could her life have changed this quickly? Just a few days ago she was serving drunken college boys pancakes, and tonight she was going to a little wine bar in Montmartre with this glamorous woman.

"So, until this evening," Chloe said, standing.

"Yes, um, could I bother you with one more thing?"

"You do not bother me, Jenny."

"Well, I wonder if you could tell me where you got that dress you're wearing?" Jenny asked, her cheeks getting hotter.

"Yes, yes," Chloe said, "it is right here on this street. Just go left out the door and walk past three streets and it is there. De Chance."

"De Chance," Jenny repeated. "Thank you. I mean, *merci*." She was very aware of how bad her French sounded, devoid of all the lovely musicality. To Jenny, it sounded like she'd just said *mercy*, not the lilting *merci*.

But Chloe smiled and said, "*De rien*."

Moments later, Jenny was standing in De Chance, holding the mustard linen dress, a short-sleeved flowered one, and a blue one with a puckered top that tied at the neck. As soon as she got back to the hotel, she would throw out that awful suit from Casual Corner, she decided. She tucked the sunflowers into the shopping bag the clerk handed her.

"*Merci*," the clerk chirped.

"*De rien*," Jenny said.

But when she went to the desk at the hotel to pick up her room key, there was a message waiting for her from the American Hospital. "Please call," it said. "Urgent."

CHAPTER EIGHTEEN

Paris

Nick, 1974

Nick did not remember anything after he showed the girl the painting and explained that they needed to find Camille. Had she argued with him? Or refused to help? Had she asked him what had happened to Laurent? He showed her the painting and told her about Camille and his ears started ringing and the girl was talking but he couldn't hear her because the ringing was too loud and then he thought he saw Camille, standing right there behind her, smiling. "Camille," he'd said. Or maybe he thought it. *Camille.* She looked as young and beautiful as she'd looked all those years ago when she'd brought them a warm loaf of bread. Nick was smiling back at her, and the next thing he knew he was staring up into the solemn face of a gray-haired doctor.

"He's coming back," the doctor said.

Nick tried to sit up, but the doctor put his hands on Nick's chest and pushed him down, firmly.

"No, no," he said. "You are not going anywhere, Mr. Burns."

The effort of trying to sit up left Nick gasping for air. He closed his eyes and took slow, deep breaths. When he opened his eyes again, the light from the window had shifted. It was early morning now. Without attempting to sit again, he looked around the room. Standard hospital room. But the daily calendar on the wall in front of him read, AVRIL 15. Avril. Okay, he was in France. He was in a hospital in France.

The next time he opened his eyes, the light had changed again, and the girl—he couldn't think of her name—was sitting in a teal-colored chair beside the bed. She appeared to be very upset.

As soon as she saw that he was awake, she jumped up and glared down at him.

"Did you know this whole time that you were sick? Did you hire me even though you knew?" she was saying, but Nick had no idea what he was supposed to have known.

"Well, I'm not going back. I'll stay here and I'll find a job and you can just go home and die."

Before he could think of a reply, she started to cry. "Oh, that was a horrible thing to say. I'm so sorry. I take it back. I don't want you to die."

Nick tried to think. They were sitting at the café. They ate omelets. He showed her the painting. He thought he saw Camille standing right behind the girl. Now he was here, and from the sound of it, he was dying.

"Mr. Burns?" she was saying. "You told me we needed to find a baby."

Hadn't his ad specifically said that he wanted someone who didn't talk a lot?

"And then it's not a baby at all, it's a woman," she continued.

Nick searched for his voice, which seemed to have vanished. He opened his mouth and a wheeze came out.

"I mean, do you actually think it's fair to get my hopes up? To have me believe we had a particular mission and that we would complete that mission together?"

"What," he finally managed.

Finally, she stopped talking.

"What," he said again.

She bent her head toward him, as if to hear him better.

"Mr. Burns?"

He took a big breath and felt a sharp pain deep in his lungs.

"What is your name?" he managed to get out as he exhaled.

The girl pulled back from him, surprised or insulted or both.

"My name? You don't know who I am?" she said.

He wanted to tell her that he knew who she was. He wanted to say, *You're the girl who answered the ad. You're like a character from an old movie with your can-do attitude and cockeyed optimism.* But it was all too much. He just closed his eyes again and went to sleep.

A young nurse in a pale blue uniform brought him a bowl of watery soup, and when his hands shook too much to get a spoonful to his mouth, she fed him, brusquely. For watery soup, it tasted delicious. In the early years of their marriage, Lillian used to make vichyssoise as a first course when they had dinner parties. She'd serve it in small chilled yellow bowls, the soup thick with potatoes and leeks and cream, a garnish of snipped chives on top. One summer night they had their little party in the yard. Nick strung twinkling lights in the trees and placed lanterns on the tabletops. Instead of the vichyssoise, Lillian served cold melon soup, orange cantaloupe nestled beside pale green honeydew, like a yin and yang in the bowl. "Delicious," Patty Young said. "But not your vichyssoise."

"What are you laughing at, Mr. Burns?" the nurse asked.

"My wife. She made the damn best soup," he said. Then, to his surprise, he burst into tears, knocking the spoon full of soup out of the nurse's hand and spilling it on the crisp white sheet.

"Oh dear," the nurse said under her breath.

Nick wiped at his cheeks and eyes. He'd been a terrible husband, and now Lillian was dead.

"Ah," the nurse said. She looked up and brightened. "Your daughter has arrived."

Nick followed her gaze to find the girl bustling in. Jenny. That was her name.

"Jenny," he said. "I'm feeling better."

"I will be back with clean linens," the nurse said.

"I'm glad you feel better, Mr. Burns," Jenny said. "Because you're very sick."

She was wearing such a pretty dress. The top of it was a soft blue, like the sky on a hot summer day, and puckered. The bottom was the same blue with white dots and went straight to her knees. Much better than that god-awful suit she'd been wearing.

Jenny sat on the teal chair, her arms crossed over her chest.

"I'm dying," Nick said.

"How could you not tell me that? I gave up everything to come with you and find this baby you said you were looking for."

"Well," Nick said, "you gave up a waitressing job at the International House of Pancakes."

She looked embarrassed, but so be it.

"And I am looking for a baby," Nick said. "I was going to explain everything to you at breakfast the other day."

"The doctor said you can go home tomorrow," Jenny said. "There's nothing more they can do for you," she added softly.

"I know," he said.

"You should have told me," she said, her voice still soft.

"You may not have taken the job if you knew."

Jenny gave him a little half-smile and shook her head. "Well," she said, "I'm here now."

"Right." He didn't tell her how glad that made him.

"Do you know a town called Mézy?" she said.

She pronounced it wrong, like *Messy*. "What do you know about it?" Nick asked.

The girl opened her purse and took out a piece of paper.

"I know that someone near Mézy has a painting by Camille Chastain," she said, handing him the paper. "I met with two gallery owners last night, and apparently your mysterious painter is a bit of a legend in some art circles. Her paintings are worth anywhere from twenty thousand to fifty thousand dollars, simply because she seems to have vanished into thin air."

Nick felt suddenly weaker.

"Are you going to faint again?" Jenny said, rushing to his side.

He managed to shake his head.

Jenny filled a glass with water from the pitcher by his head and pressed it to his lips. "I'll get the nurse," she said.

Nick grabbed her wrist. "I know Mézy," he said. "Get us train tickets there for tomorrow afternoon."

"Okay," she said, waiting for him to release her wrist. But he didn't. He held on tight and looked at her hard.

"The baby," he said.

"Is the baby in Mézy?"

"The baby is a man now. He must be almost sixty," Nick said.

"What? We're looking for a sixty-year-old man?"

"Obviously," Nick said. "Do the math!"

He released her wrist and laid his head back on the pillow. Was it really going to be this easy? Had Laurent somehow ended up back at the farm, maybe even with Camille? If he had tried harder, maybe he could have found them sooner. Maybe they would have forgiven him.

"I need to sleep," he said.

He heard Jenny sigh. "I'll be back tomorrow to pick you up."

"Get the train tickets," he said. He squinted his eyes open a little and saw the sky-blue dress disappearing out the door.

CHAPTER NINETEEN

The Museum of Tears

Enzo, 1957

The first dead face Enzo ever saw was that of Enrico Caruso; he was embalmed and lying in a glass sarcophagus at Santa Maria del Pianto cemetery.

His mother insisted this was impossible. "You were too young to remember such a thing," she would say.

But Enzo could describe that face perfectly: the bushy eyebrows and slight jowl and the white pillow his head lay upon.

"It was so hot and crowded," Enzo recalled. "And then later or maybe earlier he was brought through the streets on a horse-drawn carriage."

"You saw photographs somewhere, Enzo," his mother insisted.

But no, Enzo remembered it all. If he closed his eyes, he could clearly conjure the dead face of Enrico Caruso.

Maybe that early introduction to opera was why he became such a fan of the tenor Mario Lanza. After he heard a recording of Lanza singing "O Solo Mio" he suggested that Massimo make a figure of him for the Nativity. With Massimo, he had to suggest, not tell.

"We have Caruso," Massimo said dismissively. "Why would we add an American singer?"

"Mario Lanza is the next Caruso," Enzo said.

"Just because he played him in a movie?" Massimo kept painting the robes of a Wise Man, a sign that the conversation was over.

"Did you know that his last movie, *Serenade*, sold better here than it did in Milan? Neapolitans love Mario Lanza," Enzo insisted.

Massimo paused with the figure of Balthazar, with his dark face and heavy beard, holding the myrrh in his hand. The thin paintbrush tip was vermilion.

"Mario Lanza is from Philadelphia," Massimo said evenly.

Enzo picked up a figure. "We have Humphrey Bogart," he said. He picked up another figure. "And Mickey Mantle."

Massimo said, "I understand your point. Stop showing me all of the non-Italians we make."

"Did you know that Mario Lanza was born the year Caruso died?"

"Get me a picture of him," Massimo said, and he went back to Balthazar's robe.

"He's arriving in Naples any day, so there will be plenty of pictures of him in the newspaper. But I will bring you his record album, because I think he should be painted singing."

Massimo paused again. "I heard that he is very fat. One critic compared him to a ravioli."

"He wears his hair in a pompadour," Enzo said. He pushed his hand through his own curly hair, tugging it upward to demonstrate what a pompadour looked like.

"A singing ravioli with a pompadour," Massimo said, surveying Balthazar.

Satisfied nonetheless, Enzo returned to his worktable and began to mix paints. It was May, and the smell of lemons and lilacs drifted into the shop, making him want to be outside. At the little trattoria around the corner they were making artichokes—fried, stuffed, in pasta. Enzo would like to sit outside and eat artichokes with a glass of red wine and watch spring settle over the city. But he didn't want to upset Massimo, which leaving work to sit in a trattoria would certainly do.

It had been like this between them forever. Even when they were chil-

dren, Massimo had ignored Enzo or refused him whatever he wanted—
fruit ices in summer, one of Massimo's trucks to play with, kicking a ball
together. Massimo made it clear that Enzo was a nuisance to him.

"You knocked him off his throne," his mother always said as an explanation. "Ten years as the king of the house. He wasn't happy when a
brother arrived."

He acted like a king too. When Massimo entered a room, he dominated
it. Both men and women flocked to him, wanting to be in his bright aura.
Still, Enzo, who most people didn't even seem to notice, bothered him. It
was true that Massimo was more handsome, with his dark curls and perfectly groomed mustache. But Enzo was taller, and his eyes were a lovely
pale green that people always commented on. These things also upset
Massimo, who at five feet seven inches hated having to look up at Enzo
when they spoke.

"You favor him!" Massimo would tell their mother when she gave Enzo
a little extra calamari or a second *sfogliatella*.

"Mama's boy," he'd taunt Enzo.

Their father treated them both with equal coolness. He'd lost a hand in
the war, and until they were old enough to help out in the shop, he'd made
all of the Nativities alone, with just one hand, sometimes working sixteen
or eighteen hours a day to keep up. "*Così è la vita*," their father always said
when Massimo complained about Enzo or insisted that their mother loved
him more. It was the same thing he said when his hand cramped from
working so much or when their mother told him they needed more money
to live. *Così è la vita*.

Here they were, middle-aged men now, and these childhood grudges
had not faded. Massimo had a wife and a mistress, and they both treated
Enzo with the same lack of respect he did. Only his daughters, Aria and
Sofia, adored Enzo.

"Bad enough to have only daughters," Massimo had told him once.
"But I have daughters who adore you."

Now, with his nieces both teenagers, out of the blue Massimo's wife was
pregnant again.

"Just like us," Enzo said. "So many years apart." He inhaled the scent of lilacs and lemons.

"Spring has arrived," he said, not expecting Massimo to answer him.

Two weeks later, Mario Lanza was due to arrive on an ocean liner, the *Giulio Cesare*. The whole city seemed to celebrate his arrival. Buildings were decorated with red-and-green bunting and streamers. Banners that hung from doorways and windows said, "WELCOME MARIO!" and "NAPLES LOVES MARIO!"

The newspaper headline read, "CARUSO'S SUCCESSOR HAS ARRIVED!" Enzo showed it to Massimo, proof that Mario Lanza deserved a place in the Nativity.

"Come with me to the dock," he suggested to his brother. "It will be exciting."

"No, Enzo, I don't want to battle a crowd just to glimpse a fat singer. Besides, Philomena isn't feeling well, so I should stay near home."

The baby wasn't due until the summer, but Philomena's pregnancy had been *indietro*—backward. Healthy at the start and then sick at the end. Just last night their mother had told Enzo, "I'm worried for Philomena. A pregnancy that is *indietro* doesn't usually end well."

It was backward, she'd explained, because in the early months, when Philomena should have felt ill and tired, she'd blossomed. She'd looked beautiful and healthy and had been full of energy, knitting an entire layette.

"Not even a burp," Philomena had said at Christmas Eve dinner as she ate second helpings of all the fish dishes.

But in the last three months, she'd grown sallow and had lost weight, her big belly atop too-thin legs. She threw up most of what she ate, and had Massimo running around the city for her strange cravings—*arancini* from this stand, pizza only from this pizzeria, pistachio gelato, fried sardines—at all hours.

"Of course," Enzo said as he put on his white straw hat, "I will say hello to Mario Lanza for you."

By the time Enzo reached the dock, the crowd was so thick he could barely see anything, just as Massimo had predicted. He remembered that hot day of Caruso's funeral, a crowd like this one, and how his mother had held him so tightly. The memory made his heart bloom. How safe his mother made him feel that day. No, every day. Now, at eighty, she rarely left the apartment, though she still cooked three meals daily without fail. She made her own gnocchi, his favorite, pushing the hot cooked potatoes through the ricer, then adding just enough flour, adjusting how the dough felt beneath her hands, with their swollen arthritic knuckles. As a boy, it used to be his job to roll the cut dough off the tines of a fork to make its ridges.

On Sundays, Massimo and Philomena and the girls came for lunch, his mother laying out the antipasto—prosciutto and sharp cheese and fennel and olives—then the pasta, the secondo of roast veal or rabbit, the *dolci*, the espresso. Usually Massimo made an excuse to leave right afterward—to go to his mistress, Enzo and probably his mother knew—but Philomena and the girls always stayed until evening, playing cards or knitting socks and scarves.

A cheer rose from the crowd, reminding Enzo that he had come to glimpse Mario Lanza, not stand here and be wistful.

"Renato Rascel," the woman beside him said. "That's him, the tiny figure on deck."

Enzo craned his neck, but it was impossible to make out any figures from this distance. Renato Rascel, the actor-comedian known as *il piccoletto nazionale* because he was so short, no more than five feet one or two, usually wore an enormous, oversized coat, as if to show off his diminutive size. *The Seven Hills of Rome*, which he was starring in with Mario Lanza, would be his first movie for American audiences, even though "the tiny Italian" was one of the most famous and beloved actors in Italy.

"You can tell it's him by the coat," the woman said to Enzo, as if she knew he doubted that anyone could be seen from here.

"Ah, yes," he said, just to be kind.

"From here, they are all going to the Internazionale for a luncheon," she said, satisfied with her role of know-it-all.

"Ah," Enzo said again. "*Grazie mille.*"

He decided he would leave the harbor and go to the Internazionale and wait to see Mario Lanza there, without all these people. He began to push his way through the crowd.

But apparently lots of other people had the same idea, because when he arrived at the waterfront restaurant, reporters and photographers and another crowd of fans had already gathered. Still, he would have better luck seeing Mario Lanza and Renato Rascel here than back at the dock.

Eventually, Lanza and his entourage arrived, and the crowd shouted, "We love you, Mario!" as he approached with his wife, Betty, Renato Rascel, and other glamorous people that Enzo didn't recognize. Here, he could make out the singer's face, so handsome, and he took a mental photograph of it so that he could better describe it to Massimo for their figure.

Even after they all went inside, the crowd did not disperse, hopeful for another glimpse. People wondered aloud what they were eating and drinking. Some stood on tiptoe to try to see them. One man even ventured inside, and returned to the crowd to report that Mario Lanza was laughing and drinking and eating with gusto.

Then a song floated out to them. It was not being sung by Mario Lanza but, rather, by Renato Rascel.

"*Arriverderci, Roma, good-bye, good-bye to Rome . . .*"

The words and the tune were so beautiful that some in the crowd began to weep. Enzo lifted his face upward, as if the song could touch his cheek.

Later, after the song had ended and the entourage of celebrities had gone, stopping to wave and throw kisses at the fans, Enzo began to make his slow way back home. But he had not gone very far when he came upon a very old woman standing in the shade of a lone tree, tears wetting her cheeks.

Enzo called to her, and to his surprise her face lit up with a smile.

"Young man, young man, please let me share what has happened to me today."

"Of course," he said, going to stand beside her. The shade felt good after so much time in the sun, and he took out his handkerchief and wiped the sweat from his forehead.

"Today I went early to the docks because I had to see Mario Lanza," she began.

"So did I! But the crowds were too thick—"

"No, no. I went very early. I planted myself at the gangplank and I waited. And waited. And waited."

She let out a laugh that reminded Enzo of small bells. It was the laugh of a much younger woman.

"You see," she continued, almost conspiratorially, leaning closer to Enzo and lowering her voice, "I am an old, dear friend of the Carusos. You've heard of Enrico Caruso?"

"Of course, signora," Enzo said.

"All these years, I am the one who brings flowers to his tomb on anniversaries and his birthday and the like. The family gave me a locket many years ago, a silver locket with his picture on one side. A treasure," she added, touching her neck.

"May I see it?" Enzo asked her, because she seemed to want to share it with him.

"No, no, I don't have it anymore."

"Signora, it's lost? Do you need help finding it?"

She laughed again, with that beautiful tinkling sound. "I gave it away. To Signore Mario Lanza. Today! I waited at the gangplank, and when he approached, I stepped right out in front of him and I explained who I am, that I've known the Carusos for over seventy years, and I presented him with the locket."

"Just today this happened?" Enzo said, joining in her enthusiasm.

"Yes! I said, 'I admire you as I admired him.' "

"You said that today to Mario Lanza?"

"Yes! And I gave him the locket with the picture of Caruso on one side, and a picture of Mario Lanzo on the other that I put there myself."

Enzo was grinning with excitement. "What did Mario Lanza do?"

"He invited me to lunch!"

"The lunch there?" Enzo said, pointing toward the Internazionale.

"Yes! With all the celebrities and the press and everyone. Renato Rascel stood up and sang the most beautiful song, and there was so much food and wine." She smiled and looked up at Enzo. "Now I can die happy," she said, tears falling again onto her soft, wrinkled cheeks.

"Signora," he said, "but you are crying."

"Tears for a long life and a happy death," she said. "Tears for Enrico Caruso and Mario Lanza."

Enzo took from his jacket pocket one of the vials he now carried everywhere he went, and he told the old woman about the Museum of Tears.

"You want an old woman's tears?" she asked him.

"I do," he said.

Later, in the museum he wrote on a slip of paper: TEARS FOR A LONG LIFE AND A HAPPY DEATH. TEARS FOR ENRICO CARUSO AND MARIO LANZA."

He had been so overjoyed by her story, he had forgotten to ask her name, so he simply wrote: AN OLD WOMAN WHO WAS A FRIEND OF THE CARUSO FAMILY.

Enzo could not know, on that glorious May afternoon when he saw Mario Lanza blow kisses and heard Renato Rascel sing "Arriverderci, Roma" for the first time and came upon an old woman crying beneath a lone pine, that by the end of that week, it would be his own brother Massimo's tears he would collect. Beneath them, he would write: "Tears for the deaths of wife, Philomena, and unnamed baby boy. May 7, 1957. My brokenhearted brother, Massimo."

CHAPTER TWENTY

France

Nick, 1974

How could this village, Nick wondered as he stood in the town that he had vowed to never set foot in again, be so peaceful, so normal? Ordinary people walked past him as if nothing had ever happened here. They crowded the sidewalk cafés, drinking wine and beer with such casual care that he had to fight the urge to go up to them and knock their glasses out of their hands.

"Pretty," Jenny said.

He'd forgotten she was standing beside him.

"Pretty?" he repeated.

He supposed that the stone buildings, with their red tiled roofs, the winding streets and views of distant fields of wildflowers—the red poppies and lilies and wood violets—would indeed be pretty, if there weren't a patina of death and war over it all.

Jenny pointed to a storefront across the street. "That's where we're meeting him," she said, holding the paper with the name Charlie Reynolds and an address on it in front of Nick's face.

He batted it away.

"Let's go then," he said.

Where was the well? he thought, glancing around. Everything seemed familiar and strange at the same time. He could remember stumbling along a street not unlike this one, except it had been empty of people, the shops shuttered. He remembered trying to find the safest place, safe yet also open enough so that the bundle would be found. The bundle. He winced, realizing that for all these years he'd called that little baby *the bundle*. Probably to ease his guilt somehow, the way during the war they called Germans *krauts*, a terrible pejorative that allowed them to forget that those were real people they were shooting at. Funny how at the end of your life you understand so much but you can't undo any of it. What was the point of this newfound wisdom?

Jenny was striding ahead of him in her blue dress, walking toward a ridiculous-looking guy with an enormous mustache. A real hippie, like those Nick saw on the TV news reports of sit-ins and protests.

"Mr. Reynolds?" Nick heard her say.

"Charlie," the man said.

Charlie Reynolds was an American tour guide with the unfortunate job of showing veterans around the World War I battlefields—a grim way to spend your days, Nick thought.

"Nick Burns," Nick said, shaking Charlie's hand. The mustache, the curly hair beneath a floppy straw hat, the sandals. None of it gave Nick any confidence that this guy was going to help him.

But Charlie gripped Nick's hand firmly and looked him right in the eye.

"I'm always grateful to men like you," he said. "For what you did. For returning here."

Embarrassed, Nick retracted his hand.

"As I told . . ." Charlie glanced at Jenny.

"Jenny," she said.

"As I told the lovely Jenny on the phone"—he smiled when she gave a groan at that—"I've been kicking around Europe for a couple of years. At first, I was just doing the Eurail thing with a friend, backpacking and sightseeing. We made it all the way to Morocco, and she decided to stay there. I thought about going home, but instead I came here. My French is pretty good, and one thing led to another, and here I am, giving these World War I tours to guys like you."

The kid's energy exhausted Nick. But despite himself, he was warming up to him. Behind all the hair and the hat, there seemed to be someone intelligent. And kind. Not the worst person to spend a day with.

"We can have a coffee and go over our plan for the day," Charlie was saying. "Or we can head straight into the countryside."

"A coffee would be wonderful," Jenny said.

"Let's not waste any time," Nick said.

He saw the look that passed between the two of them, but he didn't care. His time was too valuable.

"Then away we go," Charlie said.

Nick followed him and Jenny, both walking at a lively pace. He supposed he'd be bringing up the rear all day. They were chattering away like old friends already. He hoped they'd shut up once they got in the car. Except, he saw when they stopped, it wasn't a car at all. It was a jeep, canary yellow, no windows, soft top. Jenny was already climbing into the back.

"Your chariot awaits," Charlie said, holding a hand out for Nick.

He wanted to slap the kid's hand away, but truth was, he needed the help. In fact, Charlie had to practically hoist him into the passenger seat.

"Enough men come back so that you can support yourself?" Nick asked once he'd settled in.

"I have some money to fall back on," Charlie said, "but you'd be surprised how many do return."

"You know a lot about the area, then? The history of the place during the war?"

"Yes, sir."

"He was a history major," Jenny said.

"Yale," Charlie said. "As the designated black sheep in my family, I did the proper thing and dropped out three months shy of graduation. Otherwise, I would have been class of sixty-nine."

"Yale. Huh. Then I have a question for you," Nick said.

Charlie brought the jeep to a halt. He put his hand on Nick's arm. "Before you ask me your question," he said, "I want to show you something."

Nick looked around. They were in the middle of nowhere. A country road, rolling green fields, those wildflowers everywhere he looked.

"Follow my finger," Charlie said, tracing something in the distance with his pointer finger.

Nick struggled to focus. All that green grass made it difficult.

"I don't see anything," he said finally.

But Charlie wouldn't give up. His finger paused in midair. "Look at twelve o'clock and move clockwise to about four."

Nick tried again. Twelve o'clock, his eyes sweeping slowly right.

"What the hell?" he said softly.

"What is it?" Jenny said. She was standing up in the back now, looming over Nick. "What are we looking at?"

"You see the indentation?" Charlie said.

"But what is it? Cutting right through the field like that?" Jenny asked.

Nick's eyes burned—from staring so hard, yes, but also from the tears that had unexpectedly started up.

"It's a trench," he said. "It's a goddamn trench."

Nick couldn't believe how far the village was from the farm. More than an hour's drive. From time to time Charlie pointed out other trenches, narrow dips in the fields that gave the topography a nauseating undulating look. Once Charlie pulled over to show them the stone remains of a German fort. In Nick's memory, he had walked across fields—these fields, he guessed—stumbling and confused. He'd clutched the bundle close to him, worried that the boy would wake up and cry and they would be discovered by the Germans, taken prisoner. Killed. But he hadn't realized just how far he'd walked. When the village had come into sight in the silvery dawn light, the baby had wakened, and Nick had placed his pinkie in its tiny bow-shaped mouth to suck, which it did, fiercely.

As they drove, Charlie and Jenny chatted away like old friends. When there was finally a lull, Charlie looked over at Nick

"You said you had a question," Charlie said.

"What?" Nick said.

They were passing farms now. Stone walls. Stone farmhouses. Cows. The smell of earth and shit.

"Back there," Charlie said. "You said you had a question."

All of the houses and all of the land looked alike, but Nick felt sure that one of them had been Camille's. His body tingled with recognition, and he could almost taste the fear he'd lived with in that trench.

"Are we almost there?" Nick asked, fighting the urge to jump out of the jeep and run. As if he could run anywhere. He could hardly walk. And even if he could muster the energy to run, where would he run to? An image of Camille floated in front of him, like a mirage, wavering, barely there.

Then Jenny was sticking a bottle of Coke in his face, leaning forward into the space between him and the driver.

"Drink some of this," she said. "You're looking pretty pale."

The Coke was warm from sitting in her bag, but he drank it greedily, letting her tip the bottle up as he gulped.

"That stuff will fix anything," Charlie said. "Even takes the rust off car parts."

"You okay, Mr. B?" Jenny said, her face scrunched with concern.

Nick nodded. He took the soda bottle from her and with his other hand reached into the empty space where Camille had appeared.

"You sure?" Jenny said.

She was a hoverer, a worrier, a pain in the ass. Nick nodded again.

"Good," Charlie said, "because we're here."

He turned the jeep onto a narrow gravel drive that wound between two pillars of stone, and they bumped along until they reached the barn. A short distance away sat the house, square and stone and unremarkable, except that looking at it made the hairs on Nick's arm stand up.

"What is this place?" he said, wondering how his throat could be so dry after he'd drunk almost an entire bottle of Coke.

"This is where the lady who has the picture lives," Jenny said.

For a crazy moment Nick thought the lady with the picture must be Camille herself. She'd fled that night, but of course eventually she would have come back. It was her home, wasn't it? Maybe she had tried to find him? Because how else could she find out what happened to her baby?

Now a woman was walking toward them. Middle-aged. Stout. Her dark hair braided and then tied back into a bun. Camille, Nick thought, and took an unsteady step forward.

"Whoa," Charlie said, grabbing his elbow.

But as the woman neared, Nick saw that it wasn't Camille after all. (And how could it be? She would be an old lady by now, old like him.)

"You are the ones who called?" she was saying in heavily accented English.

Charlie stepped forward and made the introductions. Nick didn't listen, just looked at the beautiful apple trees and cherry trees and fragrant lilacs as they walked to the house.

"What's this tree?" Jenny asked the woman.

"*Amande*," she said.

"Almond," Charlie translated.

Jenny shook her head, as if they had just told her the most marvelous thing. "An *almond* tree," she said.

Inside, the house was cool and dark. The woman—somehow they had learned she was named Madeline—led them to the kitchen and invited them to sit at the enormous wooden table. Clusters of herbs and flowers hung along the walls, drying, and the room smelled of vinegar and lemons. So many niceties—offering cake and coffee, making the coffee and heating milk, pouring it all into heavy cups, cutting the cake—before she finally sat.

"You have the painting?" Charlie said.

Madeline hit her forehead and laughed. "Of course! The painting!"

Then she disappeared out the door, hopefully to retrieve it. After several minutes she returned.

"Here it is," she said, and placed the tiny painting on the table.

It had the vivid, saturated colors of Camille's paintings. In this one, two chickens pecked at the ground. At the edge was a slice of coop, and beyond it that flash of blue.

"How do you know it's Camille Chastain's?" Jenny asked.

Nick couldn't stop staring at the picture. The splotches of vibrant yellow amid the brown dirt and green grass. The speckled black and white of the chickens, their bright red combs and wattles. There were dark stains in one corner. Water damage, perhaps.

"Because it was here when we moved in," Madeline said. "My mother always said that it looked as if she had dropped it accidently. It was out back, in the grass, but oddly protected from the elements somehow. You see there's just some damage here."

"Your mother bought the house from Camille Chastain?" Jenny asked. She was taking notes in a little notebook, all seriousness and efficiency.

"Not exactly. You see, after the Great War, many villages were totally destroyed. Erased, really. And many farmhouses were abandoned. Like this one. When my parents took it over, it was mostly destroyed, but it could be bought for a very little money from the town if you fixed it up and lived in it. It was an effort to bring life back here, you know?"

"This was Camille's house?" Nick said.

"She and her husband and baby fled when the Germans came. No one ever saw them again," Madeline said. "My mother found the painting in some undergrowth when she was clearing the land."

Nick stood, confused about where the door out was, looking around frantically.

"How do I go there?" he managed.

"To where she found the painting?" Madeline said, getting to her feet. "I'll take you."

She was a practical, matter-of-fact woman, heavy-footed but swift. In no time she had led all of them down a wide stone-floored corridor, to the back of the house and out the door. Nick was vaguely aware of dark rooms as they moved through, of narrow shafts of light with dust motes dancing in them. Then a patio with an oven, also made of stones, and dark purple lilacs and the smell of lilacs everywhere and then the long stretch of grass, with woods stretching out in either direction and Madeline talking about what a mess this had all been when they'd moved here in 1930, when she was just a little girl.

Somehow Nick was walking past the rest of them, toward the long, narrow indentation between the fields up ahead. He knew this place. He knew it. Those woods where he had seen Camille running away. The moon had cast a hazy light down on all of this. He heard Jenny calling for him, but he kept walking until he reached it. The trench where he'd spent all those weeks, where Camille had tossed down bread to him, where he'd painted that picture in order to hold on to something real.

What would you do if you had to make a life-or-death decision? she had asked him. *Would you make the right choice?*

Nick dropped to his knees, dug his fingers into the grass. He remembered himself then. Confident. Certain. Idealistic. Hopeful. Romantic. His true self, Nick thought as he felt the warm dirt in his hands. He wanted that person back.

Jenny and Charlie were both suddenly kneeling beside him, one on each side.

"I thought you'd fallen again," Jenny said, breathing hard.

But Charlie looked at him steadily. "You were here, weren't you?" he said, his voice soft and tender, like he was talking to a baby.

Nick nodded. He closed his eyes and let the boy's strong arms lift him to his feet.

On the way back to the village, Nick pretended to sleep. He insisted that Jenny sit up front so that he could stretch out in back, and he immediately shut his eyes. There was just the bumpy ride, the murmur of voices from the front seat, the warm air on his face. They had come this far, only to learn that no one knew what had happened to any of the Chastains. Vanished, just like the boy in that trench.

"I'm the black sheep in my family too," Nick heard Jenny say.

This surprised him. She was so thorough. So efficient. So . . . he couldn't find the words for it, but Mary Poppins came to mind. He opened his eyes just enough to watch the two of them: Jenny smiling and leaning closer to Charlie, and Charlie taking his eyes from the road to look at her.

"I can't believe it," Charlie said. "You are the girl who always does everything right."

Jenny laughed. "You have no idea," she managed.

When they finally arrived in town, Charlie invited them both to dinner.

"It's simple, rustic food," he said, "but it's better than anything fancy you tasted in Paris."

Jenny eagerly accepted. But when Nick said he just wanted to go to the inn and sleep, that he'd stop at the boulangerie and get a sandwich to bring to his room, Jenny said, "Is it okay if I go to dinner, Mr. B? I've only had that cake all day."

He told her to go and eat. He didn't tell her he was glad to be rid of her, of both of them.

They walked him to the door of the inn, stopping along the way for a *jambon-buerre* and a bottle of beer for him to take with him.

"Good night then," Nick said brusquely.

But he had not even stepped inside when Charlie stopped him.

"What did you want to ask me?" Charlie said. "About the village?"

Nick studied the kid's face. The ridiculous mustache. The light brown hair beneath that stupid straw hat.

"I just wondered," he said, weighing if it was worth it to ask. Another dead end and then what would he do?

Charlie's arm was holding the door open, and the sour smell of his sweat wafted up to Nick's nose. He turned his head slightly.

"Did you ever hear a story about a baby being found here? During the war, I mean?"

"Of course," Charlie said. "Everyone in this village has heard that story."

Nick turned back toward him, the sour smell somehow stronger, making him swallow air.

"During the second battle here," Charlie said. "Italian soldiers found a baby right over there, by the well."

Nick followed his gaze. Down the street a way stood the well, just as it had looked all those years ago. Why hadn't he recognized it sooner?

"He was dressed so carefully, and swaddled. Not even crying, that's what they say. Like he was just waiting for someone."

"It was a boy?"

"That's what they say," Charlie said.

"He was alive?" Nick asked softly, looking up into Charlie's face.

"Alive."

"And what happened to him?"

"No one knows. No one really knows if the story is even true. One of those crazy war stories, you know? A perfect baby found placidly waiting for . . ." His voice trailed off.

"For what?" Nick said.

Charlie shrugged again.

"Need anything else, Mr. Burns?"

"Go," Nick said.

Charlie touched the brim of his hat in farewell and walked away. Nick stood a moment, clutching the bakery bag. Then he walked back outside and down the street to the well. He stood there for a long time, staring.

CHAPTER TWENTY-ONE

France

Jenny, 1974

Jenny sat at a table at the outdoor café the next morning. An enormous bowl of frothy café au lait and a blue plate with a buttery croissant sat in front of her. She kept her head down, trying to focus on the postcards she was writing, each of them with the same picture of this very street cast in a golden light.

> *Dear Vera, France is everything I hoped it would be! You would love it here—the wine and food and boys, all divine!*

She read what she'd written and winced. Would Vera love it here? Jenny had no idea. She wasn't even sure why she was writing a postcard to Vera. Certainly not because Vera had told her to send *a million postcards*. Maybe she just wanted to be that person sitting in a square in France, sipping coffee and writing postcards to the people back home. Or maybe she wanted to prove to Vera that she wasn't someone who had messed up her life after all. Jenny looked down at her own careful penmanship and shook her head. What divine food had she eaten? The chicken in last night's coq au vin had not looked like any chicken she'd ever seen before, and the salad dressing had tasted like mustard. As for the boy part, Jenny winced again and glanced upward. No Charlie, thank goodness.

She picked up her pen and began the next message.

Dear Mom, I saw the Eiffel Tower! It looks exactly like it's supposed to. Now I'm in the countryside, sitting at the exact café in the picture, eating breakfast. How is everything at home?

Jenny turned the postcard over and made an X to mark the café. When she turned it back, she couldn't think of even one more thing to say. Should she explain to her mother what her job actually was? Or was searching for an artist who had vanished and a baby abandoned half a century ago the sort of thing that would just add to her mother's disappointment? Jenny stared at the words she'd written, so banal. Then she added, *Love, Jenny*, and began eating her croissant.

"There you are," she heard Nick say in his raspy voice.

Jenny looked up and found not just Nick standing there, but Nick and Charlie. Her cheeks burned and, she was sure, reddened. Quickly she went back to work on the croissant, which was so flaky that crumbs fell onto the table, her chin, and down the front of her new mustard-yellow dress.

The two men joined her at the small table, Charlie taking the seat right beside her.

"Sleep well?" he asked.

She focused on wiping up the crumbs and mumbled something that was intended to mean *Shut up.*

"So I've hired Charlie for another day or two—" Nick began.

"What? Why in the world did you do that?" Jenny blurted. A barrage of wine soaked-memories from last night flooded her. The kissing. The groping. The shedding of clothes. Thinking she'd never see him again, she'd really let herself go, doing things that sitting here in the light of day with her boss made her want to disappear.

"He's going to help us, that's why," Nick said in his crankiest *you're an idiot* voice.

"Help us do what exactly?" Jenny said. "Find this sixty-year-old baby?"

Charlie had the audacity then to cup her chin and turn her head so that she was looking right at him.

"That's exactly what I'm going to do," he said.

She wanted to knock that twinkle out of his eyes, even though she realized that she was the one who had put it there.

The plan was to play pétanque. The old men of the village played every day in the little park at the outskirts of town.

"It's like bocce," Charlie explained to Jenny as the jeep headed toward the park. "You know bocce?"

"Kind of," she said.

She still was working hard to avoid eye contact with him. If she even caught a sideways glimpse, an image flashed through her mind: those soft curls tickling her neck; that head thrown back, eyes closed; those hands around her waist, lifting her onto him. He was only the second boy she had been with, and nothing they did felt anything like all those times at the golf course with Russ. Despite herself, Jenny's body tingled at the memories. Why do our bodies betray us this way? she thought.

"Same principle," Charlie was saying. "Two or three pairs of players. One guy throws a little wooden ball about twenty feet, and everyone takes turns throwing the bigger balls as close to it as possible. All the hills and dirt and clumps of grass keep it exciting."

The park appeared up ahead, and Charlie stopped the jeep, seemingly in the middle of the road.

"Here we are," he said, jumping out and helping Nick extricate himself from the back seat, where, to Jenny's dismay, he had insisted on sitting.

"By the way, Jenny," Charlie said, "women aren't allowed to play, so you just get to drink wine and watch."

"Sexism lives on in pétanque," she said.

About a dozen men were playing, and with the exception of a couple who appeared to be middle-aged, all of them were Nick's age or even older. Jenny felt like she had walked into a scene in a French film. The park, with its plane trees and flowering bushes, made a perfect movie set. The men wore berets and had cigarettes clamped between their lips. A small kiosk, covered with chipped blue paint, had unlabeled bottles of red and rosé wine, small juice glasses, and a bowl of olives. Even the faded, scuffed-up wooden balls looked like props. Jenny sat on one of the benches, also covered with chipped paint, while Charlie made introductions and the men sorted out who and when Nick and Charlie would play.

Except for various shouts of disappointment or victory, it was pretty dull to watch. Jenny helped herself to a glass of rosé and wished she'd brought a book to occupy herself. She took out her little notebook and opened to a blank page, but she couldn't think of a thing to write. Instead, she pulled out another postcard.

Dear Annette, Wow! France is like a movie with stylish women and dashing men and beautiful lights.

She read what she'd written. It sounded so fake that she put the postcard away. When had she ever described men as *dashing*? Besides, *dashing* was not the word that came to mind for Charlie. *Primal*, maybe. *Simian*.

"*C'est bien!*" Charlie shouted, forcing her to look over at the pétanque game.

He was anything *but* dashing, with his floppy straw hat and cut-off jeans.

Jenny took the postcard out again.

I had a crazy night with a guy in the countryside. Blame the wine?

That, at least, was true.

A bee buzzed somewhere nearby, and birds sang from the trees.

Dear Russ,
Everything is so different here.

You have no idea, she thought, images from last night assaulting her again.

Her thoughts drifted to Daniel then, somewhere in South America. She tried not to think about him too much, or their night wandering the East Side of Providence together. It was foolish to waste her time imagining that he might be thinking about her too. Or that she would somehow, impossibly, show up at that information booth and find him waiting for her there. The events of the last two years had made her very cautious about feeling hopeful or indulging in dreams.

She heard her name being called and was snapped out of her reverie. Charlie was waving her over to a small table across the pétanque field where Nick and three of the men were already sitting.

"Grab a bottle of wine and five glasses, would you?" Charlie called.

"What am I? Back at IHOP?" she grumbled, though she did as he asked and made her way across the uneven, dusty ground to them.

The three men looked ancient, grizzled and droopy and missing more than a few teeth.

Everyone happily accepted the wine and greeted Jenny, their voices guttural and hoarse, like they'd been talking for centuries. After they'd all made small talk, most of which was lost on Jenny and her high school French, Charlie refilled the glasses and asked them, *"Connaissez-vous l'histoire du bébé abandonné?"*

Even Jenny could understand that he was asking about the abandoned baby. The men immediately said, *"Oui, oui. Mais bien sûr!"*

"But not *abandonné,*" one of the men said. He was dark-haired, burly, and bearded. *"Volé."*

Charlie looked at Jenny. "Stolen," he said.

The big man nodded. *"L'enfant volé."*

"Someone stole him from his mother," another man said in heavily accented English. "Stolen by the Italians." He shrugged.

"Le petit chou," a man leaning on a cane said.

This was more French that Jenny didn't understand, but Charlie translated: " 'The little cabbage.' It's a term of endearment for baby boys."

He turned his attention back to the men. *"L'histoire est-elle vrai?"*

Without hesitation they again said, *"Oui, oui!"*

The story is true.

After Charlie and the men had talked for some time, with Nick chiming in, Jenny refilled their glasses again and waited to hear what they'd said.

"The story goes that a soldier, maybe American, maybe British, stumbled into the town square with a baby boy," Charlie finally told her. "A baby boy he must have stolen. Some say he dropped it down the well, not to hurt it but to hide it. Put it right in the bucket and lowered it halfway. Others say he left it on the ground nearby, with a note. Victor's wife was here, in the village, at the time, and she told him the story."

At the sound of his name, Victor began speaking again.

"But his wife is dead," Nick translated. "So, we can't ask her about it and he only remembers the basic details."

The burly man spoke now, Charlie nodding from time to time.

"It seems that what everyone agrees on is that the baby was fine, not even upset or crying. And that an Italian platoon stole him because it was the Italians who arrived in the town that day," Charlie said. "But there the story falls apart. One version is that a childless village woman took the baby from the sergeant and ran away with him. Another version says that the Italians turned him in to the French authorities somewhere."

"And then there's the crazy story that *le petit chou* wasn't a baby at all but some kind of goddamn angel sent to bring peace to the village," Nick said. "When he was found, he flew away."

Victor was nodding. *"Oui. Comme un papillon."*

"Right," Nick said, draining the wine in his glass. "Like a butterfly."

"And the village was spared from ever seeing war or shedding tears again," Charlie added.

"Because of the stolen child," Jenny said.

They needed a plan. Jenny noticed that the waiter had already set a carafe of rosé on the café's table, so she immediately poured herself a glass. Then she opened her notebook, ready to get Nick to help.

"I suppose Charlie is joining us," she said, hoping her tone sounded casual.

Nick laughed. "He has other plans this evening."

"What plans?" Jenny said. "Like a date?"

"I believe a mademoiselle is involved, yes."

How could she feel so wounded when she'd been nothing but rude to Charlie all day?

"Hmmm, looks like you've maybe got a thing for our Charlie," Nick said.

"Hardly."

She turned the page of her notebook, trying to look nonchalant.

Jenny took a breath and leveled her gaze directly at Nick. "Mr. Burns," she began, "in order for this mission to be most successful—"

"Let's order," he said, motioning to the waiter.

The same waiter seemed to work here all day and night. He had a long, sad face that made Jenny think of a basset hound, and the sleepy, long-lashed eyes her mother called bedroom eyes. His hair was long and black, like that of a man on the cover of one of the romance novels her mother liked so much, except he didn't have the godlike physique of those heroes. This guy was tall and thin and slightly stooped. And he always seemed bothered to have to wait on them.

"Just the onion soup for me," Nick said.

Jenny glanced at the menu, which was the same for lunch and dinner. "*Croque monsieur?*"

"Are you asking me? Or telling me?" the waiter said.

"*Croque monsieur, s'il vous plaît.*"

"Very good," he replied, sounding exhausted.

"Charming fellow, isn't he?" Nick said.

"Where was I?" Jenny said.

"A successful mission?"

"Right." She put a Roman numeral I on the top of the page. "In order to have a most successful mission, we need a plan. I wrote this list of questions to help us."

To her surprise, Nick laughed. "Oh, I knew girls like you. Straight A's, right? Class president or editor of the school paper. Maybe both? Am I right?"

"I was voted Most Likely to Succeed," Jenny said.

"No offense intended, but you kind of got derailed, didn't you? One semester of college, waitressing at—"

"Thank you, but I know my own résumé, Mr. Burns."

"Let me see your questions."

She slid the notebook across the table and watched him as he read.

With a sigh, he slid the notebook back to her.

She uncapped her pen and prepared to write something next to her Roman numeral I. Minutes passed. Nick just sat there, chewing his bottom lip.

"It was me," he said finally.

"Okay?"

"I left *le petit chou* right over there," he said. He pointed toward the well. "And I want to find him. Or at least find out what happened to him."

"He was your baby?" Jenny said. Her chest felt tight, and she had to work hard to breathe evenly.

Nick shook his head. "Not mine. Camille Chastain's."

"The painter?"

"The Germans were coming and the forest was on fire and she told me to protect him. It looked like hell that night, with the flames and the artillery and the darkness all around us. I panicked. I left, and I didn't stop walking until I reached this place, right here, and then I laid him by the well, where I thought he'd be found."

"But why didn't she take him with her?" Jenny said. That tightness in her chest wasn't going away, and she put one hand on it as if she could calm her heart.

Nick shrugged. "I don't know how a woman gives away her baby like that."

"Maybe to give him a better life?" Jenny said. "Women do that all the time, you know."

"Whoa!" Nick said, holding up one hand.

Jenny took a long sip of rosé.

"It was like she knew I would mess it up," Nick said. "Just a week earlier she'd told me I wouldn't know what to do if I had to make a life-or-death decision. And I guess she was right."

"If she didn't trust you to do the right thing, she wouldn't have handed her baby over to you," Jenny said. "I think it was just the opposite. She forced you to make the right decision."

"Leaving a newborn baby like that was the right decision? It's ruined my life. And who knows? Probably a whole lot of other lives."

Jenny squeezed her eyes closed until she saw squiggles on the backs of her eyelids. After her father died, she'd started doing that to keep from crying, and it still worked.

When she opened them again, Nick was looking at her, hard.

"Maybe it helped some people. Gave them a better life," she said.

"How so?"

She shook her head and tapped her notebook.

"So first thing we do is figure out who found him, I guess," Nick said. "The Italian soldier or the sergeant."

Next to *I*, she wrote: *Find soldier(s)*.

On the next line she wrote: *II*.

"Well, I guess then we go to talk to him," Nick said.

Just these two simple steps already made Jenny feel better. Out of the corner of her eye she saw Charlie and a girl, his hand on the small of her back, guiding her to a table a few feet from them. Instead of sitting down, he came right over to their table, the girl following. Thankfully, the waiter arrived at the same time, and there was the placing of plates and the rear-ranging of wine and glasses to distract Jenny.

"This is Pippa," Charlie was saying. "I took her and her grandfather around right before you two arrived. They're off tomorrow."

"It was grand," Pippa said in a lovely British accent. "Heartbreaking, but grand. Have you found it so, sir?"

"I haven't seen the grand part," Nick said gruffly, and in that moment Jenny wanted to hug him.

Pippa, all long, straight, dark hair and minidress with miles of legs, turned to Jenny.

"Will you be going to the American cemetery? I walked through and it's lovely, with a reflecting pool and a chapel with stained glass windows that have . . . what are they exactly, Charlie?"

"The American units' insignias," Charlie said.

Pippa took his hand and squeezed. "He was a real peach and brought me there while Grandfather napped."

"Our food is getting cold," Nick said. He picked up his spoon and pushed it through the layer of bubbling cheese.

"See you tomorrow then," Charlie said.

"Why are we seeing him tomorrow?" Jenny asked after they'd walked away.

Nick tapped her notebook, which was still open on the table between them. "Number one of our big plan," he said. Then he slurped his soup, noisily.

CHAPTER TWENTY-TWO

France

Nick, 1974

Two things were clear to Nick. First, the girl had slept with Charlie. Not that he cared, but Jesus, it was a bad idea. Now she was awkward around him, making snide comments, blushing at the tiniest thing. Nick did not want to discuss this with her, not in the least. It embarrassed him, and it was none of his business. He understood, of course. Jesus, did he ever understand. He had that same longing, that desire for another person's touch. It wasn't even sexual, really. It was . . . Nick struggled for the right word. It was human, he decided. He missed those casual intimacies he'd had for a lifetime with Lillian—her fingers resting on his arm, his hand on the small of her back, the gentle way she'd push his hair off his forehead, and the warmth of his knee against her leg as they slept.

Nick sighed with the thought of those lost moments. Sometimes, even now, he saw a woman and imagined being with her. Not sexually, necessarily. Though, sure, there was that desire too. But when he saw a woman who looked like someone he might like, he thought of them walking hand in hand or settling into a comfortable silence, shoulders touching. He'd read somewhere that the need for touch is one of a human's most basic, primal needs. Didn't his old college friend Joe Downey get a dog after his wife died because a doctor told him it would help him with "touch deprivation"? And Nick, still married and young, had laughed at the idea. Touch deprivation.

So Jenny had taken care of her touch deprivation. But if they were going to move down that list of hers, they needed Charlie's help. And they needed to work with Charlie. What was it these kids had these days? Free love. What a contradiction in terms. Love was never free, and sex had even more entanglements than love. You don't spend an afternoon with a person, have dinner, and jump into bed with him. If you do that, what do you expect is going to happen? Love? Friendship? Disappointment, that's what's going to happen. Case in point: Jenny and Charlie.

The second thing he knew, or maybe didn't know with the certainty that he knew that Jenny had slept with Charlie but *felt*, was that they were never going to find that baby or Camille Chastain. He used to think—in macabre moods, he almost hoped—that she'd been killed that night. After all, she'd run, foolishly, blindly, *toward* the Germans. Even if she'd avoided getting killed then, what had lain ahead for her? Capture? What would soldiers do with a beautiful woman in a blue dress? He didn't want to even consider it. If she hadn't been captured, then she'd kept running? But where to? Sure, people did it. But most of them starved to death or died from illnesses. That long-ago dealer had told him she was supposed to have a show but had mysteriously disappeared. Surely, Camille Chastain was long dead.

He supposed they should just go home. It seemed impossible that they would find the baby who was now almost sixty years old. But here came Jenny in that blue dress, sauntering across the small plaza toward him, backlit by the sun. She'd acquired a straw hat with a black band. Not a silly floppy one like Charlie's, but a good-sized one that looked perfect on her head. Her thick auburn hair looked more red in this light, making Nick think of the sparklers he used to play with on Fourth of July when he was a kid. The bright sparks would light up the air like that.

Nick sighed, deeply. No, he decided, they would keep at it for a while longer. All that awaited him at home was his death. Although he'd imagined it many times over the years, craved it even, sitting here in the sun-light in the French countryside, he found that the idea of postponing it for a bit seemed right.

"Nice hat," he said to Jenny.

Her hand shot up and touched its crown. "Does it look ridiculous?"

"No. It's a nice hat," he said, sounding more annoyed than he felt. His voice always sounded annoyed, he realized. Had Lillian thought that too?

Jenny didn't look convinced. She sat down beside him, touching the hat lightly as if deciding whether or not to take it off.

"We need to talk," she said.

For a moment he thought she was going to quit. Why would she want to be on this wild-goose chase with someone as cantankerous and miserable as him? But when he looked at her face—the pink of a blush already on her cheeks, the cloaked eyes—he understood.

"It's all right," he said. "I figured it out."

"You did?" Now she looked horrified.

"I'm old, not dead," Nick said.

"We drank two carafes of wine," she said.

She covered her face with her hands, and Nick carefully removed them.

"It's okay," he said. "Just don't make a habit of it."

"Mr. Burns, I am not that kind of person," she said, with the serious voice that always made him see the kind of girl she'd been in school: effi-cient, task-oriented, straight A's, a pain in the ass.

"Good," he said, "because you and Charlie are going to a town about twenty-five miles away where they have records from the war. You might be able to figure out which Italian or British troop arrived here. Then you can track down all those men and see if one of them happened to find *le petit chou*."

Jenny pulled herself up straighter. "I will do that, Mr. Burns. You won't be disappointed."

Despite himself, he smiled. Was this kid for real? She already had her notebook out, and he saw her write: *III.*

———

Every morning for three days Jenny climbed into Charlie's yellow jeep and off they went, leaving Nick sitting in the café with a coffee and the *International Herald Tribune*. More than once he almost got up when Charlie arrived and went with them. But the jeep's bumpy ride made his whole body ache, and if one of the ever more frequent waves of nausea hit him, he would be stuck in a town hall twenty-five miles from his bed. Besides, poring through the records was tedious work. "My eyes cross and burn after a couple hours," Jenny had told him.

On the third day he looked up from the newspaper to find a woman standing there, staring down at him. She was old, though not as old as him, wearing a hat very much like the one Jenny had started wearing. That must be the only hat they sold in this town, he decided.

"I see you sitting here every day, some days with your granddaughter and some days alone," the woman said. "No one stays in this town that long. There's nothing to do here."

"You're American," he said, surprised.

"Better than that. I'm Texan," she said, and winked.

"If no one stays, what are you doing here then?"

She motioned to a chair. "May I?" she said, sitting before he answered her. "I actually live in a smaller village nearby. Moved here twenty years ago to paint, and well, here I am."

"I was a bit of an artist myself," Nick said.

"Were you?"

He didn't like that she looked amused. "In my youth," he added, as if that gave it some credibility.

The same waiter as usual appeared, and the woman ordered a carafe of wine. One of the big ones, Nick noted, thinking of Jenny's description or excuse.

"Madame," Nick said, "it's only ten o'clock in the morning."

"Oh, you see I'm quite wicked," she said.

She was big-boned, with hair the ash blond women of a certain age had and clear blue eyes. Her name was Everleigh Greer.

When the waiter brought the wine and two glasses, Nick thought, *What the hell* and poured them each some.

Everleigh was divorced—a *divorcée*, she said, like it was the most wonderful thing to be—and with her settlement had left Dallas and moved here. By the time they finished lunch, four hours later, Nick had told her about Lillian and how wrong his marriage had gone. He'd told her that he'd fought right nearby, how he'd spent those weeks in the trench on that farm. He'd even told her about Camille. Not about the baby and what he'd done, but about her bringing him bread and laughing at his painting.

"You were in love with her," Everleigh said, leaning back as if to get a better look at him.

Nick surprised himself by saying yes, he had been in love with her.

"Come on," Everleigh said, carelessly throwing some francs on the table and standing up.

"Where are we going?" Nick said as he stood too.

She had already started walking away, but she glanced over her shoulder at him and said, "I'm going to show you my etchings."

The house was stone, simple, and everything in it was yellow and blue. Behind it was another stone building, which was her painting studio, though he had not in fact gone there to see her etchings. She had led him directly here, to the well-worn velvet sofa, and poured them each a glass of rosé. Everleigh set a bowl of wrinkled black olives on the table, sat down, and immediately popped one in her mouth. Nick watched as she worked the pit out and spit it into her hand. Those simple motions seemed the most sensual things he'd seen in a very long time.

"Why are you staring at me?" she said, dropping the pit onto a napkin on the table.

Nick shrugged, embarrassed that she'd noticed.

Everleigh smiled. Wickedly, he thought.

"It gets lonely, doesn't it?" she said softly.

"God, yes."

Then he reached over and covered her hand with his, like a schoolboy on a first date. Her hand wasn't soft, like Lillian's. It was dry and rough, a hand that worked hard. Nick let himself sink into the feeling of his flesh on hers, the warmth that radiated from their hands. There was a time, he thought with a pang of sadness, when he would have leaned over and kissed a woman this lovely. But now there was just this: a warm hand in his.

"Your granddaughter," Everleigh was saying. "Is she good company?"

"Actually, she works for me," Nick said.

Everleigh's bright blue eyes were focused on him, waiting.

"Ah," Nick said. "It's complicated. She's doing research."

He couldn't tell if she accepted that explanation or not. But she nodded and slipped her hand from his.

"Come," she said. "I really will show you my etchings."

Everleigh's paintings were enormous canvases with bright splashes of blues and yellows, like her house. Nick thought of Camille's tiny ones, the opposite of what he was looking at now. He could hold them in the palm of his hand. Back at college, he'd learned that in Japan they called very short stories palm-of-the-hand stories. *They focus on feelings rather than understanding*, the professor had said, and the image of Camille's small paintings had risen in Nick's mind so vividly that he'd had to leave the classroom. *Feelings rather than understanding.*

"Before I came here," Everleigh was saying, "I painted still lifes. A bowl of lemons. A pomegranate cut in half with its seeds spilling out." She paused, standing in a stream of bright afternoon sun. "You said you paint?"

Nick felt embarrassed; he hadn't painted since that mural in the trench. When he'd gotten home, he had tried, but nothing had come out right anymore.

"When I was younger," Nick reminded her, hoping she wouldn't pursue the topic.

She did. "Did you study art? Gave it up when life kicked in and you had a family to support, a mortgage to pay, that sort of thing?"

"I did take some classes," Nick said.

"I got my degree at Parson's," Everleigh said. "Parson's School of Design? But before I knew it, I was a wife and a mother and painting was just my hobby."

"I gave it up after the war. In fact," he said, "my last great work of art was right nearby. I painted on the wall of the trench where I waited for weeks on end. It kept me sane," he added.

Everleigh cocked her head. "You do know they're finding all kinds of art in the trenches, don't you?"

"What do you mean?"

"They've uncovered some drawings and the like. Maybe you could find yours again."

Nick felt suddenly weak. He must have grown pale too, because Everleigh rushed over to him with a glass of water.

"Sit," she said, urging him toward a wicker rocking chair that looked more like a pram than a place a man would sit.

"Dizzy spell," he managed after several sips of water.

"It's damn hot in here, isn't it?" she said. He was grateful for her politeness.

They didn't talk again about his painting. Instead, they went back to the house and she laid out a board of cheeses and charcuterie with cornichons and a grainy mustard and small rounds of bread. To Nick's surprise, they ate and drank with great ease, as if they had known each other for a long time. He thought back to his conversation with Jenny, how he hadn't understood such casual sex. *Free love*. But it was just like this, an afternoon together, a slow, lazy supper.

By the time they were putting things back in the fridge and rinsing glasses, it was dark out.

"I suppose I'll have to take you back," Everleigh said. "It's after ten."

How he wished he were a younger man, Nick thought as they made their way to the village. He would stay the night, make love, maybe even paint beside her in the sunlit studio. But he was old, and dying, and tired. There would be no tomorrow for the two of them.

As she pulled into the darkened square, he said, "I'd like to see you again before we leave."

Everleigh chuckled. "You're sweet. And so old-fashioned. It's 1974, Nick. The boy doesn't have to promise to call."

"No, no," Nick said. "I want to spend more time with you."

It seemed imperative, as if seeing her again was a way for him to snub death. As if he were saying, *See! I'm alive!*

Two figures were running toward the car; it wasn't until they passed under the dim light of the café that Nick saw that it was Charlie and Jenny, their faces frantic and worried.

"Where have you been?" Jenny was saying as she yanked the car door open. "We've looked everywhere. We've called the police and the hospital and—"

"Whoa," Nick said. "I'm fine. Better than fine."

Everleigh leaned across him, filling his nose with her lavender-honey smell. "I'm afraid I kidnapped him," she said.

To his surprise, Jenny burst into tears and pulled him into a hug.

From behind her Charlie said, "Man, she lost her mind with worry."

Nick extricated himself from Jenny's clutches. He wanted to say something that would make it all right, but exhaustion coursed through him so hard and fast he thought he might fall over right there.

"I've had quite a day," he said.

Before she drove off, Everleigh called to him.

"Tomorrow then?" she said.

With great effort that he prayed she didn't notice, he nodded and lifted his hand to wave farewell.

"I guess I can't leave you alone for very long, Mr. Burns," Jenny said.

There were so many things Nick wanted to say to this girl, about sunlight streaming through windows and the beauty of tanned, freckled arms and how splashes of yellow and blue were the most calming thing he'd known in a long while. But he was too tired. He just went into his room and fell onto the bed. In the morning he found a note slid under the door.

> *We have a list of names of the Italian troop that arrived here on that very day. Gone to the library to start to track them down.*
> *—J and C*

CHAPTER TWENTY-THREE

Rhode Island

Jenny, 1972

Jenny entered the Home for Wandering Girls on Valentine's Day. The irony was not lost on her. Instead of roses and chocolates, she was sent into hiding for the next two months, thanks to her romantic transgressions. The Home was big and brick and looked like a high school. Inside, too. Some girls were as young as thirteen, though most were closer to Jenny's age.

They all grew bigger and rounder while playing endless games of Scrabble or gin rummy, piecing together jigsaw puzzles of castles or lakes, drinking endless bottles of Fresca or chocolate milk, and monitoring the eruption of Mount Etna in Sicily as it threatened to destroy villages. For those two months, these girls were Jenny's best friends. She learned who their babies' fathers were, what the girls planned on doing when they left here, what name they called the child they would never see again. They rubbed baby lotion on each other's bulging stomachs to prevent stretch marks and soaked their swollen feet together in warm water in lasagna pans pilfered from the kitchen. When someone's water broke or labor pains started, they held hands until a nurse arrived and whisked them off to the maternity ward. Once a girl left the Home, no one ever saw or talked to her again. It was better that way.

Laura, Betsey, Deb, Alexis, Mindy, Jill, Gabrielle, Paula. All of them with their young, pretty faces and incongruously pregnant bellies. Jenny depended on them to get her through to April 14, when she would be the one off to the maternity ward and then out of their lives. Annette's sister Pam had been at the Home for Wandering Girls just a year earlier. That was how Jenny's mother had learned of the place. When Pam left home to help with an aunt out of state, mostly everyone guessed she was pregnant. She'd always been wild, the girl caught skipping school and smoking pot and shoplifting lipsticks and earrings. Pam was two years younger than Jenny. By the time she came to the Home, she had dropped out of school and was working at the record store at the mall.

"Mrs. LeClerc told me where they sent Pam, and it's a good place with good people who will take care of you, " Jenny's mother told her.

"Pam had a baby?" Jenny said. By this time she was six months pregnant and everything seemed alien to her: her mother, her childhood bedroom, her own enormous breasts and round shiny belly with the belly button popped out.

"Last year," her mother said. "I guess you weren't paying attention." She shook her head. "An aunt in Chicago? Really?"

No, Jenny thought, *I wasn't paying attention to Pam LeClerc. I was paying attention to graduating and going to college.*

"We can come up with something better for you," her mother was saying. "Something that won't sound like you're pregnant and going to a home for unwed mothers."

"How about a semester abroad?" Jenny said.

Her mother, who had looked at Jenny mostly with disgust ever since she'd found out, actually lit up.

"Yes. A semester abroad. London, maybe?"

Jenny sighed. The baby inside her somersaulted. She thought of pictures from her old teen magazines of Carnaby Street and Twiggy and girls in Mary Quant ads.

"That would be good," she said.

It was arranged, and while she waited for Valentine's Day to go to the

Home, outside Boston, her body kept changing and becoming more alien. Dark veins appeared on her breasts. Sometimes she couldn't catch her breath because the baby seemed to be squeezing her lungs. She felt tired most of the time and stayed in bed, alternating between imagining what Vera was doing on campus and what a life in London would be like.

The pamphlet the doctor had given her told her that the baby was transforming cartilage into bone, tasting what she ate, listening to her talk, and even telling light from dark. The baby had gone from the size of a pear to the size of an actual baby since she'd come home from school. "You will think the baby can't get any bigger because you can't believe you can get any bigger, but he will just keep growing! And so will you!" the pamphlet threatened.

Waiting for Valentine's Day so she could leave, and then waiting for the baby to be born, Jenny felt like she was losing things she'd never get back. Her once-flat stomach and boyish hips. Months and months of her life. Her belief that she was a girl who would live an extraordinary life.

For almost two months, her days were a blur of trying to get to the triple-word square on the Scrabble board, reading magazines, eating bland food—eggs, grilled cheese sandwiches, meat loaf and mashed potatoes—and watching the smoke rise from Mount Etna. She needed a haircut. The ends of her hair looked like fish tails. During long afternoons doing jigsaw puzzles, she picked up a strand of hair with a split end and pulled the two strands apart. Then another. The girls around her discussed baby names. Heather was popular for girls. Also Amy. Everyone liked Jason for a boy. Jenny kept her baby's name to herself, because no one would ever call her that anyway. Some of the girls cried over having to give up their babies. They made elaborate escape plans that they never attempted. Jenny just wanted this to be over. The baby was abstract, even as it kicked and punched her all night.

Then, right on schedule, as she tried to make a seven-letter word and beat her own highest score, a gush of warm water flooded down her legs. Like Jenny, this baby showed up right when she was supposed to, even though most of the girls hadn't gone into labor until well past their due dates.

The girls moved into action. That week, five of them had gone into labor. The girls were experts. Someone called the nurse. Someone helped Jenny clean herself up. Someone went for her little powder-blue bag with her nightgown, slippers, robe, brush, and toothbrush in it. Jenny had read about women having natural births, playing Simon and Garfunkel music, squatting in a tub. But that was not what the Home for Wandering Girls did. She was brought to a hospital room, her feet went into stirrups, they shaved her pubic hair off and gave her an enema, all of it horrible except that with each step this ordeal came closer to ending.

There was pain, worse pain. After what seemed like forever, a nurse slapped a mask over her face and ordered her to breathe. All of the nurses were nuns and seemed to Jenny that night beatific.

Jenny inhaled an overly sweet smell that reminded her of rotting peaches. The next thing she knew, she was nauseated and sitting up and a different nurse was handing her a baby swaddled in a white blanket.

"A girl," the nurse said, her voice achingly kind.

Jenny didn't know what to do, so she took the baby in her arms.

Vera, she thought, but couldn't bring herself to say it out loud. The baby stared up at her, looking so much like Russ, with dark hair standing upright on her head and eyes the same shape, a dimple in her left cheek. Jenny had expected the baby to look like the picture on Gerber baby-food jars. Or maybe to look like her. But no, this baby was all Russ. Even though that disappointed her, it made it easier when, three days later, after Jenny had spent a while holding Vera and feeding her a tiny bottle of formula and watching her sleep, a man in a suit came in with the doctor, opened a briefcase, and showed Jenny where to sign. She was, he told her, free to go.

Her mother sat waiting in their dark green Ford Galaxie. When they had arrived at the Home for Wandering Girls, Jenny had entered through a different door, and in the bright spring sunlight she couldn't even figure out where that was.

"Well, that's done," her mother said once Jenny was out of the wheel-chair and settled into the front seat.

Jenny stared out the window as they drove away. She'd asked if she could take a picture of the baby, but that wasn't allowed. She was empty-handed, as if the last nine months hadn't even happened.

"The weight will come off quick," her mother said. "You'll see." She patted Jenny's knee reassuringly.

By summer she was working at the International House of Pancakes and watching *60 Minutes* with Russ every Sunday night, waiting for her mother to go to bed so they could have hurried, quiet sex on the sofa. Jenny wondered how long it would take to feel something again. Anything but this numbness, this somnambulism that hung over her constantly. Shouldn't she ache for her baby? Shouldn't she feel sad or guilty or frustrated? Once, she was sitting in the basement rec room with Annette, stoned and watching reruns of *Bonanza*, fantasizing about living on the Ponderosa with Little Joe, when Pam came down the stairs.

Jenny's stomach twisted. "Pam," she said.

"What?" Pam always sounded like she was mad at you. She had a bracelet of small bells around her ankle that jangled as she stomped across the rec room.

Jenny looked at her, the words caught in her throat. *Do you miss your baby? Do you ever think about her? Are you okay?*

"What?" Pam said again, her hands on her hips like she was ready to fight.

Jenny opened her mouth, but the words still wouldn't come out.

Pam shook her head. "Annette, is that my pot you two smoked?"

"No," Annette lied.

The three girls' gazes drifted toward the television. Little Joe and Adam were protecting a saloon girl from an angry mob.

"Oh, Adam," Pam said. "I loved him. Why did he leave the show anyway?"

"He said he didn't grow as a character," Annette said.

Jenny looked sideways at Pam. She seemed fine, Jenny thought. Like nothing had happened. Like maybe she had grown as a character.

One afternoon at the end of that summer, Jenny was driving home from work in her old VW Bug, thinking of nothing, a feat she seemed to have perfected. *Don't think of Vera getting ready to move back to school. Don't think of the courses you wanted to sign up for sophomore year, British Literature, World Religions, The 1920s, French III. Don't think of the Home for Wandering Girls, how it smelled of a weird combination of vinegar and fruity shampoo. Don't think of the maternity ward. Don't think of the baby. Don't think. Don't.*

She turned the car left, up the hill that led to home. She drove past a group of kids running through a sprinkler in their driveway, squealing and shouting. She drove past Bingo, the mean German shepherd that patrolled his yard from the end of a long chain. She drove past the house with a shrine of the Virgin Mary in the front yard. Then, without pausing, instead of turning left onto her street, Jenny kept driving.

She found herself on the winding roads of a housing development called Love Lane Estates. The houses were set back from the road by stone walls or cedar-post fences. Bushes and trees bloomed in the yards. The air smelled like hamburgers cooking on the grill. Except for a few houses with white pillars and red doors, most of them were modern, low and rambling with lots of windows. Mailboxes sat at the foot of the driveways, almost stately with their red flags and curlicued house numbers.

Jenny slowed at a house with periwinkle hydrangeas and two cars in the driveway and a handsome man mowing the lawn. She used to imagine living in New York City or San Francisco. She still had all of those notebooks of ideas cut from magazines: how to decorate a studio apartment, lists of the items needed to set up a kitchen, the best way to frame museum posters of art to hang on apartment walls, *Glamour*'s Dos and Don'ts. Watching that man and that house, Jenny decided that these must be the people, the family, that had taken her baby. Vera would grow up happy here.

The blue front door opened. Out stepped a woman. An ordinary woman with blond hair that hung to her shoulders, a white T-shirt, red shorts, bare feet. She held big clippers in her hands, and she walked to the closest hydrangea bush and cut three stems of flowers. She would put them in a crystal vase, Jenny thought, and place them on a table shiny from lemon Pledge. In the distance, Jenny heard wind chimes clanging together. The woman paused, stared in Jenny's direction. A chill ran up Jenny's arms. Jenny counted that as the day, the moment, the numbness lifted from her. *Make a plan*, she thought as she left Love Lane. *Save yourself.*

CHAPTER TWENTY-FOUR

The Museum of Tears

Enzo, 1962

Enzo's niece, Sofia, had been chosen to dance the tarantella in Sorrento on the terrace of the Grand Hotel Excelsior Vittoria, high on a cliff overlooking the Bay of Naples during the Festival of Piedigrotta on September 8. The Grand Hotel Excelsior Vittoria sat on the very spot where Emperor Augustus had his villa in 27 B.C.

"To think, *cara mia*, you will be dancing where the first Roman emperor lived," Enzo said to his niece. "Augustus, as I'm sure you know, laid the foundation for the Pax Romana, one of Italy's greatest periods."

Sofia laughed. "Zio Enzo, I care only about the tarantella. Not so much about things that happened almost two thousand years ago."

She was beautiful, this girl. At sixteen, she still possessed the clear complexion and sparkling eyes of a younger girl. But she was tall, like her mother had been, with dark wavy hair and strong brows and cheekbones. Lately, she'd grown tired of the long Sunday family lunches, restless to be outside for *la passeggiata*, strolling with her friends along the seawall or high up in the Vomero. But tonight she'd stayed after they'd eaten because her grandmother was sewing the tarantella costume Sofia would wear in the competition.

"To dance during the Festival of Piedigrotta," her grandmother said, bursting with pride. "This is an honor."

Sofia sighed the exasperated sigh of all young, dreamy girls.

What are you dreaming of, Enzo wanted to ask her. *What do you see as you sit there by the window staring out?* But, always awkward around girls, even his own niece, he said nothing.

"I thought Candida Pensa would ask me to sew her costume," Nonna said. Her fingers never stopped, the needle and thread moving quickly through the air. Like liquid silver, Enzo thought.

Another exasperated sigh. "Candida Pensa hates me," Sofia said. "And I hate her."

"What?" Enzo blurted. "She has been your best friend since before you were born. Your mothers walked together, arms linked, their bellies growing big. And then the joy of you both being born on the very same day."

"She's jealous of me," Sofia said, so matter-of-factly that her grandmother dropped the needle she was holding and her fingers shot into the sign of the *malocchio*, the pinkie and index finger extended, the thumb holding down the middle and ring fingers. The *malocchio*, the evil eye.

"She is, Nonna!" Sofia said, looking fierce, her eyes suddenly ablaze. "For one thing, I dance better than her. Don't look at me like that! I do."

"It isn't good to brag," Enzo said gently.

"I'm not bragging. It's the truth." Sofia paused, considering, then said, "And Davide Bianchi is in love with me, not her."

The room fell silent. Nonna stopped sewing and stared at her granddaughter, who wore a satisfied expression, as if she'd won a prize. Ever since Philomena had died, Enzo's mother had worried for Sofia and her sister. Girls, especially teenage girls, need a mother. For advice and comfort and discipline and love. Massimo's girlfriend, his former mistress who he now flaunted openly, wanted nothing to do with either of the girls. Ines remained jealous of Philomena, even though Philomena posed no threat any longer. She had forced Massimo to remove all pictures and mementos of Philomena, to put them away in boxes for when the girls got older and had their own homes. It was as if Philomena had died twice, Nonna often thought. Now here they were, right where she'd feared, Sofia rootless and brazen.

"The Bianchis are a nice family," Enzo offered. "Every year the mother comes to the shop and carefully selects new figures for their Nativity, which I have heard is so elaborate that neighbors are invited to see it and the priest blesses it."

"The Bianchis work for Luigi Campolongo," Nonna said.

What she didn't say, what she didn't have to say because the three of them knew it well, was that Luigi Campolongo was also known as Mr. Naples or, more importantly, as Mr. Mafia.

"And your point is what?" Sofia said, her voice hard and challenging.

Nonna went back to her sewing. "You understand my point," she said quietly.

"You understand, Zio Enzo, don't you?" Sofia said a few nights later as they stood on the crowded street, waiting for the parade to begin. "Girls like handsome boys and nice things."

The night was unusually hot and humid, and the air smelled of sweat and fried food and salt from the sea.

"I don't know the ways of the heart," Enzo told his niece. "I think those things are tempting, but other traits, like loyalty and honor, matter more in the end."

"You sound like Nonna," she said, but she didn't sound angry. " 'When you are broke or when you grow old, love flies out the window,' she always says. But I believe in romance. Flowers and presents and champagne."

Champagne? Enzo thought. What did his niece know about champagne?

The illuminated floats depicting historical events appeared down the Riviera di Chiaia, and the crowd began to cheer. From somewhere in the distance came the sound of a man singing "O Solo Mio." Enzo's heart filled. He had always loved this festival, even more than the Festival of San Gennaro, later in the month. That one celebrated the liquefaction of

San Gennaro's blood, a miracle that ushered in good luck for Neapolitans. The celebration was somber, with a crowded Mass in the morning and the cardinal parading the vial of liquefied blood down the church aisles, all of the people waving white handkerchiefs as he passed.

In 1528, when the blood did not liquefy, plague devastated the city. When the miracle did not occur in 1939, World War II started, and the blood did not liquefy the next year or in 1943, when the Nazi occupation began. For Enzo, the blood miracle caused anxiety and fear. Even the year Sofia was born, on San Gennaro's birthday, and there was much to be happy for and to celebrate, he'd rushed to the church to be sure the blood had liquefied. "Such a worrier, my little brother," Massimo always told Enzo. But Enzo knew the blood mostly kept Naples safe. "Mount Vesuvius erupted in 1631, and the lava stopped right at our city gates because of the blood of San Gennaro," Enzo liked to remind him.

But this festival was a happy one, with the floats and the lights and the singing and the tarantella. And it commemorated the appearance of the Virgin Mary six hundred years ago. That was the kind of celebration Enzo enjoyed.

As children in their paper costumes passed them behind the floats, everyone threw candy.

"I used to love this part," Sofia said, sounding more like the little girl she had been than the teenager she'd become.

The tarantella imitated the efforts of Neapolitans curing themselves of the bites of venomous tarantulas. They believed that only music and dance could neutralize the spider's toxins. The dance started with a slow tempo and gradually built to a frenzied climax. Massimo had come to Sorrento early with his girlfriend and younger daughter because Ines had insisted on lunch at the hotel. He'd invited Enzo, who had begged off under the false pretense of helping their mother move a piece of furniture. In truth, the restaurant at the Grand Hotel Excelsior Vittoria was far too expensive for him. Knowing Ines, she would order expensive wine and the dearest items on the menu. Enzo was happy to eat *pasta fagioli* with his mother, then make his way to Sorrento, arriving just as the dancers began to take their places.

The men and teenage boys in their knee-length breeches and vests of contrasting colors were lining up. Enzo immediately recognized Davide Bianchi in a brilliant red hat, sapphire breeches, and a yellow vest, standing tall and arrogant among the others. Davide had a constant look of disdain on his handsome face, as if he were better than anyone around him. Here came the women now in their magnificent dresses of embroidered gold fabric. The handsomest couple would be crowned king and queen of the tarantella.

Enzo did not have to search hard to find his niece. Sofia walked with great confidence right up to Davide, who smiled when he saw her and took her hand in the formal, traditional way. Enzo saw Candida Pensa too, pretty in her costume, but not nearly as beautiful as Sofia. Poor Candida, Enzo thought. She wore the look of the brokenhearted even as she gracefully took her partner's hand. The music began, the tambourines and castanets starting slowly as the tarantella dancers stepped forward.

For the next hour or longer, the dancers danced the beautiful tarantella as the crowd cheered them on. Enzo watched Sofia, her hair with its red ribbons flying, her face aglow, her feet in perfect step. He was not even a little surprised when she and Davide Bianchi were named the king and queen. At the sound of their names, Candida let out a cry, and ran from the huddle of dancers with her hands over her heart. Enzo tried to pretend that the satisfied look on Sofia's face came from winning, not from hurting her longtime best friend.

After the coronation, Enzo pushed his way through the crowd to get to his niece, who stood like true royalty, the gold crown slightly crooked atop her head. When he reached her, he saw that she was crying and smiling at the same time. Davide stood nearby, collecting his own congratulations.

Enzo hugged her and congratulated her. "But why are you crying?" he asked her.

"Because I won, of course! Because I was crowned queen! And the boy I love loves me," she said.

What did a girl so young know of love? Enzo worried for a moment about his niece and what kind of future she would have with the likes of Davide Bianchi. But she was smiling up at him, reminding him of the little girl who used to always be so eager to sit on his lap and listen to him read a book to her. Davide arrived, cocky and smug, and put his hands around Sofia's waist with barely a nod toward Enzo.

"Sofia," Enzo said, taking a vial from his pocket. "For my museum?"

"Silly Zio Enzo," she said, and she leaned close to him so that he could collect her tears.

Enzo did not like the way Davide kept his hands firmly on Sofia's waist, like she was his possession. But what could he do amid the cheering crowd except make way for others to congratulate them?

He was one of the few to leave the festivities early. Enzo made his way down the winding hill, the air pungent with lemons, as it always seemed to be in Sorrento. Walking slowly in front of him was the figure of a tarantella dancer, her costume seeming less magnificent away from the others. As he neared her, Enzo realized it was Candida Pensa, making her own way home alone.

"Candida," he said, drawing up beside her.

She turned her tear-streaked face toward him. "Zio Enzo," she said.

He didn't ask why she was crying; he already knew.

"I don't mind losing," she said quickly. "I'm not ungracious like that."

"Of course," he said. "And you danced beautifully." This was true. Candida had danced beautifully.

"And I'm sure Sofia would think I'm crying because she and Davide are in love," she continued.

"Aren't you, though?" he asked, confused.

Candida stopped walking and faced him directly. "Of course not," she said. "I have a schoolgirl crush on him. Every girl does. But my mother would kill me if I went with a Bianchi."

"What then, *cara mia?*" Enzo asked.

The tears began again, harder now. "I'm crying over Sofia. Over the loss of our friendship."

Enzo was so surprised and moved by this that he didn't know what to say.

"There's no greater loss," Candida said.

Enzo spent many hours thinking about what to label the tears he collected that day in Sorrento. Finally he decided. TEARS OF JOY, QUEEN OF THE TARANTELLA, SEPTEMBER 8, 1962, he wrote on one vial. TEARS OF A TRUE FRIEND, SEPTEMBER 8, 1962, he wrote on the other.

CHAPTER TWENTY-FIVE

Rome

Jenny, 1974

B efore arriving in Rome, Jenny had imagined a city of beautiful ruins, marble buildings, maybe even sculptures and paintings everywhere. She'd imagined people kissing on street corners, golden sunshine, the hum of history. What she hadn't imagined was snarled traffic, horns blaring nonstop, people shouting, and nondescript streets and buildings. Before they'd left France, Charlie had given her a beat-up copy of *Let's Go: Italy 1970*, with lots of notes scribbled in pen and highlighter throughout it. One of Charlie's clients had left it behind, and although some of the information was probably outdated, Jenny had marked the sections on the Colosseum, St. Peter's, the Trevi Fountain, and other sites that had not changed since 1970. But where were all those ancient places in this clogged, modern city?

No sooner did she think that then the cab driver screeched to a halt, setting off a cacophony of horns and shouts aimed at them, and pointed out his window.

"Signorina, il Colosseo!"

Jenny leaned across Nick to see what the driver was showing her, and there, rising fifty yards from an ordinary street, was the Colosseum. Despite the partially intact walls and crumbling façade, she could picture it as it might have looked almost two thousand years ago. Just like Paris when she'd first arrived there, Rome took a while to reveal its charms.

From then on, the taxi driver stopped and pointed out other sights: the Roman Forum and the Pantheon and the dome of St. Peter's off in the distance. By the time they reached their hotel, Jenny had decided that surely Rome was the most beautiful, most fascinating city in the world. What good luck she'd had coming here. They had almost three weeks to find *le petit chou*, and that would leave her in Italy with enough time to make her way to Capri and stand by that kiosk. Not that Daniel would be there. But Jenny had decided she would, just in case. It was, at least, something to look forward to. It felt good to dream again. And terrifying.

She and Charlie had managed to track down the whereabouts of twenty-one of the twenty-four soldiers who had arrived in the village. Eighteen were dead, three were unaccounted for—no obituaries or official records to be found—and three were back in Italy, presumably still alive. The first of those men, Ermanno Conte, lived in Rome. When Charlie had called him and explained that an American World War I veteran wanted to meet with him, Signore Conte was so enthusiastic that he invited Nick and Jenny to lunch at his home and offered to send his grandson to take them on a tour of the city when they arrived. Nick had grumbled about the tour—*We didn't come all this way to go sightseeing, you know*—but relented when he saw how disappointed Jenny looked.

The next morning they waited, sipping strong cappuccino in the hotel lobby, with its murals of Roman gods and goddesses and maroon velvet chairs and sofas and ornate tables.

"I can't believe you talked me into this," Nick said. "You know I don't like strangers. And I don't like talking to them all afternoon, either."

"But we're in *Rome*," Jenny said. "We have to see everything."

"I think the cab driver gave us a damn good tour," Nick said.

"I think Signore Conte's grandson will give us an even better one," Jenny said.

"Try to keep your hands off the poor guy," Nick said.

"Look who's talking," Jenny said, nudging Nick with her elbow. For a moment she actually thought she heard him chuckle.

A voice cut through the air: *"Americano?"*

"Jesus," Nick said. "Everybody's looking at us."

But Jenny jumped to her feet and waved to the chubby, sweaty boy named Alessandro making his way toward them. He looked no more than fifteen or sixteen, and very unhappy to be stuck with them.

"Come on, then," he said.

By the time they returned to the hotel, almost twelve hours later, Jenny was barefoot and holding her shoes in her hands, just like she used to do after a double shift at IHOP. They had walked through piazzas and crooked streets, across cobblestones and broken stones, into dark, empty churches and bright, busy bars. Fairly early on, Nick took to finding a table at an outdoor café or a bench by a fountain and happily sitting with a gelato or an espresso while Alessandro and Jenny walked from place to place. Alessandro had lived in America for most of his life and was only here visiting his grandfather for the summer, with his parents and little sister. His conversation was filled with slang and idioms. Nixon had his head up his ass. McNamara was a war criminal. With his soft accent, every vowel got pronounced, producing a lyrical sound even if he was telling her the history of ancient Rome.

They ate rigatoni carbonara and whole fried baby artichokes and saltimbocca. *"Saltimbocca*: jumps in your mouth," Alessandro translated, and the pounded veal stuffed with prosciutto and sage did just that.

Too much food, too much wine, too much walking. All Jenny wanted was to get into bed. Poor Nick had fallen asleep in the car on the way back to the hotel, and Alessandro had to wake him and bring him up to his room. As tired as she was, she decided to go down to the lobby bar and jot down her memories from the day, maybe write postcards. Decompress, she thought as she took a seat at a table and ordered a *sambuca con mosca*, the way Alessandro had done for her after dinner.

Dear Vera, Forget Paris! Rome is even more heavenly! Even though the Sistine Chapel is mostly dulled from almost five hundred years of candle smoke, it's breathtaking. I think I could have stared up at it all day. Our tour guide Alessandro said they are considering cleaning and restoring it, but that will take years, so I'm glad I got to see it, even damaged.

Jenny reread what she'd written, wondering why she always sounded so pretentious, so artificial, when she wrote to Vera. She'd made Alessandro seem wise and mysterious instead of like a sixteen-year-old boy with a mild case of acne and a big case of being full of himself. And that last line made it sound like she was talking about her own damaged self somehow. Why hadn't she written the note on a postcard of the Sistine Chapel instead of on one of those that had all the famous landmarks crowded onto it, like a bad collage? Why, Jenny wondered, did she even bother to write postcards to Vera at all? Why did she feel the need to prove to her that she was the girl Vera had thought she was when they were roommates and not a big screwup?

Jenny didn't finish the note to Vera, and instead started one to her mother on a postcard of the Colosseum lit at night. As she was writing, she thought she heard someone call her name. Ridiculous.

Dear Mom,
Rome is everything I imagined and then some!

"Jenny!" she heard, closer this time. "I cannot believe I found you," the voice said.

Jenny looked up, and there, standing in front of her grinning, was Charlie. He didn't have the straw hat on, and his hair was a wild mane of curls. She remembered that he was a Leo, which seemed, she thought, too perfect.

Jumping up, she banged her knee on the edge of the marble table and yelped.

"Crazy, right?" Charlie said.

Jenny rubbed her knee, where a bruise had already started to blossom.

"How in the world—"

"Everleigh Greer," Charlie said.

He put a bottle of Peroni on the table and took a seat beside Jenny.

"I got to thinking about you two stumbling around Italy. Neither of you speak Italian. Nick isn't in the best of shape. What if this guy isn't who you're looking for? How are you going to get to the next guy, the one outside of Siena? How are you even going to call him and tell him what you're doing?"

"So you came to Rome?" Jenny said, hardly believing he was sitting here next to her.

"I asked Everleigh if she knew where you were staying, and she did, so . . ."

"I don't even know what to say."

"I believe here it's *grazie*?" Charlie said.

"Right. *Grazie*."

"Don't worry. I'm not stalking you. I'm staying at a *pensione* in the Trastevere."

Jenny sucked on one of the coffee beans from her sambuca, trying to decide if she was relieved or disappointed.

"They put three beans in for health, happiness, and prosperity," Jenny said.

Charlie patted his shirt pocket and said, "I almost forgot. This came for you. The hotel in Paris forwarded it."

He handed her a postcard with a picture of Machu Picchu on it.

Give me your hand out of the deep zone of your widespread sorrow . . .
Love, D

"'The deep zone of your widespread sorrow'?" Charlie was saying as she read.

"Thanks for reading my mail," Jenny said. She was trying to calm her heart, which had started to bang against her ribs as if it were trying to get out.

He had found her. She didn't know why he was at Macchu Picchu, which she was pretty sure wasn't in Mexico or Chile. She didn't even know what the line meant, though she assumed it was from a Neruda poem. All she cared about was that across all these miles, Daniel had found her. Maybe he *would* be waiting at that kiosk.

"Boyfriend?" Charlie asked.

Jenny shook her head. "He's studying Pablo Neruda," she said.

Charlie shrugged. "Never heard of him."

"Only the most brilliant contemporary poet," Jenny said.

"So you're not a fan of Bishop? Or Ginsberg?" Charlie said.

"I am," Jenny admitted. "But Neruda is different."

"Okay," Charlie said, motioning to the bartender to bring him another another Peroni. "And another sambuca?" he asked Jenny.

She thought of France, of how on more than just that one night she had fallen too easily into bed with Charlie.

"I'm good," she said.

Eventually he finished his beer and put his arm around her, pulling her close.

"I don't think so," Jenny said.

He raised his eyebrows. "Is it because of this Neruda guy?"

Jenny shook her head. "I hardly know him."

She wondered how to explain to Charlie that someone she barely knew felt more possible to her than someone she liked. A lot. How sitting here with Charlie was fun, but she didn't want any more than this— conversation, friendship. Walking that night with Daniel made her want to gobble up the world. She'd felt alive.

"I get it," Charlie said.

She looked up, surprised. "You do?"

"Back in the States, I have this pal, Lydia. She's maybe my best pal. We can stay up all night talking and laughing, or sit on a beach and say nothing at all, and it's perfect. But it's not exciting. It's not that thing that makes you think crooked, that white heat that blinds you."

"Yes!" Jenny said.

Charlie laughed ruefully. "Don't sound so enthusiastic. One of us in this room feels that white heat."

He gave her a little squeeze, then released her. "Two roads diverge and all that," he said.

She kissed his cheek, which was scruffy from a few days without shaving.

"Thank you for understanding," she said.

Charlie sighed and stood up. "*Ciao, bella,*" he said, then left for his *pensione*.

It was well after midnight, but Jenny didn't want to go to bed yet. She ordered another sambuca con mosca—three coffee beans for health, happiness, and prosperity—and she studied the postcard, the picture of Machu Picchu, and Daniel's small, careful handwriting. She tried not to pay too much attention to the fact that he'd signed the thing *Love*.

CHAPTER TWENTY-SIX

Rome

Nick, 1974

This could have been my life. That was what Nick thought as Ermanno
Conte, that fat, sweaty, grinning bastard, ushered them into his villa.
An actual villa. Oak-lined drive. Arched doorways. Marble floors. A bil-
liard room, for Christ's sake. An elevator if the sweeping staircase was too
difficult. A pool with water so blue it looked fake. Tennis courts.

"Everything is so beautiful," Jenny said. "Do you mind if I take pictures?"

"Please," Conte said. Smugly, Nick thought.

Jenny had bought a used camera at the Porta Portese flea market, and
now all she wanted to do was take photographs. She'd also bought a box
of old buttons and a brown leather jacket that had seen better days. *Is this
what I pay you for?* Nick had said when she'd shown him her stuff. Jenny
had lifted the camera and pointed it at him. "Say *formaggio*," she'd said,
and snapped the picture.

"Lunch is in the garden," Conte said. "I hope that is satisfactory?"

Nick followed the glare of his white linen shirt, beneath umbrella pines
and cypress trees, past an oval pond, over a small arched bridge, to the
long table set with mismatched china that somehow seemed to match, to
work together. He remembered how once when he'd broken a plate from
their wedding set, Lillian had actually cried.

"Can't we just replace it?" Nick had asked, confused, holding the shards of porcelain, unsure of what to do.

The pattern, so carefully chosen by Lillian and her mother, was Royal Albert "Harebell," "harebell" being the British term for the bluebell, the flower that delicately twisted from the periwinkle-blue edge.

"They stopped making it over thirty years ago," Lillian had said, as if he should know that.

"How about just replacing it with a white plate, then?"

She'd looked at him, horrified. "That's not a matching set," she'd said.

Bewildered by the broken plate, Nick had placed it carefully in his sock drawer. Ridiculously, sometimes when he'd reached for a pair of socks, he'd found himself hoping the damn thing had miraculously repaired itself. But of course it had stayed broken, and eventually he had thrown it away, tucking it deep into the trash so that Lillian wouldn't see it.

But here at Villa Mazzucco, where they had kept bees for generations, mismatched things were fine, celebrated, beautiful. When he sat, Nick saw that in fact his plate had dozens of hairline cracks running across it. He ran his hand over its smooth surface. *See, Lillian? It wasn't so bad that I broke that Royal Albert "Harebell" dinner dish.*

To his surprise, the table was soon crowded with children and grand-children, visiting friends from London and Miami, an old man and woman, and two glamorous middle-aged women whose connection to the family was unclear. No wonder when Nick had asked Conte if they might bring along a friend, he'd said "Of course" so enthusiastically. What did one more guest matter to him?

The wine was Frascati, the local white, another older woman told Nick as she poured him a glass. Instead of the long-stemmed, elegant crystal Lillian had favored, this woman served the wine in a short glass, the kind Nick drank his orange juice from back home.

The woman smiled at him. "You know this wine?" she said, her accented English musical. *Theesa wina.* She had salt-and-pepper hair that fell in lux-urious waves around her shoulders, and dark green eyes that made Nick think of Smokey, a cat he and Lillian had early in their marriage.

Nick shook his head.

"It has been made here for over two thousand years," she said, sweeping her arms when she said *here*. "The Romans called it 'golden wine.'" She picked up his glass and held it in the sunlight. "For its color, yes?"

"Don't I have the most beautiful, most intelligent wife in all of Italy?" Conte yelled from the other end of the table.

This magnificent woman in a simple cotton dress that made her somehow even more beautiful was married to fat, sweaty Conte? How could she bear to make love to him? But here she was, grinning back at her husband.

"He compliments me so that he will have some *fare l'amore* later," she said.

Everyone laughed. She looked down at Nick and said, "How do you say? The making of the love?"

"Yes," Nick managed to say before she thankfully moved on, pouring wine into glasses, tossing her hair, grinning.

From across the table, Jenny met his eye. She had her worried face on, so he shook his head and tilted his wineglass in her direction. Charlie had managed to sit right beside her, Nick noticed with some satisfaction. The kid was obviously nuts about her. Maybe Nick should give her some advice, tell her to give Charlie a chance. But as soon as he thought it, he discarded the idea.

Platters of pasta with fresh tomato sauce were passed, then porchetta with roasted potatoes, then a salad of just lettuces with olive oil and salt, then bowls of wild strawberries. The food seemed to never stop, Conte applauding his wife as each course arrived, the guests toasting her. Nick was full and drunk and sleepy by the time lunch ended. And he still hadn't spoken to Conte about the reason he'd come. Jenny looked flushed, her cheeks pink and her eyes sparkling. She'd had too much wine too, Nick decided.

"Hey," he said, trying to get her attention. "Jenny?"

She was flirting with the guest from London, a man who was too old for her.

"Jenny!" he said, more harshly than he'd intended.

She turned toward him, not angry but amused, which somehow made him angry.

"We need to talk to Conte soon," Nick said. "I'm feeling tired."

"As soon as we get back," Jenny said, touching the British guy's arm. "Richard is going to show me the bees. Did you know that to produce just one kilogram of honey, bees fly the equivalent of three times around the world?"

"Quite," Richard said.

Charlie looked crestfallen, but Jenny didn't even notice. She was getting up, using Richard's arm for support, and the two of them walked off. She was barefoot, Nick noticed. What the hell had she done with her shoes?

"Friends," Conte was saying, "Gia has made her famous tiramisu for our American guests. The inventor of it, Roberto Linguanotto himself, taught her to make it in the kitchen of Le Beccherie." He lowered his voice. "Be careful. He told her it was an aphrodisiac."

Nick groaned. Still more food? He *was* tired, and his bones ached in the new way they had started to ache. The pain was deep, as if it reached straight through each bone, stabbing. But the tiramisu was served to more sighs of admiration for Gia.

"Tiramisu," Gia said when she placed it in front of him. "It means literally 'pick me up,' because there's espresso inside."

"Good," Nick said, "because I'm about to fall asleep."

Gia tossed her head back and laughed. "You were not warned that in Italy lunch, especially Sunday lunch, lasts for several hours?"

"I really just came to talk to your husband about something that happened. In the war."

Nick thought a shadow crossed her face, but in an instant she was smiling again.

"He doesn't like to talk about it, of course," Gia said.

"I understand. But this is not about the fighting."

She raised an eyebrow.

"It's about a baby that was found by an Italian platoon. Ermanno's platoon—"

Gia laughed. "A baby? Where?"

"In France. In the town they liberated."

"If my husband found a baby, he would have told me. We tell each other everything. We grew up together, little children playing in the streets of Naples. So poor that we ate bread soup three times a day. Never did we dream that we would have all of this." Her eyes took in the garden, the sparkling pool, the land stretching out seemingly endlessly before alighting again on Nick. "We tell each other everything," she said again.

Nick tried to find some sign of the little girl she'd just described, but the elegant woman in front of him showed no trace of that child.

"Everything except this perhaps," Nick said.

"No, signore, you are mistaken," Gia said, turning to leave.

Nick caught her by the elbow. "In the town in France, they say that the platoon your husband led found this baby—"

"I am sorry," she said. "You can discuss with him, of course, but there was no baby found by my husband."

"I need to learn what happened to that boy," Nick said.

"*Mi dispiace*," she said, though to Nick she did not sound sorry at all.

Nick watched her as she served the woman beside him tiramisu. The lavender dress showed off her ample breasts, her narrow waist. She smiled broadly, talking in Italian to the woman. Somehow, in his aching bones, Nick knew she was lying.

"A baby?" Signore Conte said, and burst into laughter.

Nick watched his impressive roll of chins tremble as he laughed.

"In a well?" Signore Conte said when he'd caught his breath. But then he set forth another round of laughter.

They were in Conte's study, a room filled with leather furniture and paintings that hung one on top of another on the walls and an enormous wooden desk, which Conte sat behind in a chair that looked more like a throne, with an elaborate high back painted gold.

"Not *in* a well," Jenny said.

"*Near* a well," Charlie clarified. "In the town square."

"Ah," Conte said, somehow making that one short syllable sound both longer and sarcastic.

"With all due respect," Jenny said, "someone in your platoon found that baby. Everyone in the town attests to that. Now, it may not have been you, but surely . . ."

Her voice floated around Nick, who felt suddenly light-headed.

"Nick?" Jenny said. "Did you hear Signore Conte?"

Nick looked around at the three faces turned toward him, waiting.

"I," he began. He licked his lips. "I was thinking about coffee," he said. Dizzy, he gripped the arms of the leather chair where he sat.

"You want coffee?" Signore Conte was saying. "Espresso? Cappuccino?"

Nick shook his head. It was too much effort to explain that he didn't want coffee, that he was just thinking about the Mr. Coffee on his gold-speckled Formica counter, filling a glass pot with coffee.

"Amazing," he said.

Jenny and Charlie glanced at each other.

"We showed Signore Conte the names of the other two men, and he reported that sadly they are both dead," Charlie said.

"It was all so long ago," Signore Conte said with a dramatic sigh. "You and I, Nick, are lucky to still be alive."

Again, they all looked at Nick, waiting. But his mind couldn't focus on what they were saying. Instead, it drifted to pouring coffee into the white mug that hung on the little cup tree Lillian had used—a small metal thing made for the sole purpose of hanging coffee cups on it. He took his coffee black, two sugars; Lillian liked milk in hers, as well as the sugar. She called coffee with milk and two sugars *regular*, using an old New England-ism that he always found cute. She called milkshakes *cabinets* and water fountains *bubblers*. Why hadn't he told her how charming he thought those old-fashioned words were?

"Very ill," Nick heard Jenny say. And: "Not much time."

The next thing Nick knew, he was on his back on the beautiful cornflower-blue Oriental carpet. Nick had noticed the rug when he came in, thick and plush, with that vivid blue background and a pattern of oversized geometric medallions with pomegranates circling them. "From Iran," Conte had told him. "Heriz." And Nick had nodded like he knew what the hell Conte was talking about.

Now he was stretched out on the beautiful rug from Heriz.

"He's coming to," Jenny said, her voice sounding soft and far away.

Charlie's face loomed in front of Nick's. "Hey, there," Charlie said.

"He still seems confused," Jenny said.

They said their good-byes and helped Nick to the car.

Nick sat in the front seat with a basket filled with jars of honey and cans of olive oil and bottles of wine, all of it thrust upon them by Gia and Ermanno. Everything had a dark green label with a yellow bee flying above the words VILLA MAZZUCCO.

The car was silent now that Nick had told Charlie and Jenny that he was not, under any circumstances, going to the hospital.

"Goddamnit, you sat me in the sun and made me eat and drink all goddamn afternoon. How do you expect me to feel?" he'd said as a way to end the conversation.

His mouth was chalky from that horrible dessert Gia had served, the one Conte bragged so much about. What he would like, Nick thought, was a big piece of blueberry pie. Lillian used to make a lattice crust on her blueberry pie, carefully rolling a pastry wheel over the dough to cut strips with scalloped edges; then she'd weave the strips in and out until the top was perfect, and finally she'd crimp the edges.

"You know what I want?" Nick said, staring out the window, watching the city of Rome appear. "A goddamn blueberry pie, that's what I want."

Rome. The Eternal City. How ironic it would be to die in a place called that.

"Maybe it's time to go home," Nick said, still staring out the window. He didn't want to die here. He wanted to die in his own bed.

"But what about finding *le petit chou?*" Jenny said.

"Conte said they never found a baby," Nick reminded her.

"He also said Aldo Mori was dead," Charlie said.

"So?"

"So I spoke to Aldo Mori this morning," Charlie said. "He's expecting us in Rosaria Tuesday afternoon."

"Maybe he was wrong about Mori being dead," Nick said. "That doesn't mean he was lying about the baby."

"Let's see what Mori says," Charlie said. He glanced at Nick, at that big basket of stuff on his lap.

"If he says there's no baby, we'll go home," Jenny said, leaning forward to face him. "Okay?"

When Nick didn't answer, she said, "We've come this far. We have to follow every lead," and turned back around, away from him.

Nick sighed. "I suppose I can last a few more days," he said.

CHAPTER TWENTY-SEVEN

Tuscany

Jenny, 1974

J enny climbed back into the car after asking Charlie to stop yet again so she could take pictures of the fields of sunflowers on either side of the narrow road. Sunflowers and haystacks and trees heavy with peaches. The grapevines were the only bright green against all the gold, and then, out of nowhere, rows and rows of lavender appeared.

"If you keep making us stop, we're never going to get to Aldo Mori's," Nick grumbled from the back seat, where he half-lay, half-sat, a blanket over his legs despite the heat.

"You'll be happy to know that this was my last picture," Jenny said.

"And you're out of film? No more in that bag of yours?" Nick said.

Charlie laughed. "Don't sound so hopeful. She's got at least three more rolls in there."

Jenny didn't like how Charlie always knew everything about her.

"Don't you?" Charlie said. "You've definitely got at least three more rolls of film in there."

Jenny slid the camera's small compartment open and took out the roll of film and replaced it with a fresh one. She put the used roll carefully in the empty canister, then wrote the date on it.

The car jerked to a stop and Charlie muttered, "Some signs would be really nice." He opened the Michelin book of Italian road maps, something he'd done at least a dozen times since they'd left the highway outside Florence.

He put the car in reverse and backed up to a small dirt road they'd passed. Jenny heard Nick moan in pain as the car bumped onto the road. She tried not to focus on how Nick's health seemed to be failing more every day, how he was slower to move, how sunken his eyes looked, how cold he always seemed to be, even as the temperatures hovered in the high nineties. Instead, she stayed upbeat and optimistic, hoping that by sheer will she could keep him alive. At least until they learned the fate of *le petit chou.*

"I just have a feeling Aldo Mori will have information for us," Jenny said, forcing her voice to sound confident.

"So do I," Charlie said, shifting into second gear to better navigate the rutted road. "Aldo Mori is our man."

From the back seat, Nick let out a long breath—more like a low whistle, Jenny thought—either in frustration or pain, she didn't know which. The road climbed, twisting and turning around sharp corners. Below them, the Tuscan countryside spread across golden hills. Surely this was the most beautiful place in the world, she decided. Far in the distance, Jenny could see a dozen stone towers pointing toward the hazy blue sky.

"San Gimignano," Charlie said, slowing the car. "Apparently there used to be over seventy towers there in the Middle Ages."

"I wish—" Jenny began, then stopped herself. She'd almost made the same mistake as they'd whizzed past Florence—*I wish we could see it!* But she'd caught herself then too. It was impossible to stop and see the sculpture of David, just like it was impossible to go to this hill town with the unpronounceable name and climb one of those towers. Nick wouldn't be able to walk from a car park to town, or navigate the crowds of the Uffizi Galleries, or do anything other than get from the car into Aldo Mori's house. She tried not to think about how just a few weeks ago he had been well enough to go off with Everleigh. If he met her today, Jenny didn't think he would be able to do it.

Charlie reached over and squeezed her hand, as if to let her know he understood.

"You want to know what I wish?" Nick barked. "I wish we'd get to wherever the hell we're going."

"Ah," Charlie said, "wishes do come true."

They passed through an entry between two stone walls, then continued down a long, equally bumpy road lined with cypress trees, until a series of stone farmhouses with red tiled roofs dotted the land around them. Another turn, and the crumbling main building appeared in front of them.

"This villa is a little different from Conte's," Charlie said, cutting the engine.

Four enormous Bernese mountain dogs lazily lifted their heads from their spots in the little bit of shade against the cool stone of the house.

Charlie got out of the car, and after a moment, Jenny did too. When Aldo Mori had told them he lived on his family's farm, she had not imagined this run-down property that spread out around them in every direction. In the fields, shirtless men directed the plow behind yoked oxen. Neat rows of sheets and clothes hung from clotheslines between the houses. A donkey walked casually past them. To Jenny, it felt as if when they'd left the autostrada behind, they'd driven back in time.

An old man in a sleeveless white undershirt, loose, dusty pants held up by dark purple suspenders, and a wide-brimmed straw hat was slowly making his way toward them.

"Signore Mori?" Charlie called, and the man nodded and waved to them.

A couple of the dogs got slowly to their feet and went to meet him, but retreated back to the shade as he neared.

"*Non parlo inglese*," Mori said when he finally stood in front of them.

"*Nessun problema*," Charlie said, shaking the old man's hand. "*Parlo italiano.*"

Mori harrumphed, and continued his slow walk toward the uneven stone steps that led to the front door. Nick had managed somehow to get himself out of the car. He was pale-faced and sweating, but he refused Jenny's offer of her arm for support. She knew he did not want to look frail in front of this other man, this former soldier. Silently she prayed that they would not have to walk very far.

Inside, it was dark but cool, the massive stone walls keeping the heat out just as the shuttered windows kept out the sunshine. Mori motioned them to a long wooden table surrounded by mismatched chairs, and made downward motions with his hands for them to sit. It took Jenny's eyes a moment to adjust, but an enormous hearth eventually took shape, as did a rocking chair with a basket of yarn by its side, a picture of a haloed saint, and a few paintings, at least one of them of this very farm—Jenny recognized the building in which they sat and the sleeping dogs.

The smell of tomatoes and something sweet cooking filled the air. As Charlie explained in Italian why they had come, a tiny, hunched woman as old as Aldo, or even older, entered with a carafe of wine and four small glasses on a tray, and a plate of cookies. She smiled a toothless smile, nodded at them, and left as quickly as she'd come.

"His sister," Charlie translated for Jenny and Nick.

Jenny took a cookie; to her surprise, when she bit into it, she found it hard and dry.

Aldo laughed, picked up a cookie, and dipped it into his wine before he took a bite. "*Cantucci*," he said through a mouth full of crumbs, spilling some down his chin.

"*Grazie*," Jenny said, imitating what he'd done. The cookie absorbed the wine, which softened it, and the blended flavors were neither too sweet nor too dry. "Delicious," she said.

Charlie continued to talk in Italian with Aldo, until the old man burst out, "*Basta!*"

"What's he upset about?" Nick asked.

Charlie shrugged and began talking to Aldo again. But this time, Aldo slammed his hand down on the table and once again said, "*Basta!*"

"He says enough," Charlie said. "Enough with my questions about a baby."

"I told you this was a waste of time," Nick said. "Now will you let me go home?"

Jenny was looking past Aldo Mori, at the wall with the picture of the saint in the oval frame and the four paintings beside it. There was this house with the dogs in front, and above it the fields where the men were plowing. Above that was a painting of the long road lined with cypress trees they'd driven down. The paintings weren't very good, though they depicted the *tenuta* accurately. The perspective of the dogs was slightly off; all four of them were the exact same size, despite one being in the foreground and one near the farthest corner of the house. Above that painting . . . Jenny got up and walked over to the wall. Behind her, she could hear Charlie trying to cajole Mori, his voice soft and placating.

This painting was different from the others, its color palette more vivid, the shapes more expertly drawn. Three pigs stood in mud, heads bent. Behind them was the vague outline of a stone wall. And beyond that— Jenny peered closely—was perhaps a smudge of pale blue. In this dark room, it was hard to be sure. But she was certain that this painting was more realistic and more artistic than the other three. And it did not look like the farm where they were now.

"Signore Mori," Jenny said, still studying the painting, "is this your *tenuta?*"

To her surprise, he answered—*Sì, sì*—before Charlie translated. She turned and found the old man pointing toward one of the shuttered windows, and talking in rapid Italian.

"He says the pigs are kept over there, to the west," Charlie said.

"To the west," Jenny said, noting that from the way the sunlight fell on them, the pigs in this painting were to the east.

A crash echoed as Nick jumped to his feet, knocking over his chair as he did. But he didn't pause. He just made his way to Jenny, gripping anything he could to steady himself as he went.

"It's one of hers," he said.

"My sister, she paint these," Aldo said, also getting to his feet. "My sister, Emelia." He waved his hand vaguely in the direction from which his sister had brought the wine and cookies.

Nick looked from the painting right at Jenny. His eyes were shining and bright, his cheeks pink.

"It's one of hers," he said again. "It's Camille's."

Aldo threw them out of his house, yelling and swooshing his hands toward the door. Nick climbed back in the car, said, "I'm done," closed his eyes, and slept—or pretended to sleep—the whole way back to Florence.

At their hotel, he went to his room without saying anything except good night, and left Charlie and Jenny to figure out what to do next.

"Il Troia," Charlie said when he met Jenny back in the lobby a few hours later. "The Trough."

"As in the thing animals eat from?" Jenny said.

"As in the restaurant also known as Trattoria Sostanza. As in their butter chicken."

"Ah," Jenny said. "As in dinner." She realized she hadn't eaten anything but those hard cookies all day. "I like this plan."

They walked along the Arno, each lost in their own thoughts. Jenny struggled with what she wanted to do—stay—and what she knew Nick should do: go home. Sure, there was the dream of Daniel actually meeting her in Capri, of some great romance, of some big life far from the International House of Pancakes. But perhaps an even stronger desire was to find what had happened to Laurent, *le petit chou*, left by a well by a man whose life had been ruined by his decision.

Charlie stopped abruptly and pointed to an almost indistinguishable door.

"Here?" Jenny said.

Charlie opened the door and the smells of good things simmering on a stove and the sounds of people talking and forks hitting dishes spilled out. Jenny stepped into the tiny trattoria, with its white tiled walls crowded with framed photographs. People sat on wooden benches at tables covered with steaming platters and bowls.

"I like it," she told Charlie and followed him and a waiter to a table.

"It's been here since 1869," Charlie said, after he'd ordered for them. Wine appeared immediately, and soon their table, too, was covered with food. They ate Tuscan fennel salami, braised beans, *pasta al sugo*, tripe, and that famous butter chicken as if this would be their last meal. Which, Jenny thought as a plate piled high with whipped cream and tiny strawberries was placed in front of her, it could very well be. Tonight, Charlie, like Nick, could decide it was time to go home. And tomorrow Jenny might be on a plane back to Boston. She decided not to talk or think about it.

"How do you know so much?" Jenny asked Charlie. "About where to eat in Florence and how to speak French *and* Italian and where they make the best *cacio e pepe* in Rome?"

Charlie thought a moment, then said, "Well, you see, I'm rich. Like, trust-fund rich. Like, very very rich."

Jenny laughed. "No, you're not," she managed. "You don't look rich at all."

He pointed his fork at her. "I told you I was the black sheep of my family, didn't I? The one who dropped out of Yale and got arrested—"

"Arrested!"

"For marijuana! Ridiculous."

"I can't believe you're a felon. A rich felon," Jenny said.

"There you have it. Boarding school in Switzerland after I got kicked out of both St. Paul's *and* Groton. Family trips to Europe every summer."

"You're serious," Jenny said.

"Do you know how they make it?" Charlie asked. "The butter chicken?"

Jenny pushed her half-eaten dessert away. That wasn't just whipped cream, but meringue too, and she was as full now as she'd been hungry when they sat down.

"They grill the chicken, then dredge it in egg and flour when it's still hot, and cook it in a lot of butter," Charlie said.

Jenny looked at him in the dim light.

"I don't want to go home," she said. There. She'd said it out loud. Her heart was beating fast, and she had to press her hands into her lap to steady their trembling. *I don't want to ever go home.*

"I don't think he can make it any longer," Charlie said. "He's really sick."

She nodded, pressed her hands harder into her lap.

"What do you think all these men are hiding?" Charlie said.

"Maybe they found the baby and just left him there. Maybe they're guilty too."

Charlie leaned back in his chair, watching her carefully.

"Pietro isn't dead either," he said. "Conte lied about that too."

Jenny met his gaze.

"Then we have to go and talk to him," Jenny said.

"And what about Nick?"

They held each other's gaze until the waiter appeared again, this time with a bottle of *nocino*, the local walnut liqueur. He filled two small glasses to the brim and left the bottle on the table when he walked away.

Jenny took a sip and winced. "It tastes like varnish," she said.

"Do you know what my mother would say to that? She'd say, 'Have you ever tasted varnish?' "

"I think I just did."

"It grows on you," Charlie said.

"Do you think that he could fly home on his own?"

Charlie said, "No way."

Jenny took another sip of the *nocino*. Charlie was right: the taste did grow on you.

"This Pietro is our last hope. After him, the trail is cold—" she said.

"You sound like a private eye," Charlie said, laughing.

"I think Nick will do it. It's his last chance for answers."

"I don't know if he *can* do it, even if he wants to."

"When can Pietro meet with us?" Jenny asked, her mind racing. If it was just a matter of days, then maybe Nick would be able to manage it.

"Well, that's the thing," Charlie said, refilling their glasses. "I haven't actually spoken to him."

"So we're just showing up on his doorstep?"

"No one answers the phone," Charlie said. "I've called a million times."

The wee bit of hope that had bloomed in her vanished.

"Maybe no one answers the phone because Pietro's dead?"

"He's still in the phone book," Charlie said.

"Charlie, people stay listed in phone books, sometimes even after they've died."

He caught the waiter's eye and said, *"Controlli, per favore."*

"We can't convince Nick to stay a little longer and take him on a wild-goose chase, Charlie."

"I just know that Pietro is the answer," Charlie said. "He has to be alive."

While Charlie busied himself with the check, Jenny tried to imagine herself on a plane headed home with no answers to anything—not *le petit chou*, not Daniel, not, in some mysterious way, to herself. But what if Nick died in Italy as they chased false leads? What if they showed up at Pietro's and he was dead and those few days kept Nick from making it home?

"As badly as this could go," Charlie said as they walked along the Arno toward the hotel, "it could also solve the mystery. Nick could die knowing where his actions led. He wouldn't die happy necessarily, but he would at least know."

"Try Pietro again in the morning?" Jenny asked.

"I will. But if I don't reach him, I say we still go."

The next morning, Jenny found Charlie at a table in the restaurant on the hotel roof, eating breakfast. The Duomo soared beside them, so close that Jenny felt she could reach out and actually touch it.

Charlie looked up as she approached.

"Nick took coffee in his room," he said, defeated. "And I still can't reach Pietro."

Jenny sat across from him. The sun was warm on her face. In the distance, church bells rang. She took some cheese from his plate and rolled a piece of prosciutto around it.

"Last night I thought I'd never be able to eat again," she said, taking a bite of the salty meat and cheese.

"Did you hear me?" Charlie said.

"Charlie, we have to go to find Pietro."

She reached into her big leather bag, which she'd bought on the street in Rome, the smell of leather wafting up to her when she opened it.

"Look," she said, putting an envelope in front of him.

Frowning, Charlie opened the envelope and removed the stack of pictures she'd had developed.

"I just picked them up," Jenny said.

Charlie sifted through them quickly, until one made him stop. He held it out to her.

"The next one too," Jenny said, placing the photograph on the table between them. Charlie put the next one beside the first, and they both studied the pictures. Most of the roll was from their lunch at Ermanno Conte's. Close-ups of food and wine, panoramas of the landscape around them, candid shots of the people there. Then pictures of the inside of the house, Conte at his desk in the thronelike chair, the rug with the pomegranates.

Jenny put her finger on one painting on the wall, almost hidden among the larger, more grandiose ones in Conte's study.

"There," she said.

She touched a second photograph. "And there."

Charlie grabbed her hand. "Camille painted those."

They looked at each other for a long moment.

"We'll show Nick," Charlie finally said, not letting go of her hand, holding on tight.

"Yes."

"And he'll want to find Pietro too."

"Yes," Jenny said.

"And to think Nick was fed up with your picture taking."

"What's this about her goddamn pictures?" Nick said from behind Jenny.

"See for yourself," Jenny said.

He took a seat at the table with them and picked up the two pictures.

Jenny watched him studying the photographs. He looked better today, she thought. Freshly shaven, his linen jacket pressed. Nick looked up from the photographs, his brown eyes clear and shining.

"That lying Conte," he said.

"Yup," Charlie said.

"So when do we go and talk to the next guy? Pietro? I'm thinking he's not dead either," Nick said.

That wee bit of hope bloomed again in Jenny's chest. She thought she might actually cry, so she looked away, out at the red tiled roof of the Duomo. She'd read in her guidebook that it was the largest brick-and-mortar dome in the world, bigger even than the Vatican's. A dome that large had never been built before, but in 1420, Brunelleschi claimed he could do the impossible. And he did.

"We could leave this afternoon?" Charlie said.

"Tomorrow," Nick said, waving to a waiter for some coffee.

"Why wait?" Charlie asked him.

"You're in Florence," Nick said, looking at Jenny. "You at least need to see the *David*."

"Really?" Jenny said.

"Things are getting interesting," Nick said with a happy sigh. "Why the hell not?"

Jenny grinned at him.

"What are you smiling about?" he said, without his usual gruffness.

She pointed to the Duomo. "Brunelleschi," she said. "He built two domes, one on top of the other, and a herringbone pattern with a system of chains inside, kind of like a barrel, so the weight could be distributed evenly and self-support."

"They said it couldn't be done," Nick said.

"Yup," she said.

Nick's gaze drifted toward the Duomo. "Audacious, wasn't he?"

She took the used *Let's Go: Italy* book from her bag and opened it to the section on southern Italy. Lemons. The Camorra. People preserved in ash for two thousand years. *Naples, Italy,* she read, *is considered to be a very dangerous place.*

The Museum of Tears

Enzo, 1970

It was as if the city were imploding, Enzo thought as he rushed through ankle-deep water, the rain pounding him and the flooded streets. Out of nowhere, giant holes appeared. Entire streets collapsed. Sewers broke and overflowed. The air smelled of garbage and shit instead of the salt from the bay and the particular scent of January rain in Naples. Just a few days ago, a man in Afragola had been buried alive when a sewer near his house had exploded. This city is ancient, Enzo thought. It can't sustain all the people and buildings that keep coming here.

Drenched, he finally reached the shop, where Massimo sat, dry and dapper, carefully painting the figures of John Lennon and Yoko Ono.

"You look like a water rat," Massimo said, barely glancing at Enzo.

"I have never seen rain like this. Never."

He snapped his umbrella closed, sending a stream of rain everywhere. More water poured off his mackintosh and his hat when he took them off, and still more from his black rubber boots.

"You've brought the storm inside," Massimo said, shaking his head as if Enzo were responsible for the bad weather that had seized the city these past few weeks.

Enzo decided to ignore him and make some coffee to take the chill off.

He pulled on the sweater he kept here for cold days like this one, a worn gray one that his mother had knitted for him long ago. The elbows needed repairing and there were holes at the hem, but he loved the old thing. He set about making coffee in the little back room, unscrewing the top chamber of the Moka pot from the bottom one, filling the bottom half with water, and pressing the coffee into the basket. Rituals like this, the making of coffee, always brought him serenity. He struck a match and turned on the gas on the old stove, the smell, like the sweater, comforting him. How many times had he lit this stove to make afternoon coffee or a simple dinner of *pasta pomodoro* when he and Massimo worked late? Those nights when they took turns sleeping for a few hours on the little cot they kept back there. Countless times, Enzo thought with a sigh. All the hours here, all the figures painted and coffee made and scowls from Massimo. For what?

Carefully, Enzo screwed the top chamber onto the bottom one and set the pot on the stove.

"I hope you're making more than one cup," Massimo called to him.

Enzo shook his head. He always made more than one cup because Massimo always wanted some. Even when he said he didn't, as soon as the smell of coffee rose and the hiss of steam started, he changed his mind.

"Of course I'm making two cups," he said, but not loud enough for Massimo to hear.

Sometimes Enzo saw other men—other brothers—playing bocce together on the courts in the Vomero or standing side by side at a bar sipping *caffè corretto*, or weaving home drunkenly, arms tossed around each other's shoulders, singing in harmony. Why had God decided to give him Massimo, a brother who barely tolerated Enzo's dreaminess and romanticism? A brother who hardly ever even smiled in his direction, never mind sung with him late into the night?

"Don't burn it," Massimo called to him. "It smells like it's burning."

Enzo shook his head again. He never burned the coffee. He made perfect coffee. Massimo knew that. He took two cups from the shelf above the stove. They were old, their glaze a spider web of fine cracks, their rims chipped. *Like us*, he thought. The coffee began to bubble and hiss, and he turned off the flame. A bottle of anisette was also on the shelf, and he put a splash in both of their coffee cups. On a cold, wet day like today, as the city imploded around them, a little anisette in the coffee would be appreciated.

Just as he placed a cup beside Massimo, the door flew open. The wind whistled loudly, and the rain fell relentlessly behind an image dressed all in yellow, as if the sun itself had arrived.

The young woman who stood in the doorway—for it was a woman holding a lemon-yellow umbrella decorated with white flowers and wearing a long yellow raincoat that ended just where tall yellow rain boots began, and its dripping hood framed pale blond hair—struggled with the door. The wind fought her from closing it, and when she finally won the battle, it banged shut, hard.

"My goodness! The weather!" she said, in an accent that was neither American nor English. It rolled and trilled in her mouth, like the sea.

"Typically," Enzo said, "we get rain in January. But just a drizzle, not this."

She was busy closing her umbrella and lowering her hood now, and Enzo watched her, mesmerized. If it wasn't for the coffee steaming in his hand and the smells of gas and espresso and anisette, he might think he was dreaming. Lovely women cast in sunshine did not usually burst into his life.

"There," she said at last.

"Enzo! Take her coat!" Massimo said.

"It's fine. I'll just hang it here?" she said, slipping the coat off and hanging it on the hook beside Enzo's.

She wore a thick sweater, not yellow but a color somewhere between white and tan and gray. Massimo would probably know the name for such a beautiful color, but Enzo did not. Intricate cables snaked up the sweater; the woolen skirt below was a pale yellow that made him think of sunflowers in September, how they darkened after a summer of dry sun.

"Offer her a coffee," Massimo stage-whispered.

Foolishly, Enzo stepped forward and held out his own cup to her. Close up, he saw that she wasn't as young as he'd first thought, but was more likely thirty or even thirty-five.

"*Idiota*," Massimo muttered.

"Oh, no thank you," the woman said. "I detest coffee. But if you have some tea, I'd happily have a cuppa."

Enzo found he had to tilt his head to better understand her.

"Forgive me," he said, his head cocked. "We do not have tea."

She didn't show any disappointment, if she was in fact disappointed. Instead, she smiled and announced: "I am looking for the Museum of Tears."

"What?" Massimo blurted. "You can't be serious."

Her smile turned to a frown, though her eyebrows were so light and delicate it was more like a whisper of a frown. She reached into her raincoat pocket and pulled out a small pad, the kind stenographers used. Flipping the pages, she spoke softly under her breath, and Enzo found himself leaning his head even more to try to hear her.

"Here it is!" she said, and burst into another smile.

She held the pad out to Enzo, who took it and looked at the page she'd opened it to. There was the address of the shop and the words *The Museum of Tears* written below it.

"You see, I'm a travel writer," she said. "For the *Irish Times*. And I'm writing an article about unusual museums in Italy. Mostly its saints' heads and other body parts. Though the one with all the taxidermied animals in Florence was quite wonderful. Anyway, my friend was here a couple of years ago, and she told me I absolutely could not miss the Museum of Tears in Naples. 'Just wait,' Aoife says—Aoife's the friend—'there are actual *tears* in these vials, and the most peculiar little man runs around explaining whose tears they are.'"

She looked around the studio, perhaps for the first time since she'd entered. "But this looks more like a shop than a museum," she said. "Even though I did see a sign outside."

Enzo straightened, pulling himself tall, though he still wasn't nearly as tall as this beam of sunshine standing in front of him.

"I am Enzo Piccolo, the proprietor of the Museum of Tears," he said in a loud, clear voice.

Behind him, Massimo laughed. "The peculiar little man who runs the thing," he said.

"Where are my manners?" the woman said, her cheeks turning the loveliest shade of pink, which made Enzo think of cherry blossoms. "Geraldine Walsh," she said, thrusting her hand out.

Enzo stared at it, unsure what to do. He paused for an instant, then took her hand in his free hand—the one not holding the now-lukewarm coffee—and kissed it, quite gently. To his surprise, her fingertips were hard and callused. But the hand itself was white and almost transparent, the blue veins on top like a map of tributaries.

"*Idiota*," Massimo muttered again.

"Well, my goodness!" Geraldine said. "I was warned that Italian men might freely pinch my bottom, but not that they would be so gallant." She pronounced it *ga-lant*.

Now that Enzo was holding her hand, he wasn't sure what to do next. Thankfully, Geraldine took charge. She gave his hand a little squeeze, then removed hers from it and said, "The museum?"

"This way," Enzo said, sweeping his arm grandly to point the way.

Standing here in the shop with Geraldine Walsh walking toward him like a beam of sunshine, with the faint, lingering smells of the gas from the stove and the coffee filling his nose, Enzo felt younger, eager, ready. Ready for what, he did not know.

"Let me tell you about the day I happened upon the great opera singer Luisa Tetrazzini crying on a park bench," he said, taking Geraldine's arm in his and leading her forward.

Just three days earlier, it had seemed to Enzo that the world was ending. The torrential, relentless rain. The sewers bursting and the roads collapsing. But today, just three days later, it seemed to him that the world was, in fact, just beginning.

To his utter astonishment, Geraldine Walsh had been struck by the same bolt of lightning as Enzo was. He showed her the museum, and she touched each vial with a reverence that he had thought only he had for all of these shed tears.

"I will buy you dinner!" he announced when it appeared she was going to leave.

Never had he been so bold with a woman. Never had he felt so desperate to keep a woman near.

Geraldine smiled and said, "I thought you'd never ask."

"I'm leaving," Enzo told Massimo. "I'm taking Signorina Walsh to dinner."

Massimo looked as surprised as Enzo felt. "*Buono fortuna, fratellino,*" he said as Enzo held the yellow raincoat open for Geraldine to slip into.

Enzo wondered when Massimo had last referred to him with the affectionate *fratellino*, "little brother." Enzo might have even said something to him, something like "Brother, this makes my heart full," if Geraldine hadn't been standing there in her yellow coat, waiting for him.

They ate *mozzarella di bufala* and *pasta alla genovese, parmigiana di melanzane* and bitter greens. They drank carafes of cold red wine, and all of this while the sky poured down that violent rain. The next day, for the first time in his life, Enzo did not go to the shop. He instead brought Geraldine a *sfogliatella* from his favorite bakery and then they walked around Santa Chiara, the famous monastery and museum. In the beautiful tiled cloister garden, he kissed her for the first time. And for the second and third.

Yes, there was the kissing and the food and the wine and the rain, but for Enzo it was the conversation that most mesmerized him. Never had he spoken to anyone for so long about so many things. Important things, inconsequential things, trivialities and opinions. In Dublin, she told him, her friends called her Gerry. "No!" Enzo said. "Gerry is an American cowboy name!" In Dublin, she said, they ate French fry sandwiches that they called chip butties. Enzo shook his head. "You," he said, "are a savage," and he lifted a piece of pizza Margherita to her lips.

What they both understood was that their time together was limited, and as such it had to be speeded up. Under normal conditions, Enzo would have courted her by taking her to dinner on Saturday nights. It might be weeks before they kissed in the cloister garden at the Santa Chiara Monastery. It might be months before he found himself lying beside Geraldine in the small bed in the Pensione Napoli. The Pensione Napoli was, unfortunately, located near the train station, in a dangerous neighborhood where creatures such as Geraldine shouldn't venture, especially at night. Especially alone. But when they walked in the heavy rain through the terrible neighborhood, Enzo gripped her elbow hard and strode boldly, as if to let every thug and drug dealer and pickpocket know to stay away from someone so precious.

He stared down at her now as she slept, her face lit only by the dim bedside lamp, the sound of the rain pounding the roof and street. She snored, letting out a funny little sound that made him smile. Enzo had never spent so much time with a woman, and every moment delighted him: the surprise of finding stockings drying over the shower rod, the way her hair was tangled in the back when she got out of bed, the lotion that smelled like wet grass that she slathered over her body after a shower. All mysterious and intoxicating.

The first night, after lovemaking and whispering about nothing in the dark, her stomach had grumbled. And why not? They hadn't yet eaten.

"Listen," Enzo had said. "Your stomach is talking."

Geraldine sighed. "You aren't supposed to point out these things to your lady."

"Really?" he said, confused.

"It's embarrassing. Women want to present an illusion of gentility and grace, Enzo. Men shouldn't tell us we have a hair on our chin or our stomachs are grumbling."

"But it sounds so nice," he said, and he laid his head on the dip of her stomach, nestled between her hip bones.

"Let's just get some food so it will stop," she said, slapping him gently on the side of the head.

Enzo knew he couldn't tell her about the snoring. He had to just enjoy it on his own.

Geraldine's eyes fluttered open slowly. "Are you staring at me again?" she said.

"No," Enzo said. "I am drinking you in."

She smiled. "You are a poet. Like Yeats, you are."

In that way that had so soon become second nature, he tilted his head to better understand her.

Geraldine wrapped her fingers in his hair. "Come away, O human child," she said softly. "To the waters and the wild, something, something / For the world's more full of weeping than you can understand."

To Enzo's surprise, his eyes filled with tears. Geraldine saw them, and wiped them away with her fingertips.

"It's from 'The Stolen Child,'" Geraldine said. "By William Butler Yeats." She traced his cheek, his chin, his nose, thoughtfully. "You should put that on the sign!" she said. "For the museum. 'For the world's more full of weeping than you can understand.'"

Enzo bent and kissed her. "Yes," he whispered into her mouth. "'The Stolen Child' by William Butler Yeats."

Geraldine pulled him to her, and it was some time before they stepped outside into the night and the rain again.

What Enzo had not been prepared for was that she was leaving.

They walked along winding Via Posillipo, down Via Marechiaro, and then down the steps to the spot that offered the most beautiful view in all of Naples. They had done this today because it was the first day without rain, even though puddles still dotted the streets, and the sky remained gray and cloudy. Before them stretched the Bay of Naples and the islands that Enzo had pointed out to her: Capri, Ischia, and Procida. He had been imagining taking her to Capri, showing her the famous lemons there and the Grotto Azzurra, the natural sea cave with the tiny entrance—so narrow and shallow that the skipper of the rowboat that takes you there orders you to lie down when you enter. He would take her to the Casa Rossa in Anacapri, where the ancient Roman statues found there were displayed. Another unusual museum for her to write about, Enzo had thought excitedly.

He was about to say all of these things to her when Geraldine said, "I'm going to miss Naples." She said this without looking at him, her eyes fixed on the view below them. "I have to leave in five days. I've got a job," she said, when he looked surprised. "And an apartment in Dublin. And a cat. Maudie will be wondering where I've gone to, won't she?"

"But you can't leave," he said.

Enzo took her face in both his hands and turned it toward him. He looked her squarely in the eyes and said, "I love you." Then, for good measure, he said it in Italian: "*Ti amo.*" This declaration, under normal conditions, would have occurred in a year or two. But it seemed to Enzo that their time together was moving past him so quickly, he could almost see it disappearing before him.

"*Is breá liom tú,*" Geraldine said, meeting his gaze.

He tilted his head.

"I love you," she said, touching his chin.

"So you will stay," Enzo said. "I will take you there," he said, pointing to Capri. "And there," he said, pointing to Ischia.

"No, Enzo. I can't stay. But I'll come back. Soon."

"When?"

"I don't know," Geraldine said. "But soon. I promise."

They stood staring out at the sea for a very long time, hand in hand. Enzo wondered how he could be so happy and so sad at the same time. She had said *I love you.* That meant everything, didn't it? But what kind of love lived apart? He tried to picture leaving here, going to Ireland. But what would his mother do without him? What about the shop, three generations in his family? He didn't even know what Dublin looked like. Was it on the sea? How could he ever live the rest of his life with his head tilted just to understand what people were saying? How could he live the rest of his life without Geraldine Walsh in it every minute?

Before she left, she gave him a small sign with the Yeats quote on it to hang inside the shop at the entrance of the Museum of Tears. She kissed him good-bye, lingering over a long kiss that would have to last until she returned.

"Soon," she whispered at the airport. "I love you," she whispered. Then she walked away in her yellow coat.

Enzo's heart pounded recklessly until he yelled, "Stop! Geraldine, stop!"

He saw people staring at him.

"Stop!" he yelled again.

Geraldine stopped, and turned, her cheeks that pink of cherry blossoms.

"*Ti amo!*" he called to her. "*Ti amo, Geraldine Walsh!*"

The crowd—all those people going to and from their gates—seemed to pause, and in unison broke into applause.

Tears were streaming down Enzo's face.

"I will wait for you," he said, a little more softly now.

Weeks and then months passed. Letters flew between Naples and Dublin, written on pale, thin airmail paper with colorful stamps, read and reread, carried in pockets to keep the words close. *Soon,* Geraldine always wrote. *I love you.*

As time passed, it seemed to Enzo that he had dreamed her, that beam of sunshine on one of the rainiest days in the history of Naples. He went over everything she'd said, the contours of her body. He recalled the way she smelled, the lotion that smelled like wet grass, the stockings in the shower. Thinking of her, he cried, but even he wasn't sure if they were tears of sadness or love or despair or grief or gratitude. One day he collected his own tears and added the vial to the others. THE TEARS OF ONE WHO WAITS. JUNE 11, 1971. Then he went back to waiting.

CHAPTER TWENTY-NINE

Naples

Nick, 1974

Nick knew that dying people often had a miraculous recovery just before they died. He'd seen it with his father, who had lain in a hospital bed growing weaker and weaker for over two weeks, who hadn't spoken in days. Then one morning—it happened to be Easter morning, a coincidence that would have turned into a family joke about resurrection had he truly recovered—he opened his eyes, sat up, and declared himself hungry. Nick's mother, who had been on all-night vigils that whole week, ran out and procured an entire Easter lunch of baked ham, asparagus, deviled eggs, fruit salad, and sweet bread. She even brought back chocolate rabbits for everyone. "A miracle," she kept saying. "We thought you were leaving us." "Me?" his father said. "I'm not going anywhere." He died that Tuesday.

When Nick woke in the hotel in Florence, prepared to go home, however, he felt surprisingly good. Or at least better than he'd been feeling. He recognized this surge before death. He called for coffee and rolls in his room, and it all tasted so good that he decided to go to the roof for a proper breakfast. But first he took a shower, a long, hot shower. He shaved. He dressed in his nice clothes. He even considered suggesting that Jenny go to the Uffizi and see the *David*. If you're in Florence, you should at least see the *David*.

Nick had seen the *David*, and Botticelli's *The Birth of Venus*, on a trip with his wife years ago, and he thought Jenny should see them too. She was growing on him, he had to admit. She'd lost a lot of the timidity he'd seen in her at first, and had grown bolder, more confident. He almost hated to make her go back home, where surely something bad had happened to her. She'd dropped out of college after only a semester. A smart girl like her. And then waitressed at an International House of Pancakes. Yes, something had gone wrong in her life.

Nick ran a bit more Vitalis through his hair. His hairline had receded, but he still had most of his hair, a point of vanity. He glanced in the mirror. Not bad for a dying man, he thought. In the elevator up to the rooftop restaurant, he decided that he would send Jenny and Charlie off to the Uffizi and he would take a slow walk along the Arno. Maybe stop for a cappuccino and watch people walk past. When he and Lillian were here with the Pierces, he'd bought Lillian dangling blue glass earrings at a stall on the Ponte Vecchio. She'd worn them every day for the rest of the trip.

On the roof, he spotted Jenny and Charlie immediately and walked over to them, still feeling stiff and achy, but hell, at least he could fake a stride today.

Jenny looked up at him, her eyes narrowed, almost on fire with excitement.

"Look at these," she said.

Jenny was spreading out photographs in front of him, pointing and telling him to *Look! Look!* Right there in Conte's study, one of Camille's paintings. And then another.

"The bastard," Nick said.

Now both Charlie and Jenny were looking at him with intensity.

"So," Nick said, "it looks like we're going to Naples."

Jenny jumped up and threw her arms around him. "See? You've still got plenty of life in you," she whispered, holding on to him a little too tight.

"I'll go check out then," Charlie said.

"Hold on," Nick said, stepping away from Jenny. "You're in Florence. You at least need to see the *David*."

"Really?" Jenny said.

They left him soon after, even before his cappuccino was delivered to the table, rushing to put on their comfortable shoes and get to the museum before he changed his mind.

After resting in his room for a while, Nick picked up a map at the front desk and followed the maze of streets until he was at the Arno. Then he slowly made his way to the Ponte Vecchio, stopping to watch a man giving a puppet show with a Pinocchio puppet and browsing in shop windows at leather coats and bags and shoes that didn't seem possible to walk in. The day was hot and humid and a stench rose from the river, fetid and thick. But sidewalk cafés were everywhere he looked, and he was happy to sit at one and drink a cold beer. The waiter, officious and too serious, also brought small triangles of focaccia and a little bowl of very green olives. The focaccia was sprinkled heavily with salt and rosemary. Delicious. Eating it warranted another Peroni, which came with still more focaccia.

Nick sipped this one more slowly, stretching his legs out and bending them at the ankles, which were swollen and pink. He watched the people strolling past, no one looking like they had anywhere to be. What a life! To wander Florence all day, to pop into churches or museums at your whim, to sit in the early afternoon sun and drink beer and eat focaccia and olives. He had worked at jobs he didn't like and locked himself into a routine that was deadening. Why hadn't he thought to come to Florence and live? His eyes scanned the apartments, with their wooden shutters painted lovely shades of blue or yellow and flower boxes bursting with geraniums and petunias. He could smell food cooking. Rosemary, maybe. And tomatoes simmering. He should have moved here and been a painter and strolled the city on summer afternoons with Lillian.

Lillian. Would she have agreed to such a lifestyle? Would she have left her family and childhood friends to live an expat life here with him? She was the one, after all, who'd planned all those European vacations. Once she'd suggested that they go to India and see the Taj Mahal and he was the one who said absolutely not. Why hadn't he said yes? Now he would never see the Taj Mahal. Never live in Italy. How sad life was. When it was too late, you figured out everything you should have done.

Like that baby.

What Nick knew for certain was that he should have taken that baby to a police station. Handed it over to the authorities. And left France knowing that someone had taken care of it. Someone had found the baby a home, maybe even found Camille. Instead, he'd wasted almost sixty years wondering if the baby had died.

Nick drained his beer and sighed. Too many regrets for a dying man.

He left some lire on the table and stood, wobbly on his swollen ankles and from two beers drunk in the heat. He consulted his map again and slowly continued along the river until, up ahead, the Ponte Vecchio came into view. The arched stone bridge looked golden in the sunlight, and Nick stood staring at it for a moment before he resumed walking. That day with Lillian and the Pierces they'd taken a walking tour of the city. It was hot then too, and the tour was boring. The guide waved around a red umbrella when he wanted them to follow him, and Nick felt like a kindergartener on a field trip. He didn't remember much from that tour, except that there had been a bridge in that spot since Roman days and that it had originally housed butchers, who were pushed out in the sixteenth century and replaced with goldsmiths and jewelers. The guide had somberly recited all the years it had been destroyed by floods, something Nick had recalled a few years ago when he'd read that the city had once again been damaged by flooding.

The crowds here were thick and close. Nick moved with them, pushed forward by their propulsion. Once on the bridge, he broke free and leaned against a stall selling souvenirs: more Pinocchios and key chains with the boot shape of Italy striped red, green, and white. Postcards and cheap aprons with the *David*'s body on them, presumably the wearer's head completing the statue. The air smelled of sweat and the sewage-like stench from the Arno, making the beer rise in Nick's throat, sour.

He considered turning around and going back to the hotel. But he'd come all this way. He would walk the length of the bridge and then get a taxi. Jostled and sweaty, Nick walked past stalls thick with gold bracelets and necklaces, more of the same cheap souvenirs, sparkling jewelry. Then something caught his eye. An entire stall wall of glass earrings, just like the pair he'd bought Lillian. Delicate and shiny, in jewel tones. They came in different sizes and shapes, some with tiny flowers painted on them, but Nick liked the plain ones, just that sparkling glass on a thin gold wire. When he touched the blue ones, he could still picture Lillian's face, lit with delight at opening the small bag and seeing them.

"You like these?" the saleswoman asked him wearily. She was thick and solid and tired and hot.

Nick nodded.

"For your girlfriend?" the saleswoman joked, smiling.

"No," Nick said, confused. "No."

"The blue is very nice," she said.

His fingers moved to the next row and a yellow pair that would match that dress Jenny had bought in Paris and wore all the time.

"These," he said.

She unpinned them, wrapped them in paper, and slid them inside a bag fast, before he could change his mind.

Nick handed her the lire and she handed him the earrings.

"*Grazie mille*," she said, her eyes already drifting to the next potential customer.

"*Prego*," Nick said.

He put the bag in his pocket and hobbled to the end of the bridge, where a line of taxis sat waiting. He closed his eyes as the taxi lurched forward. Lillian's face floated before him, smiling, the blue glass earrings dangling, catching the light, making her eyes look bluer still.

Five and a half hours to Naples, Charlie had told him. If there was no traffic. Straight down the A1. But there was traffic, and they crawled south, the air hotter and more humid than in Florence and Nick's ankles swelling even though he had done nothing but sit in this back seat all morning. Was it his kidneys failing that caused the swelling? he wondered. Or his heart? Maybe it was just this oppressive heat. He watched the yellow earrings sway slightly against Jenny's auburn hair as the car bumped along.

She'd looked so surprised when he'd handed her the little bag at breakfast that morning.

"A present? For me?" she'd said, and then she'd just sat there holding it. She had crumbs on her chin, which made her look like a kid. Which she was, Nick supposed.

"Open it," he said.

"Thank you," she said, her eyes teary even before she opened the bag.

When she finally did take the parcel out and unwrap the paper, she began to cry hard. "They're beautiful," she managed, already removing the silver hoops she always wore and putting on the yellow glass earrings. "I'm never going to take them off."

Nick felt almost embarrassed. They'd only cost about ten dollars, trinkets really. And she seemed so grateful.

"Where's my present?" Charlie asked.

"You? I'm going to let you drive all the way to Naples," Nick said.

"Wow! Thanks," Charlie said. He reached out and touched one of the earrings. "Pretty," he said.

Nick watched him, wondering if he meant the earrings or the girl.

Jenny started reading from that damn guidebook again. She'd already told them that pizza had been invented in Naples. "We have to try pizza Margherita. It was named for the queen in 1889," she'd said. "Tomatoes, basil, and fresh mozzarella. Did you know that they make mozzarella from water buffalo milk here?"

"Stop it," Nick grumbled. "It's past lunchtime and you're making me hungry."

"Pizza as soon as we get there," Charlie said.

Now Jenny was on to street food: fried pizza, potato croquettes, zucchini blossoms, anchovies, and mozzarella, specifically. "These treats are sold on every corner in brown paper cones called *cuoppo*," she read.

Nick closed his eyes, her voice full of excitement and facts floating around him pleasantly. The next thing he knew, Jenny was saying, "How ugly! This can't be Naples."

He opened his eyes and saw block after block of concrete triangular-shaped apartment buildings coming into view.

"The Vele di Scampia," Charlie said. "Sails of Scampia. Not a place you want to visit. Unless you're looking to buy or sell some heroin. I think the idea was well intended. Build something beautiful and life will be beautiful. But it's been a disaster. I read that eighty thousand people live in those seven buildings."

"Beautiful?" Jenny said.

"Modernist architecture," Nick grunted.

In no time, the Vele di Scampia was behind them and the Bay of Naples glittered before them.

"Don't even tell me that in the fog over there is Mount Vesuvius," Jenny said.

"Smog, not fog," Charlie said. "But yes, there she is."

Nick was afraid Jenny would start reading from the guidebook again, but she didn't. She just stared out the window, grinning.

Charlie told them parking in Naples was impossible, and car theft common, so a taxi dropped them in front of Antica Pizzeria Port'Alba, which Jenny couldn't resist telling him had opened in 1830.

"They used to line the ovens with lava rocks from Vesuvius," she gushed, but then caught herself and stopped talking. God, she could be annoying.

The waiters were grumpy, the pizza was thin-crusted and soggy—though Charlie told him that was how it was supposed to be—the red wine served cool. Jenny was practically swooning over every little thing, and Nick started feeling grumpier than the waiters. They hadn't come to Naples to eat at the oldest pizzeria. They'd come to find Pietro.

"So? When will he see us?" Nick said after Charlie ordered a second pizza Margherita.

Charlie glanced at Jenny, the quick look letting Nick know the news wasn't good.

"The thing is," Charlie said, "he's still not answering the phone. I tried all afternoon."

"Maybe he *is* dead then," Nick said. His stomach rolled slightly, and he felt dizzy. *Here we go*, he thought, and squeezed his eyes shut.

"You okay?" Jenny asked him.

He opened his eyes. "Pizza's not agreeing with me," he said. He was starting to sweat.

The waiter slammed the second pizza on the table, along with another carafe of wine.

"*Grazie mille*," Jenny said, and smiled at him.

He paused and looked at her and then, to Nick's surprise, he smiled back at her. "*Prego*," he said.

Nick looked at Jenny too then, and saw what the waiter had seen: a pretty girl in a summer dress, happy. She'd pulled her thick auburn hair back and fastened it with a big tortoiseshell clip, and the yellow glass earrings dangled from her ears.

"All bark and no bite," Jenny said as she picked up another piece of pizza, folded it, and took a bite. "Like you, Mr. B," she said, through her pizza.

"Do you want to go back to the hotel?" Charlie asked Nick. "I can get you a taxi."

"No, I don't want to go back to the hotel," Nick said.

What he wanted was to sit here amid the excitement and good cheer of the two of them. Gorging themselves on pizza and wine. They'd probably take a walk by the bay when they got back. Maybe have a gelato. Maybe have sex, for all he knew. He hoped they would. He hoped they'd grab every minute they had, gobble it up. Jenny was laughing at something Charlie had said, her head thrown back slightly.

"What's so funny?" Nick said, wanting to be in on the joke. Wanting to laugh. Not wanting, to his great surprise, to die.

Late the next morning, the three of them stood on a narrow street, gazing up. The sun was blazing white and hot, and sweat trickled down Nick's neck and underarms. Unlike the modern Excelsior Hotel, this part of the city made him feel like he'd stepped back in time. The small streets. The laundry strung across the balconies, faded shirts and sheets and panties. Bunches of dried red chilies hung beside each door. Kids in shorts and T-shirts and socks and scuffed black shoes kicked a ball around, bouncing it off the buildings and each other. It was loud here too—so many scooters and horns and people shouting. The air smelled like strong coffee and flowers and diesel and garbage. Nick glanced at the buildings, their walls covered with posters covered with graffiti covered with city soot.

This was the Quartieri Spagnoli, the old part of the city. According to Jenny and her guidebook, it dated all the way back to Roman times. And this was where Pietro lived, in one of these buildings. Above them, a woman leaned over her balcony and called to the woman across from her, who also stood on a balcony. They both had cigarettes in one hand and clothespins in the other, and they shouted happily back and forth to each other, reminding Nick of the way Lillian used to have the neighborhood ladies over for coffee and cake some mornings, early in their marriage. He could almost smell the almond cake she used to bake, and the bitter smell of percolator coffee bubbling. He could picture Lillian in that green dress he always liked, a moss-green one with buttons down the front and a belt at the waist. Nick reached out, as if he might find Lillian standing there in her green dress.

Charlie was trying to figure out which building matched the address, but he wasn't having much luck. Most of them didn't have numbers on them, and the numbers he could find didn't seem to go in any particular order. Finally he gave up and called to the boys playing ball.

A gaggle of boys ran up to him, and Nick thought of the kids in France during the war, how they'd flock around the Americans and the soldiers would give them chewing gum. For an instant he felt confused, felt like he was in a village in France and these boys had never seen Americans, and he reached into his pocket for the gum he kept there but found only a few lira coins. He checked his other pocket. No gum.

"*Je suis désolé*," he said to the boy closest to him, a kid with a buzz cut and long dark lashes.

"*Cosa stai dicendo, signore?*" the kid said, laughing.

Nick stared at him. Blinked. He wasn't in France, was he? He looked around, at the laundry and the scooters and the graffiti.

"Quartieri Spagnoli," he said softly. "The old part of the city, dating back to Roman times."

"*Cosa stai dicendo, signore?*" the kid said again, louder and more agitated.

Nick shook his head. "*Niente*," he said.

The kid waved his hand at Nick, as if to shoo him away, and moved closer to the other boys, gathered around Charlie. The leader of the group was taller than the others, and instead of the shaved summer haircuts the others had, he still sported a head of dark curls.

He read the address silently, his lips moving as he read.

"Ah," he said. "It's here. Up this street, then left." He pointed as he spoke, making a sweeping gesture to indicate up the street, then a sharp cut through the air for left.

"I'll take you," said the kid who'd spoken to Nick. "*Cinquanta lire.*"

The tall boy repeated, "*Cinquanta lira*," and pointed to each kid with both hands.

There were probably ten kids total, Nick thought. Not even a dollar if he gave them fifty lire each.

"Okay," Nick said. "Ten each if you take us straight to this address."

Immediately the boys started shouting and heading up the street, calling, "*Seguimi!*" and "*Su questa via!*"

One boy, the youngest, took Nick's hand in his small, sticky one.

"*Su questa via*," he squeaked, tugging Nick's hand to urge him forward.

As they walked, lagging behind everyone else, the boy patted Nick's hand with other one.

"*Nonno*," he said.

Nick only understood a smattering of Italian, but he knew that *nonno* meant "grandfather." Unexpectedly, tears sprang to his eyes. He blinked them away, and let the boy lead him up the steep street.

Charlie and Jenny and the other boys stood waiting for him where the street leveled off ever so slightly. It had taken Nick twice as long—who was he kidding? more like three or four times as long—to get there because he had to keep stopping to catch his breath, to regain his balance, to lift his feet briefly out of his loafers. As he approached them, he was struck by how young, how healthy, how *alive* they looked, the hazy sun casting a halo-like shadow around them. Whereas he was drenched in sweat, their faces glistened from it. At some point, Jenny had pulled her hair into a bun that made her look fresh and cool rather than hot and tired. Charlie, in his strange long khaki shorts with pockets everywhere, straw hat, and huarache sandals, could have been the guide on an African safari.

Now that he was standing in front of them, Jenny's face appeared worried. But Charlie patted him on the back congenially, as if they'd just played a round of tennis.

Nick thanked the boys and handed out lire to each of them. Most of them scattered immediately, excitedly discussing how to spend their money. But the leader and the little one stayed put.

"Maybe you will need a translator," the leader said.

"We're good," Charlie said. "*Parlo italiano.*"

The boy frowned. But Charlie had turned his attention to the buzzers outside the door. His fingers ran along them until he found the apartment number he was looking for; then he pressed it and smiled at Nick.

"Here we are," he said.

"Maybe they're not home," the leader said when there was no response.

Charlie just pushed the buzzer again.

"Or maybe the buzzer is broken," the little boy offered.

They stood in awkward silence a moment more; then the little boy stepped in front of Charlie and pressed all the buzzers. Immediately they were buzzed inside.

The little boy grabbed the door and yanked it open, stepping aside gallantly to let them enter.

"*Grazie*," Charlie said.

"*Prego.*"

Nick slipped the boy fifty more lire. Why not? At least they were inside, thanks to him.

The entryway through which they stepped was dark and hot, the bulb hanging from the ceiling turned off. The smells of many dinners from many nights filled the air: meat frying mixing with onions mixing with something sour and even something that had maybe gone bad. In front of Nick, steep steps disappeared into darkness. He did not think he could climb those stairs. He would just sit here and let Charlie and Jenny find Pietro.

But to his great relief, Charlie said, "It's this corner apartment," and walked past an oversized baby carriage, a variety of shoes, and a mop sitting in a bucket to reach the door, which he knocked on several times, firmly.

The door opened right away, and a young woman who appeared to be around Jenny's age peeked around it.

Charlie spoke to her in Italian; Nick could make out his own name and Pietro's. Her eyes lit with surprise. She opened the door a little wider and wedged herself between it and the jamb. She was plain-looking except for her hair, which was a mass of long curls that seemed to have a mind of their own, sticking out everywhere, untamable.

"My grandfather is Pietro," she said softly.

Despite being so hot and so tired and so weak, Nick grinned. They had found this guy, the last person who could help them.

"Is he home?" Charlie asked her.

She shook her head.

Still, Nick felt elated. Somewhere, just beyond this door, lay the answer to what he was looking for.

"We can wait for him," Charlie said.

The girl's hand patted at her curls, as if she wanted to contain them. Her dark, thick brows were furrowed. But she opened the door wider still and let them inside. They were standing in a living room filled with big, dark wood furniture with worn upholstery in either faded moss green or maroon, lacy doilies over the arms, two footstools with hand-embroidered cushions, and lots of throw pillows in different shapes and colors.

She stretched her arm out and said, "Sit."

Charlie and Jenny sat on the sofa and Nick in a high-backed, over-stuffed chair. But the girl didn't sit. She stood and blinked at them like they had just landed here from another planet.

Charlie cleared his throat. "I'm Charlie," he said, touching his chest. "This is Jenny, and he's Nick. He's the one who was in the war, like your grandfather."

"I am Aria," she said.

Such a lovely name for such a plain girl, Nick thought.

She pointed above the couch. "My grandfather," she said. "And my grandmother."

Nick's eyes followed where she pointed. In a heavy gold frame, an old black-and-white photograph of a solemn bride and groom stared back at him. The bride was young, her eyes slightly startled; an elaborate veil covered her head, and she clutched a bouquet of calla lilies in her hands. The groom had an impressive handlebar mustache and a mischievous look about him—eyes twinkling, lips turned up slightly.

Charlie and Jenny turned to look too, and Jenny said, "How lovely."

"She . . . my grandmother . . . is only fifteen."

"Fifteen!" Jenny said.

"Arranged marriage. He has a good business."

"When was this?" Charlie asked.

"Old," Aria said. "Nineteen . . ." She hesitated, then said, "Around 1907, I think?"

Nick frowned. This guy—Pietro—was easily ten years older than him. If he got married in 1907, and by the looks of him, he had to be at least nineteen . . . Nick glanced at the picture again. No, older than that. Twenty-five? Ten years later, in the war, he would have been thirty-five, which would make him over ninety now.

Charlie was frowning too, probably doing the same math as Nick.

"And he's coming back soon?" Charlie asked.

"Coming back?" Aria repeated.

"Here," Charlie said. "Returning here."

She looked confused for an instant, and then she threw her head back and laughed.

"My English is not so good," she said, wiping at the corners of her eyes. "My grandfather is not coming back. He's dead."

Nick gasped for air, and bent over slightly.

"Nick?" Jenny said.

He lifted a hand to tell her he was okay. He was okay even though the world had just stopped suddenly. This was it. The end. He would never know what happened to that baby.

Nick took deep breaths, and when he could sit upright again, he pulled himself together and thanked the girl for her time.

"I had so hoped to meet your grandfather," he said softly.

"I'm sorry," she said. "I thought you knew him. In the war. And you came to tell us about him."

Nick shook his head. "I didn't know him. I thought our paths had crossed, in a way."

He got slowly, shakily to his feet, and Jenny and Charlie stood too. But as Charlie was thanking Aria, the door opened and slammed shut.

"Aria?" a woman called.

Aria said something—*Americans*, Nick heard.

"Americans?" the woman said, and now she was walking into the living room, her eyes as startled as they were in her wedding photograph. She carried a net bag bulging with fruits and vegetables and wore—oddly, in this heat—a thin black cardigan over a flowered dress. Her silver hair was in a thick braid wound into a low bun at her neck.

"Americans?" she said again.

After Aria explained the situation to her, she said, "You are looking for Pietro?" in slow, careful English.

Charlie met Nick's eyes, waiting for a signal of what to do.

"Why not?" Nick said. "We're here."

He didn't expect anything from this old woman, but he didn't want to give up. That was clear to him. Just a moment ago, he had believed it was over. But what if Pietro had told his wife the story of finding a baby by a well in a town square in France? What if he had told her what had happened to that baby? What if, after all this time, here was the one person who actually knew?

The woman's grip on her net bag full of groceries tightened, as if she were holding on to the edge of a boat in rocky water.

"We think he knew something about a baby abandoned in France during the war," Jenny said.

"Why would you think such a thing?" she said.

Charlie explained in detail the research he and Jenny had done at the library back in France. He told her about the people they'd spoken to in the village, the stories about this baby boy. As he talked, Jenny watched the woman's face. The scared eyes. The set jaw. The tight grip on that bag.

When Charlie finished, the room was silent. Somewhere a clock was ticking. But otherwise, no sound.

To Jenny's surprise, Nick took a few steps toward the woman and spoke into the silence, his voice soft but firm.

"Listen," he said, "the truth is, I'm responsible for that baby being left like that. Imagine it, Signora. The Germans are advancing and I'm nineteen years old and as scared as a person can be. Listen," he continued, "I didn't want to die. I wanted to go home and marry my sweetheart. My Lillian." His breath caught, and he took a few sharp inhalations before going on. "And we'd been in this hole, a hole in the ground on a farm, for weeks. We all stank of sweat and piss and dirt and fear. But the woman who lived in that farmhouse came and talked to us. She was the most beautiful creature I'd ever seen. But tough. Hard, you know? And pregnant. She wanted to go to Paris and become a painter, she told me that. But she couldn't get canvases because of the war, so she cut the ones she had into these small ones, no bigger that this"—here he held up his hands to make a square—"and she painted what she saw. The cows and the fields and the haystacks and the flowers. Vivid. Colorful. Real. But there was always a vague blue figure or shadow in them, looking at the landscape, the farm, like a ghost. Like something that didn't belong there."

The old woman was listening carefully as Nick spoke, whether from interest or an attempt to understand him, Jenny couldn't tell. But she dropped her bag to the floor and sat, stiff and erect, in the faded maroon chair. She took the round, shiny celery-green pillow from it and placed it in her lap. Nick waited until she had arranged herself, and then he went on.

"When the Germans came close, she ran to the trench and she gave me the paintings wrapped in linen. But she gave me something else," he said, his voice cracking.

Jenny saw him swallow hard, and she considered asking for some water for him, but thought better of it. He needed to finish, she calculated. If she interrupted him, he might not continue. The spell would be broken. That was what it was like in this stuffy, warm room with just the whisper of a ticking clock and Nick's voice. It was like a spell had been cast here.

"She handed me her baby," Nick said, and his voice had something like awe in it, as if even after all this time he could not believe this had happened. "He was wrapped in a soft white blanket. Asleep. So tiny. And the sky was lit with artillery shells and the sounds of fighting and Stan Danes, who had been down there with me all these weeks, pissed his pants and the smell of it mixed with the gunpowder and the fear and she said, 'He is Laurent,' and she said, 'Save them.' And then she was gone."

The woman's face remained unchanged. Scared eyes. Set jaw.

"I turned to the guys, to ask them what the hell I should do, but Stan

Burns was twisted into a fetal position, sobbing, and the fighting was getting closer, and Tommy Pratt had his gun ready and he jumped out and in that one second he was dead, shot right in the face, and so I crawled out of there—crawled in the dirt and the animal shit, clutching the bundles and I tried to think of what to do."

Nick went over to where the widow sat so straight with the pillow on her lap, and he bent close to her and he said, "Do you know how impossible it is to think straight when you are about to die?" At that, a harsh laugh escaped his throat. "Like now," he said, "because, Signora, I'm about to die anytime now, and all I want to know is if that baby survived. Because I left him in that blanket by a well in a village square, and anything could have happened to him. Anything."

He straightened and closed his eyes briefly, as if to keep out the images of what might have befallen Laurent.

"Mister," Aria said, "why would my grandfather have anything to do with this baby?"

Charlie spoke then, once more explaining what they had found out. "If anyone found that baby," he said, looking not at Aria but at Pietro's widow, "it was your husband and the men in his troop."

The widow stood and placed the pillow back on the chair. Her eyes had changed to two hard stones.

"*Esci*," she said. "Get out."

She raised her arm and pointed toward the door. "Now," she said.

"Please," Charlie said, "please. If you know anything at all—"

Her stoic face rearranged itself into one of rage, twisted and red. Her finger, still pointing, shook, and she screamed as loud as Jenny had ever heard anyone scream: "*Esci! Esci! Esci!*"

Charlie grabbed Jenny's arm and urged her out of the room, but she shook him off. Nick was still standing there, taking the woman's wrath, his face wet with tears.

"Come on, Nick," Charlie called. And when Nick still did not move, Charlie went to him and tugged at him, murmuring "Come on, come on," even as the woman continued to scream, "*Esci!*"

Finally, the three of them were outside the apartment, moving through the hot hallway, and then out the door and into the blazing sunlight.

The two boys were still there, and when they saw the Americans emerge, they hustled over.

"You need to find your way?" the leader asked Charlie.

Nick, dazed from the heat and the scene they'd left behind, leaned against the building, with its posters covered in graffiti.

"Nick?" Jenny said. "What do you need? Tell me what you need."

His gaze moved slowly toward her. He seemed to be gone somehow, his eyes distant and foggy.

"She knows," he said.

"Pietro's widow?" Jenny asked him. "You think she knows what happened?"

Nick slowly slid his body down the length of the building until he was sitting.

"Nick, no," Jenny said. "The ground is so dirty."

But he just looked up at her as if he had never seen her before.

"She knows that those soldiers found a baby who had died because he was abandoned. She looked at me like what I am. A murderer. That baby died because of what I did," Nick said.

Was that right? Had her fear, and then her rage, come from reconciling a story her husband had told her with the actual man who was responsible for that baby dying? Had she been horrified that such a person had come into her home?

"I'm ready now," Nick said.

His cheeks and eyes were sunken, and his body seemed smaller, more fragile.

"I'm ready to go home."

CHAPTER THIRTY

Naples

Jenny, 1974

The Neapolitans had named this heat wave Lucifer. A perfect name, Jenny thought as she stood on the small balcony of her hotel room and watched the heavy, humid air over the bay. It was midafternoon and it felt like hell—hot, miserable, relentless. Their travel had slowed down due to Nick's waning energy, and the blasted heat. Today was August 18, one week from when she had foolishly promised to meet Daniel at the information kiosk on Capri. She could see it out there, Capri, cloaked in heat and smog, just twenty miles away from her. Her house to IHOP was almost as far. But both of those things seemed like they were from a distant lifetime ago. Capri was real, right there, with its lemon trees and impossibly blue water. "On Capri," her guidebook said, "you will experience some sublime moments."

Jenny sighed and walked back into her room, the cold blast of air-conditioning sending shivers up her arms. A floor below her, Nick was packing his suitcase, preparing to go home. He'd booked the two of them on the earliest flight to Boston tomorrow morning, and had growled at her to leave him alone. He didn't want to join them for dinner at Trattoria da Nennella, even though it was one of the few restaurants that still made traditional *pasta e patate con la provola*, and even though the waiters served fruit at the end of the meal in a replica toilet bowl. He didn't want to meet them after dinner for limoncello in the hotel bar. He just wanted to not talk to anyone, to sleep and then to wake early and take a taxi to the airport. "I'll see you in the lobby at five-thirty," Nick had told her. "Sharp."

She flopped onto the bed, with its fluffy white duvet and mountain of pillows, and closed her eyes. She needed a plan. Of course she could simply not show up in the lobby at five-thirty sharp tomorrow morning and let Nick make his own way to the airport and onto the plane and then home. But the image of him, feeble and shaking, navigating all of that alone made her immediately discard that idea. She could try to convince him to stay a little longer, if a week constituted a little longer. It seemed to stretch before her endlessly. How would it seem to Nick? A week at the end of a life? And what was her reason for asking him to stay? *I might be meeting a guy I haven't seen in a year on Capri.* That wouldn't convince him of anything. Why should he pay for a hotel and meals for another week on the off chance that a guy she hardly knew might be standing at the information kiosk on Capri?

A third option came to her: Go to Capri this afternoon. Go to Pablo Neruda's house and hope that Daniel would be there. The idea made her sit up, smiling. Until she played it out fully in her mind: She would have to catch the ferry. That would be fairly easy. Then she would arrive on Capri and ask for directions to Neruda's house. Also easy. She would walk there or take a taxi, and then walk inside and . . . Here her plan faltered. And what? Ask for Daniel? And what if no one even knew who he was? Or, worse, what if he was there and had forgotten all about her? But no, Jenny decided, that was impossible. He had sent her that postcard. It was possible, though, that he'd changed his mind about seeing her again, or seeing her here. Maybe he had a girlfriend now. Maybe he'd fallen in love. Not everyone liked surprises. Especially one that involved a girl you didn't know very well showing up unannounced.

Jenny turned and looked out the window. The smog had lifted some-what and Capri appeared brighter, closer. Once again she considered Plan C. She could take the ferry to Capri and a taxi to Neruda's only to discover that it was closed to visitors. Or only open certain days or hours. Then there would be no one to ask about Daniel, and she would do what? Sit there and wait for the place to open? Which could be days or even, she reminded herself, never. *Let's Go: Italy* didn't even mention the house. She couldn't very well wander the island of Capri, hoping to catch sight of him or asking strangers if they knew where she could find an American boy who loved the poetry of Pablo Neruda.

She needed to think. She would go into the city and look at some of the sights she had carefully marked in her guidebook.

She quickly rejected the National Archaeological Museum, despite its relics from Pompeii, because she didn't have the focus a museum of that size took to navigate. The Cappella Sansevero was a possibility. It had one famous sculpture, *Veiled Christ*, and two strange anatomical machines built on real skeletons. The walk there would be long, which would give her time to think. And the reward would be both macabre and fascinating. Maybe she could even buy a postcard of those skeletons and send it to Vera.

Paging through the guidebook, she moved quickly past pictures of castles and cathedrals and catacombs—too big, too far, too creepy—and finally paused on the *presepi* shops on Via San Gregorio Armeno. She had marked this page because these Nativity figures could be good, cheap souvenirs to bring home, as well as "an experience in local life and culture," according to the guidebook. The figures were made by artisans who had learned their craft from their fathers and grandfathers. Besides the usual religious characters, there were typical Neapolitans—sausage makers and pizza chefs and vintners—and famous people. "Don't be surprised if you find Frank Sinatra or Pope Paul standing next to Mary and Joseph with a cobbler and a pizza guy behind them," the book warned. Jenny smiled. The *presepi* shops sounded like the perfect distraction, and they were far enough away that she'd have a good long walk with lots of time to think.

She picked up the small pad with the hotel name and address on it and tore a piece of paper from it to mark the place in the book. As she stuck the page inside, she saw that she'd highlighted something at the bottom of that page: "Don't Miss If You Like the Odd, the Unusual, or the Weird:

The Museum of Tears is a quirky, offbeat museum tucked into the back of a *presepi* shop. Vials—most of them empty now—that allegedly once held the tears of a person crying are arranged chronologically on old wooden shelves with labels like 'The tears of a little girl who has dropped her gelato, 1956' and 'The tears of an American soldier, 1944.' Tears from actress Sophia Loren and soprano Luisa Tetrazzini are also displayed. Added Bonus: This shop makes some of the most beautiful *presepi* in Naples."

Perfect, Jenny decided. She dragged a comb through her hair, put on her French straw hat and the oversized sunglasses she'd bought from a street vendor, and headed out. She would figure out how to stay in Naples, and she would buy terra-cotta figurines for her mother and Annette. And she would even see Sophia Loren's tears.

All this because Pietro's widow had thrown them out.

Jenny had misjudged how far it was from her hotel on the bay to the shop on Via San Gregorio Armeno, so by the time she turned onto the street, she was covered in sweat and city dirt. *Lucifer, indeed*, she thought. The walk hadn't even helped her make a plan—the streets of Naples felt too threatening, with groups of teenagers huddled on corners, garbage everywhere, and a general atmosphere of danger. More than once she opted to avoid checking her map, afraid that as a tourist she would be obvious prey. Instead, she made missteps and wrong turns, and finally arrived more than an hour later, wanting nothing more than her air-conditioned room and a shower.

But here she was. And the sight of the street lined with *presepe* shops almost made the whole ordeal worthwhile after all.

Nativity figurines seemed to spill from every storefront, filling wooden bins and shelves. Just as the guidebook had promised, fruit vendors and pizza makers and butchers joined Mary, Joseph, and the three Wise Men. There was Richard Nixon, Mickey Mantle, Pope Paul, Dean Martin, as well as cork and wells and electric-powered waterfalls, bridges and towers and houses. The windows of the shops had enormous displays, with things that moved and lit up and spun. Jenny stood staring at them, imagining what she would bring back for everyone. Her mother would like the traditional ones, but wouldn't figurines of the Rat Pack make her smile? Annette would love Mick Jagger; Jenny could picture her throwing her head back and hooting with delight at the terra-cotta Mick with his shirt open to the navel and his lips cartoonishly large. For Vera she would have to find actors. Maybe Italian ones, though Jenny didn't really know who they might be. There were so many figures she didn't recognize, dressed in sparkling gowns or military uniforms or dark suits.

Wait. Why was she trying to impress Vera? Why was she even bringing souvenirs home for her, someone who, in truth, she didn't even really know very well? Not well enough to tell her why she'd so suddenly left school or ask her for help. Not well enough that Vera even bothered to stay in touch. Jenny thought of the two of them in their dorm room, she trying so hard to be cool, to be someone like Vera. "Vera does not like this music," Vera would say when they walked into a party. She'd survey the room with disdain and announce, "This is not for Vera." Instead of staying anyway, Jenny followed Vera out, to the small, dark bar at Bonnet Shores that had a jukebox full of music from the forties. They sat at the bar there, smoking those horrible clove cigarettes Vera preferred, and drinking ridiculous cocktails that Vera ordered for them. Lillet with a slice of orange. A kir royale.

Why hadn't Jenny stayed at the party with the keg and the blue-jeaned people like her? Why had she seen some better, more interesting self in someone like Vera? And who refers to themselves in the third person? How pretentious! How ridiculous! Jenny found herself actually laughing at her memories of Vera. She felt suddenly light, as if she were shedding an old skin. And with that feeling came such clarity that Jenny, hot and sweaty and dirty, standing on a street hundreds of years old, surrounded by Nativity scenes, knew that she was not returning home. Not with Nick tomorrow morning. Not at all.

"Jenny," she whispered, "is staying."

———

The shop she was looking for was halfway down the street, as old as all the others and just as crowded with bins and shelves of figurines. But the display in the window—a large cork-and-straw manger with the requisite holy figures, animals, and baby Jesus, as well as a shimmering lake, tall palm trees, and Neapolitan and pop culture characters—showed more artistic talent than many of the others. The colors were more realistic, more sophisticated, and the faces were more expressive. Standing behind Mary was the figure of a man in a black suit and bowler hat, his face both beautiful and tragically sad. Jenny tried to place him. Was he that French mime? Or an actor from old silent movies? She didn't know. Above the door, a cracked terra-cotta sign read, THE MUSEUM OF TEARS.

Inside, the shop was hot and stuffy, despite two fans strategically placed to blast air on incoming customers. The air was warm and stale, however, so Jenny stepped deeper into the dark shop. An old man sat at a workbench, carefully mixing colors, a line of terra-cotta figures placed in front of him. Other than him, she was the only person in the store, which wasn't surprising. Though this street would be jammed with thousands of people before Christmas, on a hot August day it was mostly empty, except for a few tourists like her.

Even though a bell had tinkled when she'd walked in, the old man paid her no mind, so she browsed the shelves with the smaller figurines on them, carefully choosing traditional ones for her mother, then adding a pizza maker and a sausage maker. She paused with John Lennon and Yoko Ono both in her palm. How would she get these to her mother and Annette if she wasn't going home? Just as carefully as she'd chosen them, she put each figure back. She would return before Christmas and buy them and mail them home as gifts, she decided.

As soon as she decided that, something settled deep inside her. She remembered that night with Daniel, how he had asked what her purpose in life was, and she hadn't known. Except to escape, she could not see a future for herself then. But standing here in this crowded shop in this hot, noisy city, she knew that she wanted to stay. Stay and do what, she could not yet say. But these weeks of travel and intense living had shown her that her world needed to be bigger, different, even mysterious. She had to stop herself from taking out her notebook and making a To Do list. *Learn Italian*, she would write. *Find a job. Make a life.*

Jenny glanced around the shop, her eyes now more accustomed to the dark. She didn't see the Museum of Tears that the guidebook had described as tucked away in a corner. But something else did catch her eye again. The figure of the man in the black suit and bowler hat with the beautiful, sad face. She picked it up. She would buy it, she thought, looking into its eyes. How did the artist put so much expression in such a small thing? The artist who, she supposed, was the old man at the workbench.

"Buongiorno," Jenny said as she approached him.

"Buonasera," he said curtly, without looking up.

Right. It was afternoon, not morning. "Sorry," Jenny said. "Do you by any chance speak—"

"English. Yes."

"Can you tell me who this man is?" Jenny asked, feeling properly scolded.

The old man paused finally and looked at the figurine she was holding out to him.

"He is nobody," he said. "Just a silly romantic man."

"Oh." Jenny stared down at the face on the figurine. "He doesn't look silly," she said. "He looks sad."

"Well, romantics get their hearts broken, don't they?"

"I suppose," Jenny said.

The old man went back to mixing his paint.

"I'll take him," Jenny said.

The man sighed and put his brushes down. He had mixed blues with different shades of white to produce a color that made Jenny think of the summer sky. Or, she considered, the Virgin Mary's robe.

She watched as the old man got up and made his way over to the ancient-looking cash register, an enormous thing with an ornate gold design and a heavy lever on one side. He slowly wrote out a bill on a piece of paper.

All this for what amounted to about fifty cents, Jenny thought as she converted the amount of lire he'd written down on the paper that he now was thrusting into her face. She retrieved the coins and waited as he carefully wrapped the figure in brown butcher's paper.

When he finally handed it to her, she thanked him with a rushed *grazie*, afraid of being mocked again.

"*Prego*," he said wearily, and began to make his way back to his workbench.

"*Signore?*" Jenny called after him.

She pulled the guidebook out of her purse and followed the man.

"I was looking for this," she said after he was seated again. She showed him the page she'd marked, pointing to the yellow highlighted paragraph at the bottom. "The Museum of Tears?"

"Ha!" he said, knocking the book away. "There's the Museum of Tears."

She followed where his chin had jutted and saw nothing at all like what the book had described. But the man was now mixing a new color, squeezing a maize shade and then a lemon yellow onto his palette. Jenny made her way over to the alcove in the corner. A dusty sign above the entrance read, FOR THE WORLD'S MORE FULL OF WEEPING THAN YOU CAN UNDERSTAND. Yeats, Jenny thought. "The Stolen Child." She'd read it in her Modern Poetry class, and she'd torn it out of the textbook she'd bought at the Co-op, where students bought and sold used books. She had tucked that scrap with the poem on it into her suitcase when she'd gone off alone to the Home for Wandering Girls. She'd left it there, in her top dresser drawer, for the next girl to find.

Jenny reached up and wiped the dust from the sign. Then she stepped into the alcove.

To her disappointment, there was nothing there but empty glass vials in crates on top of dusty shelves. Pushed into the corner of one shelf was a black fabric box, the kind someone might keep important papers in, and inside the box were dozens of index cards with dates and a few sentences written on them in an ornate penmanship. Jenny shuffled through them, noting that some were from as far back as the 1930s and others stretched all the way up to last year. Out of habit, she put the cards in chronological order, the first one from 1935 and the last one from June 11, 1973. Although most of the cards were written in Italian, the more recent ones were written in Italian and English. LE LACRIME DI CHI ASPETTA. And below it: THE TEARS OF ONE WHO WAITS.

Lacrime. That word appeared on every card. Jenny looked around at the empty, neglected room. She was standing, she realized, in what had been the Museum of Tears.

CHAPTER THIRTY-ONE

The Museum of Tears

Geraldine, 1973

For one thing, it was more than a cat that sent Geraldine back to Dublin. It was a husband. Hugh. Hugh, who was as unlike peculiar little Enzo—which was how Enzo's brother had described him—as anyone could be. Hugh played rugby, spent late nights at the pub around the corner, smoked harsh cigarettes he rolled himself. "You are a cliché," Geraldine told him, often. In response he would grab her ass and pinch. "Oh, Gerald," he'd say, "you love me so much, don't you?" To which she would answer, "Not really."

But she did love him. Or had. Until she got the job for the *Irish Times* writing about far-flung places. She'd fought hard for that job, desperate to get off the ladies' pages, with its recipes and stories of Americans returning to the homeland. She sent the editor, tough Joe Sullivan, three story ideas every day. Nothing too hard, like covering the Troubles or investigating crimes, but nothing too soft, either. Every day, he ignored her and her ideas. Sometimes she'd wait by his office door and buttonhole him when he walked out.

"Did you see my idea about interviewing Francis Bacon? I could go to London and—"

"Crab toes," Sullivan growled.

"Excuse me?"

"People love crab toes. With lots of butter, right? And garlic?"

"I guess," Geraldine said, knowing where this was going.

"Some guy in Kerry somewhere cooks them in saltwater."

"Okay."

"Find him. Get the recipe, requisite story, et cetera. I'll run it next Tuesday."

He grinned, showing most of his tobacco-stained teeth, and walked away.

Geraldine took a deep breath. Crab toes. Fine. She put on her yellow raincoat and hat and made her way through the drizzle to Heuston Station and Kerry.

Even though Sullivan wouldn't reimburse her train fare, he liked her article. And her moxie. He told her so himself as he passed her desk, which Geraldine knew one didn't pass by accident; her desk was in a far corner, away from all the real reporters. She looked up when Sullivan passed, muttering the compliments. But before she could respond, he was already a blur of gray wool in the distance.

She complained to Hugh often—over dinner, over pints, after sex. "Keep at it," he'd tell her. "Tenacity, Gerald," he'd say.

Meanwhile, she loved Hugh and their little garden flat with the bright blue front door and brick patio out back. She loved kissing the length of his long, lean body and the way he whispered, "Come here, Gerald," and pulled her toward him. She loved their cat, Maudie, a gray-and-apricot tortie with an extra toe on each paw. She loved her friends, all of them flatmates back at university and now living mostly in the same neighborhood with their husbands or boyfriends. They went for boozy lunches on Grafton Street and helped each other pick out dresses and shoes. They had dinner parties that always ended with someone crying in the bathroom and a couple fighting in the kitchen and someone passed out on the sofa.

She loved telling people that she was a reporter, even if all she wrote about were recipes and old knitting patterns and sappy stories.

"I could go to the Aran Islands," she told Sullivan one evening when she saw him, by accident, on the street, waiting to cross just like her. She actually tugged at his sleeve. "They say each family had a pattern so they could identify their loved ones who died at sea. They say—"

"People like those sweaters, that's for sure," Sullivan said. "Go to that shop down on Drury Street and ask Mrs. O'Toole to share their most popular Aran sweater pattern, maybe with a little background? I'll run it on Tuesday."

The light changed and he was gone.

But a few weeks later, Sullivan showed up at her desk again. She'd written about the Aran sweater pattern and had woven in an adjacent story about how Mrs. O'Toole had grown up on Inishmaan and had known the playwright J. M. Synge, who'd lived there when she was a girl. "He told my mother it was Yeats who sent him. 'Go to the Aran Islands, and express a life that has never found expression,' Yeats told him. And he did, didn't he?" Dutifully, Geraldine included a pattern for a Cassidy sweater, not because it was the most popular but because it looked impossible to knit, with its four different cable stitches.

"What are you doing this weekend?" Sullivan barked at Geraldine.

She didn't know what to say. Was he asking her to work overtime? Or, God help her, to meet up with him?

"Well?" he said.

This weekend she and Hugh were going with everyone to the pub on Friday night as usual, she had a girls' lunch and shopping on Saturday and a dinner party that night at Barry and Kate's, and then there would be a hangover to nurse for most of Sunday.

"Not much," Geraldine said.

"Good." He reached into his pocket and handed her an envelope. "You know Desmond Shea?" He didn't wait for her to answer. "He's in hospital and I need someone to cover his story."

Geraldine did not know Desmond Shea, but she knew he was the paper's travel writer.

Sullivan cocked his chin toward her. "Flight's Friday morning. Don't miss it."

When he walked away, she opened the envelope and found a round-trip ticket to Copenhagen and an assignment sheet. Nyhavn was being transformed from a working port with the city's red-light district into a "museum harbor" with cafés and restored houses. Desmond Shea—or, rather, Geraldine—was to stay at three different nearby hotels, eat at eleven restaurants, go to six cafés and as many bars as possible, and write about the transformation.

Poor Desmond Shea died in the hospital over the weekend, and when Geraldine returned to work, full and exhausted, on Monday morning, she was the new travel writer.

"Even though you're a sexy girl," Hugh said to her that night over too much champagne.

"Even though I'm a woman," she corrected him.

Two days later, she was on a flight to New York City to go to a rock concert in a town more than a hundred miles away. The roads were clogged and she couldn't get even close to the concert, so she turned her rental car around and went back to the city, where she wrote an article about not going to Woodstock and missing the biggest cultural event of the 1960s. She had scribbled down restaurant suggestions from friends who had been to New York, so she flipped through her notebook and randomly chose a place called Fanelli's, on Prince Street. The guy sitting next to her at the bar worked on *The David Frost Show*, and when he saw how impressed she was by that—*You work on an American television show? Really?*—gave her tickets to the show, where Nina Simone sang and a comedian named Rodney Dangerfield made jokes about his wife.

One of the guests was a mind reader named Johnny Tremain. He stood in front of the audience and said things like "I have someone here going to Disneyland," and "Is there a Paul here?"

When someone answered, he moved into the audience and talked right to the person.

"Yes, Paul, you are going to get that job. Take it! Why are you hesitating?"

Paul blushed, and the two men shook hands. As Johnny turned to leave, his gaze settled on Geraldine, in the next row.

"Your life is about to change," he said to her.

She looked at the lights and the camera, at David Frost on the stage. She was in America, on a television show.

"It already has," she said.

He kept looking at her until she finally looked away.

"You have no idea," he said.

Between that night and the rainy afternoon she walked into the Museum of Tears, she traveled to every continent except Antarctica. After each trip she returned home to her little garden apartment and Hugh and Maudie and resumed what she thought of, at first, as her real life, and then later as her other life, and then, by the time she went to Naples, her old life.

Even if she hadn't met Enzo that day, eventually Geraldine would have left Hugh. She knew that. He seemed to be shrinking in front of her eyes, becoming a shadow or a ghost. He still talked and laughed and pinched her ass. He still called her Gerald and pulled her onto him at night. She could feel him and smell him and taste him, but he was vanishing.

Sometimes Geraldine thought her ideas for travel pieces were more and more designed to keep her away from home. Like the one that led her to Enzo: unusual museums in Italy. "Three weeks?" Hugh said. "How will I survive it?" He was, Geraldine knew, only half-joking. Lately he had been watching her as if he might catch her at something—carefully, intensely, constantly.

The museums, as it turned out, were marvelous. Saint Catherine's head dressed in her wimple staring out at Geraldine. Saint Anthony's vocal chords blooming like calla lilies. The wax anatomical figures in Florence and the skull of Pliny the Elder in Rome. She ate and drank her way around the country in her rented yellow Fiat 500. The men there, so easy to find, so willing to share cigarettes and rides on their Vespas. Over grappa or Punt e Mes, they flirted, teased, gesticulated. How she loved it, all of it. Geraldine imagined staying here, driving her own Vespa along cobblestone streets, eating and drinking long into the night.

The sun was low, the air warm and damp. She was in Rome, and the idea of returning to Dublin, to the gray skies and Hugh and the predictability of her days made her shiver. She had to find a way to stay. Or to go home and settle things and then return to a new life here. The next morning she got in the little yellow car and headed south to Naples, and the Museum of Tears.

She had not been prepared for the torrential rain that fell on Naples so relentlessly, day after day. After she returned the car to the rental agency (she would be flying back to Dublin from here and parking and car theft were both problems in Naples), she spent her first night in her shabby hotel room by the train station hoping to wait out the rain. But when it showed no sign of letting up the next day, she pulled on her rain boots and raincoat, grabbed her umbrella, and headed out. Rain could not deter an Irish girl, she thought as she hurried through the downpour.

The museum was difficult to find, hidden in a small shop on a street of shops that made and sold Nativity sets. If it hadn't been raining so hard, Geraldine would have paused to look at some of the scenes in the windows, enormous things with moss and cork and waterfalls. She walked past the right shop three times—none of the numbers lined up in any order that she could determine, and she had trouble locating the sign that was supposed to hang over the front door—before bursting inside. The wind took hold of the door and tore it from her hands, slamming it shut just as she stepped inside.

Two men stared up at her. One was handsome, brooding, sitting at a table of terra-cotta figures. The other was somewhat taller, with a gentle face and large, pale green eyes. Geraldine let her gaze linger ever so briefly on the more handsome one, imagining him offering her a cigarette, a Campari

"My goodness! The weather!" she said, looking away from him.

The other man spoke. "Typically," he said, "we get rain in January. But just a drizzle, not this."

He was holding a cracked white mug. The air smelled of turpentine and licorice.

"There," she said when she finally closed up her umbrella and shed her dripping coat and hat.

"Enzo! Take her coat!" the handsome man said sharply.

"It's fine. I'll just hang it here?" she said, slipping the coat off and hanging it on a hook beside another wet coat.

The three of them stood awkwardly for a moment as Geraldine glanced around the shop. She did not see a museum, or anything like a museum. Despite the sign, perhaps this was the wrong place after all.

"Offer her a coffee," the handsome one said.

The taller man stepped forward and held his own cup out to her.

"*Idiota*," the handsome one muttered.

"Oh, no thank you," Geraldine said. "I detest coffee. But if you have some tea, I'd happily have a cuppa."

"Forgive me," he said, his head cocked. "We do not have tea."

Geraldine smiled at him and said, "I am looking for the Museum of Tears."

"What? You can't be serious," the handsome one said.

She reached into her raincoat pocket and pulled out a small pad, the kind stenographers use, flipping the pages until she found what she was looking for.

"Here it is!" she said and held the pad out to the man who still stood before her with his mug of coffee. He took it and looked at the page she'd opened it to, which had the address of the shop and the words *The Museum of Tears* written below it.

"You see, I'm a travel writer," Geraldine explained, still loving how those words sounded, how important they seemed. "For the *Irish Times*. And I'm writing an article about unusual museums in Italy. Mostly it's saints' heads and other body parts. Though the one with all the taxidermied animals in Florence was quite wonderful. Anyway, my friend was here a couple of years ago, and she told me I absolutely could not miss the Museum of Tears in Naples. 'Just wait,' Aoife says—Aoife's the friend— 'there are actual *tears* in these vials, and the most peculiar little man runs around explaining whose tears they are.'"

She looked around the studio again. "But this looks more like a shop than a museum," she said.

The man standing in front of her straightened and announced, "I am Enzo Piccolo, the proprietor of the Museum of Tears."

Behind him, the other man laughed. "The peculiar little man who runs the thing," he said.

"Where are my manners? Geraldine Walsh," she said and thrust her hand out.

Enzo Piccolo looked startled. But then he took her hand in his free hand—the one not holding the coffee—and kissed it, quite gently.

"*Idiota*," the other muttered again.

But something happened to Geraldine when he kissed her hand. It felt as if he put a tiny arrow into her vein and sent it shooting straight to her heart. She thought of Cupid. She stood very still, trying to collect herself. Her hand and her wrist and her arm burned slightly, and her heart was growing warm too.

"Well, my goodness!" she said. "I was warned that Italian men might freely pinch my bottom, but not that they would be so gallant."

She thought she could stand there like this for a very long time, her hand in this man's—Enzo's—and her whole body burning. But she gave his hand a little squeeze, then removed hers from it and said, "The museum?"

"This way," Enzo said, sweeping his arm grandly to point the way.

Geraldine fell in love. That was the only way to explain the white heat that Enzo sent into her hand that day and that never left. Everything he said seemed marvelous to her. He had an almost childlike way, laughing at the sounds her stomach made and tracing her face and staring at her as if he wanted to swallow her up. Do it, she thought. Swallow me up.

What Geraldine also knew was that if she told Enzo about Hugh, he would be crushed. She couldn't hurt him, not in such a grand way. Not at all. She wanted nothing more than to hold his hand and walk with him, to kiss him and watch him watching her. She imagined a life with him, though these fantasies always took different shapes. They would live here in Naples and she would give him babies, six or eight, an endless parade of round, fat babies. Or he would come to Ireland, and they would live by the sea there, somewhere remote, like Donegal or Cape Clear, with no electricity and no people around them, and they would make love on beaches and in fields. A dozen lifetimes unfolded in her mind as she kept changing her plane ticket to Dublin, moving it back a day, then another, then another.

Until finally she knew she had to leave. She had to go home and tell Hugh she didn't love him anymore. She would say that to soften the blow, but what Geraldine realized was that she had never loved Hugh, or any-one, until she met Enzo.

"*Ti amo!*" Enzo shouted to her as she made her slow, sad way to the gate at the airport. "*Ti amo, Geraldine Walsh!*"

"I love you!" she said, that white heat burning her up. But she said it so quietly that she knew he could not hear her.

Geraldine felt like a character in an old-fashioned novel, falling even more desperately in love through the letters from Enzo that flew to her across the hundreds of miles. The thin blue envelopes crackled in her hand when she pulled them from the mailbox, and she would hold the letter close to her chest as she rushed inside to read it. Enzo wrote like a poet. His letters were full of metaphors comparing her to the sun or daffodils or the sea. Always he ended with *please: Please, please, my darling, my love, my heart, return to me.*

So why couldn't she? What kept Geraldine firmly in the same place as ever? She tended her little garden and knit sweaters for her friends' babies and put the kettle on for tea. She went to work and pitched ideas for articles on going to see the midnight sun and watching the America's Cup race, even though the paper had cut back and most of her assignments were closer to home. Was God, Geraldine wondered, keeping her home to save her marriage? Especially when Sullivan gave her three assignments: the opening of the Kingston Bridge in Glasgow, a walking tour in the Cotswolds, and the pubs of Dublin. "The pubs of *Dublin?* Seriously? I'm a travel writer, remember?" she reminded Sullivan. He coughed the phlegmy cough he'd recently developed and said, "Cutbacks. Remember?"

She went to Glasgow and the Cotswolds and the pubs of Dublin and she made love to her husband and had lunch with her friends and got drunk at dinner parties, all while the words *Go! Go!* whispered in her ear. "I'm coming back in a month," she wrote Enzo. Then: "I will be there in the fall." And: "Soon." But she did nothing to actually leave.

Until a week passed with no letter from Enzo. Then another. She reread his last letter for some clue or indication that he had finally grown weary of waiting for her. But it was like all the others, filled with declarations of love and descriptions of his lonely heart. He ended with his plea for her to return to him. But over a year had passed. Why shouldn't he give up on her? she thought. Perhaps he had finally seen through her empty promises. Perhaps he had met someone else, someone there.

She called in sick to work and booked a one-way flight to Naples for that very afternoon. How could she have stayed away so long? Geraldine berated herself as she threw clothes into her suitcase. What had paralyzed her like this? Fear of change? Fear of love? Whatever it was, she would change it right now. She kept thinking of his face when she walked into the shop. *Finally*, he would say. And he would take her into his arms and all of the waiting would vanish.

Geraldine scribbled a note to Hugh: *I'm sorry, Hughie. I just can't anymore.*

She stared down at it amid the newspapers and candy wrappers and empty packs of cigarettes in the rubbish can and felt as if she had shed some part of herself. With each step forward—into the airport, at the ticket counter, down the terminal to her gate—she seemed to shed yet another layer.

By the time Geraldine took her seat by the window on the plane, she felt lighter, as if she could float all the way to Naples on her own. She looked out the window as the plane lifted off, and watched Ireland grow smaller and smaller, until it was gone and below her was England, and then France, and then Italy. She imagined the cities whooshing by. Milan. Genoa. Rome. And then the plane was descending and Naples appeared, sprawling and sparkling and stretching before her as if it had been waiting for her to return too.

CHAPTER THIRTY-TWO

Naples

Nick, 1974

Nick looked at Jenny's face, twisted with some emotion he couldn't quite land on. Worry, maybe? Guilt? He knew what she wanted to tell him, and he knew he should try to make it easier for her. But he couldn't. She had knocked on his door, and when he opened it, she stood there with her eyes intense and she held out a small bouquet of periwinkle-colored flowers. He recognized them: hydrangeas. Lillian used to grow them, but hers were pink.

"Did you know that hydrangeas represent gratitude?" she said after he took them and walked back into the room.

Jenny followed, closing the door behind her. But she didn't come inside, just lingered by the door. For a fast getaway, Nick thought.

"I didn't," he said.

Ridiculous to bring someone in a hotel room flowers, wasn't it? He didn't exactly have vases laying around. Nick tossed them on the bed, then waited.

"Let me put them in water," Jenny said, more to herself than to him. She picked up the silver water pitcher, went into the bathroom to fill it, and placed the flowers inside.

"There," she said as she put them by his bed, pleased with herself.

"There," Nick said.

He realized his arms were folded tightly across his chest. He considered dropping them to look less defensive, but decided against it. He *was* defensive. *Just say it*, he thought.

"I had an interesting afternoon," Jenny said, still sounding like she was thinking out loud rather than talking to him. "I walked over to the street where artisans make these incredible Nativity sets. Hand-painted figures. Mangers made out of straw. But also pizza makers and vintners and vegetable sellers. They even have these over-the-top figures of the pope and the Beatles and, well, anyone you can think of."

Nativity sets? Really?

"It was so far. I completely misjudged the distance. The hotel map isn't exactly to scale. And it's about a million degrees out."

"Lucifer," Nick said.

"Right."

"So you bought a Nativity? The wise men and the donkeys and the baby Jesus? All of it?"

Jenny shook her head. "I actually went to see this museum I read about in my guidebook. The Museum of Tears, it's called. Some eccentric guy has collected tears for decades, and he puts them in these vials and displays them with an explanation of where they came from."

Obviously tears would dry up over decades, Nick knew, but he didn't say anything.

"Except when I got there, the museum was in shambles. The cards with the descriptions had been tossed in a box, and the vials were in a heap."

"And where were the tears?" Nick said sarcastically.

Jenny looked at him, and he saw that she herself was crying. Her cheeks were wet and her eyes shiny.

"Gone, obviously," she said. "But the tears aren't really the point, are they? It's more the recording, the witnessing, of human sorrow. One card said: *Tears of a boy who dropped his ice cream cone, 1956*. Another one said: *Tears of a man who has been lost for a lifetime, 1949*."

She reached into her bag. "Here, I'll show you."

To his surprise, she pulled out a fat stack of cards.

"You took them?" Nick said. "From the museum?"

"The dreadful man who runs it, or at least runs the shop, was so awful that I was afraid he would just throw them out someday," she explained. "I rescued them. The vials too." She paused, then said softly, "All those tears."

"You stole them," Nick said, not adding the obvious question: Why?

"I asked the man where the proprietor of the museum was, and he laughed at me!"

"That gave you the right to steal these?"

"It made me think," Jenny said. "I took all the cards and vials and I put them in my bag and I walked out. My feet were killing me because I'd already walked so far, but I walked even more, until I found a place to sit down and think."

Sitting, Nick decided, was a very good idea. He plopped onto one of the wingback chairs by the window. Better.

"I laid those cards across the table and I read each one. And do you know what I realized, Nick?"

"I can't even begin to guess," he said, feeling disoriented. He thought she had shown up here to tell him she wasn't going home with him in the morning. Instead, she was yammering on about Wise Men and boys dropping ice cream cones.

"There is so much sorrow, Nick. So many tears spilled. I have my own heartbreak, you know? And you have *le petit chou*."

Nick started to protest, to say that the baby wasn't his heartbreak, what he had done was. And how that one stupid act had broken so many hearts over the years. But the words got tangled up in his throat and he couldn't untangle them.

Jenny took a big breath. "What I decided, Nick, is to take over the museum."

"The museum?" he asked, confused.

"The Museum of Tears," she said.

"The empty vials?"

Jenny nodded.

"What about the dreadful man?" he asked, even though he was think-ing, *What about me?*

"I haven't sorted that out yet," she said. "I've written down my options. One, I could go back and ask him if I could rent the space. The little alcove in the back of his shop, I mean. Two, I could go back and get the name of the original curator and track him down. Three, I can just find another spot and start over. To that end," she said, "I have these."

She reached back in her bag and pulled out just two cards. She handed him one.

A foolish girl who gave up her baby, 1971.

Nick frowned. "You mean 1917."

"No," Jenny said. "Not Camille. Me."

"You?"

He thought about how sad her eyes always used to look, and how he had never understood why someone so smart and organized and quick-witted worked at an International House of Pancakes.

"Yes," Jenny was saying, pushing the other card into his hand. "And now you."

He looked down at the blank card.

"I was going to write, 'The man who left *le petit chou* by the well, 1917.' But I don't think it's mine to write, do you?" she said.

She put a pen beside him, and picked up all of the other cards, and started to walk away.

"You're not coming home with me, are you?" Nick said, his heart breaking. Really. He felt his heart physically shattering.

Jenny turned. "No," she said, "I'm not."

She would take him to the airport, she told him. She would make sure he got safely on the plane. And, she added, she would call his nephew to pick him up at Logan. Jenny tried to convince him that he should join her and Charlie for dinner, but he refused, not only because he wanted to sulk alone in his room, but also—mostly—because he just wasn't hungry. As the day had worn on, Nick had felt more and more tired. Even walking across the room to let Jenny out was a great effort, and now he wanted to get into bed and stay there. He hoped that after a good night's sleep, he would be able to get up in the morning, pack, and make it to the airport. He hoped he would be able to endure the long flight home. All of it, he thought as he climbed into bed, seemed impossible. But thinking of home, that messy old house that needed a new roof and a plumber to fix the drippy sinks, made him almost happy. He wanted his own bed with the faded striped sheets he'd slept in for years and the decorative pillows he placed on the chair by the bed each night. Yes, he wanted home.

Nick had forgotten to close the shade. From bed, he could see the early evening sky, lit deep lavender and pink, and the dark hulk of Vesuvius in the distance. Lights twinkled at him, and for a moment Nick imagined staying after all. He imagined getting out of this bed and dressing for dinner, striding across the lobby and out the grand front doors into the warm summer air. He thought of a meal of grilled octopus and *baccalà* and cold, dry white wine. Thinking of it made him salivate, as if he could taste that wine, the salty fish, the smoky char. Beyond the table where he'd placed himself was the harbor filled with gleaming white boats. Nick closed his eyes, hearing the flapping of sails and the lap of the waves.

As a young man, he used to go sailing often. There had been so many summer days with Lillian and her brothers on Cape Cod back then. Remembering, he could feel the lines in his hands as he hoisted the sails and the gentle rocking of the boat. His toes clenched, as if keeping him balanced. Lillian would pack delicate sandwiches—watercress, cucumber, smoked salmon—and thermoses of lemonade, to which her brothers would add profuse amounts of gin or vodka. She'd lay out the picnic on the small table: the sandwiches and celery filled with cream cheese topped with raisins—what did they call that? ants on a log?—and the shortbread her mother was famous for baking. How they ate and drank on those excursions! Sometimes they went all the way to Martha's Vineyard, dropping anchor in Edgartown and going ashore for cold beers at that little

bar . . . The Fox and Hound? Or was that in Nantucket? They had a pot
of cheddar cheese with pimiento mixed in at the bar, and Ritz crackers.
Whatever the bar was called, it was surely long gone, Nick thought, suddenly missing it—the beers and the cheese and the Ritz crackers and the
sawdust on the old wooden floor.

Suddenly, Nick missed Lillian too, missed her with a pain bigger and
deeper than what he'd felt when she'd first died. And her brothers, he
missed them too, all of them dead. Funny Richard, with his bright red hair
and freckles. Malcolm, who'd lost one eye to a slingshot when he was a
boy and wore a patch, which earned him the nickname Bluebeard as a kid
and later Blue. After Blue married, his wife sewed him variously colored
and patterned eye patches to match his shirts. She was dead too. Agatha?
Agnes? Nick couldn't recall, though he did remember how she'd worn
her hair in an intricate braid that wrapped around itself several times and
ended in a bun on top of her head. The face of Lillian's youngest brother
floated into Nick's mind. Toby. Just a baby during the Great War, but old
enough to fight in France twenty-six years later. And to die there. Forev-
ermore when anyone spoke of him they called him Poor Toby.

Nick felt the gentle rocking of the sea, Lillian's hand warm on his arm
and her brothers laughing in the distance. He wouldn't have to get up in the
morning and make the arduous trip to the airport. Instead, he would stay on
this boat and eat a sandwich. A thin round of cucumber, a lot of butter, crusts
removed, and the bread cut into a circle with the rim of a whiskey glass.

From far away, Nick heard his name called. He didn't know if a few minutes or a few hours had passed, but he still felt the boat swaying.

"Nick!" he heard again.

A lot of noise and hubbub followed, but Nick didn't care. He just kept
his eyes closed and enjoyed the movement, which also felt like a cradle
rocking. In fact, he felt like a baby—carefree, soothed, light.

"Oh, God," a woman said, closer now. "Nick?"

Go away, he thought. *Let me be.*

CHAPTER THIRTY-THREE

Naples

Jenny, 1974

When Nick didn't answer his wake-up call from her in the morning, Jenny went to his room. As she walked down the hall, she tried to convince herself that he had just overslept. Or was in the shower. Surely he was fine. He was finally going home. Maybe he'd even gotten up early and was right now sitting on the roof, finishing his breakfast.

She knocked. And knocked again. But no answer.

Jenny pressed her face close to the door and called to him. Nothing.

Her heart was beating hard, and her hand, paused to knock again, trembled.

"Nick!"

She rushed to the elevator, which took an interminable amount of time to arrive, and went up to the rooftop breakfast area. As soon as she stepped into the sunshine and looked around at the few people eating this early, Jenny knew he wasn't there. Still, she made her way through the tables, just in case. A waitress smiled at her and asked if she wanted a cappuccino. Jenny didn't pause to answer her. She walked quickly back inside, pushed the button for the elevator, and waited forever for it again. This time she took it to the lobby, where Charlie sat waiting to help her take Nick to the airport.

As soon as he saw her face, he jumped up and ran over to her.

"What happened?" he asked.

"We need to get into his room," Jenny said, her voice shaking. "He's not answering his phone or the door—"

"Maybe he's having—"

"I looked. He's not there. We're wasting time," she said and rushed to the desk, cutting in front of a couple in the middle of checking out.

"We need help," Jenny said. "We need a doctor. Now. Please." She had started to cry, certain that Nick was in trouble. Or worse.

The startled clerk hesitated, then picked up the phone and spoke in rapid Italian. *Dottore*, Jenny heard. *Emergenza*.

"Room number?" the woman said, pressing the telephone receiver to her chest.

Jenny told her, and the woman repeated it in an urgent whisper, the phone once again at her mouth.

"The *dottore* is on his way," she said after she hung up. She wore carefully applied red matte lipstick and smoky kohl around her eyes. Like an Italian movie star, Jenny thought. The hotel uniform was navy blue with a red silk scarf, all of it suddenly seeming out of place.

"On his way?" Charlie said. He had joined Jenny at the desk at some point without her even realizing it. "Isn't he here at the hotel?"

The woman shook her head. "He is on call."

Time slowed down; the minutes waiting for the doctor seemed like hours. The woman went back to checking the couple out of their room. People arrived, handing their luggage over to the bellmen. Sitting on one of the couches in the lobby, Jenny focused on the revolving door, willing the doctor to come through it. It spun and spun, like a slowly moving globe, spitting people into and out of the hotel.

"They should break down the door," Charlie said, jumping to his feet. "Why didn't we think of that?"

Just then, a small man with a pencil mustache entered officiously. Carrying a very large black medical bag, he strutted across the lobby toward the desk. Jenny ran to meet up with him, introducing herself and telling him Nick's room number all in one breath. He didn't even pause, just tipped his hat—a funny black bowler with a feather in the band—to the woman at the desk and continued to the elevators, Jenny and Charlie close by his side.

In the elevator, Jenny explained that Nick was almost eighty, and sick. "But he's been feeling really good the last couple of days," she added.

As soon as she said it, she realized that Nick was probably fine. He had been in the shower, no doubt, and was going to be spitting mad when they burst into his room with a doctor. By now, he'd never make it to the airport for his flight. Jenny smiled, imagining Nick's face as he scolded her.

Even as they walked quickly down the corridor, the doctor did not say a word. Maybe he didn't speak English? Maybe he hadn't understood a thing she'd told him?

From his pocket, the doctor retrieved a key and slipped it into the lock.

"He's going to be so mad at us," Jenny whispered to Charlie. She expected him to laugh or even just agree with her. But his face remained worried, a frown deepening as he stepped into the room even before the doctor.

Time slowed again. Charlie's arm reaching back to keep Jenny from entering. The doctor bustling in, his footsteps clicking across the floor like tap shoes. An odd smell, both sour and sweet, filling her nostrils. Charlie held his arm firmly in place, so that she had to crane her neck to see inside the room. The doctor bent over Nick, touching his neck, his wrists, his eyes. Nick's face. Nick's handsome face, still and pale.

"Oh God," Jenny heard herself say. "Nick."

She watched the doctor open his big medical bag and pull out a stethoscope. The room was bathed in sunlight, the curtains and shade opened wide, and the stethoscope gleamed. Even though she saw now that Nick had not simply been in the shower, that he might even be gone, she held her breath, expecting him to slap the doctor's hand away or sit up at any moment. The doctor pressed the stethoscope to Nick's chest and then to his neck. He shook his head ever so slightly, reached for the phone on the bedside table, and, standing now, dialed a number.

"*Urgenza*," Jenny heard him say.

She didn't know how long she stood in that doorway, pressed against Charlie's arm, before the distinctive wail of European sirens neared. Not a long shrill sound, but a *wee-oww-wee-oww-we-oww* that reminded Jenny of someone keening. Then there was a burst of activity in the hall and the rush of footsteps and a gurney bumping along. Charlie and Jenny stepped aside to let the emergency workers in. She tried to see what they were doing, but Charlie put his arm around her shoulders and moved her away from the door.

"*Uno, due, tre,*" a gruff voice counted, and Jenny could picture these men lifting Nick onto the gurney, the way she'd seen on the television show *Medical Center* when Dr. Joe Gannon appeared during an emergency. But this was all too real, and that black-and-white image immediately vanished when the gurney rolled out of the room, two emergency workers on each side and one at the head, directing it. On it lay Nick, his face white, his shirt opened to reveal his pale chest. Before Jenny could think what to do, the gurney headed down the corridor to the elevator. She thought they should be moving faster. Wasn't this urgent? Hadn't the doctor himself said that?

"Run!" she called after them, but they did not pick up their pace.

The doctor put his hand on her arm. "I am sorry," he said. "Prepare for the worst."

His voice was silky and soft. A beautiful voice, Jenny thought.

The elevator dinged. She looked down the hall, and the gurney with Nick on it was gone.

CHAPTER THIRTY-FOUR

The Museum of Tears

Enzo, 1973

E nzo described to Geraldine how the seasons changed in Naples, the Christmas markets that sprang up around the city, how on the last day of February there were hearts and flowers everywhere.

"Do you know who Befana is?" he wrote her. "She is a good witch who brings the children of Naples sweets on January fifth. If you are here on that day, I will bring you to the Piazza Mercato and buy you chocolates from the candy vendors."

"My dearest Geraldine," he wrote, "How could I have been so remiss, my love? You love museums, yet I neglected to take you to Museo di Capodimonte, the terra-cotta palace built by the Bourbons. Not only does it have Carvaggios and Titians, but when you step out onto the terrace the view of the city will make you weep. I will gather those tears, my beloved, and I will put them in the Museum of Tears. *Tears of a woman beholding the beauty of Napoli.*"

Geraldine always wrote back, though her letters were short and hard to decipher. When she described the rain, was she really describing her tears of loneliness? When she wrote about getting battered or stocious at the pub, did she mean that she was drunk on love? He puzzled over each letter, looking for clues and codes that might give him an indication that she would arrive soon. But the only things he could hold on to were her closing lines, which always told him how much she loved him. "I long for you," she ended one letter. Or: "I'm hungry for you." Or: "How do I love thee, Enzo? Let me count the ways." These words he held on to. They kept him going, forced him forward to the shop and the museum and home to his mother's. Aria, Massimo's younger daughter, had moved in with them, and at night he sat with her and played scopa, Aria always keeping one card from her sweep faceup to taunt him as he scored the game.

Sometimes they could convince his mother to play, but typically she sat nearby and knitted, shouting at them from time to time.

"You can't play that six, Enzo! There's a two and a four on the table," she might say, even though she appeared to never look up from her knitting.

"In America, they call this backseat driving, Nonna," Aria explained. She, like so many of the young people of Naples, dreamed of moving to America, the way her sister, Sofia, had after Davide Bianchi left her for another girl.

Enzo would look around at his niece, with her plain, serious face, and his mother, bent over her yarn so that she could see the stitches better, and the cards spread across the table—the knaves and the aces and the one his niece had put faceup—and he would picture Geraldine here. Perhaps she would play scopa with them. Or sit by his mother and knit one of the intricate cable sweaters she favored. Or perhaps she would stand beside him in the kitchen as Aria did her homework and his mother attached squares together for a blanket, and he would show her how to make gnocchi, how to roll the dough into long snakes and then cut them into bite-sized pieces. He would show her how to roll them off a fork just so, leaving the tine marks on each one.

Time kept passing. The pile of letters in their thin airmail envelopes grew, filling the drawer in the table beside his bed. Still, Enzo did not give up hope.

One evening as they were leaving the shop, Massimo insisted that Enzo join him and his wife, Ines, for dinner on the waterfront later that night.

"You can't sit home with an old lady and a sullen girl night after night," Massimo told him. "You need fresh air, and you need good food and wine."

Massimo leaned close, his breath still with the hint of the sardines he'd had for lunch. "You need a woman," he said softly, elbowing Enzo in the ribs. "Am I right?"

Enzo opened his mouth, ready to remind his brother that he had a woman. She was at this very minute in Ireland, tying up loose ends, as she'd written in her last letter.

But Massimo kept talking: "Not someone thirteen hundred miles away, either. Someone in your bed every night." Massimo laughed. "Or at least in your bed some nights."

Enzo started to protest the dinner invitation. Their mother was expecting him; she had no doubt cooked dinner already.

"Eight o'clock," Massimo said, veering off in the direction of his own apartment. "Dress nice, Enzo. Maybe a woman will take notice of you."

Angry, Enzo turned in the opposite direction. He didn't like Massimo's wife, the vulture who had seized on Philomena's death as an opportunity to marry her longtime lover. Almost immediately, she had a son, and then another son, and then a daughter, one after the other without pause, having babies as easily as lemons grow along the coast. To Enzo, this woman and these babies were an insult to his dead sister-in-law, who gave her life trying to have a son.

Just last week, Massimo had not shown up for work until the afternoon, and Enzo could tell right away that he was drunk.

"Another one," Massimo groaned. "She's pregnant again. All of these babies are making me go broke, Enzo. You were smart to never marry or have children."

That night, Enzo went to Philomena's grave and placed a dozen hot-pink peonies there as an apology for his brother's thoughtlessness.

Now he was stuck having to endure an entire dinner with Massimo and Ines, who would no doubt act smug in a too tight dress, rubbing her belly and flaunting her fertility, her low-cut neckline showing off her ample cleavage. Massimo would drink too much and talk too loud, and Enzo

would sit silent and miserable. He thought of Aria and his mother playing scopa without him. He thought of Geraldine in her local pub in Dublin getting stocious (a new word for him from a letter a few weeks ago:
My mates were hammered, but I was positively stocious). He would rather
be home or in Dublin, but instead, he would go to the restaurant at eight,
dressed in his church clothes, just as Massimo had asked him to do.

Perhaps, Enzo thought as he began the steep climb home, he always
did what Massimo asked in the hopes of finally pleasing him. The thought
made him pause. That was it, he realized. A lifetime of wishing his brother
might notice him, approve of him, like him. But Enzo knew as he stood
there, smelling the stench of garbage and sewage that filled the air, that no
dinner would change that. Nothing would change that. Massimo simply
did not like him. It was freeing to finally understand this.

More lighthearted now, Enzo continued toward home. He had
to sidestep the garbage that overflowed from full bins, but he hardly
noticed. Tonight, he decided, would be the last meal he would share at
Massimo's orders.

Ines's cheeks were flushed from the Punt e Mes she was drinking, her
third. As Enzo had predicted, she wore a serpent-green dress that was too
tight across her stomach, which had already started to grow, and cut low
enough to show off her large, soft breasts. They were so white and so big
that even Enzo found it hard not to look at them. As much as he loathed
Ines, he had to stop himself from thinking about what those breasts would
look like freed from the confines of the green dress. Enzo could tell that
every man who passed the table had the same thought.

They ordered anchovies to start—battered and deep-fried, sautéed with
olive oil, lemon, and oregano, and *alici indorate e fritte*, the raw boneless
ones in vinegar, oil, parsley, and garlic that were Enzo's favorite. As soon
as the anchovies arrived, a woman appeared at the table. Ines shrieked
with surprise and got up to greet her.

"This is Paulina," Massimo said dismissively, waving his fork with a speared anchovy on it in the women's direction. "Ines's second cousin. She lived in Ravello for years, but then her husband died and she came back home." He glanced at the woman, then returned to his fish. "Pretty, isn't she?"

She was not pretty, Enzo thought. She was pointy—nose, chin, shoulders poking from her sleeveless dress, and even her breasts, which he knew looked pointy because of a certain type of bra some women wore.

"Very pretty," he said, because why insult this woman.

The *alici indorate e fritte* were perfect, tangy and garlicky, and Enzo turned his attention to enjoying them. But he'd hardly swallowed one when the chair beside him was sliding out and Ines's cousin was sitting down into it, smiling her heavily lipsticked lips at him, revealing two crooked front teeth on top, a flaw he might have found attractive under different circumstances.

A party-like atmosphere settled over the table, with Ines's loud voice and her cousin's loud laughter and Massimo's grandstanding. Bottles of wine appeared, and Enzo, miserable as predicted, decided to get very drunk. After all, he reasoned, this was the last time he was going to let Massimo force him to do something he didn't want to do. Why not make the most of it?

Bowls of spaghetti with clams and pasta with squid arrived, and Enzo filled his plate and his wineglass, leaning over to fill Paulina's too. That was the first time she seemed to notice him. She lowered her eyelids and glanced at him from beneath them in a practiced way that he supposed was meant to be sexy and said, softly, "*Grazie mille.*"

"I understand that you lost your husband," Enzo said when there was finally a pause in the frivolity.

Paulina nodded.

"I am sorry," Enzo said, and made a quick sign of the cross.

"Are you married, signore?" Paulina asked, turning in her chair so that she faced him fully.

With all those points, she was not a pretty woman, but her eyes were large and flecked with gold, which had a startling effect.

"Only in my heart," Enzo said.

"Widowed?"

He shook his head. "She is away. Tying up loose ends."

Paulina raised her eyebrows, or what she had for eyebrows, which were two very thin lines that seemed to be made of velvet.

"I await her," Enzo said.

"So, you don't have a brood at home like those two," Paulina said with a wicked smile.

Perhaps she wasn't as shallow as he had first assumed. She too found Massimo and Ines ridiculous.

"Just my mother and my niece," Enzo said. "His daughter, who fled his house when your cousin arrived and began making babies."

A waiter appeared with more wine, and cleared away the plates and bowls.

"Do you like to dance, signore?" Paulina asked him.

Enzo blinked. Her face was a bit fuzzy, an effect from too much wine.

"No," he answered.

A different waiter placed a bowl of *mussels all'impepata* in front of him, and Enzo squirted lemon on them. He liked the simplicity of this dish, how the mussels were quickly steamed with lots of black pepper and then served immediately. Paulina, he noted, had ordered the *polpi alla luciana*, as had her cousin. This didn't surprise him. The octopus was rich with tomatoes and spicy from chili pepper. Spicy like Ines and, in a different way, Paulina.

"Please," Enzo said, "taste a mussel. They are especially delicious tonight."

Paulina scooped three from his bowl, and he watched her pry the meat from the shell and slurp it into her mouth, tossing the empty shell into the silver bowl the waiter had provided.

"They taste off to me," she said, though she ate all three. "Perhaps because I've had so much chili pepper and my tongue has gone fuzzy."

She didn't offer him any of her octopus, though she did pour him more wine, which he drank down too quickly.

"I'm afraid I'm quite stocious," he said, the faces at the table and the food before him spinning slightly. "Do you know this word? Stocious?"

Paulina shook her head, seemingly uninterested.

Enzo leaned close to her and said, "Intoxicated," then attempted to lean back. But he was off-balance and instead leaned right into her. The smell of her—lilies, maybe? and hair spray?—made his stomach roll. Rather than lurch back into his seat, he moved his face toward the vicinity of her neck.

"Signore," she said, but she did not move away.

Enzo nuzzled her.

"Your mussels," she said. "They will grow cold."

With great effort, he straightened and rearranged the napkin on his lap. He could feel Massimo staring at him, and to Enzo's surprise, when he looked up, his brother was smiling approvingly. Massimo lifted his wine-glass a tiny bit in a private toast, and Enzo did the same.

"Don't toast with an empty glass!" Ines said and reached over to refill his wineglass. "It's bad luck." She was too late; he had already clinked Massimo's glass with his. But he accepted the wine and a grateful eyeful of her beautiful breasts.

The noise at the table buzzed around him, and Enzo gave himself over to it. Tomorrow he would return to his simple life, free of Massimo's judgments and disappointments. Tonight he would drink this glass of limoncello Ines was handing him and then stand shakily and make his crooked way across the restaurant to the door, Paulina's arm tucked in his.

The salt air felt good against his face, and Enzo inhaled it deeply, greedily, hoping it would calm his stomach. The four of them walked together, Ines still going on about whatever she went on about and Massimo laughing and chomping on a cigar, until Ines announced that they needed to go this way. She kissed Enzo and then Paulina on both cheeks, as did Massimo, who gave Enzo an unexpected quick hug too.

"*Ciao*," Enzo called to their backs. "If this is the last time we ever share a meal like this, then know that it was delicious and enjoyable."

Ines turned and called to him, "Good night, Enzo, you funny little man!"

But Massimo just lifted his hand in a wave without even looking back.

"I go this way," Enzo said, pointing.

"As do I," Paulina said.

They continued walking, her arm now holding his more firmly. He had the desire to shake it off, but then how would she feel? Insulted, no doubt. Hurt.

"Wait," Paulina said after some time. "I have something in my shoe. A pebble."

She leaned on him and removed one high-heeled shoe. It was slender and also pointy. He watched her shake it, then slip it back on.

"Better," she said.

The next thing Enzo knew, she had tilted her face toward his and was kissing him. Not softly, but hard and deeply. She had both hands on his face and she was holding on as if he were breathing life into her.

Oh, he was so drunk. Why had he decided to get stocious? Why was he so eagerly, so readily, kissing this pointy woman? Why was Geraldine so far away?

"I'm sorry," Enzo said, pulling away from her.

The smell of lilies was overwhelming, making him nauseous.

"My heart," he said, touching his chest, "it belongs to a woman named Geraldine. I love her," he added softly.

"Wonderful," Paulina said. "Just wonderful."

Her face changed right in front of him, from soft and open to hard and angry. She shook her head and turned away from him, heading up her street.

"Wait!" Enzo called. "Let me walk you home!"

Waves of nausea washed over him, and stomach cramps took his breath away.

"Don't bother!" she called back without even pausing or looking over shoulder.

His stomach heaved and tossed as he stood watching her, unsure whether or not to follow. Luckily, Paulina lived practically around the corner from him. His stomach was about to explode. Perhaps he could make it home in time.

Standing there on the street, at the fork, he couldn't hold down his vomit any longer, and he bent over and retched. He just made it home and into the bathroom for the rest. But to his surprise, it didn't seem to end. The pains in his stomach grew worse, and the sweating more profuse. As soon as he tried to get up, he had to sit back down again and more came out of him. Doubled over, he heard himself moan. So did his mother, who knocked on the door and asked him what was wrong.

"I just had too much to drink," Enzo groaned.

"Fool," his mother muttered, and he heard her walk away.

By morning, he was too weak to sit, and lay on the cold tiles of the bathroom floor. His arms and legs ached, as if he'd carried something heavy a great distance. But he closed his eyes, unable to move or call out.

At some point, the door opened and his mother looked down at him, disgusted.

"Why do you always do whatever Massimo tells you to do? He drinks like a jackass, so you have to drink like a jackass?"

Aria also appeared, and the two of them helped him to his feet and into bed. His mother put a cool cloth on his forehead.

"After you sleep it off, you can clean up the holy mess you made in the bathroom," she said.

"*Zio?*" Aria said when his mother left, "can I bring you anything?"

He managed to shake his head, but as she too started to leave, he said, "Paper? And a pen?"

Aria hurried back with a pad and pen and kissed his forehead.

"You feel warm," she said.

"No, no, I'll be fine in no time."

"Do you remember what today is?" she asked.

"Tuesday?"

"No. Well, yes, but it's the day I start at the shop. Papa is going to let me help paint the figures. Remember?"

Enzo smiled. "You will do beautifully," he said. His lips and tongue were so dry that he wanted to ask her for water. But he saw that she already had her coat and hat on, eager to get to the shop, so he said nothing.

It took all his strength, but he started a letter to Geraldine. "My heart," he wrote, "love of my life, I am too sick to write a proper letter today. I was, as you say, stocious last night. And this morning I am paying the price. Please come to me, Geraldine. If you were here . . . if only you were here . . ."

He would finish later, after he slept. He folded the paper clumsily and stuck it in his jacket pocket, because his mother had put him to bed fully clothed. Then he laid his head back on the pillow, another wave of cramps gripping him. Tears sprang to his eyes. He couldn't make it to the bathroom this time. He lifted a piece of paper to his eyes and let it catch his tears, but he was too sick to write what he was thinking: *Tears of a fool.*

CHAPTER THIRTY-FIVE

Naples

Jenny, 1974

To her utter surprise and relief, Nick had not died. Yet. The doctors at the hospital advised that he stay there until the end. "He is so near," one of them told her gently. But Nick wanted to go home. He had grabbed Jenny's arm with a strength a man so sick shouldn't be able to muster and said, "Please. It's your last duty. Get me home."

She'd spent hours on the telephone with Alitalia, making the special arrangements a flight for such an ill man required, and then hours on the phone with his nephew, Dr. Bill Casey, for the preparations when Nick arrived, and then hours filling out hospital forms. But she had done it. Nick was on his way back home, somewhere over the Atlantic Ocean, flying to Boston, where his nephew awaited him. Even though she had failed to find *le petit chou*, she had completed this last task perfectly.

Alitalia had let her accompany Nick, in a wheelchair, onto the plane. As she'd watched a steward help him into his seat, she couldn't help but remember the cantankerous man she'd left Logan Airport with a few months ago. How much he'd changed, she thought. How much she'd changed.

"Bon voyage," she whispered to him as she kissed his sallow cheek.

His brown eyes met hers. "Don't give up," he said.

At first, she thought he meant in a general way: Don't give up on life, on herself. But then she understood.

"If he can be found," Jenny said, holding his gaze, "I will find him."

Now she was back in her hotel room, desperate to sleep even though it was only midday. But someone was knocking on the door.

The man standing at Jenny's door looked like he'd rather be anywhere else. He wore the same uniform all the hotel employees wore, though it hung large on him, as if it had swallowed him and just his head and hands remained. In those hands, clutched in front of him, was what looked like a laundry bag stamped with the hotel logo.

"We did you the service of cleaning out the rooms of Mr. Burns for you," he said gallantly. He gave a little nod, and turned to go.

"*Grazie mille*," Jenny said, holding the bag close.

Jenny sat on the bed and opened the bag. Inside were neatly laundered and folded clothes, Nick's wallet, and other things carefully wrapped in tissue paper.

She placed the bag on the desk. She didn't want to go through it. Not now. Not ever. Maybe Charlie would do it instead. Though she hated asking him for any more favors. He had translated all the paperwork and instructions, spoken with the airline and the Italian authorities. Helped her track down the nephew. Now, without Nick or their mission to find out what happened to the baby, Charlie should go back to France, not stay here with her.

She looked around the room, the growing dread of having to leave the hotel heavy inside her. Nick had paid all of her expenses. Without him, she had to pay her own way. That didn't include living in an expensive hotel. Nick had paid up through the end of the week; then Jenny would have to find somewhere to go. He'd paid her for the whole month, thankfully. And she hadn't spent much during their travels. Even so, she needed to be frugal and not blow all of her money on a fancy hotel room.

The weight of the future forced her into the stiff, goldenrod-colored chair by the window. She would do what she always did, she thought, staring out at the bay. Make a plan. She would write a list of what she needed to do, and then she would just do it. She got up and walked back to the desk, ignoring the bag waiting to be opened and gone through, its items thrown out or sent to the nephew or maybe just given away.

In the desk drawer was hotel stationery, thick, creamy paper with the logo on top, and a monthly calendar, also with the logo on it. Each month could be filled in and then torn off, revealing the next month beneath. Jenny stared down at the top sheet. August. She had lost track of time these past days, and she even struggled to figure out what day it was today. Her fingers traced the days, each inside its own square with space to write in appointments or activities. Nick had gone to the hospital on a Tuesday. She moved her pointer finger down the column of Tuesdays, realizing that more than a week had passed already. The time since she'd stood at Nick's hotel door with Charlie blocking her from entering and the doctor inside the room was a blur. But that was *this* Tuesday—Jenny tapped the day—and now it was *this* Wednesday. Eight days later.

Her finger froze on today. Wednesday, August 28.

She glanced back at the top of the page to be sure she was looking at the right month. There it was, in three languages, one on top of another. *Agosto. Août. August.*

She looked back at where her finger still rested. Then her eyes slid to the day before. And the day before. And then settled on three days before. August 25. The day she was supposed to meet Daniel at the kiosk in Capri.

CHAPTER THIRTY-SIX

Naples

Geraldine, 1973

For her return, Geraldine had wanted to wear her yellow raincoat and the cable-knit sweater she'd worn when she'd first walked into the shop. Enzo had loved that coat and sweater. "You look like a beam of sunshine," he'd told her every time she put them on, which was frequently, as it had rained almost her whole time there. But the September day she returned was warm and sunny. The sky was wrapped in a silvery haze that made Geraldine think of fairies and magic. Dressed instead in a flowered sundress and a straw hat with a red band from which hung a bunch of darker red cherries, she made her way from the same *pensione* where she'd last stayed to the shop. She could have upgraded to someplace nicer, but like her, Enzo was sentimental. He would be as happy as she was to lie together in that same narrow bed and walk those same streets arm in arm.

In her bag—also straw—she had the article she'd written for the newspaper on offbeat Italian museums, with the Museum of Tears featured prominently and accompanied by a photograph she'd taken. She had thought of sending him the clipping, but selfishly she wanted to watch his face when he first saw it, listen to him read the article, or at least the part about the Museum of Tears, in his soft, melodic voice, and see how happy it made him. Thinking of that, she walked faster, eager to get there, to him, at last.

Now Geraldine was on the street of Nativities, passing all the shops with their windows of crèches and bins of painted terra-cotta figures. Her heart raced as she neared his shop. Should she open the door slowly, suspensefully? Then peek her head around it? Or should she burst right in? Shout his name? Open her arms? But there was the matter of the snarling brother, who would sneer and mock her if she entered so boldly. Perhaps just an average entrance, like she was any customer stepping inside. The door would open. The little bell would jingle. And she would step inside, smiling.

She was at the shop now. She paused, deciding. Yes. She would arrive like she was no one special. Her legs were trembling. She paused to steady herself. She closed her eyes, imagining Enzo's happy face when he saw her, conjuring it in her mind. Despite the warm air, goose bumps shot up her arms. "A ghost just walked by," her ma would say. Geraldine shook her head to get her mother's voice out of it. These goose bumps were from anticipation, from desire. "Cross yourself quick," her ma would say. And just like that, Geraldine found herself making a fast sign of the cross before she grabbed the door handle and pushed the door open.

The bell tinkled. She stepped inside. Immediately, Geraldine knew something was very wrong.

The girl at the worktable where Massimo usually sat glanced up from whatever she was painting. She was plain-looking, her dark hair pulled into a low ponytail and held in place with a fat tortoiseshell barrette. She didn't have on any make-up, though small diamond earrings sparkled in each ear. Her smock was paint-splattered, and dingy beneath the splatters, as if it had been washed far too many times.

"Where's Massimo?" Geraldine heard herself ask. Why had she asked for Enzo's brother and not Enzo?

"Not here today," the girl said in a soft voice.

Geraldine looked around the shop. Everything seemed the same—the displays, the figures, the paints and cork and painted backgrounds in garish colors—but also entirely different. The door to the Museum of Tears was closed, the sign she'd given Enzo hanging above it. The lights at the end of the shop were off.

"And Enzo?" Geraldine said, looking not at the girl but at that dark area in the back.

The girl startled.

Geraldine swung her gaze in the girl's direction. "Enzo?" she said again.

"*Morto*," she said matter-of-factly, even though her eyes filled with tears as she said it.

Geraldine stared at her. "No," she said, just as matter-of-factly. "He is not."

The girl chewed her lip, thinking. Then she picked up a newspaper and walked around the worktable to Geraldine.

She tapped the paper, which was folded into thirds so that the picture of Enzo and six other people was prominent.

"I can't read Italian," Geraldine said. But she could make out enough to understand that seven people had died from cholera, and that Enzo was one of them.

"Mussels," the girl said. "Bad mussels."

They both stared at the newspaper.

Geraldine glanced away first. Disbelieving or just defiant, she strode across the shop and turned the lights on in the back, where Enzo should be. She yanked open the door to the Museum of Tears and turned that light on too. It hesitated before illuminating, and when it came on she saw that the museum had been dismantled. All the vials of tears and the carefully written index cards cataloging them were gone.

She didn't realize the girl had come up beside her until she spoke.

"My father put it away," she said. "Too painful."

"Your father?"

"Massimo," the girl said.

They stood side by side in the doorway, looking into the empty room. Geraldine didn't know what to do, or where to go, or even what to say. She mumbled how sorry she was, but her mind was racing with the idea of bad mussels and Enzo's face in the paper and this sad room.

Suddenly, it seemed very important that Massimo know that she had come back. She took hold of the girl's arms and shook her gently.

"Tell your father Geraldine came today. Geraldine. Have you got that?" The girl nodded. "Geraldine."

"Give him this," Geraldine said, releasing the girl's arms and retrieving the article she'd written.

The girl took the newspaper but didn't even glance at it.

"All right," she said.

Days later, Geraldine would come back to the shop. Again Massimo was not there, but the girl was, and she assured Geraldine that she'd given her father the message and the newspaper. Geraldine walked across the shop to the museum, and pulled open the drawers where Massimo had put all the tears. From her big straw bag, she took out a vial, half full, and a small card. She placed them both in the drawer. Then she went around the shop, choosing objects and figures. When she'd paid the girl for them, she left quickly, hailed a taxi, and returned to Ireland.

Before long it was Christmas, and Hugh laughed as she assembled an enormous crèche, with the usual Wise Men and shepherds and holy family and barn animals. But also with figures of the pope and John F. Kennedy, a jester and a sausage maker, a drunk and a pizzaiolo, and a sad-eyed man who looked exactly like Enzo. She turned on the waterfall and stood back to watch as it flowed and the lights on the bridge twinkled.

"Why are you crying, Gerald?" Hugh said.

Instead of answering, because she could not answer, she went into his arms, seeking the tenderness she had lost. She couldn't find it with her husband, not that night, not ever again. But that night she got pregnant, and the next September she gave birth to a son, who she named Labhras. Every Christmas for the next three years, Geraldine spent hours putting up the Nativity scene and crying, a glass of whiskey in her hand, staring out the window, trying to see beyond this little house, trying to see all the way to Italy, to the Museum of Tears, where she'd left a vial of tears and a card that read: *Tears of a woman who delayed for too long.*

CHAPTER THIRTY-SEVEN

Naples

Jenny, 1974

Jenny ran. She ran out of her room and down the hall to the elevator, where she pressed the down button over and over, as if the more she pressed it, the faster the elevator would come.

From somewhere above, she heard dings as the elevator stopped on a higher floor, then another.

"Come on, come on," she whispered.

Her mind raced too. Had Daniel shown up at the kiosk at noon three days ago? *Ding!*

Maybe he had left her a note? Surely he wouldn't have just walked away if she wasn't there. He would consider a late ferry, a mix-up on the time or the day. He wouldn't—he couldn't—give up on her so easily.

This time the ding announced her floor, and the elevator door creaked open. Jenny squeezed in among people with oversized luggage and pressed the lobby button as many times as she'd pressed the down button.

Come on! she thought.

After a stop on the floor below—more people, more suitcases—finally she reached the lobby. Unencumbered, she was able to get off first, and as she walked quickly through the lobby, she made a plan: Take the next ferry to Capri. Go straight to the kiosk. Ask if a boy had left a note or instructions for her. Leave her name and contact information. Here, her plan faltered. She had no contact information. The hotel, yes, for now. But in a few days, she would be gone, and she had no idea where.

"Signorina!" someone called.

By the sharp tone of his voice Jenny could tell he had been trying to get her attention.

She turned and saw the concierge waving to her from his desk.

"I'm in such a hurry," she said when she reached him.

"Signore Reynolds asked that I give you this," the concierge said, obviously insulted by Jenny's terseness.

It took her a moment to realize that Signore Reynolds was Charlie.

The concierge was holding out an envelope, which Jenny immediately recognized as the hotel stationary.

"For you," he said.

Puzzled, Jenny took the envelope from him. Her name was written across the front and underlined with a flourish.

"*Grazie*," she said, already moving away from the desk.

"*Prego*," the concierge said sharply.

Jenny stuffed the letter into her purse and picked up her pace again. *Ferry*, she thought. *Capri. Daniel.*

On such a hot summer day, Marina Grande, where the ferry docked in Capri, was crowded with arriving tourists. Mount Solaro rose above the brightly colored buildings that lined the piazza. Jenny stood still, her eyes settling on the small fishermen's boats, then the houses and stores and cafés, until finally she saw a sign that read INFORMAZIONI and headed through the crowd to it.

Clustered together were the kiosk that sold tickets for the funicular, another that sold bus tickets, another for taxis, and there, finally, the tourist information kiosk.

The line was long, full of people asking for directions, booking rooms, seeking restaurant recommendations. Even though she was three days late, Jenny kept searching the crowd for Daniel. But, of course, she didn't see him. Not for the first time, she wondered if he'd even shown up on the appointed day and time. Standing in the long, slow line under the hot August sun, Jenny began to think that her rush to get here—to come at all—was foolish.

If it wasn't her turn at last, Jenny might have gotten right back on the ferry, now bound for Naples. But here she was, the bored man inside the kiosk staring at her, waiting for whatever she needed from him. What did she need from him? Jenny thought, staying silent.

"*Pensione?*" he asked. "Hotel?"

Jenny shook her head.

"Bus tickets there," he said, pointing vaguely to the right. "Funicular tickets there." He pointed vaguely again.

"No, I'm . . . I'm looking for someone."

The man cocked his head, frowning, seemingly studying her.

"A boy. An American boy working at the Pablo Neruda house," she said.

He narrowed his eyes, then held up his hands—one just above his eyes, one just below, as if he was narrowing his gaze even more, to focus on her face.

Unnerved, Jenny said, "How would I get there? To the Pablo Neruda house?"

"Via Tragara," the man said, this time pointing upward. "Taxi. Bus." He shrugged. "It doesn't matter because it is closed on Wednesdays."

"Oh no," Jenny said, her heart sinking.

From behind her, someone cleared his throat, loudly. She was taking too much time. The line was even longer now, the people in it hot and impatient.

"Okay," Jenny said, trying to think of what to do next.

The man behind her nudged past her so that he was in front of the kiosk window.

"I need a room with breakfast included," he barked in a harsh American accent. "Preferably in Capri Town."

Instead of answering the tourist, the man in the kiosk picked up the heavy black telephone beside him, consulted a number, and slowly dialed. Presumably finding the tourist a room. The man's eyes followed Jenny, the receiver pressed against his cheek, as she stepped out of the line. He was starting to give her the creeps.

"Hey, buddy. My room?" the American said.

Defeated, Jenny considered having a glass of wine at one of the busy cafés and making a new plan. But what would that plan be? To come back tomorrow? *Foolish*, she told herself. Slowly, she made her way back toward the ferries.

> *Dear Mom,*
>
> *I have been on quite an adventure. I don't even know where to begin . . . Mr. Burns (the man who hired me) was searching for things from his past. He was so sick, Mom, and I helped him. A lot. To try and find what he needed. To make him comfortable. Sadly, he got too sick to continue the trip. But I managed to get him home safely. Mom, he liked me. He thought I was special. I feel like I'm a different person than the girl I used to be. I feel like you would be proud of me.*
>
> > *Jenny*

Jenny sighed and turned the postcard over, staring at the famous Grotto Azzurra, which she had not gone to. She hadn't boarded one of the small wooden rowboats that took tourists into the cavern where the water was so blue that, legends declared, it could hypnotize you. She was, instead, on a noisy, smoke-belching ferry with a hundred other sweaty, sunburned people, heading back to Naples. Jenny reread what she'd written, her eyes burning with tears.

Although Jenny wanted nothing more than to climb under the cool sheets in her hotel room, with the shades drawn and the AC blasting, and sleep the rest of the day away, she had to keep moving forward. That meant making a plan with Massimo. Her day had been so disappointing already, why not get this over with too?

———

Jenny was surprised to find not Massimo in the shop but Aria, the young woman they'd talked with at Pietro's house what seemed like a lifetime ago.

"I remember you," Jenny said as soon as the girl looked up at the sound of the bell's tinkling. "You're Pietro's granddaughter."

Aria didn't answer. Her face remained impassive, unreadable, as before.

"Your grandmother got so angry that day," Jenny said.

The girl held up a hand. "Stop. I do not want to discuss this."

"That's not why I'm here. I've come to talk with Massimo," Jenny said. "About the museum."

"My father isn't here today," Aria said.

Jenny saw that Aria's smock was splattered with paint; six medium-sized figures stood glistening in a row in front of her, drying.

"Did you do these?" Jenny asked.

For the first time, a small smile crossed Aria's face.

Unlike the usual Nativity figures, in somber, traditional colors, these wore modern clothes. The Wise Men looked more like rock stars than Magi, with shoulder-length hair, droopy mustaches, tie-dyed shirts and jeans. Instead of gold, frankincense, and myrrh, they offered daisies, a peace sign, and a dove.

"My father says no one will buy them," Aria said.

Beside the Wise Men were Joseph and Mary, who looked rather like Sonny and Cher, in bell-bottoms and vests.

"I think lots of people would buy them," Jenny said.

"My uncle taught me how to paint. He was more talented than my father, I think. He told me that a work of art that did not begin in emotion is not art." She blushed. "Well, Cézanne said that. My uncle just repeated it. But this is why my father's work is so . . . so ordinary. There is no emotion in it. He just paints the same things the same way."

Jenny glanced around the shop, which was overflowing with figures. "I suppose you're right," she said, remembering how impressed by the items she'd been when she'd first walked in here. But now they did seem ordinary. Especially compared to the vibrant, ironic ones Aria had painted.

"My uncle was relegated to running errands and mixing the paints, perhaps because my father knew he would eclipse his work if he let him paint. He never complained, though. He used to say that he who works with his hands and his head and his heart is an artist."

"Cézanne?" Jenny said.

Now Aria smiled wide. "Saint Francis."

"Your uncle sounds wise," Jenny said. "I'd love to have met him."

"What did you want to talk to my father about?"

"Taking over the museum. I would fix it up and advertise it so that people would come. Perhaps it's your uncle's greatest work of art. He created it with his hands and head and heart."

Aria considered this for a moment. "My father is at the Caffè del Professore," she said. "He holds court there every Wednesday." She took a pencil and pad and began drawing a map. "Piazza Trieste e Trento is here. This is the fountain there, in the center. You just go straight down here until Via San Biagio dei Librai, then turn right . . ."

Jenny followed along as Aria labeled piazzas and streets.

"Or you can take the bus from—"

"I'll walk," Jenny said.

Aria tore the paper from the pad and handed it to her.

"Good luck," she said.

As Jenny maneuvered through the streets, she wondered if Aria had meant good luck locating the café or good luck talking to her father. After twenty minutes of walking, struggling to read Aria's handwriting and to find street signs, she thought it could easily be either.

Aria had said her father held court at the Caffe del Professore—the actual name was Il Vero Bar del Professore, which added to Jenny's confusion—and she was exactly right. Outside at a table covered with a red cloth,

Massimo sat at the center, surrounded by men. All of them were dressed in suits and had sleekly styled hair. Most of them smoked cigarettes. Their voices rose loudly above the chattering of the other patrons, Massimo's loudest of all.

Before Jenny could decide how to approach the table, Massimo's eyes landed on her.

"You!" he called to her, motioning with his fat hand for her to come to the table. "The girl who is obsessed with my brother's foolish museum."

The men turned and watched her as she walked toward them, some of them laughing.

"This girl took all of the tears off my hands," he said to them.

"Tears!" one of the men said. "A bunch of empty paint vials, that's all."

"I didn't realize you knew they were gone," Jenny said to Massimo.

"Of course I know. But I don't care. Keep them. You are foolish, like my brother."

Another man leaned close to Jenny and said in a stage whisper, "His brother, Enzo, was a hopeless romantic."

That brought even more laughter.

"I wonder if we could talk privately?" Jenny said softly to Massimo.

"No," he said. "Say whatever you have found me here to say."

Jenny took a deep breath, the air smelling of espresso and hazelnuts and heat.

"I would like to run the museum. To fix it up, I mean, and advertise it so that people come."

"Oh," Massimo said, nodding. "To make it a proper museum."

"Yes!"

"In the back of a *presepe* shop."

"Well—"

"So people will come."

"Please don't make fun of me," Jenny said.

"But how can I resist? You are being ridiculous." He shook his head. "Again, like my brother."

She took another deep breath.

"I'd like you to give me six months. Then we can renegotiate."

Massimo looked around the table dramatically. "Renegotiate? She wants six months—"

"Give it to her," one of the men said. "Why not?"

"You can charge her rent," another one said. "For the space."

Massimo grinned. "How does that sound? I'll charge you rent for the space, and if your museum is a success, we can renegotiate the rent."

Jenny stuck her hand out to him. "Deal," she said.

To her great relief, Massimo took her hand and shook.

"Oh, and I'll be living there too," Jenny said.

"Where?"

"In the shop. In the space I'm renting from you," she said.

The men broke out in laughter again.

"I said you could run a museum there," Massimo said. "A small, worthless museum that no one wants to visit. Not move in."

"*Grazie mille*," Jenny said as she walked away.

She could feel their eyes on her, but she didn't turn around. She kept walking, hoping they couldn't see that she was trembling.

The more she walked, the more confident her stride became. *I found my purpose, Daniel*, she thought. Thinking it, she could imagine the Museum of Tears with a line of people clutching *Let's Go: Italy* books waiting to come inside and see all the tears that had been shed by so many people over so much time. And picturing it, she smiled, and kept on walking.

Back at the hotel, Jenny called Charlie's room. No answer. She drew a very hot bath and poured in all of the bath salts from the jar at the edge of the tub. From her bag, she pulled out the Italian-language book she'd bought. It was for a child, the kind kids here used in second or third grade. Perfect for her.

Jenny sank into the tub and opened the book.

There was the letter the concierge had given her earlier, forgotten after this long day. She placed the book on the chair beside the tub and tore open the envelope. Jenny read Charlie's letter through, then read it again.

Shakespeare, he wrote, *was wrong: parting is not sweet sorrow. It's sad. Heartbreaking, even. Better to make a French exit, which is to leave without saying farewell. I will never forget Nick. Or le petit chou. Or you.*

This was it, then. She was completely alone. Completely on her own. Jenny let the idea sink in, expecting to feel panicked or frightened. But all she felt was complete calm, as if all the cells in her body had finally fallen into place.

CHAPTER THIRTY-EIGHT

The Museum of Tears

Jenny, 1974

Jenny knew that at any time Massimo would order her to find a place to live. But for now they had found an uneasy coexistence: Massimo and his daughter worked in the shop, and Jenny set about re-creating the Museum of Tears. She painted the walls a shade of yellow that reminded her of the fields she'd seen in Tuscany and trimmed them with a soft white. She'd found the museum prominently mentioned in an *Irish Times* article about quirky museums in Italy that was in one of the cabinet drawers, and she neatly cut it from the newspaper and had it framed. She did the same with the sidebar from *Let's Go: Italy* and with the small article in Italian *Vogue* about her reopening the museum. "AN AMERICAN GIRL GIVES NEW LIFE TO MUSEUM," the headline read. The three of them hanging on the wall made the room seem important, official.

Most days, Jenny worked on trying to figure out the best way to display the vials of tears and the cards with their descriptions. She tried glass cases and wooden shelves, drew blueprints, rearranged the vials chronologically and then thematically and then back again. When she took breaks and moved through the neighborhood, she marveled at how Enzo had found so many people crying and willing to talk to him and let him collect their tears and their stories. In the weeks since she had arrived, Jenny had not noticed anyone crying. If she had, she didn't know if she would have had the nerve to approach them, never mind actually ask for their tears. But she knew that she would have to begin to seek the hurt and the broken-hearted, the joyful and the confused, so that she could continue to build the museum. *Soon*, she thought as she moved through the tangle of streets. She would get to that point soon.

For now, it was enough taking in the gorgeous fruits and vegetables arranged on carts, the deep purple eggplants and bright red tomatoes, the bright green basil and giant lemons; to watch the people talk and barter and fight; to sit outside in the warm late summer afternoon and sip cappuccino or eat a big bowl of simple pasta tossed with tomato sauce and sprinkled with cheese.

Sometimes, Jenny allowed herself to stare off at Capri, shimmering in the distance. She wouldn't let herself dwell on her failed trip there to find Daniel, but instead looked upon it with a mix of regret and hope, as if somehow Daniel were looking back and feeling the same things. More than once she found herself imagining that somehow he would find her, and when she thought that, she felt something deep in her start to crack and try to emerge. But she always stopped it, always shoved it back into that place where it needed to stay locked away.

At night, Jenny slept on the narrow cot in the museum. From a nearby shop, she'd bought pale blue linen sheets and a white duvet with light blue stripes. They were soft from washings and smelled of lavender, the combination of their softness and that smell sending Jenny into the deepest sleeps she could ever remember having. Even the scratching of mice in the walls and the street noise and sirens that cut through the night did not bother her.

Jenny was on the cot, asleep, when something startled her—footsteps, a shadow crossing over her, a feeling that something was wrong—and she sat up, quickly. It was so hot that she'd gone to bed in just a white camisole and her panties, and she clutched the duvet close to hide her near-naked self as well as for protection.

"Signorina," a voice whispered into the dim room.

As Jenny's eyes adjusted to the light and to waking up, she saw Aria standing a few feet from the cot, a nervous look on her face. She, too, clutched something close to her chest.

"You scared me half to death," Jenny said, also in a whisper.

"I'm sorry," Aria said. "But I had to speak with you before my father arrived."

It wasn't the middle of the night, Jenny realized, but dawn.

"Is something the matter?" she asked the girl, who still stood there, unmoving.

Aria shook her head. She hesitated, then took a few steps closer to Jenny and stretched out her arms, the white bundle she'd been holding in her hands now like an offering.

"Please," she said. "For you."

Confused, Jenny took what she saw was a small blanket from Aria. Embroidered in light blue thread were six words: two words on top of two words on top of two words:

Aime-le.

Lo amo.

Love him.

Jenny looked up at Aria, who had moved closer.

"I don't understand," she said.

"May I?" Aria said, motioning with her chin toward the cot.

Jenny moved over to make room for Aria to sit.

"There is an opening here," Aria said, taking the blanket from Jenny as she sat.

She showed Jenny the small button that held the opening closed, and then unbuttoned it.

"*Guarda,*" she said, holding the edges apart so Jenny could see. "Look."

Jenny reached inside and took out the few papers and photographs that were tucked there. She spread them out on the small space between her and Aria. A handwritten note. An official document of some kind with an elaborate red seal. Two black-and-white photographs.

"I don't understand," Jenny said.

"The baby you call *le petit chou*," Aria said.

Jenny's heart began to race. She looked down at the items on the cot. The document. It was a birth certificate.

"Yes?"

"He was my uncle. Enzo," Aria said, her voice cracking.

To her surprise, Jenny felt the heat of tears in her eyes, felt them flow down her cheeks.

"He was found," she managed to say.

"Yes," Aria said. "It is a very long story."

The early morning light streamed through the slats of the shutters, sending soft beams across the floor. Jenny picked up the photographs. One was of a solemn-faced baby. The other of a beautiful but sad woman holding the baby, mostly hidden among yards of white clothing and blanket. Camille. And *le petit chou*. Then Jenny remembered. *He is Laurent*, Camille had told Nick. *Save them.*

She looked back up at Aria.

"Tell me," she said. "Tell me everything."

"My grandmother almost died when she had my father," Aria began. "And so the doctor forbade her from having any more children. This," she added, "was a heartbreak."

Jenny had made them strong coffee with steamed milk, and Aria held the chipped bowl in both her hands, pausing to take a sip before continuing.

"She cried about it all the time, and spoiled Massimo because he was her only child. Precious." Aria gave a small smile. "This is why he is so impossible," she said. "Her sister Gia had married into a rich family, the Contes from Rome—"

"Ermanno Conte?" Jenny said, picturing him in his fancy villa, lying to them.

Aria looked surprised. "Yes. Ermanno Conte. How did you know?"

But Jenny just shook her head and asked her to continue her story.

"Gia only came home to visit on holidays. She had become very fancy, flaunting her clothes and her jewelry, and Nonna thought her sister didn't care about her sadness over not having another baby. That was why she was surprised when Ermanno's fancy car pulled up on an ordinary day. Not Christmas or Easter but just a normal Wednesday."

Aria paused, smiling again. "Nonna remembers this specifically because on Wednesdays she always did the laundry, and she was on the balcony hanging the clothes to dry when her sister arrived."

She paused again, this time long enough for Jenny to prod: "And?"

Aria sighed. "And Gia had an offer for her. An offer of a baby."

"Laurent," Jenny said.

"Her husband was high up in the Italian army, and it seemed he had stumbled upon a newborn baby, left by a well, wrapped in that blanket."

She pointed to the blanket in Jenny's lap.

"And inside he'd found the birth certificate with the names of the boy's parents, and those photographs, and that letter, written by the mother."

Jenny picked up the letter, but it was written in French and the ink was too faded to read.

"She explains that they had to flee the Germans and that she had entrusted Laurent to an American soldier."

At this, Jenny shivered. Camille had believed that Nick would make sure the baby was safe, but he hadn't.

Aria picked up the letter and ran her finger across the lines as she spoke, as if she had memorized what used to be there.

"Perhaps he has handed Laurent to you, placed him in your arms. Perhaps he has left him for you to find at a hospital or apothecary or on the doorstep of your home. However you have come to have him now, please be sure he is taken care of, safe, loved. If you cannot do this yourself, perhaps you will give him to someone who yearns for a child more than anything else."

"Your grandmother was that person," Jenny said, putting the pieces of the puzzle slowly together. "But how did her sister come to have Laurent? Conte brought him back to Italy with him? During a war?" Even as she said this, she knew how impossible it would have been.

"As I said, he was very high up in the army," Aria continued. "He was able to get the baby to his wife through . . . what is the idiom? Pulling threads?"

"Strings," Jenny said. "He pulled strings to somehow get the baby safely out of France and into Italy."

"With the intent of giving him to my grandmother. If I know him, he probably said something coarse like *This will finally shut her up about her sorry life.*" Aria didn't even try to hide her distaste. "He is a greedy show-off and a buffoon."

Another piece slipped into place. "We were there, at his estate."

"Villa Mazzucco," Aria said.

"We spoke to him, and he denied knowing anything about this. So did his wife."

Aria nodded. "Because of what he did," she said softly.

"I'm sure taking a baby out of the country like that breaks all kinds of laws. But during wartime, these laws are broken all the time, aren't they?"

"I suppose," Aria said with a shrug. "But that's not the terrible part. You see, this letter ends with a postscript. Two, actually. The first was Nick Burns's name, battalion, regiment number, and hometown in America. 'Please find him and let him know the baby is safe. Please let him know he did the right thing.'"

"He never contacted Nick, that bastard," Jenny said angrily, again feeling tears filling her eyes.

"The second postscript says that she, Camille, is going to Paris. That she is determined to get a show of her paintings at the Louis Leroy gallery, which was a very important gallery at that time, I learned."

Aria once again turned her gaze on the letter.

"You can still make out some of the words," she said. "See? The address of the gallery is here. And this."

"*Je suis désolée*," Jenny read out loud. "But sorry for what?"

" 'I did not want this beautiful baby, or my husband, or my life on that godforsaken farm. The war has freed me. Please find someone to love him like a mother should,' " Aria more recited than read.

"And he did," Jenny said softly.

How different Nick's life would have been if he'd known that Camille gave up her baby willingly! If he'd only known that the baby had been given to a woman desperate for a child, that he'd had a happy life. That he'd been loved. Jenny thought of her own baby and imagined that he, too, was in a family that loved and treasured him. She felt a connection to this woman who, almost sixty years ago, had entrusted her child to a stranger.

"What about Camille?" Jenny asked. "Did Conte ever let her know that Laurent—"

"Lorenzo," Aria said. "My grandmother wanted to keep the name Camille had given him. In Italian, it's Lorenzo. My uncle Enzo," she said, sadness sweeping across her face.

"Did he tell Camille that Enzo was placed in a loving home?" Jenny said.

The sadness on Aria's face was quickly replaced with anger.

"He went to her after the war, yes," she said. "On the pretense of telling her about her baby's fate. But what had really caught his attention was that she was an artist and he learned she was about to have a show at that gallery in Paris. I don't know if he intended to blackmail her somehow, or what he hoped to gain, but knowing him, I am sure he had something sinister in mind."

Jenny thought of the lavish estate, with its fountains and manicured lawn. With its art.

"He does have two of her paintings," she told Aria.

"Two? He has them all. Except the ones he found with the baby. Those he gave as payment to the men who helped him smuggle the baby out of France."

"So he bought out her entire show?" Jenny asked, confused.

Aria gave a harsh laugh. "Bought? He stole them from her. He found her dying in a tuberculosis sanitorium outside Paris, trying to get her show together before she died. It was her dream. Her legacy." She looked hard at Jenny. "He assured her he would take care of everything. Then he stole all her work. Every last painting."

Jenny let the story settle over her, a chill spreading across her despite the warm air.

"Why did he do it?" she asked finally.

"An aura was created around the Blue Woman artist who died before her first show opened. A show that had gained a lot of excitement because of the quality of the paintings, of course, but also because of the artist's story: living in rural France, painting on tiny canvases during the war, losing most of her art when she escaped to Paris—"

"But she didn't lose it," Jenny interrupted. "She gave it to Nick that same night she gave him Laurent." She corrected herself: "Enzo."

"With the baby?"

Jenny nodded.

"I suppose Ermanno paid the smugglers off and kept all the others for himself then. As I said, he's a greedy man," Aria said. "Then after the war he went to Paris to acquire the new ones. When he found Camille dying in that hospital, it was easy to do. The story has made them more valuable over time. Who was the mysterious Blue Woman? What became of her and her art?"

They were quiet for a moment, and in that silence Jenny saw that Aria was crying. She placed her arm around the girl, thinking how different it all could have been if Camille had had that show, if Aria's grandmother had told Nick the truth, if any of the men they'd tracked down had admitted to their part in Enzo's journey.

Jenny pulled away from Aria, studying her cheeks, wet with tears, and her glistening brown eyes. She got up and went to the large table where she organized the museum exhibits and picked up an empty vial from the rack where Enzo kept them. When she turned, Aria was standing there.

"Yes," Aria said.

Jenny gently placed the vial to the girl's tear-stained cheek.

"The tears of a girl mourning her uncle," Aria said.

When Jenny stepped outside later that morning, the air buzzed with excitement. The streets were crowded with people dressed in their Sunday best, all moving in the same direction. Noticing the confusion on Jenny's face, an older woman dressed in black with a large cameo pinned to her blouse said, without even pausing, "*Festa di San Gennaro.*"

The Feast of San Gennaro. Jenny had read about it in *Let's Go.* On September 19, the two sealed ampoules of San Gennaro's blood were brought out of the reliquary in the cathedral and everyone waited for the priest to declare if they had liquefied. If they hadn't, disaster of some kind was predicted for Naples. Jenny let herself get swept up in the crowd, moving along with everyone through the old streets of Spaccanapoli to the Piazza del Duomo.

As she stood and waited with all of the praying people—women clutching rosary beads, children with their palms pressed together and their lips moving silently, murmuring men with their eyes closed—Jenny thought about miracles, about how hope and faith could sustain a person. It was almost one month since she was supposed to have met Daniel by the kiosk on Capri. Three weeks since Nick had returned home. So many things had changed in these few weeks. So much from just this morning. Her life, which had been stalled for such a long time, was suddenly filled with new things, new ideas. Hope.

Almost in unison, the crowd pushed forward, and a swell of excitement filled the air. Ahead of them, at the front of the cathedral, Jenny could just make out the figure of a priest in full regalia with several men around him. She saw him lift his arms, heard the crackle of a speaker and the tinny sound of him talking. Before she could try to figure out what he'd said, the crowd burst into shouts and tears of joy and the church bells began to ring. The blood had liquefied. Naples and its people were safe for another year.

It took Jenny a long time to separate herself from the elated worshipers.

The streets were full of people and noise and stands selling all kinds of food and candy and trinkets. Hot and sweating, she finally found herself away from the revelers and was able to make her way to a post office.

Inside, she sat at one of the pay phones that lined a far wall. Around her, voices in different languages mixed into a loud, cacophonous din. She pressed one finger in her ear to muffle the sounds, then placed her collect call to the States.

Since Nick had gone home, she had called him collect once a week, each time holding her breath until she heard his voice, weaker each time, say he would accept the charges. Even though his nephew had promised he would let her know when Nick passed, she worried that somehow she had missed it.

Jenny sat as the phone rang, once, twice, three times.

Please answer, she thought.

Four times. Five times.

And then finally.

"Hello?"

Jenny sat up straighter. This was not Nick's voice.

She listened as the international operator asked the man who'd answered if he would accept the charges from Jenny.

"Yes, yes, of course," he said.

"Go ahead," the operator told Jenny.

But before she could speak, Dr. Bill Casey was telling her that Nick didn't have much time left.

"I'm surprised he made it this long," he said. "When he got here, I thought he wouldn't last a week, never mind a month. But my wife and I are here with him. And there's a nurse round the clock. We're taking good care of him," he added.

"Can he talk to me?" Jenny asked.

"I'll hold the phone for him," Bill Casey said.

She heard him explaining to Nick that she was on the phone, and then she heard Nick's voice in her ear.

"Mr. Burns," Jenny said in her best voice, "I found him."

After she told him the whole story, every detail, there was a pause.

Then Nick's faint voice, sounding happier than she'd ever heard him, said, "I knew I made the right choice when I hired you."

Back outside, Jenny paused to catch her breath, and there, rising up across the bay, was the island of Capri. Without hesitating, she began to run toward it, down the steep streets, to the port and the ferry that would take her there.

One hour later, Jenny was in the bustling port, Marina Grande, still without a plan. She did what she had done three weeks ago: made her way to the kiosk Daniel had described to her that night in Providence. The same sullen man sat inside, looking bored.

In a mix of English sprinkled with Italian words, Jenny tried to explain that she was looking for someone, a boy who had perhaps left her a message of some kind.

Just like last time, the man shrugged.

She tried to ask where Pablo Neruda's house was, but the man only handed her a map.

Discouraged, she found a seat in an outdoor café and spread the map open on the table. She already knew that the house wasn't marked, but maybe there was some clue or reference she had missed.

When the waiter put a cappuccino down right on top of the map, she looked up at him and asked, "Neruda?"

He also shrugged.

Jenny moved her fingertips across the map and tried again. "Pablo Neruda?"

"I don't know him," the waiter said.

"No, no, he's a poet. A famous poet who lived here. I'm looking for his house," she said in a rush.

But the waiter shrugged again, smiling sadly, and walked away.

Jenny knew how futile this was, but she couldn't bring herself to take the next ferry back to Naples. Her coffee grew cold as she sat, alternately studying the map and watching the people disembarking and boarding the boats. The crowd at the port thinned as the day-trippers left for their hotels in Sorrento or Naples, and still Jenny stayed, without a plan or any idea of what to do next.

"Signorina," a voice said from behind her. "I believe this is yours?"

Jenny turned, expecting to find the waiter ready to ask her to order something else or leave.

But instead, Daniel stood there, grinning, holding up three one-dollar bills.

"I think I owe you this?" he said, putting the bills down and topping them with two dimes, a nickel, and four pennies.

She tried to speak, but her voice caught in her throat, until finally, after he'd pulled up a chair and the waiter had arrived with a carafe of wine and two glasses and then retreated, she managed to croak out, "How?"

Daniel poured them each a glass of wine and clinked his against hers. "*Salute*," he said, and took a sip.

"I came every day," he said. "Every day until I felt like an absolute fool for believing that a girl I hardly knew would actually show up at a kiosk on the island of Capri. Even though I sent her a dozen postcards—"

"A dozen? Really?"

"You didn't get them," he said.

"Just one."

"After a week without you coming, which I chalked up to a mix-up of the day or the time, because of course you were going to come, I paid off Antonio, the guy who runs the kiosk. I told him that if a girl who looks like Elaine from *The Graduate* ever showed up, he had to call me immediately."

"And he knew what Elaine looked like?" Jenny said.

"As luck would have it, the outdoor movie they showed last month was *The Graduate*—"

"No way," Jenny said, shaking her head.

"Then, two weeks ago, I saw Antonio at the outdoor movie, which was *Casablanca*, and he told me that a girl who looked a little like Elaine from *The Graduate* had shown up and asked him about Pablo Neruda. Maybe this was the girl I was looking for? I almost throttled him! Until he told me that he *had* tried to call me before you got back on the ferry, but that was the day I'd gone over to Ischia for a thermal soak."

Jenny remembered how the man had studied her face and picked up the heavy black telephone. She remembered the man behind her snapping at him to hurry.

The waiter replaced the empty carafe with a full one, and Daniel stopped talking only long enough to refill their glasses. The sky was streaked with violet and orange, and the air had the slightest chill as the sun began to set.

"I could only hope that if you had come once, you would come again. So I kept paying him until today. He called me and said, 'I am looking at the girl who really has very little resemblance to Elaine from *The Graduate* but who is sitting at the café on the corner studying a map.'"

"And here I am," Jenny said.

Daniel smiled. "Here you are."

"Now what?"

"Now we will eat the best *pasta alle vongole* you have ever eaten," Daniel said.

He reached across the table and took her hand, the first time they had touched since he'd appeared beside her.

"And after that, we will go up there"—he pointed to the steep hill above them, where lights twinkled—"and do everything I have imagined doing with you since that long-ago night."

"I have so much to tell you," Jenny said. "I don't know where to begin."

Daniel leaned across the table and kissed her. "We have plenty of time," he said.

And just like that, for the first time since the day she'd found out she was pregnant, and had left school, and her world had ground to a halt, Jenny saw a future appear before her.

Dear Vera,

If you are ever in Italy, come to Naples and see the museum I run here on
Via San Gregorio Armeno. My boyfriend is writing his PhD thesis on

the Chilean poet Pablo Neruda. Have you read his poetry?

I won't be writing to you again, Vera. You became a symbol of some-thing for me to hold on to, to strive toward, but the last time I saw you, you weren't even nice to me. The truth is, we knew each other for four short months, and you were never a very good friend.

So farewell, dear Vera. Thank you for what you, unknowingly, gave me.

Un abbraccio,

Jenny

Dear Mom,

This is the museum I own. I hope you will come and visit us someday. I would love to show you around my little corner of the world.

I love you.

Jenny bought two postcard stamps at the post office and affixed them to the postcards, from a new batch that had only recently arrived: a picture inside the shop of the entrance to the Museum of Tears.

"*Un abbraccio,*" she whispered as she slipped the postcards into the box for international mail.

Outside, Daniel waited for her. She had one more thing she needed to do, and Daniel was going to help her.

Jenny and Daniel had found a small apartment not far from the museum. Two rooms plus a kitchen and a tiny bathroom, on the fifth floor of a build-ing that had once been grand—the sweeping marble staircase that circled the center of the building, leading to each floor, was testament to that. But now the paint in the hallways was chipped and the floors scuffed. Still, they painted their walls a soft white and Daniel painted the bedroom ceil-ing a pale blue with white swirling clouds. They rescued a red enamel table with four chairs, all of it with broken legs that needed to be fixed, put out on the sidewalk for trash pickup, and covered the old sofa that had been left behind in the apartment with a colorful blanket Daniel had brought from Mexico. Aria managed to talk her grandmother out of a rocking chair and an old chest of drawers, which Jenny painted green, with hand-drawn daisies. One night, a kitten cowering on the fire escape cried outside the window, and by the next afternoon it had moved inside too.

With Pablo the kitten snoring softly beside them on the bed, Jenny opened Nick's suitcase. The plastic bag sent from the hospital had held what he'd had on him that awful day: clothes, wallet, passport, watch, college signet ring. But someone from the hotel had repacked the suitcase, carefully folding all of his clothes and placing his shoes in soft chamois bags that closed with a drawstring. His Dopp kit, with all his toiletries and shaving paraphernalia, the Old Spice and Listerine and Vitalis, was also neatly packed and zipped.

It felt intrusive to go through such personal things, Jenny noticed as she lifted out Nick's shirts—dress, golf, and the one red Hawaiian shirt that she teased him about whenever he wore it. Here was his seersucker blazer and his navy blue one, his two striped ties, and, beneath, white boxers and T-shirts. She had told the nephew that she would send everything to him, but he had said not to bother. "But if I come across money or valuables—" Jenny had begun, but he'd said it didn't matter. "I didn't know the guy really," he said. "You spent more time with him than anyone except my aunt. Keep it."

But she couldn't bring herself to open the suitcase, especially after she'd emptied that laundry bag, spilling the remnants of Nick's life onto a table in a hotel room, everything looking both ordinary and oddly profound at the same time. The creased brown leather wallet with his driver's license (expired, she noticed) and credit cards for gas, Jordan Marsh, and a local men's clothing store had lire and francs and dollars in separate compartments. A section meant to hold four pictures had just one: a graduation photo of a young blond woman in a cap and gown with a wide white collar, smiling confidently at the camera. On the back, in ornate cursive, she had written:

For Nick, With Love, Lillian
May 1922

More than fifty years later, and ten after she'd died, this was the only picture Nick carried.

Jenny shivered, remembering how she'd tucked the photograph into her own wallet, unable to discard it.

"We can donate the clothes," Daniel said. "Maybe to a church that can distribute them to people who need them?"

Jenny zipped up that section of the suitcase. In the other section were paperback novels—*The Winds of War, The Day of the Jackal, Ball Four*—all bestsellers.

"Funny," Jenny said. "I never once saw him with a book. But these have all obviously been read." She flipped the pages to reveal turned-down corners and coffee stains.

"Let's keep those," Daniel said. "You can never have too many books."

She threw her arms around him and hugged him hard.

"Someday," he said, "we will have a room just for books."

She closed her eyes and nodded against his chest, inhaling the smell of him—harsh detergent and something musky and male. *Someday.*

"What the hell?" Daniel said.

Jenny opened her eyes and sat up straight, watching as Daniel lifted beige linen from the zippered compartment between the two main parts of the suitcase.

Before he even opened the linen, Jenny knew what they would find. In all the time that she had been with Nick, listening to him tell the story again and again about Camille and the baby and that night, she had never thought to ask, and he had never volunteered, what had happened to the paintings. But she knew that Camille had given him two bundles and asked him to save them.

She placed her hand on Daniel's, to stop him for a moment. She had told him everything about Nick and his search to find out what had happened to Laurent. She had described their visits to the men who she now knew had either found him or helped to smuggle him out of France, who had been paid off with a painting and a warning to never tell anyone what had happened to *le petit chou*. And she had told Daniel about Camille, the beautiful, mysterious artist known as the Blue Woman.

"They're her paintings," Jenny said.

Daniel's eyes widened. "Camille's?"

"Nick never told me what he'd done with them. But he kept them and left the baby. That was the choice he made that haunted him the rest of his life."

She slowly unwrapped the tightly rolled linen, thinking of how it reminded her of the way people swaddled babies.

Jenny untucked the last corner, and the linen fell open, revealing a dozen small square paintings, their colors still bright and vivid. In the paintings were images of cows and potatoes and a desolate farmhouse, withered sunflowers and a field of lavender. One she picked up was all dark night and sky. Jenny had to study it to make out the shapes: tall poplar trees, a distant fence. She looked harder. A long hole in the ground? The perspective was looking into the hole from above, and there was a man, hidden in shadow, gazing upward.

"It's the trench," Jenny said. Her finger touched the face of the man, who she could now see had brown eyes. "And Nick."

The figure looking down was either never finished or purposely meant to be a streak of dark blue, holding something out to the man.

"A loaf of bread?" Daniel guessed.

Jenny shrugged, unable to take her eyes from the painting until Daniel handed her another one.

The scene was the same, except this time the focus was inside the trench. Three or four shadowy figures were in the background, but the center image was clear: Nick. Nick, young and in uniform, crouching beside what looked like a mural of a day in a park. *A mural down there?* Jenny thought. *Impossible.* But for some reason Camille had chosen to paint one there, with Nick.

"What do we do with these?" Daniel asked her.

"We hang them on the walls. And when we leave here, we hang them on the walls of wherever we go next."

"But they're valuable, right? Didn't you say they were considered lost?"

Jenny looked at this man who had waited every day for nearly a month to find her, this lover of poetry, and of her.

"Yes," she said. "But now they're found."

She swept the paintings onto her lap, every one of them, already imagining them on the wall over the couch with the Mexican blanket, and the walls of apartments and houses miles and years away from now. She thought of Nick. And the tears of the man who forgave himself.

ACKNOWLEDGMENTS

Ten years ago I went to the Musée d'Orsay, in Paris, and fell for the painting *Ploughing in the Nivernais* by Rosa Bonheur. Painted almost two hundred years ago, it somehow reached across the centuries and sent my writer's imagination into wondering about female artists in a male-dominated field in France. A few years later, my son, Sam, who shares my endless interest in and curiosity about World War I, shared a *National Geographic* article about trench art—literally sketches, carvings, caricatures, and relief sculptures discovered in abandoned World War I trenches in France. The article led Sam and me to Jeff Gusky, an ER doctor and photographer in Texas who photographs this art and posts his pictures on Instagram.

These two serendipitous events collided with an idea I'd been mulling for quite a while: How many tears have I shed in my lifetime? Thus, the fictional Museum of Tears was born and placed in Naples, Italy, where I long ago became fascinated with and began collecting the *presepi*—Nativities—made on Via San Gregorio Armeno. That plus a female painter from the turn of the twentieth century and a World War I soldier drawing on the wall of a trench in France brought me to write *The Stolen Child*. I stayed as close as I could to accurate historical details, but please forgive any straying for the sake of the story.

Of course I must first thank Sam for leading me to those abandoned trenches, and for sharing my enthusiasms and passions with me not just here, but in all of life.

Endless gratitude goes to my agent, Gail Hochman, and my wonderful team at W. W. Norton: Jill Bialosky, whose editing is always exactly what my story needs; her assistant, Drew Weitman; and my fabulous publicist, Erin Lovett. The support and love I receive from all of these great women is truly special and a writer's dream.

Thanks too to my daughter Annabelle, who always, always asks the right questions about story and characters and pushes me to go deeper and write better. And, of course, thanks to my marvelous husband, Michael Ruhlman, who reads more drafts than anybody should have to and whose love holds me up every day. Thanks too to Robin Kall: See, Robin! I added it!